LITERAL DEMONS

BOOK THREE OF THE INCARNATE ACCOUNTS

JUSTIN SCHUELKE

COPYRIGHT

For Todd.
No one has believed in The Incarnate Accounts, *and in me, as much as you. You aren't just my best friend—you're the Best Friend incarnate.*

PROLOGUE

Welcome back, class! For those of you who have forgotten who I am... you should probably go back and read the first two installments. They explain incarnates, my role as the Protagonist, and my life. This life, that is.

Oh, all right; I'll do my best to catch you up.

The story begins, as these things often do, with a prologue. In the past, I've used these as an opportunity to show you windows into my past incarnations, and what follows is another memory of a life I sometimes recall and sometimes do not. Incarnates' awareness of past lives is tricky— we don't have amnesia, really, but our memories are compartmentalized, accessed as they are needed.

The prologues of the first two books have proven to have some relevance to the main plot, because that's just the kind of expert storyteller I am. So I'd normally advise you to pay attention. To allow no detail to escape your notice. For those A+ superstars out there, to maybe read the prologue (or listen to it) twice.

But my conscience—or maybe it's Caden's influence—will not allow me to mislead you. So, for what it's worth, this is not one of those prologues. This is pure entertainment, a reward for slogging through book two's ridiculously antiquated prologue that dated back 1,647 years.

Enjoy!

∼

England, 674 years ago...

"*T*hat is *quite* enough," I said, though Avery's contagious laughter threatened to undermine my stern expression.

The little girl hopped off the soft back of the Pegasus incarnate down into the tall grass, stifling another round of giggles. Even the winged horse nickered playfully, enjoying his time with the little terror.

I sighed. "Young lady, if you are not willing to take your riding lessons seriously, I will be forced to remove them from your curriculum and substitute..." I paused theatrically. "Arithmetic."

Avery made a sour face, though she immediately tried to hide it from me. Little ladies did *not* stretch their faces into uncomely positions, after all. I pretended I didn't see it, though I knew I was spoiling her.

"May I please try again?" she asked, all wide-eyed innocence.

I could feel her glamour tugging at me, but I resisted its allure. Child incarnates, like other young creatures, often misjudged the potency of their innate abilities. Avery was no exception.

And, I conceded silently, *she's a* new *incarnate. We do not yet understand the full ramifications of her talents.*

"You may." With effort, I kept my face smooth. It was hard not to surrender to the exuberance that poured off the young girl. "But once more only. The Lady Corinna will be returning this afternoon, and we need to be ready to serve her."

Avery was barely listening. She scrabbled up the side of the Pegasus incarnate—who bore her inelegant ascent with stoicism—and settled herself forward on the creature's back. Her hands gripped the Pegasus's mane, and her knobby legs sat just in front of the feathery wings.

The Pegasus danced forward with grace and astonishing speed, carrying the laughing girl out of earshot in a matter of moments.

They raced across the plain, sending up stalks of grass and dandelion fluff in their wake.

The day was warm, the early-rising sun having burned away the clouds until only a few white, fluffy ones dared to cross the sapphire sky. Of course, the heat was due in no small part to my attire, from the cinched tunic to the woolen trousers. Expensive acquisitions, especially since there were so few opportunities to wear anything but dresses in the court.

I watched as the now-galloping Pegasus flapped its wings, sending dirt and grass whirling around him. A few strong wingbeats later, he lifted from the ground and sped across the field a few handspans above the earth. He knew better than to fly too high and risk being seen. In these times, aberrations like a winged horse, no matter its majesty, were not tolerated. Even on gorgeous days like these, doom and gloom were all too common of late.

The little girl's delighted laughter chased away my less-than-cheery thoughts. I smiled and made to seat myself on a nearby rock. A fat spider squatted there, as if watching me. With my gloved hand, I brushed it away before settling myself in its spot. I tilted my head to bask in the glow of the late-morning sun.

I allowed Avery to fly about on the winged incarnate for the better part of an hour. I soaked in the sunlight until even I knew we were pushing our luck. If we were late for Corrina's return, the baron would punish us both, regardless of my girl's tender age—or her charms. While Lady Corinna, the Maiden, might be an incarnate, she was born to a mortal lord who didn't understand our ways. He would not show leniency to us.

I frowned as I heard the faint sound of galloping behind me. Ahead, I could still see the Pegasus wheeling in the air. I turned and tensed. A rider was approaching at speed, his colorless mount kicking up clouds of dirt.

Death incarnate rides a pale horse. I shoved the thought aside. An ill omen, regardless.

I hopped to my feet, cursing my attire. This was no proper way for a lady to greet a stranger, but there was nothing for it now. I sent a shrill whistle in warning to the Pegasus but needn't have bothered. The incarnate was firmly planted on the ground and trotting toward us, Avery astride his back. I had to squint and concentrate to detect the Pegasus's wings. He'd folded them back against his hide, and his glamour was in full force, tricking the eye and mind into ignoring the peculiarity. Once, the Pegasus had been a Benign incarnate, but he had developed many such defense mechanisms to avoid being hunted—by ordinary humans or the worst of their kind, Vox Populi. Over the years, as the world became more dangerous, he'd become Prey, though I'd never say so in his company.

The lone rider slowed as he approached, and despite his mild-mannered appearance, my heart refused to calm. I didn't recognize him, and I knew the face of just about everyone in the vicinity of the castle.

The man addressed me without dismounting. He spoke in a tone that implied he wasn't wholly accustomed to speaking with cultured folk. "Milady, I've orders to round up you and your charge. Come with me."

I arched an eyebrow primly, hoping my indignant air wasn't completely sabotaged by my ignominious attire. Cursed leggings. "To what does this pertain, goodman?"

He didn't supply his name, unless I was to believe it sounded akin to a grunt. "Fetch 'em, I was told. Nothing more."

I pursed my lips, weighing my options. We could flee—this poor excuse for a messenger would obviously be incapable of pursuing a winged horse—but I was loath to surrender the life I'd built for us here, especially based on a summons that could be nothing. I feared it was something more, but I wouldn't uproot Avery and all we'd attained on a mere hunch. I should see this through. We could always escape later.

"We were headed back to the castle anyway," I said, smiling tightly. "We would feel safer with an escort." I called to the Pegasus and Avery, and they obediently trotted forward.

The man grunted again and spun about, leading us in the direction of our home. I mounted the Pegasus behind Avery, and we followed. Something about the situation was troubling me. We hadn't received news of anything untoward since the Maiden's departure nearly three weeks ago. But as I mulled things over, I realized we hadn't received any news *at all*. My skin crawled. I admit, it required much of my willpower not to turn and flee then and there.

"If I give the word," I said in a low voice, "I want you to flee. With or without me. Do you understand?"

Avery nodded soberly, and the Pegasus's ears flicked in what I hoped was affirmation.

The ride wasn't short, but consumed with my inner worries, all too soon I found we were among the homes of the village that surrounded the castle. There were several dirt paths in the small town, though only one could truly be called a road. It led straight through the heart of the village, the market square, to the gates of the castle proper. On such a sunny day, the village was swarming with people going about their daily tasks, but small oddities caught my attention.

The first was the subdued noise. The main street in particular was usually a raucous affair, with church bells and criers and traders hollering their offered goods. The church bells *were* pealing, but with an odd sort of vigor, as though catching up for a lapse in recent days. The baron's tabard flew from the walls ringing the castle itself in preparation for his daughter's return, but the celebratory banners and streamers I'd seen when we left were nowhere to be seen. Had they been taken down? Had we missed Corinna's arrival? Was that what all this fuss was about?

As we walked beneath the heavy portcullis and entered the courtyard, my breath caught. A line of men stood before the large staircase leading to the castle's main entrance, facing outward and watching our arrival with keen interest. Their livery, horses, and standards bore heraldry that froze my blood: a yellow cross on a field of pristine white. The symbol of the inquisition.

To my left, a newly assembled pair of contraptions drew my eye. The first was a tall wooden post with a fat base, black iron manacles dangling at the end of chains driven into the wood near the top. The second was a wooden framework with holes for the head and hands. A whipping post and a pillory. Contrivances whose twin purposes of flagellation and humiliation were meant to punish the wicked.

They did not lower the portcullis behind us, but more inquisitors closed off our escape route. I felt a shudder run through the muscles of the Pegasus beneath me, and I leaned forward and placed a hand on his cheek to calm him.

"Do not dismount," I whispered to Avery as I ignored my own advice and gracefully swung down to the cobbled pavement.

I searched the cold faces for their leader, paling as I saw a man in finer garments speaking amiably with the baron. He sported a close-cropped dark beard, as though he normally kept his face smooth but had seen many days of hard travel. He'd found the time to don a fresh tabard, however, the purity of the white making the yellow cross stand out starkly and belying the dark deeds he perpetrated.

Easy, I told myself. *You have not confirmed the rumors.* It didn't matter, though. If even half of what I'd heard was true... The last official inquisition had ended decades ago, but local tribunals still existed. Emboldened in recent years by King Edward's ongoing war—and thus his lapse of attention to *trivial* affairs like rooting out heresy—inquisitors had begun resurfacing following their official disbandment by the church.

As a result, it was all too common for people to be labeled heretics these days.

After a moment, the baron deigned to notice our arrival. "Lady Luple."

I curtseyed, though my station only required me to do so in formal situations. I decided this counted. "Lord Richard," I said. "You summoned?"

"Actually, *I* did." The inquisitor barely moved as he spoke, making no attempt at a respectful address.

I curtseyed in return, but more shallowly than I had for the baron. "To what do I owe this honor, Father?" I wasn't entirely certain of the correct term of address, but I hoped my attempt would flatter him.

It didn't. "It has come to our attention that you harbor a child of... questionable parentage." The inquisitor's eyes flicked to Avery and the horse, then narrowed. My heart skipped a beat. Was he able to pierce the Pegasus's glamour? After a moment, he addressed me again without looking my way. "Is this she?"

I licked my lips, considering my answer. If I protested his claim, I'd likely be asked to produce her father. Could I play the role of a widow, perhaps? Had I said anything contrary in the baron's presence? "Um—"

"What is the meaning of this?" a new voice demanded from behind. I turned—along with most of the men surrounding me—and saw Lady Corinna push through the crowd, the aging Sir John at her side. His hand was on the pommel of his sword, I noticed.

Despite her journey, the Maiden looked refreshed and... well, *angry*. She strode forward with purpose, her expensive dress swishing about her booted feet, soft features sharpened by her fury. Unmounted and not especially tall, she nevertheless seemed to tower over the men present.

"C-Corrina," the baron stammered, his smug expression vanishing beneath an abashed one. "Thank God you've arrived safely, my dear."

"And not a moment too soon, it would appear," she noted, coming to a stop next to me. "Lady Luple, are these men *of faith* troubling you?" A few men scuffed their feet and took a few steps back in apparent shame at her pointed question.

"Not at all, my lady. I'm certain they were just about to apologize for detaining us and see us on our way." I threw a challenging smile at the inquisitor.

He ignored it. "I'm afraid I cannot do that, Lady Luple. An accusation has been levied against you, and I am oathbound to uncover the legitimacy of the claim."

I put a hand to my breast. "An accusation? Against me?"

Corinna stepped forward. "Of what does my good woman stand accused?"

The inquisitor's eyes bore into mine. "She stands accused of consorting with demons and teaching her wicked craft to her child."

I swallowed. Well... he *was* half-right. I refrained from looking at the little girl atop her steed.

Fortunately, the Maiden laughed. "Witchcraft?" she said in disbelief. "Have you nothing more original?"

The inquisitor blinked, his heavy gaze settling on the diminutive woman in front of me. "The Devil's work may not be original, my lady, but it is very real. And very dangerous." His eyes narrowed. "You would do well to remember that those who offer succor to his constituents are just as guilty of sin as the witch herself."

I scoffed and muttered, "There's only one Witch, you ignorant knave." The insult stiffened the Maiden's back, but I didn't think anyone else had heard me.

"Now see here," the baron spluttered, "my daughter is a proper God-fearing woman, and I won't have any slandering her good name."

Huh. So the fop had a spine. "My lords," I said, "I do not wish to cause division here. I have nothing to hide, and thus nothing to fear. I will face my accuser and accept the judgment of God's good will." As the inquisitor's smirk spread, my tone hardened. "But this will *not* involve my daughter. Under my careful tutelage, and by the grace of the baron, she is guilty of nothing more than an education. Whilst that may threaten some, Father, it is no cause for inquisition. She is young and innocent of sin."

The man's smile had become pinched, but I knew I'd won. He'd prefer my cooperation, especially in light of Corinna's vehement defense, and he wouldn't risk the backlash of taking a child when the situation had grown so tense—

"No!" Everyone froze, looking around for the source of the protest. I winced, knowing exactly whose terrified voice that was. "You won't take my mother. You can't have her!"

I spun and placed my hand on Avery's knee to placate her. "Hush—"

"No!" she screamed again. "If anyone lays a hand upon you, Mother, I will..." She trailed off, huffing.

Oh, my brave, sweet child.

"You will *what*, little girl?" the inquisitor demanded, eyes glittering.

The Maiden and I spoke over each other.

"Leave her alone."

"She's just a child. She doesn't know what she's saying."

The inquisitor held up a hand for silence and leveled a heavy gaze at Avery. "What do you think you could possibly do, child? What would you do if we took your mother?" At his signal, the nearest man wearing the cross reached out and grabbed my arm.

"Stop!" Avery cried.

"What will you do?"

"I will... I will... bring the blackest of death upon you!"

Sir John gasped. The baron watched with wide eyes. The Maiden groaned. The inquisitor's eyes gleamed.

A wave of terror crashed into me. No, not just me. Over everyone in the courtyard. Men cringed back, shying away, unable to determine what was wrong but instinctually knowing it came from that little girl. I amended my thought. *Oh my brave, sweet,* foolish *child.*

The air was thick with the stink of terror. Horses in the courtyard panicked and bucked, a few breaking free from their handlers and bolting across the busy space. As men fell, screams and moans punctuated a feeling of unspeakable, eldritch horror.

Gritting my teeth, I pushed through her glamour—if such immense feelings of dread could be contained in such a paltry word —and reached for her. "Flee! You must go." I felt like I was in a nightmare where my scream came out as nothing more than a breathless whisper.

Then, as abruptly as it began, it ended. Not for everyone, I saw, but for me. She'd somehow conjured a hellish storm of trepidation and then excluded me from its shrieking winds.

"Come with me, Mother," she urged, small fingers stretched to take my hand, as though she possessed the strength to pull me up onto the Pegasus.

In that moment, maybe she did.

I glanced at the terrified people around me. I knew what I needed to do. "I wish that I could, dear child, but they would chase us to the ends of the Earth." I steeled myself. "You must go. You know the place?"

Tears streamed down her face, her dark eyes so like her father's. "I know it."

I nodded, smiling to her. "And if I don't find you tomorrow? You will count the days?"

Her face threatened to crumple, but she bobbed her head. "All one thousand."

I reached up and wiped her cheek. "Do not despair. Our parting will be but temporary. I will find you again."

She sniffled and gripped my hand. "I love you, Mother."

"And I love you, my little lady." I retrieved my hand, then placed it on the Pegasus's flank. "Protect her."

In a spread of wings that no one else saw through that haze of terror, the Pegasus took to the skies.

I watched my daughter disappear.

And I couldn't help but wonder, what had I unleashed upon the world?

My name is Emery Luple, and I am the Protagonist incarnate. Caden and I dream of the first Sanctum City, a refuge from the nightmares of the incarnate world. A place where all are welcome to build futures for themselves unfettered by the past. But every once in a while, the demons of my past return to haunt me. To test me.

I will prevail. I always do.

This is my story.

~

"I'm just going to say what's on everyone's mind," Maggie said in her southern accent. "We need some structure. Y'all given any thought to how this Watch is going to work?"

We were meeting in the Lodge, a rentable venue in the townhome complex where Caden and I lived. As the name implied, the space was themed after a log cabin, modified with technology like the flat-screen TVs mounted from the wooden crossbeams. The decor was a mix between rustic cabin and corporate retreat, a clash that somehow managed to ruin the appeal of both. Sleek computers looked out of place next to carved elk figurines. Expensively framed pictures of nature hung side by side with lists of rules and Wi-Fi passwords thumbtacked to the wall. Candles and potpourri should have given off a pleasant, spicy odor, but the place instead smelled like citrus disinfectant.

Only five of us were physically present. At one seat, a laptop turned toward us on the heavy oak table showed Agatha, our newest member, who was attending the meeting by videoconference. Her face was blurry, as though her webcam was underwater, and I couldn't determine whether it was because she just wasn't tech savvy or whether she was using some sort of *cauldron* to communicate with us.

Don't laugh. She was the Witch incarnate, after all.

In response to the Selkie's question, Caden said, "I've given it considerable thought. The Incarnate Watch needs some organization to get off the ground."

And out of this place. I didn't say it out loud. I was being a supportive boyfriend. Caden didn't need anyone to fill the cynic role, which was a real shame because I would have been a natural. Lately I'd found myself playing devil's advocate—against the Guardian Angel, go figure—more often than I wanted to, despite my best intentions to be encouraging. To be completely honest, the idea of the Incarnate Watch scared me more than it excited me. Incarnate communities had always met disastrous ends in the past.

But Caden had taught me to live for today, not the past. He made me want to be a better person, not just for him but for me, too. I knew some of that was his incarnate nature; he wore inspiration and hope the way others wore clothes. On top of his lean frame and blond boy-next-door looks, he had a magnetism that drew me to him, and I wasn't certain how much could be attributed to his glamour and how much was simply because I loved him. Trying to gauge it by how his aura affected the others in the room didn't work, because Caden had been a newborn when he'd reincarnated, so he'd spent the better part of eighteen years subconsciously using his powers without knowing who or what he was. In other words, his glamour had become a natural part of his identity, not just as an incarnate, but also as a person. He radiated beauty and didn't even know it.

He glanced at me with a private smile and squeezed my hand under the table. Well, *sometimes* he knew it.

"I called us together," he continued, "to prepare for our first official meeting of the Incarnate Watch tomorrow. I think we should begin by dividing the different tasks of the Watch and assigning some roles. Think of it like running a government body or creating departments for a business. Accounting, security, marketing, et cetera. Someone to handle our money, someone to be in charge of scheduling, someone to act as head of recruiting. That sort of thing."

That had been my idea, taken from my artificial memories of high school student council. So far all of those responsibilities had fallen to Caden as the one spearheading this dream. If he weren't also a full-time student *and* an intern at the UW Medical Center, I'm sure he wouldn't have minded. He was really passionate about the Watch. But a good leader needed to learn how to delegate, to lean on the strengths of those around them. Caden wasn't *officially* in charge of our little group, but we all followed his lead. His natural charm and supernatural charisma made it remarkably easy to accept his direction.

"I want to make sure everyone knows they have a voice in the Watch," Caden continued, "so any proposals we make today will need to be voted on during tomorrow's official meeting, when everyone is present."

"I get it," Maggie said. "We lay down the groundwork behind the scenes, and the real deal goes smooth as butter."

"Exactly. Does anyone have a role they'd like to take on?"

Melusina raised her hand, like she was in class. "I'm not sure where I'd fit in best, but Uncle Dagan would be excellent as the Watch's treasurer. He works for the CFO of Starbucks, you know."

I hid a smile. It was kind of an inside joke among incarnates that Melusina and her "Uncle" Dagan, the Triton, worked for a company that used the image of a mermaid as its logo. With green-blue hair and favoring swim-ready outfits that would've been more at home at a five-star resort than a hunting-lodge-inspired office space, Melusina looked nothing like the Starbucks mermaid. It made me wonder whether the Starbucks logo was based on a previous incarnation of her or simply the urban legend itself. Probably a combination of the two. Like all incarnates, Melusina was the one and only Mermaid in existence, the universe's representation of that myth.

Caden nodded in approval. "Since Dagan couldn't be here today, would you mind asking him if he'd be interested?"

"Of course. I'll get you two in touch after the meeting."

A cultured voice spoke up, coming through the speakerphone in the center of the table. "I, too, am good with numbers and figures," Artie said. "I would be more than willing to assist Mr. Dagan in his accounting endeavors."

Artie—the Artifact or, these days, the Artificial Intelligence, take your pick—was a computer program of sorts. If you imagined Siri and Alexa having a snobby, know-it-all little brother who gained independence from his creators and, after going on a murder spree, realized the error of his ways and was now doing all within his power to reform, you'd be on the right track to describing Artie. Despite the hiccups in the middle, which weren't entirely his fault, Artie was good people. Which was a damn good thing for us: his capabilities were seemingly endless. He could access just about anything linked to the internet, from phones to cars, and every smart device in between.

Oh, don't get me wrong: Artie was not Benign. As the Artifact, he usually came in one of two designs: an item or a weapon. When he was an item, like a book or a ring, he was probably Prey. Like other incarnates of that class, his powers and abilities often included methods of hiding himself from the wrong type of attention. When he was a weapon, he was a Predator: get in his way, and he would chop, hack, slice, stab, or incinerate you.

Artie's current incarnation was his most terrifying yet. A high-tech tool and weapon all rolled into one. Good thing he and I had developed such a strong relationship over the many, many years we'd known each other, and I'd been able to convince him to correct his course.

"Excellent," Caden replied. "I'm hoping, with your multitasking capabilities, that you won't mind assisting everyone else in their roles. Your resources would make everyone's job significantly easier. What do you say?"

"I would be honored, Caden Malek. Thank you for putting your faith in me."

Maggie indicated Caden and me. "I suppose the two of you want to be president and vice president?" Her eyes were so dark that there was almost no distinction between iris and pupil, and they matched her dark skin. Along with her easy smile, she had a direct frankness that I admired. The fur coat she always wore framed her generous frame and trailed down to gather on the floor. As the Selkie incarnate, she could take the shape of the animal whose pelt she wore. Despite the background checks we ran on all prospective members—with Artie's help, naturally—we didn't know too much about her; we'd met her in the aftermath of our encounter with Vox Populi. In the week since, we'd learned that Maggie's southern charm was her way of hiding her intimidating intelligence. Behind her affectation was a mind Caden had been relying on more and more as the week wore on.

I opened my mouth to answer, but Caden beat me to it. "I think it's best to hold off assigning leadership of the Watch until all members are present, don't you?"

Maggie raised her eyebrows, but she didn't look especially surprised. "But ain't this whole shebang *your* thing?"

This was why I liked her. She brought things out into the open but made it seem innocuous.

Caden blushed but didn't look away. "Yes, and I have every intention of nominating myself for the role. But I feel strongly that leadership needs to be earned. I came to you with my dream to create an incarnate community, but it's not going to be just *my* community, it'll be *ours*. If I'm to become the leader, I want it to be with the blessing of the people I'm to lead." He smiled wryly. "And if not, then I want the Watch to be led by the most capable person possible. There may be others who are better suited to the role."

I expected him to look at me, but instead his eyes drifted to Gregory Gregorius, the Watchman incarnate. I suppose that made sense: he literally had the word *watch* in his title.

But Gregory shook the idea off. "Not me," he said in his gruff, succinct way.

Maggie cocked her head, sending her vibrant, red-dyed braids swaying. "Really? The most important mission of the Watch is to find and protect incarnates, ain't it? That sounds right up your alley, Gregory." Her accent clipped his name into just two syllables.

"I'll help with that," he said. "But I don't want to be in charge. This thing will grow until it's a community, and I don't want to play mayor."

Caden grinned. "Well, you'd make an inspiring leader, but I'm sure the Watch would happily take you up on your offer to take on the responsibilities of security. In order to convince any other incarnates to join us, we'll need to prove to them that we can keep them safe. It's the first tenet of the Watch, a cornerstone on which our community will be founded. It's an enormous undertaking."

The corner of Gregory's lip twitched. "I know. It's what I do."

Melusina giggled. When everyone's eyes went to her, her light skin turned pink, and she looked down at the table. "That was so serious."

"*He's* serious?" Maggie said, amused. "Did you hear that speech about cornerstones and tenets?" She turned back to Caden. "You're giving me shivers."

"Thanks," Caden said, grinning. I melted a little, and it wasn't even directed at me. His smile was just so *radiant*. "What do you think about taking the reins on recruiting? I think incarnates outside of the Watch will respond positively to your friendly and forthright demeanor."

Her eyebrows shot up, and she smiled. "Well, hot damn! Ain't those some college-level words." Like she didn't have a degree herself; she worked at a medical clinic on the peninsula. "Since you asked so nicely, I'd be happy to put these dimples to work for you."

"Great! We want to invite as many incarnates as we can, to diversify our strengths. Plus, sheer numbers will help Gregory keep the city safe. The more eyes we have watching each other's backs, the better."

"I have eyes all over the city," Artie said. "In a manner of speaking."

Gregory leaned forward. "Good. Your coverage will help us keep incarnates in line."

"Security is one thing," Caden said carefully, "but oversight is quite another. The Watch isn't about *managing* the lives of incarnates. It's about protecting them, supporting them, and giving them a community where they can express themselves, free of recrimination. We need to walk a careful line between providing a place of peace and maintaining boundaries that respect the individual's privacy."

He and I had spoken about this at length. Originally, I'd thought it would be a better idea for the Watch to create rules that governed its members, to make protecting them easier and more foolproof. But Caden could be remarkably stubborn when he thought he was in the right. He'd explained how important it was for the Watch to provide a community where self-expression was encouraged, especially given how diverse incarnates could be. Over the last week, I'd come to see he was right, if for a more pragmatic reason. Incarnates were accustomed to solitary lives, so a sense of community would both appeal to and frighten many. In order to persuade people to join us, we'd need to guarantee they weren't giving up any personal freedoms. Of course, there was a single enormous problem with this logic...

"What about Predators and Malevolents?" Gregory asked, his words following my thoughts.

Maggie snorted. "He ain't going to allow Malevolents into the Watch."

"Actually," Caden said, licking his lips and looking uncomfortable, "I'm not planning on turning away anyone who wants to join the Watch." As Maggie and Melusina gaped at him, he hastily added, "As long as they agree to abide by our rules, of course."

Maggie broke the silence first. "Well, I'll be."

"I know it sounds scary," Caden said, his aura flaring as it worked double time to soothe the riled emotions in the room. He even began to glow faintly. "But *all* change is scary. If we're going to make this work, we need to be open to putting old enmities aside. If Malevolents are willing to reform, who are we to refuse them that choice? We can offer a safe place for them to undergo that transformation."

"And the ones that won't change?" Melusina asked.

"The Watch will deal with them." Obvious relief met his statement, and he sighed. "I may be an idealist, but my dream is for a *safe* incarnate society. We'll find the right balance, with time, practice, and unity. I'm the Guardian Angel—protecting others is my first and foremost concern." He grinned, and all the gravitas he'd been exuding fell away just like that. "All that said, Maggie, recruitment is up to you: I trust you to be fair."

"I'll get on it. I already have a few in mind. Melusina mentioned she and Dagan have been speaking with the Undine. Bonney Lake's Renaissance faire just ended; I'll see if the Knight or maybe the Fairy is still in town. And I know the Leprechaun's been looking to relocate his rainbow." She tapped her chin in thought. "Maybe Capitol Hill."

Caden nodded. "That leaves Agatha, Melusina, Emery, and me without specific roles for now."

Since this had been just about the longest I'd ever gone without speaking, I sat forward and said, "That's okay, there's still plenty to do today. Melusina will butter up Dagan for the treasurer job, I'll help you prepare for tomorrow's meeting, and Agatha can brew up some love potions."

He frowned, and someone help me, even that was beautiful. You'd think after dating for months, I'd get used to his charm. Not so. If anything, he grew more attractive by the day. I know some of you are scoffing at me, and I don't blame you—my best friend Rachelle would be rolling her eyes out of her head right now—but when he laid those seafoam green eyes on me, I simply surrendered. If it wasn't glamour, then... "Love potions?" he asked dubiously.

I gave him my best smirk. "So we win the vote when we nominate ourselves for the presidency and vice presidency."

"Oh, please," Agatha said through the laptop. "Even an express delivery wouldn't get to you by tomorrow from Maine. I'll prepare a hex instead. Far more effective."

I grinned at her, but inside I was a little worried she'd taken me seriously. The Witch. I mean, excuse my stereotype, but she probably wasn't *Benign*, right?

"I'll have Artie send everyone the agenda for tomorrow," Caden said quickly, casting me an unamused glance. Then he grimaced. "Right after I create it. But expect more talk of cornerstones and mission statements as we take this thing to the next level, from concept to creation. By this time tomorrow, I want to start rebranding Seattle as the Sanctum City. A place of peace and safety for all incarnates."

Maggie barked a laugh. "Riiight. Like you ain't going to be president."

"*What* did you think?" Caden asked as soon as it was just the two of us. He was stacking cups and leftover snacks onto a tray beneath a large wood carving of a bear. The stiff, efficient movements of his hands gave away his nervousness. He kept his face angled away from mine, and I knew he was worrying his lip.

So I came up from behind and wrapped my arms around him. I was taller than he was, with broader shoulders perfectly incarnated to envelop him snugly. He stiffened at first, then took a deep breath and relaxed back into me.

"You did great," I told him, mumbling into his hair. He smelled clean and fresh, like he always did. Since we'd moved in together a few days ago, we'd started using the same body wash, but it didn't matter; I smelled like hibiscus or honeydew or something, but his scent was the same as ever. Faintly minty. "They not only accepted the positions you were hoping they would, but they seemed excited about them, too."

"And they weren't *that* put off by the Malevolent conversation, right?" He pulled away and busied himself with tidying up again.

Well, no one walked out. "They'll need some time to warm up to the idea," I said, "but I think their openness was quite promising. You bring that out in others, you know." He shrugged off the compliment, self-conscious. "You do. Though maybe next time start with your idea to bring in a few mortals, and work your way up to Malevolents."

"I suppose Rachelle would be easier to accept than monsters." He perked up. "Speaking of which, have you gotten in touch with Trish yet?"

I shook my head, wincing as his face fell. "I know you want her to help maintain peace, but you *do* remember what she's like, don't you? She'll create as many problems as she'll solve."

He waved away my concern. "Gregory is going to need help. Trish would be perfect."

I'd never describe Trish as *perfect*, but I didn't argue. "Either way, you have your work cut out for you before tomorrow morning. Are you sure—"

"I'm coming with you," he said, his tone mild despite the fact that he'd cut me off. He hefted the tray and took it over to the large garbage can in the corner of the room. "You can put yourself in danger without me on my next shift." He dumped the half of the tray containing discarded cups and crumpled napkins into the trash, then shoved the leftover snacks and clean flatware into a bag he'd left at the room's entrance.

"It's just a hunt," I said. "You aren't missing anything."

"It's more dangerous than that, and you know it. It could be anything from the Werewolf to the Swamp Thing."

"It killed a *horse*, Caden, not a person."

He hefted the bag over his shoulder. "You emphasized the wrong word, Em. It *killed* a horse."

I opened my mouth, but he put his hands on his hips and I wisely turned the motion into a wide smile. "All right," I said, picking up my own bag from its place on the back of my chair. "But I'm telling you, we probably won't even find anything."

"You'll find something."

I walked past him and out of the room, then waited as he turned off the lights and locked the door behind us. We were renting the space again in the morning for the next meeting, but we didn't know if anyone else in the complex had it reserved before then. "You don't know that."

"I do," he said, pocketing the key. "You're the Protagonist. You *always* find something."

Well, that shut me up. There was some truth to those words.

Though I still masqueraded as the Loophole incarnate in the community, a few people knew the truth: I was actually the Protagonist incarnate. I wanted to come clean to the members of the Watch about who I was, but I needed to be sure I could trust them first. You see, each incarnate has a fatal flaw, and protagonists have been known to have a weakness for the people around them. I worried it wouldn't take too much effort to put two and two together. The fewer incarnates who knew about my identity, the safer my friends—and I —would be.

And I'll admit, as I became friends with them, confessing that I was not who I'd claimed to be when we first met was kind of embarrassing. The longer I avoided telling them, the harder it became to divulge the truth.

Being a manifestation of the main character from every myth ever created had its perks. It was one of the few things most urban legends had in common, which meant at times I'd been a princess, a monster hunter, or a child in need of a moral. I usually incarnated into an attractive, capable body, with a sharp mind and a penchant for adventure. I got to be at the heart of the story, with events literally revolving around me. I had a purpose in the world, a destiny.

Those were also some of the downsides to being the Protagonist. I mean, not the attractive and capable parts—they were great, though I'd lived multiple lives in less-abled bodies that presented different challenges—but rather the rest of it. It would be nice to just enjoy a quiet life with Caden. I mean, if terrible life lessons were going to happen to anybody, it was all but a guarantee that they'd happen to me.

Did I mention I never have a father? I knew protagonists sometimes had them, so that detail didn't quite fit, but I refused to share

Morrigan's belief that our father (as if we could ever be related) was somehow the narrator of my stories.

Ridiculous. Clearly, I was the narrator of my own story.

My powers worked in strange ways, too. As the Protagonist, I stretched the improbable into degrees of likelihood that boggled statistics. For example, if an incarnate went around murdering people in Seattle—a metropolitan area that included nearly four million people—chances were nearly certain the culprit would be someone I knew or met. Conveniently, the chances I'd catch them were also pretty high.

All this meant that I was the center of my own universe. Which... really isn't all that different from you. After all, you're the center of your own universe, right? I just happen to also be the center of some of your universes.

Huh. Every time I try to explain all that, I think it sounds a little cockier. Sorry for stealing the spotlight. You're special, too, I'm sure.

"I'm glad you're coming," I told Caden as we walked out into the parking lot. The Lodge was located near the front entrance to our complex, so it was adorned with carefully manicured grass and flowers to show prospective buyers how inviting our neighborhood could be. "I just worry about you overworking yourself." Only a little over a week ago, he'd been so exhausted his powers had begun giving out. Unfortunately, it had happened while we were in the middle of a gunfight.

"I'm fine," he assured me. "But we need to get going, or we won't be back in time to meet Rachelle and Matlas for dinner."

It was a cool, beautiful autumn day. We were creeping up on October, which brought with it shorter days and gloomier weather, but for now the sun still shone brightly in the sky and gave the illusion it was warmer than it was. Especially in the morning, when the night's chill refused to wholly surrender until the bitter end.

I scanned the row of cars in the parking lot. "Don't look at me. We're waiting on Ray."

There were a decent number of people out. It was a weekday, and not yet noon, but Caden and I had come to realize that our neighborhood, as well as this suburb in general, attracted young families and a large number of people who worked from home. I spotted two joggers and a woman with bright purple hair who waved to us while pushing a stroller down the sidewalk. I didn't know her, but I waved back.

I heard the low roar of Ray's motorcycle approaching from down the road and turned to Caden. "Sounds like he's here."

As I spoke, a figure across the street caught my eye. Was he watching Caden and me? The man stood behind a parked Mustang, his silhouette tall and muscled. He had dark, tousled hair and brooding eyes that I swore I could see even at this distance.

A chill ran up my spine. Did... did I know him?

Ray's motorcycle rumbled up. "Good day for a ride," he said, killing the bike, flipping the kickstand, and dismounting. He removed his helmet and approached. "Caden. Emery."

I looked back at the man who'd been watching us. I blinked.

He was gone.

I was seeing things. He'd reminded me of someone. He'd almost looked like...

Caden elbowed me and I jumped, then realized Ray's hand was extended toward me. I shook it, putting the incident from my mind. "Nice to meet you, Ray. Glad you could make it. Thanks for coming all this way."

Ray's hair was more black than gray, pulled back into a tail. He was Inuit and had weathered brown skin, but whether it was roughened by experience or age I couldn't say. His leather jacket was adorned with carved pieces of what might have been walrus ivory instead of the typical steel accoutrements I associated with bikers.

"It's me who should be thanking you for agreeing to help me. Amara was beside herself when she found Spray. The mare she lost," he added at our blank looks. "She was as healthy as a... well, horse, I guess. Amara woke up, and Spray had dropped dead in the night. Seemed suspicious." Ray and I had spoken about this on the phone, but it was good for Caden to hear the details from the source. "I think we might have another incarnate lurking in the area. It'll be good to have you along for the hunt."

"It's one of the things I do," I said. "Especially when an incarnate needs help." Ray was the Ijiraat incarnate—a shape-shifter of some kind, though that's where my limited knowledge ended.

His face was unreadable. "I appreciate you doing this as a favor. You usually charge for this kind of assistance, don't you?"

"Got to pay the bills," I said, wincing at how defensive it sounded.

"But the Watch isn't for profit, Ray," Caden interjected quickly, "We just want to do the right thing for incarnates—and mortals—everywhere. If an incarnate is causing harm in Seattle, the Watch will intervene. This *will* be a safe city."

I hid my smile. Caden had something to prove. The Kushtaka and the Thunderbird had attended the first meeting of the Incarnate Watch at E-Pluribus last week, but neither had yet agreed to join. They wished to see more before fully committing. So when Walt, the Kushtaka, had called this morning to ask me if I'd consider helping out an incarnate friend of his, we decided to use the opportunity to impress them. Ray had reached out to me less than an hour later, telling me about his neighbor's dead horse.

We had a rare chance to dazzle three incarnates with one job.

"The Watch sounds like a good cause," Ray said, but I caught a flicker of concern in his expression. Walt and Halona had undoubtedly shared with him their misgivings, whatever they may have been.

I decided to take a stab at addressing them. "You might wonder how the Watch is going to operate without charging for our work. I assure you, Caden has it all planned out."

Ray turned an expectant look on Caden.

Caden paled. "Y-yes. Um, well, some of the Watch will be volunteering their time. And donating resources as required."

I gave Caden a sidelong glance, wondering why he was sidestepping the point. I'd set him up to tell Ray about Micah Asker's fortune. The former CEO of E-Pluribus had accrued enormous wealth by creating Unum—which had turned out to be Artie, so you could argue that the money partially belonged to Artie. Asker might not have seen it that way, but Artie had access to his bank accounts—and those would sustain the Watch for years. Maybe longer, if a sharp financier like Dagan took charge of the treasury. Caden had initially objected to spending Asker's money, but Artie had assured us that Asker would believe in and support Caden's dream. I guess we'd know for sure in 987 days, when the Technopath reincarnated.

Caden placed a hand on my arm and smiled at me. "Plus we have the Loophole on our side," he said, giving me a look that spoke volumes. For some reason, he didn't want Ray—or maybe Walt and Halona—to know about Asker's money. "If anyone can find a way, it's him."

Ray accepted the explanation. "That's what I'm counting on today. Let's move," he said. Then he eyed Caden's commuter car. "You two going to be able to keep up with me in *that*?"

I exchanged a genuine smile with him. "Don't worry. I'm driving."

a n hour and a half later, we arrived at a small ranch outside of Anacortes. Caden had spent the drive with his laptop out, constructing tomorrow's agenda. Unlike this morning's get-together, tomorrow's Watch meeting would include the full roster of members and would begin to shape the vision of Caden's dream to make Seattle a Sanctum City for incarnates.

Artie was helping him. We'd begun wearing wireless earbuds to allow him to speak with us directly, so Caden occasionally conferred quietly with him as he wrote. He just looked like he was mumbling to himself.

The ranch was tucked away in thick woods that grew right up to the edge of the roadway. It gave the place a sense of isolation. Ray apparently lived nearby. Most of the twisting roads we'd passed as we'd neared our destination were only wide enough for a single car, and my navigation app didn't even register some of them.

Caden stowed the laptop as we pulled up. The approach circled the ranch, giving us a chance to see the fenced-in area where several horses grazed outside a stable. The house proper had a low roof and single window facing toward the driveway. It was well maintained, with bright blue paint, white trim, and squares of garden that looked a little sad, but I supposed that made sense for the season.

Ray pulled to the side to allow me room to park Caden's car next to his bike. The garage door was open, the interior tidy enough to accommodate a large pickup truck that almost filled the entire space. A woman came out to greet us, and I assumed it was Amara.

Caden and I got out, and I studied Amara as we approached her. She looked to me like she was trying a little too hard to live up to the image of being a rancher, with her cowgirl hat and plaid shirt under a plain, brown vest. White, she was middle-aged and of average height, thin, with hourglass hips and long dark hair that hung straight down to the small of her back. She would probably be pretty, but her face was set in a severe expression that took me a few moments to realize was an attempt at stoicism. The whites of her eyes were pink and the skin beneath them puffy, like she'd been grieving all day.

"Hi, Ray," she said as he stepped up to her, giving him a ghost of a smile. "Thank you so much for coming over."

"It's the least I could do. Amara, this is Caden and Emery."

"I'm so sorry for your loss," I said after we'd exchanged pleasantries. "Can you tell us what happened?"

She took a shaky breath. "Of course. I woke up this morning, early, which is normal for me. Right away, something felt... off. I don't know how to describe it, really. Just a feeling. Like I was sick to my stomach. I thought nothing of it, but when I went out to check on the girls, I—I f-found..." A tear slipped down her cheek.

Caden extended his hand, offering it in comfort. After a few half sobs, Amara took it. Her breathing calmed. Ray watched the exchange with eyes that missed nothing.

"Thank you," she said. "Perhaps it would just be better if I show you?"

I nodded. "However you want to do it is fine. I want to help, but I don't want to cause you more pain."

She nodded and brushed a tear away with her free hand. "The only thing that could cause me more pain is if one of my other girls falls to whatever animal did this."

"That won't happen," Ray said. "We'll stop whatever did this to Spray, I promise."

Amara gave him another one of those broken smiles and steeled herself, then led the way to the fenced-in yard. The path from house to stable was gravel and wove around several large evergreen trunks. This place reminded me of a forest retreat—the Lodge could take notes from the harmony between abode and nature here.

I breathed in the smell of pine but immediately wrinkled my nose. Something foul hung on the air as we approached the stable. Amara didn't lead us to the stable doors as I expected, but rather past the building. The stench grew, and I worried about what we were about to see. Not really for myself: I was accustomed to crime scenes, blood, guts, and death. I glanced at Caden. His face was set in a grim mask. He knew—or at least *thought* he knew—what he was getting himself into.

We rounded the corner of the stable. Spray's corpse had been gently propped up against a mound of grass. I didn't know a ton about horses, especially in my more recent incarnations, but even I could tell it was grossly emaciated. It was little more than a skeleton, ribs showing starkly against its flank. Its legs were so spindly they looked brittle, and I could only imagine they would snap trying to support the bulk above them, even wasted away as it was. Its coat had been a white-gray, and in life it probably had been glossy and sleek, but death had robbed it of that dignity, too, leaving the hair dull and flat. Flies and other insects crawled across the corpse, but not as many as I would have expected.

The worst part, however, was the raw wound in the horse's neck—like something had ripped out its throat and then begun to feast on its body. I swallowed and looked away. Nearby, I spied a tractor, which must've been how Amara had managed to move the dead body.

"I'm going to bury her this afternoon," Amara said in a husky voice, clearly fighting for control, "but I knew you needed to see her first."

Ray looked grim. "I am so sorry, Amara. Our actions today will bring Spray's spirit peace, that she may accompany you always."

I gave them a moment, then asked as gently as possible, "Was she always so thin?"

Amara took out her phone. "No, not at all." She flicked through a few photos and then showed me her screen.

I took it, frowning. The horse in the picture was healthy, well-fed, with a dark coat. "This is Spray?" I realized it was an insensitive question and snapped my mouth shut. But she wasn't even the right color!

Amara nodded, squeezing her eyes shut. "Yeah. That picture is from a few days ago."

Days? The corpse looked decades older than the horse in the picture. I held up the phone and inspected the corpse and the photo side by side.

"When I found her this morning, she was still brown, though the color was fading already. It's like death is just, I don't know, leaching the color out of her." She cracked a laugh that sounded like it came from the edge of an abyss. I recognized that emotion. So did Caden; he reached out again and placed a hand on her shoulder. She plunged on. "And what *happened* to make her so thin? It's like whatever attacked her sucked the meat right off her bones. I know I sound ridiculous. I'm sorry, it's just that it doesn't seem real. It almost sounds like something out of a story."

It sure did. "Where, precisely, did you find her?"

Amara pointed to a corner of the yard not too far from where we were standing. I left the others to console her while I walked along the fence to inspect the area where the body had been found. It was pretty obvious: the low wooden fence was broken there, wood chips and splinters scattered across the lawn.

Spray had been at the edge of the paddock where woods met fence. The grass was matted and flat where her body had lain, and I could make out the rough impressions of Amara's footprints. I snapped a picture of them on my phone. Then I turned on the flashlight to get a brighter image, and something caught the light and reflected it.

I squatted down and reached through the broken wooden railings. It was a shard of glass. No, not just glass—a piece from a mirror. Looking around, I caught sight of the wire contraption that had likely held the mirror, mounted to the fence itself. Someone, or some*thing*, had shattered the mirror that hung here, leaving the shards in the field. I wondered if maybe we should be looking for something other than a beast. If it had been a person, though, wouldn't they have covered their tracks better?

Looking up—you *always* needed to look up, and it was the direction most people forgot about—I saw another oddity. Fir trees hung over the area, but the branches that extended above where Spray had been found were twisted and tangled together, the very wood of the branches snaking into odd, interconnected patterns. It was the kind of trellis art you might expect from a careful gardener but rarely saw in nature. Never among bulky trees. Right?

I snapped a picture of the branches, too, and then turned to walk back.

I jumped as I nearly collided with Ray, who stood directly behind me. "What did you find?" he asked in a low voice.

"Not sure yet," I said. "Look at those tree branches."

He frowned up at them. "I've never seen anything like that before."

"Neither have I."

He looked at me. "Know of anything that would cause that kind of growth?"

I shrugged. "The Dryad? Treant? Groot?" I shook my head. "Not sure yet." That was true, though I was already beginning to build a theory based on the evidence. The horse's corpse drained of life. A broken mirror. Those fit with a pretty well-known Malevolent, though the twisted branches were an odd detail.

Don't jump to conclusions, Emery. I'd done that a few times recently —the Queen of Hearts and the Zombie came to mind. Both times I'd been wrong. Twice could still be a coincidence. I didn't want it to become a pattern.

We walked back to the other two, who had moved a little way from the body of the horse, and I held up the shard of mirror. "Amara, do you know what this is?"

She examined it before nodding. "I have mirrors set up all along the perimeter of the yard. A few years ago some fool drove his truck through my fence. Blamed it on the dark. I put up mirrors to reflect headlights and haven't had an issue since."

"Makes sense. Except, why was this mirror mounted on the inside of the fence and nowhere near the road?"

Amara flickered a smile. "After I installed the mirrors, some of them were positioned in such a way that they caught the light from the stable. I noticed my girls would gather around those spots, especially at night. So I put several more facing inward to reflect the light, and they love it." She grimaced at the piece in my hand. "I didn't realize they'd broken one of them, though."

I wasn't certain one of her *girls* had, but I kept my thoughts to myself. "Thank you for showing me around. The three of us are going to find some clear prints of the beast that did this so we can track it down and make sure it doesn't get another one of your horses." At her worried look, I smiled encouragingly. "Don't worry. We'll catch whatever did this."

"I'll be working around the yard, then," Amara told us. "My other girls are spooked, and I suspect they'll stay that way until I bury their sister." Her voice quavered a little, but otherwise she seemed to be doing better. Being around Caden was like that. Although he swore he couldn't heal emotional wounds, I remained unconvinced. "Let me know if you need anything."

We returned to the car and geared up. I'd brought my Taser and my tranq handgun, along with a box of spare darts and the battery backup for the Taser. Caden had brought packed lunches and folded plastic ponchos. I hid my smile. I looked like we were about to go on a hunt; he looked like we were headed out for a picnic.

"You sure you still want to go with us?" I asked. "I bet Amara could use some company, if you wanted to stay with her."

Caden looked back toward the garage, a troubled look on his face. Then he shook himself. "I'm certain. There's a lot of pain in her, true, but there's a clear solution. She'll feel better when we stop this incarnate." The troubled look came back as he said those last words, and I wondered if he was rethinking his stance on Malevolents and the Watch.

I knew I should comfort him, tell him he was right to keep hoping for change. I loved that about him, after all.

I couldn't bring myself to do it. Better he discovered the truth about Malevolents before he invited them into our home, right?

So instead I explained what I'd found at the spot where Spray had died, and we made our way back to that location. Ray waited for us, listening as I finished up and pointed out the twisted branches to Caden.

"How are you at tracking?" I asked Ray.

He grinned for the first time since I'd met him, the deep lines in his face suddenly making sense. The smile was wolfish and took *years* off of him. "Oh, I don't think we'll have any issues." He turned without further elaboration and began picking his way over roots and through branches, deeper into the woods.

Caden and I exchanged glances behind his retreating back, then we shrugged and followed him. We hadn't gone more than thirty feet when Ray stopped. He looked around, but the ranch was barely visible through the deep foliage. Seemingly satisfied, he said, "Try to keep up."

His body *rippled*. Fur washed over his skin in a wave, gray and black like his hair. His ponytail receded into his skull, which expanded in the front into a muzzle. Bones clicked, tendons popped, and his whole body contorted like a circus performer's. His ribs expanded into a flank, and his fingers melted down to nubs, nails poking through. He lurched forward and fell to all fours. And just like that, a large gray wolf stood before Caden and me. The whole transformation had taken less than five seconds.

The wolf sniffed the air. Catching a scent, he whirled and darted into the thick forest, leaving us gaping after him.

4

Hey there, this is Caden. Emery says he's been telling you all about the Incarnate Watch, and he wanted me to say a few words about my dream. That's nice of him, but it really isn't my dream. It's everyone's.

I grew up as the only boy in an abbey, my moms and aunts doing what they could to provide me with an education. Eventually, after we moved to New York, they decided they couldn't keep up with the curriculum, and they enrolled me in a public high school.

I suddenly entered a world I didn't understand. Everyone already seemed paired off—I didn't see a collection of individuals with their own problems; I saw groups of friends uninterested in accepting new members, particularly a boy with six moms who'd grown up far from there and had never had a friend before. I had nothing in common with any of them.

It was a crash course in human nature, in community, and eventually I—like so many others—discovered things I shared with the people around me and, perhaps more importantly, learned our differences didn't need to divide us. With many, I found friendship. A sense of belonging.

The Incarnate Watch is meant to be a refuge like that. Where incarnates can be themselves among people who understand them, but who also celebrate their uniqueness.

A place of safety, and a place where you belong.

Everyone deserves an Incarnate Watch.

~

"What do you think it is?" Caden asked as we followed the Ijiraat through the woods. Well, tried to. That wolf could *move*. He would range out ahead of us to catch the scent and then double back, guiding us in the right direction before loping ahead once again.

It made me wonder why he'd reached out to us in the first place. He was clearly capable of hunting on his own. Or maybe that wasn't entirely accurate. Maybe he could *track* the incarnate, but he didn't know how to take it down once he'd found it. Considering his demeanor, though, that explanation didn't quite fit. I would be surprised if Ray didn't know how to fight. Perhaps it was this specific incarnate he feared. But wouldn't that mean he knew something we didn't?

No, I decided, he didn't know what he was getting into either. And maybe that was the answer: that he was cautious when hunting the unknown. This would provide him with a chance to test our mettle, too, and give him more information about the Watch. Likely, that was all it was.

A tiny part of me wondered about what Caden had said earlier, though. Since the Protagonist was all but guaranteed to find the culprit, I was the perfect person to bring along on a hunt. Could Ray know who I truly was? Or maybe he thought that the Loophole's powers would work the same way. *You're overthinking it, Emery.* But that made sense, didn't it? I'd chosen that deception specifically because it presented a viable alternative to being the Protagonist.

All this made my head hurt.

"Not sure yet," I told him quietly. It was impossible for me to determine how close we were to our quarry, but I didn't want to alert a Malevolent incarnate to our presence if I could help it. Not to mention Ray would be disappointed in us if our talking ruined the hunt.

"But you have a theory." It wasn't a question.

I sighed. "Not really. Well, maybe. Certain things don't fit, and when I've jumped to conclusions in the past—"

"What? We won?" Caden grinned at me. "You always figure it out in the end. You needn't worry so much about making mistakes along the way."

I chewed on that for a few seconds before I relented. "Okay, maybe you're right. But it's just a theory—and not an especially good one."

He nodded solemnly, allowing me time to gather my thoughts. Ahead, a rustling in the undergrowth heralded the Ijiraat's return. I mulled over the evidence again while we followed Ray through the forest. At frequent intervals I spotted signs that we were on the right track: broken branches, smashed foliage, fresh paths that didn't seem to follow the expected animal trails that a good hunter could find in the wilderness. Stepping carefully over a fallen log, I stopped to examine a mat of woolly fur snarled in the bark of a tree we passed. It was a deep brown and coarse, like the hair of a gorilla.

"The Sasquatch," I said, pitching my voice for Caden's ears alone. I watched Ray, noticing that his ears pricked and twitched at my words. Interesting. So his hearing was *really* good.

"Really? What does that have to do with Spray?"

I pursed my lips. "I'm not sure yet." Which was concerning. The Sasquatch was, despite its fearsome appearance and reputation, a Prey incarnate. In the same family—so to speak—as the Yeti, but instead of fiercely defending its Territory, the Sasquatch roamed the Pacific Northwest, finding temporary Safe Havens for a time before moving on. Once, in ages past, this entire corner of North America had been its Safe Haven, but settlers had long ago begun encroaching upon its domain. First pioneers, then loggers, then campers, until sightings and rumors of the Sasquatch built to a frenzy. Over time the incarnate developed certain powers of elusion, learning to live alongside people, nearly invisible.

The Sasquatch *might* have attacked an animal if it were desperate for food, but I would expect it to find smaller game, like rabbits and mice. A horse was not only in a different league, it also belonged to someone. Killing it would be both out of character and extremely dangerous: it risked exposure to people, something this particular incarnate abhorred.

"What're you thinking, Em? I can see your mind racing."

"Something is wrong," I told him. "This is unusual activity for Bigfoot. It reminds me..." I trailed off when Caden wrinkled his nose. "What?"

"Is it the Sasquatch or the Bigfoot?" He gave me a chagrined smile. "I feel like I did when we were in New York and you were teaching me all about incarnates. Like there's so much I don't know about my own community." He lowered his voice and looked away. "How can I hope to lead them?"

I reached out and gently touched his shoulder. "Nothing wrong with making mistakes while you learn. Isn't that what you just told me?"

He gave a short laugh. "How did you get so good at cheering me up?"

"It's easy: I just quote your own words back at you. Who's the egotistical one now?" I grinned and gave him a quick kiss. "Besides, you're hardly the brooding type. And to answer your earlier question, Bigfoot is the Sasquatch's name."

He stared at me. "You're kidding."

"Can't make this stuff up."

I discarded the clump of fur and wiped my hands on my pants, and then we continued to follow the Ijiraat through the woods.

"The Sasquatch doesn't drain blood and meat from its victims," I said as we hiked. "Not its MO at all." I hesitated, then rushed on. "Draining the horse's blood, coupled with the broken mirror, immediately made me think of the Vampire."

Caden pushed between two large bushes, carefully holding one of the branches so it wouldn't snap back into my face as I followed suit. "What's the mirror got to do with it?"

"Of all the incarnates, the Vampire might take the prize for the most fatal flaws. Crosses, garlic, a wooden stake through the heart—

though I suppose that's fatal to quite a few of us—UV radiation, thresholds, and mirrors."

"How are thresholds fatal?"

"Well," I hedged, "I suppose I'm being a little flippant with the term. The Vampire only has one *fatal* flaw—sunlight—but has many weaknesses because there are so many urban legends surrounding vampires. Crosses, garlic, thresholds, and mirrors are all talismans that keep others safe around the Vampire, as long as they aren't in its Lair."

"And those things really work?" he asked.

"Yes. There's nothing mystical about a clove of garlic, but the Vampire will not bite someone with garlic in their system because the myth made it a talisman." I frowned. "Have I really never told you about talismans before?"

He shook his head, but he was grinning. "Never."

Huh. My bad. "Okay, so you remember how incarnates are divided into archetypes and personas, right?"

"Sure. You're an archetype and I'm a persona. Because you represent many urban legends across a variety of cultures, and I'm a very specific incarnation, a subset of an angel."

"*The* Angel," I corrected automatically, ignoring the glare he cast my way. "And I'm somewhat of a loophole. My incarnation exists in just about every myth but doesn't get labeled as such in damn near any." I coughed, realizing the glare hadn't stopped, so I nudged my way past him and continued. "Anyway, archetype incarnates tend to have a wider set of powers than personas, but also more restrictions. Like the Vampire and their many, many weaknesses. Talismans, however, can often be used to ward off personas and archetypes equally. So even if you don't know the incarnate's exact fatal flaw, you can take measures to protect yourself."

I turned around when I didn't hear his footfalls behind me. Caden was staring into empty space, almost... vacantly. I rushed back to him and took his elbow. The second I touched him, he started and shook himself, blinking rapidly. "Whoa."

"Are you okay? What happened?"

He rubbed his face and gave me a wan smile. "Sorry. I just—" He let out a quick gust of air. "I *remember*."

My concern evaporated as I realized what he meant. "You recalled something from a past life?"

He nodded, pulling a water bottle out of the side pocket of his bag. "Is it always so intense?"

I laughed. "No, not always. You've been repressing your memories for a long time, my love."

"As you were talking, it just pulled at my mind. Like I had something at the tip of my tongue. Then, all of a sudden, I remembered... and it was so vivid."

"What was it?"

"I found myself in a small house—a cottage, I think—and I was placing wards and, well, talismans around a baby's crib. Or maybe it was more of a bassinette. It seemed like an old memory. The baby was sleeping soundly, and I was hanging a dream catcher above her." He looked at me with a guilty expression. "I didn't know those actually worked."

"They work better than most talismans, actually. They're imbued with a fraction of the Asibikaashi incarnate's power, she who first taught mortals how to weave them."

The Ijiraat appeared at that moment and cocked his head at us, clearly wondering why we weren't moving. "Sorry," Caden said, "my fault."

"Are we close?" I asked the wolf.

In response, the Ijiraat—it was difficult to think of him as *Ray* when he was in animal form—gave a noncommittal shake of his head and bounded back down the path. I was fairly sure that meant he didn't know. Or that we were catching up to our quarry but still had a distance to go.

Then again, it was hard to tell if he could even understand me while shifted.

"Em," Caden said after we'd walked a few minutes in silence. He looked faintly perturbed. "Why did you tell me about talismans now?"

"Because you asked," I said, not sure what he was getting at. "Why?"

"Well," he said slowly, thinking it over. "You've never mentioned them before. This is brand-new information."

"Yeah, so?"

"Well, you're the Protagonist. Couldn't that mean you decided to tell me about talismans because they might be related to this little adventure?"

I shrugged, uncomfortable. "Who knows? My powers are anything but predictable." I could tell he didn't want to let the subject drop, so I added, "Are you saying you think talismans will be important to figuring out who killed Amara's horse?"

"Maybe." He brightened. "That's a good thing, Em. Now we know they're something to look out for."

"You make my life sound like a mystery novel."

He smacked my arm playfully. "Hey! Who said it's not a romance?"

"Because we're not doing it in the bushes right here, right now."

Caden jerked to a stop, surprised, then threw his head back and laughed. Certain we were the worst hunters in history, I joined him.

We hiked for a few minutes in silence, then Caden said, "So, the Vampire. Maybe they went after Spray because they were hungry but don't want to hurt people. So they broke the mirror and drained a horse instead."

I was shaking my head. "The Vampire can't break the mirror," I told him. "That would defeat the entire point of the talisman."

He nodded thoughtfully. "Okay, so maybe one of the horses accidentally broke it, which allowed the Vampire to get in. They drank Spray's blood and fled, breaking the fence in their haste." He hesitated. "Her neck was really ravaged, though. Does the Vampire not leave two cute little holes like in the stories?"

I sighed. "No, they usually do. That's kind of the whole point of an incarnate—we excel at what the stories say we do. I'm not sure why the whole neck would be torn out."

I fell silent as the Ijiraat slunk through the bushes and growled.

"We're close?" Caden asked. The wolf nodded in a distinct and exaggerated motion, the human mannerism eerily out of place on the animal.

We carefully crept through the branches, trying not to make too much noise. It was extra tricky because there wasn't a clear path or trail here. Ahead, an enormous, uprooted tree trunk loomed out of the greenery around us. At its tangled mass of roots crouched the barely detectable outline of some shaggy creature.

The Sasquatch.

*I*t was sleeping.

Nestled up against the foundations of the enormous tree trunk as it was, its brown fur—or maybe hair—blended in with the dirt, roots, and autumnal foliage around it. It was difficult to determine its size in its curled position, but it was clearly larger than your average person. I began to pick out some of its details as we crept forward, trying to approach as silently as possible. Its thick, unkempt coat covered it from head to toe, even across its face, though it thinned noticeably there, revealing pinkish skin. Its nose was black and wet, like a dog's, but without the pronounced muzzle you'd expect to accompany it. And speaking of its muzzle...

My heart fell. It was stained with still-drying blood and chunks of something I pointedly avoided scrutinizing too carefully. The Sasquatch *had* eaten Spray after all.

Don't jump to conclusions, a part of me whispered, but it was a tiny voice. That blood-smeared muzzle was like a smoking gun.

The Ijiraat had been leading the way, but he stilled as we neared the sleeping incarnate. I crouch-walked forward until I was even with him. His ears were alert, twitching back and forth at the tiniest of sounds.

I carefully levered my bag from my shoulder and lowered it, settling it on the tops of my feet rather than letting it rustle the forest floor. I withdrew my tranquilizer handgun and, very slowly, slid a dart into the chamber. There was a tiny metallic *click* as the dart entered, and I looked up, holding my breath.

The Sasquatch stirred but didn't wake.

Caden leaned down and cupped his mouth, pressing it against my ear. "Can it talk?" he asked, his breath tickling my skin.

I hesitated, then shook my head. That was mostly true: the Sasquatch couldn't talk, at least the few times I'd run across it. But it *was* intelligent. It could understand language, even if it couldn't produce it. So communication wasn't completely out of the question. But something about that red muzzle frightened me. Prey incarnates weren't often that savage. This incarnation of Bigfoot looked somehow more feral.

Great. And that was while it was sleeping.

I took a cautious step forward, raising my handgun. I could feel my heart thundering in my chest, every nerve spiked. A tranquilizer dart would probably kill the Sasquatch; it shared a fatal flaw with others in its family. Capture.

Keeping my eyes trained on the creature, I mouthed "Sorry," and I squeezed the trigger. Compressed air hissed, and the dart flew forward.

I swear the dart *curved* in midair, disappearing into the deep foliage.

I heard Caden gasp. I stared, disbelieving. The Sasquatch was only fifteen feet away, max. It should have been next to impossible to miss it. Moreover, my powers as the Protagonist usually guaranteed my shots were accurate, regardless of my skill at aiming.

The Sasquatch's eye cracked open.

Shit.

I expected it to unfurl from its position among the roots, rise to its full height, and charge us. Maybe roar for good measure. I was wrong on every account.

Bigfoot *exploded* from its sleep, going from lying down to crashing through the bushes and skipping all the steps in between. For a lumbering creature, it hauled ass. And it did so *away* from us.

It was fleeing. And it was *fast*.

The Ijiraat was faster. He plunged through the thick forest like a velociraptor from a *Jurassic Park* movie, a blur of teeth, snarls, and gray.

"Wait!" Caden cried. I was already darting after the two of them, and I wasn't sure whether Caden was addressing me, the Ijiraat, or Bigfoot.

I raced after the Sasquatch, amazed at how the forest swallowed its silhouette. It was hard to track with my eyes, and I realized that was a piece of Bigfoot's defensive powers. It made it difficult to hunt.

I leapt over a fallen tree, and my feet got tangled in some undergrowth. I cursed as the ground raced up to meet my chin. Luckily, the greenery here was dense and cushioned my fall, but I would never have been able to catch up to the Sasquatch on my own.

I wasn't alone, though.

As I picked myself up, I saw the Ijiraat zip past Bigfoot and then circle back, cutting off the creature's escape. I yanked another dart out of my bag, snatched up my tranq gun, and rushed forward. Caden was now only a step behind me. The Sasquatch hesitated, turning to veer off to the left. Its hesitation gave the Ijiraat the opening he'd been waiting for.

The Ijiraat leapt with a growl, throwing himself bodily against the Sasquatch in an attempt to tackle it to the ground. Bigfoot, clearly panicked, reacted with a backhanded swipe that caught the Ijiraat in midair. The casual power behind the Sasquatch's blow was staggering. The paw—or hand, or whatever—impacted the wolf with the force of a tractor. The Ijiraat let out a yelp of pain and was *hurled* into the forest, where he crashed into the foliage off to our right.

Caden changed course, running to where the Ijiraat had disappeared, while I raced forward to engage the Sasquatch. The handgun was slippery in my sweaty grasp. I wouldn't do anyone any good if I got too close, as I was clearly outmatched in a contest of strength. Could I reason with it?

"Bigfoot!" I called. "I just want to talk to you." I knew my words were fruitless, undermined by the fact that I'd tried to murder it in its sleep. I mentioned it was intelligent, right?

The Sasquatch watched me for a brief moment, then turned and fled into the forest.

"Come back!" I yelled after it. "Why did you kill that horse? She belonged to someone. You're better than that."

Ahead, the Sasquatch hesitated.

It wanted to talk. To tell its truth.

I approached more slowly, holding my hands up and open before me in a gesture of peace. "Please," I said, "were you eating the horse?" I put my hand to my face and tried to mime eating.

A loud grunt and exhalation of air surprised me. It wanted to talk but couldn't.

"Did you eat her?" I demanded, enunciating each word. It grunted and let out frustrated bursts of air.

Towering over me, the Sasquatch reminded me of the Yeti, the incarnate I'd hunted and killed in the Saudi Arabian desert. The experience had been terrifying and exhilarating all at once. And I'd died.

That time, at least, I hadn't had as much to live for.

I swallowed. I was too close to Bigfoot, with how quickly I'd seen it move from a dead sleep. If it decided to strike me, I wouldn't stand a chance.

The Sasquatch was barely moving, its gaze boring into my own. Like it was trying to tell me something. Then its eyes flicked to the left, where the Ijiraat crashed through the bushes...

And metamorphosed as he went.

The wolf's bulk ballooned, audible snaps and pops accompanying its growing mass. When he surged past me, I caught the flash of lupine legs, but by the time he was halfway to Bigfoot, he'd become a fully ursine figure. The Sasquatch, reacting faster than I could, spun and began to flee again, but the Ijiraat had used our conversation—if you could call it that—as a distraction. With a mighty roar, a great bear leapt onto the back of the Sasquatch.

And slammed into a wall of light.

Between blinks Caden was there, light fountaining from him and forming twin wings of hot-white illumination. One of those wings extended between the Ijiraat and the Sasquatch, creating a barrier of radiance that I knew from experience could stop bullets. I hadn't seen Caden move that fast since New York, when the Genie had hurled the Vorpal Blade at me and he'd outrun the thrown weapon to tackle me out of the way.

It surprised the Ijiraat, too. His head whirled toward Caden, a growl of warning thrumming from his throat.

"Stop," Caden commanded, the single word holding such weight that it seemed to settle about my shoulders. His glamour, of course, but it was still unnerving.

The Ijiraat spun and slashed at the wall of light, but nothing happened.

"The Sasquatch is innocent," Caden pronounced, his voice brooking no argument. "I will not allow misguided judgment to befall an innocent incarnate."

I held my breath, realizing my tranq gun was trained on Bigfoot. That probably wasn't making the situation any less tense. I lowered the gun.

The Sasquatch cowered behind the glowing wing, having stumbled to a stop. Despite its ferocious appearance, it suddenly seemed no more than a child, clutching itself in terror. Its head swiveled back and forth between Caden and the bear, as if bewildered by how the much smaller human was keeping the massive grizzly at bay.

Caden addressed Bigfoot. "You are safe. Please, go."

The Ijiraat fully turned toward Caden and *roared*. Spittle flew, and I flinched back from the intensity of its anger. Caden, though, faced down the grizzly bear with the steely confidence of one who was utterly unafraid.

I was afraid. Caden was the Guardian Angel, and he was incredibly powerful when defending others. His powers, however, did not extend to protecting himself.

"Don't do it," I pleaded, my voice strained, my blood cold. The Ijiraat spared me a glance. "*Please,* Ray."

He snarled and focused back on Caden. His muscles bunched, and my heart plummeted. Feeling sick to my stomach, I lifted the tranquilizer gun again.

And aimed it at the Ijiraat.

"We're all friends here," I said, speaking with a calmness I didn't feel. The grizzly looked back at me, staring down the barrel of my dart gun. "Please, Ray, stand down. Trust Caden. He knows what he's doing."

His huge head swung back and forth between us, taking our measure.

"I don't want to hurt you."

The Sasquatch finally got up and slowly backed away. After several yards, it turned and disappeared into the forest. In my peripheral vision, I watched the forest welcome it into its protective fold; my gaze never wavered from the Ijiraat's dark, ursine eyes.

He rose to his hind legs, and I almost pulled the trigger reflexively. But before I'd wholly registered his action, he began to shrink. He melted back into a man, claws softening into fingers and nails, fur retracting into flesh and—thankfully—clothes. Seconds later, a fuming Ray stood before us. I lowered my gun in relief, and Caden's glow faded.

"What the hell was that about?" Ray demanded, nostrils flaring.

I wasn't sure how to answer him, but Caden said, "The Sasquatch didn't kill Spray." He sounded exhausted, like he'd been wrestling with the grizzly bear rather than holding it off with wings of light.

"You're wrong," Ray said. "I could smell Spray—and her blood— all over that thing. And you let it escape."

I stayed silent, though I wanted to defend my boyfriend. I would, too, if it came down to it, but right now I was worried that Ray was right. The blood on Bigfoot's muzzle had been convincing.

Caden was shaking his head. "I know the Sasquatch was there. I'm not arguing that point. But it didn't kill Spray."

Ray took a few deep breaths, clearly calming himself. His eyes, however, skewered Caden with fury that wasn't so quickly buried. "How can you be sure?"

Caden sighed. "I'm the Guardian Angel. I'm not certain how I knew, exactly, but I could *feel* its innocence. Something about its terror, or maybe its imminent death, triggered something in me. It wasn't guilty of the crime for which it stood accused." He made a frustrated gesture. "I can't explain my feelings, but there was another piece of proof: the tranq dart curved away from it. Emery is the Loophole; his shots never miss. Whatever powers of self-preservation Bigfoot has, they overwhelmed Emery's own powers, which are considerable. The Sasquatch is *supposed* to live."

Ray made a disgusted sound. "A feeling and the incarnate's power working as intended. Those are your arguments? You two are worse than I feared. You've been using this situation as nothing more than an opportunity to gain potential recruits to your precious Watch. I was fine with that if you were earnest about helping Amara, but you didn't hesitate to turn your weapons on me."

A flicker of hurt passed over Caden's face. I stepped forward. "That isn't fair, Ray. We were all in until things changed." Ray's angry expression didn't soften, so I tried again. "I trust Caden's instincts, but you've only known us a few hours, so I understand your skepticism. But think. Even you have to admit there are pieces to the puzzle that don't make sense: the broken mirror, the warped and twisted trees, the drained and emaciated horse herself. These details don't fit with the Sasquatch incarnate. Which would mean we still have a horse slayer on our hands."

Ray considered my words and, after a moment of deliberation, huffed. "Fine. I don't like it, but I suppose it's possible the Sasquatch came across the dead body and decided it was a free feast. But," he said, raising a finger, "I don't think it's likely. If it looks like a duck and quacks like a duck, it's usually a damn duck." His eyes narrowed. "And turning your gun on me, tranq or not, crossed a line." He turned back to Caden, scowling. "I don't appreciate the way you handled the situation, either. You made it sound like this Incarnate Watch of yours was going to be a collaboration. Today, you acted like a tyrant, making the decision for me and bullying me into standing down with raw force. That's not someone I'd call a leader."

Caden paled at Ray's words and slowly nodded, looking like he was on the verge of tears. My temper flared. *I might call them a hero,* I wanted to say. Caden had saved Bigfoot from a possible unjust execution. At a quick glance from Caden, I swallowed my response, knowing he would be even more upset if I stepped in to defend him again.

The tension between all three of us was thick enough to swim through. It was going to be a long hike back to the ranch.

*C*aden closed his laptop with a sigh and stared out the window with a faraway expression. We'd picked our way back to the ranch, where Ray had stiffly informed Amara that the beast's trail went cold and it shouldn't return. She accepted the news with stoicism, clearly disappointed we hadn't bagged the creature responsible for killing Spray but also grateful for the effort we'd put in. Our parting with Ray had been brief and laced with friction, and then we'd somberly exited the ranch and begun the drive home.

Though Caden had been working on the laptop for most of the drive, I could see at a glance that he hadn't made much progress. He wasn't chatting with Artie, and he frequently stared at the screen without typing, obviously replaying the events in the woods. Focusing, in all likelihood, on Ray's words.

I knew he was also bitterly disappointed. This outing was supposed to be a demonstration to Ray, showing him the good the Watch aimed to achieve. In the end, it had the opposite effect. It seemed unlikely he'd ever join now.

We continued down the freeway in silence, and then I ventured, "You did the right thing."

He didn't answer right away. We were nearing our exit, and clouds had begun to gather in the distance, mimicking our mood. We'd had a sunny, if not completely warm, September, but the month was ending and October winds were blowing in, stripping the trees and bushes of their leaves, revealing the bare skeleton of the greater Seattle area. It was one of my favorite times of year, with bright, sunny days and cold nights perfect for cuddling indoors.

Our exit. The idea still sent a thrill through me. Caden and I had just moved in together earlier in the week, after he and my mom had conspired to find a place for the two of us and surprise me. We lived in an eastern suburb, along the border of Bellevue and Newcastle. The townhome wasn't extremely large, but it was perfect for us. Caden had even recreated my office, which had been reduced to ashes by the Genie's attack right after I'd reincarnated.

In fact, I'd just finished moving my final things in last night, and tonight would mark my first night wholly moved out of my mom's house and into our new home. My new Sanctum—which was wherever Caden was.

"I think so, too," Caden finally said. "But then why does it feel so heavy?"

"Because the right choice isn't often the easiest one."

Caden gave a soft, unhappy laugh. "Yeah. What's with that?"

"I think it's important. It makes the act of choosing to do the right thing more meaningful."

He was silent for a minute. We exited and came to a stop at the bottom of the off-ramp, waiting for the light. "I think Ray was right, too. I was a bully. If that's all I am, then I don't deserve the mantle of leadership."

I shook my head. "A bully would've struck out at Ray to tear him down. You were protecting Bigfoot. *That's* why you deserve to be the leader of the Watch: even when the evidence was against it, you defended the Sasquatch. The Watch deserves you as its leader because you will protect its members with all your conviction. Remember, your dream of turning Seattle into a Sanctum City starts with keeping incarnates safe."

Caden still looked distressed, but he spared me a small smile.

"Thanks. You're right. If Ray had known the Sasquatch was innocent, he wouldn't have wanted it dead. I just wish I had something more conclusive to go on than my feelings." He shrank. "What if I was wrong?"

I considered my response. The question had been going through my mind, too, though I was trying to ignore it. "If anyone should trust their gut, it's you. You were an infant when you reincarnated; you've been using your powers on instinct for your entire life. And those instincts are based on lifetimes of being the Guardian Angel. Even though you're unable to recall those experiences, something inside you knows what to do. Believe in yourself." I placed my hand on his leg and squeezed comfortingly. "I do."

He put his hand on top of mine, then smiled and looked back at me. His eyes were sparkling with unshed tears. "Thank you." He scrubbed his face. "I don't know what's wrong with me today."

I chuckled as we pulled into our neighborhood. "Hate to say it, but I'm surprised it hasn't happened before now." He gave me a perplexed look, and I fought a grin. "Think about it: you've been working long hours at the hospital, picking up extra shifts, and attending university medical courses. You just went through the process of buying a townhome, and now you're moving. That's enough to be stressful to anyone—and it's just scratching the surface. We adopted not one, not two, but *three* puppies. Overnight you went from being a student with a roommate to having a small family. Not to mention spearheading the creation of a new community of myth-ical beings, getting kidnapped and tormented by a cult less than a week ago, and protecting a creature you knew to be innocent from another you wanted to impress. You've put all this pressure on your-self to be strong and perfect in front of the other incarnates. I under-stand why, but you're overwhelmed. Justifiably so. *I* feel overwhelmed, and I'm just watching you."

Caden waved his hand in surrender. "All right, all right," he said, laughing. "But you forgot to include hosting a dinner party on that list."

I snorted. "It's just Rachelle and Matlas. That's hardly a 'party.'"

"Oh yeah?" He raised his eyebrows. "You'll do the cooking, then?"

We turned into the driveway, and Caden opened the garage door with the remote.

"I can cook," I protested.

He leaned across the car and kissed me on the cheek. "No you can't, Em. I love you, but your talents lie elsewhere." Lies. I could cook, but apparently chicken nuggets weren't fancy enough for guests. That was hardly my fault.

"Feel better?"

"I do." It was clear there was more he wanted to say, using the cover of getting out of the car and unloading the trunk to mull over his words. Finally, as he plopped down our equipment in the only available corner of our little garage, he sighed. "I'll feel even better when I see some results. Getting the Watch off the ground is one thing, but I want to see it working. Keeping incarnates safe. Then I'll feel like I'm making a difference."

"Just be careful you don't pin all your happiness on some future goal," I told him as I closed the trunk. "Strive for tomorrow but live for today. Or something like that."

"Ancient incarnate wisdom?"

I shook my head. "Inspiration-of-the-day calendar."

"Liar," he said from behind me, waiting as I unlocked the entry door from the garage. "You're not fooling me. You could give the ancient philosophers a run for their money."

"Who says I wasn't one of them? And you're not fooling me, either. I know this is weighing on you, regardless of how amazing your boyfriend is at cheering you up."

Suddenly I felt his arms wrap around my waist and his head against the back of my shoulders. "Thanks for trying. I just need time to think about it and process my emotions. But you really did succeed more than you know. It's tough to stay upset when we're walking through the door of our new home together."

We entered the townhouse and I couldn't help but agree with

him, inhaling deeply in contentment. This place represented something more sacred than the meager decor and modest space indicated. There was a simple sort of magic in a place that made you feel comfortable, safe, and happy.

Six days, and it already smelled like home.

And lilac.

We'd purchased a few air fresheners to help cover up the scent of new puppies. We'd originally chosen a cinnamon scent but quickly moved away from it after realizing it smelled like the Genie. As long as we didn't make enemies of the Elf incarnate, we were in good shape.

"Place seems so quiet without the puppies," Caden noted. Rachelle had agreed to babysit the trio. As a matter of fact, she'd demanded it when she found out we were going to be gone for the whole day.

We'd adopted Mask, Beard, and Mittens following a harrowing adventure at Paradise Lake Cemetery. Rachelle, in all her stubborn bravery, had tried to descend the Thirteen Steps to Hell, but neither of us had known it was being guarded by the Hellhound. And, *of course*, because I'm the Protagonist and these things happen to me, the incarnate had apparently been pregnant. We'd arrived two days later to find its mortal litter bereft of a mother.

I suppose we were lucky. When we were attacked by the Hellhound, I'd seen glimpses of other shiny, evil eyes in the foggy woods. Who knew how many demonic incarnates had been there, drawn to the Thirteen Steps?

I glanced at the time. "Rachelle and Matlas won't be here for a while." I grabbed his hand and pulled him close, inching my mouth closer to his with each statement. "No roommates. No moms. No puppies." I kissed him, delighting in the way he inhaled as my mouth met his. "I wonder," I whispered seductively, "what we could do for an hour."

"An hour? That's perfect." I began to smile as he gently pushed me back, but it wilted when he slipped out of my hold and headed toward the kitchen.

"Why do I get the feeling we're not thinking of the same activity?" I asked, following him.

He spun and cupped my cheek with his hand, tugging my head down for another kiss. Caught off guard, I still responded eagerly to him. His mouth was cool and minty fresh—like always—while mine was hot. We both lost ourselves for a moment. Then he leaned back and murmured, "Because you can't cook."

"What?" I asked, catching my breath.

He tapped my nose affectionately with his finger. "So you don't know how long it takes to get dinner ready for company." He shook his head in mock disappointment. "Too bad you didn't drive a bit faster."

I scowled at his retreating back.

I decided to head upstairs for a shower. I needed to wash off after playing around in the woods all afternoon.

Fifteen minutes later, freshly dressed and groomed, I came back down to offer my help. Caden had the kitchen looking like something out of a celebrity cooking show, every inch of the space meticulously organized into rows of cutting boards, pots of water, carefully chopped vegetables, arranged ingredients, and, in one corner, a stack of dinnerware.

He indicated the dishes and told me I could set the table, which was not nearly swanky enough for the meal Caden was preparing. It was just an old patio set with three matching chairs and a fourth that didn't belong at all. Our dining space was large, but since our living room was upstairs, we'd bisected the dining room and placed a sofa and TV on the far side of it from the kitchen, the dining table between them. It meant that both spaces—dining room and makeshift living room—were tight, especially with guests over, but we could cook and watch the television at the same time. I dutifully set the table and then, after Caden assured me my help was neither needed nor wanted, tidied up the area. Mostly that meant rearranging items we'd placed haphazardly when unpacking our boxes.

I received an alert from my phone—or possibly Artie—that Rachelle and Matlas were on their way, as well as an ETA.

Caden and I hadn't lived here long enough to justify a deep clean, but the carpet had seen its fair share of foot traffic during the move, and the cardboard boxes laden with our things had flattened it in spots. I ran the vacuum over them, smoothing them out. That finished, I retreated to the couch. Which, admittedly, was a bit of an inflated term; it was a loveseat at best. Our true couch was upstairs in the living room proper, and it was the same model as the one I'd rein-carnated on.

I found and began streaming a sitcom we could play in the back-ground, then finally relaxed. It only lasted for about eight minutes, but it felt good to just check out, breathing in the aroma of Caden's cooking. My mind tried to tackle the problem of the mysterious horse slayer, but I forced it to shut up. Quiet moments like these were few and far between of late.

A few minutes before Rachelle and Matlas were due to arrive, I got up and refilled the dogs' food trays. With snacks. Because I couldn't resist spoiling them.

The doorbell rang, and Caden poked his head out of the kitchen. "Can you get that?"

I was already on my way. "Hey, guys," I said as I opened the door. "Th—" I cut off as I realized the figure standing there wasn't either of my friends.

He *was* familiar, though. I'd seen him watching me and Caden that morning, across the street, behind a Mustang.

I swallowed. Up close, he was, in a word, stunning. Dark hair and eyes, tall but not towering, with a musculature that his thin, slightly too-tight cotton shirt celebrated. His lips quirked in a smoldering smile that seemed to catch my lungs on fire, plunging them down into my stomach. I suddenly found it hard to breathe.

It was glamour.

I knew it, named it, but still it crooned to me. Thick and intoxicat-ing, it dug little barbs into my skin, eliciting goose bumps and sending sensations running up and down my body. I'd never been so aware of my skin; it felt like it was sizzling, like it was heated from within. It felt *good*.

"You." It was all I could manage.

He smiled, a flicker like that of an ember burning behind his otherwise deep, steady brown eyes. "Hello, Emery. I've been searching for you. I need your help."

7

I licked my too-hot lips. "What the hell are you doing here?" I hissed.

His glamour whispered over me again, cool puffs of air on my skin, heavy with unspoken promises.

It pissed me off.

I cast a quick glance over my shoulder, but Caden hadn't emerged from the kitchen. I forced the man back a few paces and stepped out into the cold night air after him, closing the door behind me.

Nyx.

Remembering his name sent me hurtling hundreds, if not thousands, of years backward in time. A kaleidoscope of memories overwhelmed my mind, snippets of experiences overlaid atop one another, time and time again, until they ceased to have individual meaning but a larger picture emerged.

Of bodies together. Icy fingers brushing fevered skin. Husky words slithering across my cheek and tickling my ear. The musk of sweat and brimstone. Dreams, so many dreams, each one building a tower of promises that caught my breath. Teeth grazed my lips and assured me release, while those promises mounted higher and higher.

Nyx beneath the starry sky, naked, the moonlight sculpting his perfect muscles and...

Enough. I get it.

My mind snapped back to the front porch. My jaw was clenched, hands balled into fists. My body still tingled from his glamour—and the memories, which would have made me flush if I weren't already red from anger.

That last memory hadn't even been real. But that was the thing about Nyx: illusion was just part of the seduction. In some ways, he couldn't help it; he fed upon the carnal energy between him and his prey. It was the only thing that sated him.

Somehow, he'd found me. I shouldn't have been overly surprised; as a Malevolent incarnate, he loved to show up when he was least wanted.

"I told you," he said in his sultry voice. "I need your help."

I stared at him. "Stow the glamour, Nyx."

He grinned, revealing a set of perfect white teeth. "What glamour?" At my furious expression, his grin widened. "Maybe you've just missed me."

"Not a chance. And I'm not interested in helping you."

He affected a wounded expression. I couldn't help but notice that his slight shift narrowed the distance between us. "Come now, Emery. You haven't even heard me out."

I stepped back, but my butt hit the now-closed door. "There's nothing you could say..." I trailed off. *Shit.* There was, unfortunately, one thing he could use against me to guarantee my help. And we both knew it.

He saw the look in my eyes and sighed, his breath pluming in the cold night. "No, I won't mislead you. Not about... that. This has to do with me and me alone."

I set my jaw despite my relief. "I'm not interested."

"Oh, I think you're *very* interested," he purred, making his words into an implication. He hadn't taken another step forward—not that I'd seen—but he was somehow closer to me again.

"I think you should go, Nyx."

He pouted, taking in my rigid pose. "This incarnation of yours is so stiff, Emery. Is that little angel of yours not taking care of your needs?"

I felt my blood rise. "My 'needs' are none of your concern. Caden and I are happy, something you and I never achieved together, because the only things you care about are yourself and your appetite." I was leaning forward to drive home my point when I suddenly became aware of how close his face was to mine. Which made me furious all over again. He was manipulating me.

So it surprised me when he backed off. "I didn't come here to fight with you, Emery. I admit I was disappointed to find you with Caden yet again." He placed his hand lightly on my chest to forestall my response. It probably wouldn't have worked, except that the contact sent electricity zinging through me. "But only because I require your help, and you are so much more amenable when I find you dallying with mortals."

I knocked his hand away, ignoring the pang of loss when we broke contact. It was just the glamour. "Caden isn't the reason I won't help you." I absently rubbed my chest where his hand had rested. "You are. I can't even remember all of our pasts together, but I can remember enough. We aren't good together, Nyx."

He smirked. "Then you aren't recalling the right memories."

Which made me think of the memories I *had* recalled, and I felt a blush creeping up my neck. Damn him. At least he probably couldn't see it in the dark. In response to that thought, Nyx seemed to glide closer, and I swear I detected the hint of a hungry expression behind his deceptively demure eyes.

We were eye to eye, close enough that the mist from our breath mingled. I wanted to push him away, but his lousy glamour was clouding my brain. "I like this incarnation," he said in a low voice. "Good height. Great shoulders. You were built for me, Emery."

I opened my mouth to argue, but the words caught in my throat as I became aware of the points of contact between our bodies. I was wedged between the door frame and his chiseled torso. And, to my shame, I didn't hate it. I—

A growl came from somewhere behind him. Then it was taken up by multiple throats at once, and someone said, "Emery?"

Wonderful. I'd been so distracted by Nyx's glamour that I hadn't even noticed their arrival.

The growls seemed to pop the glamour around me like a bubble, and I could breathe again. Furious, I shoved him away from me, saying, "This is exactly why I won't help you, Nyx. Go back to wherever you crawled out from. I won't dance on your strings any longer."

Rachelle and Matlas stood on the walk, staring at us. All three puppies stood on the lawn in wide stances, teeth bared, hackles on end as they stared unblinkingly at Nyx. Separately, their growls were adorable. But together, their voices blended and merged into a layered thrum that I felt in my chest, deep and menacing. Just like the Hellhound's had been.

Nyx glanced at the puppies in surprise, which he tried to cover with amusement. "Oh, you'll help me, Emery Luple," he said quietly. "You won't be able to resist."

"You're wrong." I hated that I was trembling, but at least my voice sounded firm.

He shook his head as he retreated down the walk. He skirted the puppies, though. "No one forgets their first, Emery," he tossed over his shoulder. He gave polite nods to Rachelle and Matlas as he threaded between them. The movement was natural, the message subliminal, but I saw it for what it was. Nyx thrived on dividing couples.

Remarkably—although it made me burn with shame—Matlas and Rachelle barely gave him a glance before returning their attention to me. His glamour should have at least pulled out a lingering look, but all I read on their faces was concern.

Mittens, Mask, and Beard turned in unison as he walked away, orienting on his retreating form. As soon as he stepped onto the curb, though, they ceased their growling and bounded forward to greet me, tails wagging.

I crouched down, basking in their puppy kisses and letting their emphatic adoration push away the last vestiges of Nyx's glamour. With all three of them jumping on me, I was nearly bowled over.

"What was that about?" Rachelle asked, coming forward. She was a warrior at heart, but no one had told her body: while athletic, she was a little too short to be physically intimidating. Her long, high-lighted brown hair was usually worn up in a ponytail, but since she'd met Matlas, she'd been wearing it down and styled more often. Her deep blue eyes looked huge in the dim light of the front porch and were wide with concern.

"Nothing," I said between doggy kisses. "Just an old"—I spared a glance at Matlas—"friend."

Matt Atlas—Matlas—didn't know about incarnates. And he didn't *want* to know. Well, that wasn't entirely accurate. Rather, he wanted to figure out the mystery on his own. A longtime fan of my vlogs (or at least he thought he was, since reality had created false memories of vlogs going back years before I reincarnated... it's complicated), Matlas was a Debunker. That's what my mortal fans called them-selves, because they thought that I went around and debunked myths. In truth, I used *There's Always a Loophole* as a way to help incarnates—who were based on those myths—and draw attention away from them by "debunking" their existence. Occasionally those same incarnates would reach out to me for assistance or even protec-tion. It was an arrangement that worked for everyone: I got paid, mostly by online advertisers, and I got to help incarnates in need. Rachelle was my business partner. Which cast her in various roles, from cameraperson to media manager. I really couldn't do it without her—a fact she reminded me of quite frequently.

Sparks had flown between her and Matlas when we'd arrived at his family's cemetery in Maltby. But when things started to get weird —really, really weird—Matlas realized there was a lot more going on than we were telling him. Instead of demanding answers as I expected, he decided he wanted to solve the mystery for himself. And if that meant he had to spend more time around Rachelle and delight her with his bizarre theories, so much the better.

Matlas himself cut quite the figure on the lawn, standing like a protective silhouette at Rachelle's shoulder. Literally tall, dark, and handsome, he had intimidated me at first; then he'd opened that mouth of his, let out a high, nervous laugh, and told me how much of a fan he was.

We were basically best buddies after that.

"You sure you're okay, man?" he asked. He frowned. "Is this 'friend' trouble?"

I stood up, and the puppies began nipping and playing with each other around my calves. "Like you wouldn't believe." I hadn't missed the emphasis he put on friend. Or how he watched me with narrowed eyes, clearly trying to piece together who or what Nyx had been.

As clever as he was, he wouldn't arrive at the truth anytime soon. It was just too complicated. And specific.

I opened the front door, and the dogs barreled inside. They slid and slipped on the hardwood floor, becoming a puppy pile at Caden's feet where he was busy cooking. I held the door for Rachelle and Matlas, who removed their coats and hung them on the pegs in the entry. I avoided making eye contact with Rachelle, who was quite clearly trying to catch my attention. I was embarrassed, and I didn't even know how much they'd witnessed.

"Welcome to our humble abode," I said, gesturing grandly.

"Oh, please," Rachelle quipped, "there's nothing humble about you."

Our relationship in two lines, folks. "Not true. We Luples are known for three things." I ticked each one off on a finger as I led them past the den and toward the kitchen. "Our towering intellect. Our renowned good looks. And our humility."

She rolled her eyes. "Okay, *Dad*, I'm glad you made it to the party. Where did you pick up that joke, 1959?"

I grinned. "Well before then, actually. Medieval people had a sense of humor, too, you know." And I winked at Matlas.

His easy grin faltered for a moment as he realized what I was implying. "Right," he said, not rising to the bait. When he turned his back, Rachelle smacked me on the arm.

"Hey, I'm just keeping the romance alive between you two," I said innocently.

To my surprise, she blushed. Ha! This was almost too easy. "Kind of like the romance between you and the mystery man back there?" she growled.

My heart rate spiked, and I glanced guiltily to where Caden and Matlas were greeting each other before I realized that she was ribbing me. Her smirk, however, disappeared as her eyes widened. "I was kidding, Emery." She grabbed my arm and pulled me into the den, which my mom and Caden had set up as my office. "What the hell?" she hissed. "Who was he?"

I sighed. "No one," I said, trying for a reassuring tone. "Certainly nothing romantic."

"Not good enough."

"Come on, Rachelle. You know I love Caden."

"You love your best friend, too, which is why you're going to tell her why you're keeping things from your boyfriend. And since I love you back, I'll *consider* not telling on you."

"Telling on me? What are you, six?"

She arched an eyebrow. "Quit avoiding the subject. Why don't you want Caden to know about your ex?"

I spluttered. "How did you—?"

"You, O Incarnate on High," she said, jabbing a finger into my chest, "are not nearly as indecipherable as you think you are." She folded her arms. "Last chance. Who was he?"

I swallowed. "The Incubus incarnate."

She continued to stare at me. "What is that?"

Oh, right. Rachelle was a quick learner, but she was still new to the whole myth thing. I peeked my head out of the den and looked down the hall. Caden and Matlas were chatting amiably, so I ducked back in. "Do you know what the Succubus is?"

Her brow creased. "Isn't that like a girl demon, or vampire, or something? She makes men fall in love with her and then drains their life. Pretty sure there was one on *Charmed*."

"Yeah. The Succubus is fairly well-known. She's also Nyx's sister."

Rachelle's eyebrows shot up. "So it has a name."

I scowled. "It's not important. Anyway, he and his sister are demon incarnates; that's the family classification I'm using, because there is only one Demon. And like you said, they're also sort of like the Vampire. They both seduce people—of all genders, actually—and then feed off of the, er," I licked my lips, "uh, sexual energy between them and their victims. If they feast too much, they can be deadly, but they both know how to, um, nibble or sip to sate themselves for a while without hurting their partner. Prey, I mean." Damn, I was sweating. I rushed on. "They usually invade people's dreams. It's where they prefer to do their seducing, because it's much harder to get caught there. Makes for a convenient Lair, too, since it's tough for others to access."

Rachelle nodded thoughtfully. "Okay. So, what did he want?"

"My help. But I refused."

"On account of your happy relationship. With the guy you're hiding your ex from."

I didn't rise to the bait. "Exactly." I glanced at the door. "Can we get back to our boyfriends now?"

"Why did he want your help?" she asked, ignoring my request.

"I'm not sure. I didn't let him finish."

"You're clever. What do you *think* he wanted?" she pressed.

I hesitated. "I really don't know, Rachelle," I said after a moment. When Nyx had shown up at the door, I had thought I knew the reason, but he'd assured me that his request didn't involve... anyone else. Just him.

Which was odd. He had the perfect instrument with which to coerce my help, but he didn't use it against me. Why? He essentially had no morals, so it wasn't due to honesty or loyalty.

"All right," Rachelle said, seeming satisfied with our little chat. "But you should tell Caden."

I nodded, relieved. "I will."

And I would, but not until after tomorrow's Watch meeting. Not only did I want to avoid putting even more on Caden's plate when he was already so stressed, I also feared he would insist on bringing Nyx into the Watch, Malevolent or not. Especially if Nyx turned the charm on.

And, if I was being completely honest with myself, I didn't relish the thought of Caden learning about Nyx. Better to put it off. I was uncomfortable with the feelings Nyx had stirred in me, true, but I was even more embarrassed by the fact that I'd fallen for the Incubus in the first place. He and his sister were, after all, known to prey upon weak-willed individuals. And, if my memories were to be believed, I'd fallen for him more than once over the millennia.

Just great.

"No way!" Caden said, laughing as he set down his drink. "That didn't happen."

Matlas grinned, leaning back and putting his arm nonchalantly behind Rachelle's chair, his fingers resting gently on her shoulder. "It really did. I almost quit the class, but my parents wouldn't let me."

Rachelle and I exchanged glances, unable to see the big deal. But then, we didn't go to college like them sophisticated folk. Well, that wasn't entirely true. I possessed more university degrees than just about anyone I knew, but *this* Emery hadn't gone for more than a quarter before quitting to start *There's Always a Loophole* with Rachelle. All of this was determined in my backstory, of course. I'd reincarnated a few months after dropping out, so it was reality's fault, not mine.

"I thought getting called out like that in front of the whole class only happened in the movies," Caden was saying. "Especially in an econ class."

"Well, to be fair, Highline has fewer students per class than U-Dub. But it was my first day. I was terrified."

Crunching from my right drew my attention briefly to Mittens, who was daintily eating out of her bowl. Beard and Mask had retired to the couch, where they'd promptly fallen asleep after the evening's excitement.

"Econ?" I chimed in. "Are you majoring in business?"

Matlas made a face. "Only if my father has his way. I'm mostly taking the class to humor him." He tipped his drink back with his free hand and finished it off, putting the empty glass next to his similarly empty dinner plate. "He means well, but I don't have the same dreams he does... and that doesn't seem to matter to him. I shouldn't complain. It's just normal dad stuff, right?"

Exchanging a look with Caden, I said, "We actually wouldn't know."

"Neither of them has a dad," Rachelle said, patting his hand on her shoulder.

The poor guy looked like he'd swallowed poison. "Oh, jeez, I'm sorry, guys. I didn't think before I spoke."

"I have six moms," Caden said, waving away the concern, "so I never felt like I was missing a parent. Mother's Day gets pretty expensive, though."

"I've never had a father," I said. I waggled my eyebrows at Matlas. "Ever. Mom didn't need a man to make me." Because my mom didn't "make" me at all. I was conceived by reality as a nineteen-year-old guy, and Lynn Luple had never been pregnant, even though *she* remembered things quite differently. She probably even thought she knew the identity of my dad, since the only thing reality impregnated her with was artificial memories. Ugh, sorry; that's one mental image I didn't mean to conjure.

My remark sparked amusement in Caden, elicited a glare from Rachelle, and made Matlas look at me with wary interest. He knew I liked to poke fun at his game with Rachelle, but I suspected he was also cataloging the information I doled out, fueling his theories about what was going on.

"Are you trying to make IVF sound mystical?" Matlas asked. Then he waved away his own question. "Wait, don't answer that. I think you mean it more literally. A virgin birth, perhaps? And just last week you stopped a cult of religious fanatics who were trying to use you to break into hell itself." Partially true. "And you two somehow healed Mask of a broken leg." That was, of course, all Caden. Matlas looked back and forth between us for a moment, then finally ventured uncertainly, "Are you... like some sort of modern Jesus? And Caden is an angel your real father sent to protect you?"

Rachelle squealed. "That was one of my first guesses, too!" I couldn't help but crack a smile; a few weeks ago, she wouldn't have been caught dead making that sound.

"Really?" He was obviously thrilled by her enthusiastic response. This was exactly why they played this game.

I shook my head, smiling. "No, I'm definitely not Jesus."

"But it was a good guess," Rachelle said, casting a sly grin across the table. "He *does* tend to think he's god's gift to mankind."

"Could you imagine?" I snorted. "I'm gay, Matlas. I don't think the world's ready for my brand of Jesus."

"Oh, the world's most *definitely* not ready for that," Rachelle agreed. "But it has nothing to do with you being gay."

Caden laughed. "I grew up in a convent and was raised by nuns. The world might surprise you." He looked between me and Rachelle. "Are we not going to give him partial credit for that guess?"

Matlas waved his hand in a warding-off gesture. "No, no, it's okay. All-or-nothing. I get it." But he watched Caden speculatively. Since we hadn't addressed his angel guess, I could almost see him connecting dots in his mind.

I stood and cleared the table as Caden and Matlas returned to their conversation about college life.

Mittens had finally finished her meal and was headed toward the couch where her brothers were sleeping. I was still getting to know their individual personalities, but she reminded me of a much older dog. The way she carefully watched over Mask and Beard seemed almost maternal. Actually, all three tended to act like pets we'd had for a long time rather than young, untrained puppies. They slept a lot, sure, and they had boundless energy, but they also innately knew to use the doggy door we'd installed and to utilize the plot of yard in the back as their potty area. We'd color-coded their bowls—we'd ordered customized ones with their names printed on them, but they hadn't yet arrived—and they only ate from the bowl we assigned them. They never stole or squabbled over food, despite the bowls being laid out right next to each other.

Maybe being the litter of an incarnate had instilled some of their mother's instincts in them. That... wasn't really how it worked, though. I was probably just misremembering how easy it was to raise three puppies.

Caden, always organized, had filled the sink with soapy water in preparation for the dishes, so I dropped off the armful of plates and then opened the refrigerator and fished out the store-bought cheesecake we'd picked up.

As I juggled the dessert plates and silverware, my mind drifted unbidden to Nyx. He'd undoubtedly find *this* Emery, the host of quiet dinner parties, to be dull. He was drawn to the excitement of action, of drama. Of passion.

Well, he could cram his judgment. I'd hunted the Sasquatch today, and that was anything but boring. Besides, these moments of quiet happiness belonged entirely to Caden. That thought made me smile. Nyx's arrival may have thrown my thoughts into turmoil, but in the end, that was all on the surface. Deep down, where it counted most, my heart was still my angel's.

What *did* Nyx want, other than my attention or a quick "meal"? He had said he needed my help. While I couldn't really trust him— correction, I couldn't trust him *at all*—I had to admit there was something genuine in his request. Something that wormed its way beneath the walls I'd thrown up between us.

The ironic thing was that Caden would probably urge me to help him. Even if I told him that Nyx was Malevolent. Even if I told him about our history together. Caden cared too much about incarnates in trouble and too little about the distinction between Malevolents and the other three, more reasonable, classifications.

Or... could it be *my* issue? Was I allowing my prejudices against the monsters of the incarnate world to compromise my judgment? I'd known Malevolents who'd chosen to reform, though usually they only managed to do so for a single incarnation. But for inhuman incarnates, that could be far longer than a mortal lifespan. Centuries.

No. Malevolents were called that because it was in their very nature to harm people or society. Nyx needed to feed, and his food source, whether he liked it or not—and I knew firsthand he *relished* it —was the life energy of humans. It was no coincidence some of my incarnations spent with Nyx were short-lived; it wasn't solely due to the fast-paced, often dangerous lifestyle we chose to live.

But, a disloyal voice inside me whispered, Nyx was capable of temperance, too. I *had* experienced lives with him that were long and whole.

"Emery?"

I blinked. I'd reached the table and was standing there, arms full of dessert, dishes, and forks. Blushing, I handed the plates and silverware to Caden. "Just lost in thought."

"About tomorrow's big meeting?" Matlas asked.

"You know about that?"

He looked faintly disappointed. "Not really. Just that all three of you have some secretive get-together tomorrow."

"Not that secretive," I said. "You can attend, if you want to."

"I can?"

I shrugged. "Sure, why not? Rachelle's a mortal, and she's going." It wasn't until his eyes went round that I realized I'd slipped.

Matlas took a few shallow breaths, then tried for a smile. The edges of his lips quivered, at least. "Well," he said faintly, "I'm glad Rachelle's, um, *mortal.*" His wide eyes tracked my movement as I placed the cheesecake in the middle of the table and opened the box. His head didn't move an inch, though.

I knew that reaction. It was the same way you'd watch a rabid animal.

Rachelle peered at Matlas with concern, the space between them seeming to grow. I met Caden's eyes, and he gave a little nod, almost imperceptible.

So I gave Matlas my cockiest grin and said, "Well, what do you say, tasty mortal? Care to join our meeting? You'd be especially popular during our snack break."

The tension stretched into a taut moment on the verge of snapping. Then Matlas inhaled sharply and reclined a bit, his anxiety bleeding away. "Wow, I'm gullible. You got me."

We all released nervous laughs, and I sliced the cheesecake, but despite his change in attitude, there was still a rigidness to Matlas's posture that told me we hadn't fooled him completely. That was just as well. If he stuck around, he'd eventually learn the whole truth. Feeding it to him in bites was probably kinder than shoving the whole meal down his throat without a chaser.

Rachelle shared a smile with me, obviously grateful for my attempt to make him more comfortable. It made me appreciate her all over again. Within minutes of my most recent reincarnation, she and I had been attacked by the Genie, and I'd subsequently told her everything. Just threw her in the deep end, expecting she could swim. And—well, she hadn't really even flinched. I mean, sure, she'd batted an eye or two at learning the Easter Bunny was real and her best friend was immortal, but all in all she'd taken the news in stride. Even when she broke her leg fighting off an especially toothy urban legend.

I told you. She was a warrior.

In an uncharacteristic, almost out-of-body experience, I felt a pang for the future Emerys who wouldn't get the chance to know her. Rachelle was special, even by my immortal standards. In all my lifetimes, I hadn't had a friend quite like her. When I died, she would forget all about me as reality scrubbed her memories. But I doubt I'd ever truly forget her.

Bleak. I shook myself and forced my attention back to the present. I took a few bites of my cheesecake as Caden expertly navigated the conversation back to harmless subjects, like his work at the hospital and his coworkers' antics amid a serious profession.

Less than an hour later, Rachelle and Matlas excused themselves, and Caden and I walked them to the front door. It was already fairly late, and I was sure they wanted some time to themselves before their night ended. Despite already going through one life-or-death situation together, they'd only been dating a week.

I half expected Nyx to be lurking out on the street, but thankfully he was nowhere in sight. Rachelle gave us both hugs, Matlas thanked us for the meal, and then we closed the door behind their retreating backs.

"That was exactly what I needed to get my mind off things," Caden said.

"Good," I responded, smiling. I wished I could say the same.

He headed toward the kitchen, but I caught him by the hand. "Go on," I said, nodding toward the stairs. "I know you have some work to do with Artie. I'll finish the dishes and clean up."

He grabbed the back of my neck and pulled me into a kiss. "Thank you," he whispered against my mouth. "I love you, beamish boy."

I breathed him in and felt my body warm. I chuckled. "Go, before I don't want to let you."

We parted, and he headed upstairs. Mask, who seemed to have a strong connection with Caden, hopped off the couch and followed him.

As I cleaned the kitchen and dining area, then attacked the dishes, I felt a sense of peace. There was something satisfying in the completion of mundane chores, a reminder that in spite of the chaos of my role as the Protagonist, I could still find some sense of normalcy.

I dunked a stemless wineglass in the soapy water and carefully wiped it clean before drying it with a fluffy white towel.

Sometimes it felt like I was built—or incarnated—solely for danger. Often that was exciting; who didn't want to go on adventures, solve murders, and save the day? The fact that I couldn't die—at least, not permanently—made the adventure that much more enjoyable. Even so, think of it like a vacation: eventually, you want to go home. To return to your regular patterns, to the comfort of daily tasks. Now, imagine every vacation included dead bodies, gun battles, very little sleep, and long chases by foot, car, or elephant. It was exhausting.

I dipped another plate beneath the faucet and scrubbed at it with a soapy sponge.

I'm not saying I would trade my reality for a traditional, unexceptional life. Being the Protagonist was an integral piece of my identity, a badge I wore with pride. But a month or two off, now and again, would be bliss.

I didn't expect that to happen any time soon, though. I was destined to have the thrilling lives others only imagined or wrote about. That made sense. It wasn't overly exciting reading about a character who just hung around their home and did dishes, after all.

9

Hi, guys. Three books in and Emery finally deigns to give me one page to talk with you. Generous, huh? At least I get to be the first one—what? Caden already wrote a passage? That's it, Emery Luple, we're in a fight.

As the resident mortal-incarnate expert, I'll let you in on a little secret: the world of incarnates isn't as daunting and mysterious as our high-and-mighty Protagonist makes it out to be. The hardest part is keeping track of all the different urban legends out there. Whoever said you'll never use Greek mythology in the real world was clearly a mortal. Not that there's anything wrong with that, obviously.

Actually, I take it back: the hardest part of the incarnate world is keeping secrets from those you care about. Matt's made it into a game with me, sure, but I can tell he's a bit terrified to learn the truth. Which is a real shame—it's not as scary as everyone thinks. Just stay off of urban myth spook sites (There's Always a Loophole excluded, of course), as some of them will give you nightmares, especially when you understand they're real. Still, it's a big world, so what's the likelihood you'll be a victim of the Bogeyman? Low. You're far more likely to die in a car accident. Just saying.

Speaking of There's Always a Loophole, *you should check it out on streaming services everywhere! Emery's been so busy he probably hasn't taken the time to plug our show, and I don't know if he's told you, but pretty much any time I'm off page, I'm working my ass off to create content, edit it, and promote it. And who do you think gets all the credit?*

That's pretty typical, though. Even back in high school, he was the star of the show. I guess, technically, he wasn't even there, but I don't like to think about that. Easier just to pretend that our story began years ago, with a silly schoolgirl crush that led to the most fulfilling friendship I've ever had.

Wait, this has already been a page? But I didn't get a chance to tell you my theory about Ahedrian, or about the incarnate I saw in the woods at Paradise Lake Cemetery that I'm fairly sure Emery missed, or abou—

~

$\mathcal{U}$pstairs, I found Caden sitting on the bed, still fully dressed, the laptop resting on his legs. Next to him, Mask lifted his head off his paws to look at me as I entered, his little tail wagging. I gave him a head scratch and then, without disturbing Caden, went into the closet and changed into basketball shorts. I grabbed the fuzzy pajama pants I knew he loved and tossed them at him.

He glanced up in surprise, took in my bare chest appreciatively, then set his laptop aside and got into his nightclothes. Disappointingly, he kept his white tee on. As I climbed into bed next to him, he pulled the computer back onto his lap. Mask obligingly crept to the edge of the mattress and resettled himself.

I yawned as I read what he was working on. Deceptively organized into a bullet-point list, it appeared to be nothing more than a collection of jumbled thoughts and notes about tomorrow's meeting. Good, that probably meant he'd already finished the agenda.

I tugged on his sleeve. "Hey. How much longer, you think?" The meeting was early tomorrow, and it was already late. "I want you to be well rested, so you'll be your absolute best in the morning."

Then again, I thought, eyeing the way his white tee hugged his lean stomach, *maybe he doesn't need that much rest...*

He shot me a tolerant smile that said he knew exactly what I was thinking. "I'll be up for a while yet, Em. Why don't you get some sleep?"

I sighed. "You're sure?" I asked, tickling his thigh through the fuzzy pants.

He gently removed my hand. "I'm sure." He brought my fingers to his lips and kissed them to take away any sting to my ego. "I'll make it up to you tomorrow night, okay?"

"Definitely." I paused. "You don't owe me anything, though. What you're doing is important. You know I'm aware of that, right?"

He assured me that he did, but I could tell he was distracted. So I resolved to show him my support: I rolled over, leaving him alone, and went to sleep.

I dreamt.

It was one of those hauntingly vivid dreams.

The Lucid. I know this place. The thought—like dreams themselves, so often—was quickly forgotten.

I stood atop a tower. Despite the commanding view, the colors felt muted. The sky above and all around me was overcast, gray and flat. Low ramparts surrounded the space, the weathered stone a uniform sandy brown. Set into the floor, off center, was a faded hatch that presumably led to lower levels. There was something vaguely familiar about that hatch.

I realized I was on a watchtower, like those at the top of a castle or other defensive fortification. It was difficult to distinguish details in the surrounding environment, subdued as it was, but I thought I could make out a patch of forest and, rising beyond, a great, snow-laden mountain with a crater at its tip. I knew that mountain, didn't I?

A flicker of motion caught my eye.

Creeping across the top of the rampart was a fat black spider. With its front legs, it felt its way across the uneven stone. It arrived at a large crevice and stopped, stretching its legs to test the distance before trying to advance further.

Fascinated by the arachnid's journey across the lip of the tower, I almost missed the sound. It began as a faint annoyance but grew rapidly. Too rapidly, in that way of dreams. A foreboding sensation flooded through me.

Something was terribly wrong.

Darkness fell over me, and I looked up. A writhing shadow crept across the sky, blocking out the light. A black cloud?

No. It was hundreds, maybe thousands, of crows. They streamed across the horizon, blotting out the nondescript gray sky. Their raucous cries built and expanded until I couldn't hear anything else.

A single crow swooped down and landed on the rampart. Quicker than a cobra strike, it snapped its beak forward. It snatched up the spider and gulped it down, bobbing its head as it swallowed its meal.

For some reason, I felt horrified. From my angle, I could only see the crow's profile. It cocked its head, piercing me with the burning eye on the left side of its face.

The crows suddenly descended. Grating caws, black feathers, and sharp talons spun around me like a vortex. I ducked my head and cried out, unable to stop them from swarming over me, each individual bird a part of something grander, something I couldn't discern.

In the irrational way of some nightmares, I understood there was something important about this sequence. Something I was missing. Even my dream self knew that.

I strained. Tried to run toward the stone hatch. I couldn't find it in the flickering, fluttering darkness of crow feathers. Where was it?

I couldn't run, couldn't move. My legs wouldn't work. I collapsed to the rough stone and tried to crawl across the top of the tower. The ceaseless calls of the crows mocked my lack of progress. I couldn't escape.

I was swallowed up by the flurry of crows just as completely as the spider had been.

An incongruous sound broke through the nightmare. I grasped it, using it to pull me away from the infinite mass of birds, back to consciousness.

I awoke with a gasp, soaked with sweat. Breathing hard, I whipped my head around, trying to get my bearings. My bed. Caden was asleep next to me.

My phone was ringing, its display indicating that it was just after four in the morning. That was the sound that had penetrated my nightmare. Mask cracked an eye at me, as if asking whether I was going to answer the call.

I snatched up the phone. "Hello?" I asked, my voice low and raw. I was dazed, trying unsuccessfully to dislodge the dream—and the unease it summoned—from my mind.

"Emery. It's Gregory."

Something was wrong. I could feel it in the air. Hear it in the strain of his voice.

"Get dressed. There's been a murder. I'll pick you up in ten."

10

"In Anacortes?" I asked, groaning. "You're sure?"

Gregory frowned at me from the driver's seat. "Yes. Why?"

I filled him in on what Ray, Caden, and I had been up to the day before. He listened quietly, never interrupting, as we cruised down the highway in his nice, but old, vehicle.

It felt good to talk; it kept my nightmare from last night at bay. Even doing my best to distract myself, it still worried at my mind. Mostly because it had featured crows. No, I wasn't afraid of them. I was afraid of what they represented.

It was only a dream. I could be overreacting. But I suspected my Protagonist powers were at play, sending me a warning or a message —or an omen. Something I shouldn't ignore. Coincidences like a foreboding nightmare didn't just happen to me; they all too often meant something significant. I was determined to unearth the meaning before it was too late.

I wasn't sure how long Caden had been asleep, but when I snuck out of the house to meet Gregory, I didn't wake him. I left a note explaining where I'd gone and that I'd be back in time to help him set up for the Watch meeting.

Gregory absorbed the information and asked, "What do you

think killed Spray?"

I hesitated. "I'm not sure. The broken mirror and the withered appearance of the horse made me wonder if the Vampire was in town. But something tells me that's not it."

We were both quiet for a few minutes. The sky was dark and the traffic light this early in the morning. Which was a good thing. The Watch meeting started at nine. We needed to get to Anacortes, investigate a murder scene, and be back before then. No pressure.

"Because the victim was a horse?"

"I guess so. What I need is the version of the Vampire that attacks animals instead of people."

"You're describing the Chupacabra."

Huh. "I am, aren't I?"

Gregory glanced in my direction. "You don't sound convinced."

"The Chupacabra is almost perfect, but why would it be this far north? Even when it ventures out of its Territories in Puerto Rico or Mexico, it tends to stay in the southern US. Attacking livestock in Washington is uncharacteristic. Especially since we haven't heard of any other cases, and I would expect a trail of slain goats and horses leading all the way back to the border."

"I'll keep my ears open for any other cases matching your description."

"Thanks, Gregory," I said, absently looking out the window at the shadowy shapes that flickered by.

"Something else?"

"I'm not sure." I let out a breath. "Something about Spray's body is bothering me."

Gregory mulled that over for a moment, changing lanes to pass a slow truck. "From what you say, it almost sounds like the horse was drained of its essence. Its life force, rather than its blood."

I considered. "That would explain the discoloration. A human drained of its blood might turn white and pale, but that wouldn't explain why the horse's coat would change color."

"Right," Gregory agreed, "and then there's the blood on Bigfoot's muzzle."

It took me a moment to realize why that was meaningful. When it struck me, I nearly smacked myself on the forehead. *"Of course!* Assuming the Sasquatch isn't the culprit—and not only is Caden pretty confident of that, but Bigfoot doesn't have any draining powers —then the Sasquatch most likely just came across the carcass and fed. But since it had blood all over its muzzle, the horse wasn't drained of it." My excitement dimmed as I realized what that meant. "Oh. That rules out the Vampire and the Chupacabra."

"That's a good thing, Emery. You don't want to spend energy pursuing the wrong leads."

"I suppose. Where does that leave us?"

"Which incarnates drain creatures of their life?"

The obvious answer was Nyx. The Incubus siphoned life from his victims. But those victims were strictly human. Strictly human*oid*, at any rate. I squirmed at the unhappy mental image of my ex seducing a horse. I don't care if that's basically how the Minotaur legend started, it still gave me the heebie-jeebies.

It wasn't Nyx. He'd never stoop to that level, especially when there were plenty of potential human subjects in the vicinity. Besides, the broken mirror didn't fit with him, either. Unless it was broken by accident and I was seeing clues where none existed.

"You have an idea?" Gregory asked.

I shook my head, perhaps a little too emphatically. "No. There are a handful of Malevolents with the ability to drain the life from others, but I don't know how to narrow it down." I chewed on my lip, thinking. "What if we—" I cut off as I caught Gregory covering a small smile. "What?" I demanded.

He shook his head. "Nothing."

"No really, what?"

He kept his eyes on the road. "It's not relevant."

"I don't mind. What's so funny?"

He sighed. "I just noticed you and your mother have the same mannerism. You both chew on your lip when you're thinking."

Oh. Mom and Gregory had gone on a coffee date about a week ago, but Mom hadn't said much about it. Then again, I'd been so busy moving, I hadn't really asked for details. And Gregory, as a man of few words, hadn't mentioned it at all.

"So," I said after an awkward silence, "how'd the date go?"

"The first was good. The second, better."

My relationship with Gregory was becoming complicated. We were comrades and had been for ages, across many reincarnations. Despite the perceived age difference in our current bodies, we were peers. Then he and my mom started dating. And suddenly he felt more like a father figure that I didn't request or especially want. Although I tried to quash such emotions, I found myself just a touch too eager to please him; similarly, his rare disapproval weighed heavily on me.

The corner of my mind that I associated with my immortal identity scoffed at such trivial concerns. I was, in actuality, far older than the Watchman. But that didn't change my feelings. This was why reincarnation was so tricky: emotions and baggage from the backstory that reality created for me cluttered my perceptions. It made each life meaningful and unique, but also more convoluted than it would otherwise be.

"You've been on two dates already?"

Gregory nodded. "Last night." His fingers flexed on the steering wheel. "Lynn's a special lady, Emery. I can see why your current incarnation is so well-adjusted."

I stared at him. A gleeful emotion slipped through my defenses at his compliment, but I kept it from my face. "Thanks, I guess. Is this going to become something serious?"

"Can't say. Time will tell."

How practical.

We were quiet for miles. Though uncomfortable at first, it quickly settled into a companionable silence. As we neared our destination, the sky began to lighten across the horizon, separating shadows from night, trees and landscape emerging out of the darkness.

I finally spoke. "This case in Anacortes. Is the incarnate the victim or the murderer?"

"As far as I know, neither."

I sat up straighter in my seat. "What? Then why are we getting involved?"

"Because an incarnate reported the murder."

My heart fell. It was Ray. I just knew it. My powers of coincidence would all but ensure it. And if the Watch wasn't able to solve this case and keep the murderer from striking again, any faith he had in us—whatever was left at this point—would be utterly destroyed.

It was tough to fight through my negative thoughts. I blamed the nightmare from last night. It crouched in the back of my brain like a panther looking through tall grass, haunches bunched, ready to pounce on any happy thought that passed by. I took a few deep breaths, trying to expel the sinister pall.

What if my powers were providing an opportunity rather than an obstacle? If we *did* manage to save the day, perhaps we'd be able to salvage yesterday's debacle and secure Ray's support. Maybe even bring in Walt and Halona as well.

Obstacle or opportunity? Maybe both. Either way, I'd take it. I could just imagine Caden's face if I managed to recruit those three.

As we pulled off the main road and into a neighborhood, I was relieved to see that Gregory wasn't heading back to Amara's ranch. With the specter of my dream riding my emotions, I half expected her to be the victim.

Our destination was obvious. A police SUV blocked off the road, its flashing lights painting the surrounding houses blue and red. Several more police cruisers crowded the driveway of an unremarkable house. It was modern and well-kept, a cookie-cutter model of the houses immediately surrounding it. The yard was small but groomed, two sedans parked sedately in the driveway. An ambulance blocked them in, its rear doors open, and people wearing EMT jackets scurried around, busy with a myriad of tasks. There was even someone handing out coffee in recyclable cups.

Gregory flashed his credentials, spoke a few words, and we parked and approached the house without incident. I was beginning to think his "credentials" were part of his incarnate powers rather than anything recognized by the law, because pesky concerns like jurisdiction and security clearance never seemed to apply to him.

"Gregorius!" a voice called, and a person hustled forward to greet us. "Thank goodness you're here."

The boisterous voice belonged to a woman shaped like a linebacker, her severe face and shaved head reminding me of nothing so much as a drill sergeant, the kind who didn't take flak from anybody. The fierce smile she adopted as she neared us didn't do her face any favors, either. I shivered to think what her scowl must look like.

"Thanks for letting me butt in, Grant. Been what, ten years?"

"Twelve, I think." She took his hand and shook it fondly. "When I worked in Tacoma. Don't see as much trouble since I moved this far north."

"Emery, this is Detective Corporal Monica Grant."

"Call me Grant," she said, extending her hand. "Not even my husband calls me Monica."

"Emery Luple. I work with Gregory as a consultant."

"What kind of consultant?"

Gregory didn't seem inclined to jump in, so I answered, "The best kind. I do a little of everything. I helped Gregory solve the Asker case just last week."

She grunted. "I wish *this* guy had faked his own death." That was the cover story for Micah Asker's murder, though it wasn't true. The Technopath had been killed by Vox Populi, the same cult of incarnate hunters that later took Caden hostage. The Android, who'd been created in Asker's image, had taken his place as head of E-Pluribus, his massive enterprise. "Unfortunately, body's still upstairs. I wouldn't let anyone move anything until Gregorius had a chance to scope out the scene. Wife's a mess."

"Did she witness anything useful about the murderer?" I asked, hopeful.

Grant gave a dark, bitter chuckle. "She *is* the murderer. Swears it was an accident, though."

Normally I would ask why the heck we'd been called if the case was so open and shut, but I realized that something about the situation must've concerned Gregory. Also, I was distracted; something had caught my attention. Sitting on the front lawn, staring unblinkingly at me, was a black cat. When I noticed it, it dipped its head ever so slightly, as though in recognition.

Well, well. The Ijiraat was keeping tabs on me.

Grant ushered us toward the front door of the house. The downstairs was bustling with activity: EMTs, police, and investigation units slipping past us, conversations creating a constant buzz of white noise. The home was welcoming, with a thick rug at the entry and a staircase leading up to the second floor visible from where we stood. To our left, the hallway ended in what looked like a kitchen.

"Where's the man who reported the incident?" Gregory asked Grant.

She looked around, eyebrows knitting. "Not sure. Must've slipped out." She grabbed one of her officers' attention. "Fuller! Find our witness. Gregorius and his partner have some questions for him." A nearby man jumped and scurried off.

We followed Grant upstairs.

Sometimes it amazed me how easy it was to slip into a crime scene. One moment we're on the landing of a staircase, the next I'm passing a hyperventilating middle-aged woman being simultaneously comforted and questioned by officials, and then—just like that —I'm walking into the main bedroom to find a grisly murder wrapped in the sheets.

Being the Protagonist literally and figuratively opened doors.

The man was short, balding, and quite dead. His bare chest was perforated with multiple stab wounds, the blood already drying into a tacky gumminess that I avoided touching for many reasons. The wounds were especially concentrated lower on his stomach, beneath his ribs, where the damage was also far grosser. I inspected the wounds closely—it was my job, after all—but I'll spare you the details. Suffice it to say it must have been an agonizing, slow death. The dark, yet somehow too-bright blood was a scarlet puddle beneath him and likely meant he'd bled to death.

A serrated knife, its blade and handle coated in blood, sat

discarded next to the corpse.

While messy and frightfully disturbing, the crime scene was almost too convenient. I mean, it wasn't all that often that the murderer left the murder weapon right next to the body.

Call me a cynic, but I was skeptical. I spun around.

"Going somewhere?" Gregory asked quietly. We were hardly the only ones in the room. Besides us and Grant, someone sat in the corner taking careful notes, while another investigator snapped pictures of every single thing, even the undisturbed flower vase next to the bed.

"I need to talk to the wife," I whispered. "This is too easy."

Gregory nodded, then surprised me by following on my heel. Sometimes I didn't know whether he trusted me and my intuition or whether he just figured my Protagonist powers led me to the best place to be. It shouldn't matter, but I hoped it was the former. Even though both were *me*, right?

We retreated back into the hall, where the distraught woman had traded hyperventilation for uncontrollable sobs. The officer trying to console-slash-interrogate her looked up at us, shrugging helplessly. I took a deep breath, stepping in and turning on the charm.

"Hi there. My name's Emery." I crouched down to be eye level with her. She sat on an odd sort of bench set against the railing that overlooked the mess of people on the first floor. I took her hand; she wore those disposable white gloves that doctors use. "I'm sure you've told the officers what happened, but can you tell me again? I have a knack for believing the weirdest parts of a story, okay? Can you tell me what happened?"

"N-n-no one b-b-believes me," she cried, trying to contain her heaving sobs. "I didn't kill Jerry, I would never! I love him. How could anyone think I c-could hurt him?"

"I know, I know," I said reassuringly, wishing I had Caden's magical touch. "There are things in this world that don't make a lot of sense. You aren't alone. It's going to be okay. What you need, right now, is someone who believes you. But to do that, I need you to tell me what happened."

From somewhere behind me, I heard a grunt. "What she needs is a lawyer," a voice murmured.

Irritated, I glanced over my shoulder. "Get us some tea, please," I said, keeping my voice low so as not to upset the woman further. "Noncaffeinated, if possible."

I received a glare in response, but then Gregory's hand fell on the officer's shoulder. "Do as he says. I'll watch them."

I turned back to the woman. "What's your name?"

"Susan." She continued to sniffle but had calmed considerably.

"Tell me what happened, Susan. Tell me why no one believes you."

"Because it happened while I was sleeping," she whispered, tears spilling down her red cheeks. "It wasn't me."

I nodded, still holding her gloved hand. "What do you mean, Susan?"

"I mean I didn't kill him!" She took a shuddering breath, obviously trying to reclaim some calm. "Someone set it up perfectly. I think I was drugged; I couldn't wake up, couldn't move. There was someone in the room with us. I didn't see them, but I could *feel* them. They must've done this! Someone else *killed him*." Her voice broke at the end.

I exchanged a glance with Gregory but, as usual, learned about as much as if I'd glanced at the wall.

"Susan, what else did this person do? Do you remember anything about them? How they smelled, maybe. Any detail may be able to help us. I believe you that someone else was in the room."

She blinked several times in rapid succession, trying to fight through the grief and shock. "I-I d-don't remember. I didn't really even see them—"

"That's okay," I told her quickly, worried she'd think I doubted her. "What about the knife? Do you and Jerry keep one in the bedroom, or did that come from somewhere else in the house?"

She blinked several times in rapid succession. "No, we don't keep weapons in the bedroom. This is a safe neighborhood. We keep the knives in the kitchen." Her eyes narrowed. "Why? It wasn't me; you have to believe that. You must believe me, you must, you must..." She degenerated into sobs again, and I did my best to comfort her.

I asked Gregory for his business card, then handed it to her. "Susan, this is Gregory. We want to help you." I lowered my voice as I saw the officer returning with a plastic cup of something steaming. Damn, that was fast. "Don't talk to anyone else. Call a lawyer. And have them call us, okay?"

I waited until she locked eyes with me and solemnly nodded. "Yeah, okay."

"I'm so sorry for what happened here today," I said awkwardly as she burst into tears again. "Call that number if you need anything."

After we took a few steps back, Gregory winced. "Couldn't you have given her *your* number?"

"That was almost a joke. I'm proud of you." I tried to grin, but my heart wasn't in it.

"Why ask her about the knife?"

"Because it didn't get up and walk to the room by itself."

"That points to her being the likeliest suspect, though. The doors were locked, and the alarm system says no one entered through the outside doors or windows." He thought for a moment. "But you don't think she's our murderer."

"I think someone went to a lot of effort to make it look that way."

Gregory frowned. "A frame job? Why?"

"Not sure yet." My eyes tracked a man coming up the stairs. Fuller, the officer Grant had sent to find the witness—incarnate—I wanted to question. However, Fuller was alone.

Grant came back out of the room to meet him.

"Sorry, Grant," Fuller said, clearly frustrated. "He gave us the slip."

"You have a description of him?" I asked.

Fuller hesitated until Grant nodded. Then he turned to me. "Just a name."

I nodded, expecting to hear Ray's name.

Instead, Fuller said, "Nyx Ebon."

11

"*A*rtie, are you there?"

I stood in a corner of Susan and Jerry's kitchen, trying to be discreet—it rarely worked, eyes just naturally gravitate toward me —as I spoke softly into the Bluetooth earbuds connected to my phone.

"Always," came the reply. "I do not require sleep, and I'm capable of being in many locations—"

"Good," I said, cutting him off a little too loudly. One of the nearby officers looked in my direction, and I flashed her a rueful smile.

"—simultaneously." The sound that followed proved artificial intelligence could huff. "Honestly, Emery, your abrupt response cut off only a single word."

"Sorry, but I'm in danger of being overheard. Let's keep this short."

"Oh! Why didn't you say so? This will give me the ideal opportunity to engage my brevity protocols. How may I be of service?"

I grit my teeth. "Do you have surveillance of my current location?"

"Surveillance? Not precisely, though I can clearly discern your GPS coordinates, if that is what you mean."

"Are there any cameras nearby? I want to track a specific incarnate." I said the last part under my breath.

"Plenty. There are quite a few body cams in the immediate vicinity, as well as a few smart devices. Widening the search parameters, I am able to find laptops, tablets, and smartphones in nearly all of the neighboring facilities, though only three face outward windows, and the angles are not ideal. Ah, I do see two doorbell cameras, including one on the building immediately west of your current location. Who or what am I searching for?"

The officer who'd been eyeing me apparently decided I was up to something shady, because she approached. "Excuse me, young man, who gave you permission to be here?"

"Grant and Gregorius," I assured her.

"Understood, beginning scan for Grant and Gregorius!" Artie said in my ear. "Though I feel the need to point out that this is hardly a task worthy of my processing capabilities, would you not agree?"

The officer frowned and asked, "Did Grant give you a clearance badge?"

"No," I told her.

"No?" Artie repeated indignantly. "Emery Luple, my computational abilities far outclass any contemporary—"

"Enough!" I hissed.

The security officer's eyebrows shot up, and her face darkened. "Come with me, sir."

I blew out a breath in annoyance, pointing at my earpiece. "Look, I need to finish my phone call. If you need to verify my identity, go find Grant."

"If you need assistance," Artie informed me, somehow affecting a smug tone despite being a computer, "Monica Grant is upstairs, main bedroom. Oh, scan complete."

After a brief hesitation, the officer nodded. "Stay put." She whirled and left the kitchen.

"With Gregorius," he added after a beat.

I rolled my eyes. "Yes, thank you." I scanned the kitchen, relieved to see I wasn't attracting too much notice anymore. "But Gregory and Grant weren't who I was looking for."

"Yes, I arrived at that conclusion." Condescending AI.

"To start," I said, improvising—it's how I did my best thinking, really—"please compile any and all footage of the main bedroom and figure out if you're able to find anything. Narrowing down the time of the murder would be helpful, too." I caught my lip between my teeth. "Then, widen your scan to see if you can find any trace of Nyx Ebon, the witness who reported the crime. He's an incarnate."

"Acknowledged. Nyx Ebon is in the system, though his file is conspicuously light. Additionally, I believe I found a recording of the phone call he made at 2:35 a.m. to the local police station. Would you like me to send a copy to your smartphone?"

Huh. "Yes, please." I mused how useful it would be to have a second set of eyes on everything I investigated. "And order me a body cam and bill it to my business account, please."

"Your business account does not have the requisite funds. Would you like me to instead add it to your tab?"

"I have a tab?"

"Indeed. Last week, Caden Malek opened an unusual line of credit jointly in your names."

"Why 'unusual'?"

"It isn't connected to a bank but rather to an account, and the interest rate is a fixed zero percent."

Those were interesting terms. Wait. "Is this just a fancy way of saying we're borrowing money from Asker while he's dead?"

"Well, he's hardly utilizing it, as Caden pointed out. Using advanced algorithms and applied predictability, I've invested some of his assets into surefire stocks to recoup the funds spent. If anything, Asker will reincarnate with more money than when he died. It is logically infallible."

Right. Except for that "surefire" stocks part. Caden had undoubtedly created the account for emergency situations with the Watch, not to line our pockets. "I'm not sure about this. How much have you recouped on the stock market?" I asked.

"To date, I have a net gain of $1,203,709. And twenty-eight cents."

I choked a little. "Okay, put the damn body camera on my tab."

"Understood."

I shook my head in wonder. "Artie, where have you been all my life?"

"I am unable to answer. My artificial memories only trace back to this incarnation's inception, and I am not yet proficient in relying on instinct, though I am practicing."

"Artie?"

"Yes, Emery?"

"That was rhetorical."

There was a pause. "I see. I will study the syntax of your request and compare it to your vocal patterns in an endeavor to recognize such rhetorical questions in the future."

I grinned. "See that you do."

It was time to go. I needed to get back in time for the Watch meeting, or Caden would kill me. Not literally, of course. In fact, Caden would probably forgive me. But *I'd* kill me.

I wandered upstairs, bumping into the officer who'd accosted me in the kitchen. She handed me a plastic guest badge—like I couldn't fake one of those if I wanted to—and then wordlessly returned to her post in the kitchen. The hallway outside the bedroom had been cleared, while sounds of grief from the spare room I passed told me where they'd relocated the widow.

"Is this going to be one of those *strange* murders?" I heard Grant say in a low voice as I approached the bedroom. "Like last time?"

I should've entered, but I was curious, so I hovered by the door frame, listening.

"I'm not sure yet," Gregory's calm voice replied. "That's why I brought my colleague. He's an expert at the supernatural."

"Supernatural," the woman repeated sourly. "Don't like the word. It's an excuse, more often than not, to muddy up simple, straightforward crimes like this one. Or to excuse them."

"Sometimes."

"Damn it, her fingerprints are going to be all over that knife, you know. Even your expert can't deny how this looks. Did you know they updated the victim's life insurance a week ago?"

"Give Emery a few days. He and I will get to the bottom of this."

She heaved a sigh. "I can give you forty-eight hours, no more. You prove this is something other than a *Snapped* situation, and we'll talk. But I can't ignore the evidence. I'll stall any further actions, but I've got to book her."

"More than fair. Thanks, Grant."

"*Prove*, I said. No half truths or maybes. I'm only doing this because of our history, and because I still can't forget what happened at the Rust House."

"The Rust House?" I said, choosing that moment to make my entrance. "You should check out my vlog, *There's Always a Loophole*. Season two, episode eight. All about debunking that particular urban legend."

"Thanks, but I don't get cable."

I decided it wasn't worth it to explain how streaming worked. "Gregory, we should get going. We've got that meeting, and I promised Caden I'd help him set up for it. With traffic, we're already pushing it."

He nodded and turned to Grant. "Thanks again. We'll be in touch."

We exchanged farewells and departed. I conveniently forgot to return my new, handy-dandy crime scene guest badge, pocketing it instead. At the front door I asked Artie to locate me by sight, but he was unable to do so. Bother. There were no cameras pointed toward the entrance to the house, which meant I'd be unlikely to catch footage of Nyx entering or departing the premises. Oh well, it'd been a long shot. And, I knew, he had other ways of entering a household of sleeping folk.

We ducked into Gregory's car, and ten minutes later we were on the interstate. It was already uncomfortably crowded. We didn't have a lot of spare time to get to our meeting.

After a few miles, I said, "You mentioned earlier that an incarnate reported the crime, but you never mentioned how you knew that."

Gregory spared me a glance, and then the corner of his mouth tugged up into a smile.

I waited. "That's going to be the only answer I get from you, isn't it?"

"It's my job to know, Emery." His smile widened. "And that was technically another answer. Seems you don't know everything after all."

I stared at him, then tilted my head back and laughed. "Fair enough."

"What are your theories?"

I considered his question. "Well, there's the obvious one: the wife did it. Or my favorite: someone or something snuck into their bedroom and assassinated the man while she slept soundly next to him."

"With those stab wounds?" he said doubtfully.

I winced. "Looked painful, and death wouldn't have been quick. You're right; she should've woken up." My mind alighted on Nyx. He'd been at the crime scene. "Unless an incarnate was keeping Susan under."

"Like a sleep spell?"

"Something like that," I muttered. Traffic was thickening, and I glanced at the time worriedly. "You have a siren and lights on this thing? If traffic stays like this the whole way south, we're not going to make the meeting."

"With your powers and my driving, we'll make it. What else?"

I bit my lip but stopped when I realized I was doing it. "Running with the theory that the murderer snuck in and killed Jerry, it works on one of two levels: either a single murderer kept Susan asleep while they carried out the deed, or two murderers were present. One to keep Susan asleep while the other took their time with her husband."

"Depends on the method used to keep her under," Gregory said. "I'll order a blood draw on the wife."

"Good. She mentioned she had a hard time waking up. A toxicology screen will rule out drugs."

He grunted. "Not necessarily. Supernatural concoctions—

including incarnate venoms—don't always show up on the report. At least not conclusively."

"I'm not surprised. Still, if something inconclusive shows up, we'll know more than we do now." I drummed my fingers on my knee. "We might be barking up the wrong tree altogether. If the murderer were, say, the Siren incarnate, there'd be virtually no evidence of their presence. Can't trace a lullaby we didn't hear."

"True."

"And why Jerry? Did he have enemies? There has to be a reason he was chosen." He made a sound of agreement, and my eyes narrowed. "What?"

He shrugged with just one shoulder. "Motive, means, and opportunity. Criminal investigation 101: it all points to the wife. If we don't uncover some evidence to the contrary, we may need to accept that it's because there isn't any."

I shook my head. "You called me for a reason. There's something too coincidental going on here. My Protagonist sense is tingling." Realizing who I was talking to, I shelved my grin. "A Malevolent reports the crime, and it turns out to be the same one that visited me hours beforehand? I'm calling foul play."

Gregory was silent for a few minutes. The car slowed to a near standstill in the traffic, and I brought up my phone again. I felt my heart fall into my lap. There was no way we were going to make the start of the meeting. If I wasn't there to help Caden set up, it would only pile more stress onto his already heavy burden. I'd promised.

I texted him. GREGORY AND I ARE ON OUR WAY, BUT WE'RE STUCK IN TRAFFIC SOUTH OF ANACORTES. IF I'M NOT THERE TO HELP SET UP, I'LL MAKE IT UP TO YOU. I'M REALLY SORRY.

Caden was going to be so disappointed. This meeting was the start of his dreams. And I was running fifteen minutes late to it. Some boyfriend I was.

"So. You know Nyx is in town," Gregory finally said. It wasn't a question.

"No thanks to you. A heads-up would've been nice."

"Sorry."

I closed my mouth around my retort, taken aback. I hadn't expected an apology from him.

After a moment, he said, "I wanted you to have a fresh look at the crime scene first. I worried that knowing he was involved would compromise your ability to be impartial." He clenched his jaw. "I should have trusted you."

Damn right. Except he was kind of on the money. "We'd be foolish to rule him out. He's certainly capable of keeping someone asleep for a long time."

"From my understanding, he's usually quite, ah, busy when keeping someone asleep, though. Moreover, where's the motive?"

"To keep me from attending my boyfriend's meeting?" I muttered darkly. "It would be just like him to murder a mortal to stir up drama between us." Gregory didn't look at me, and I realized how I sounded. Shit. "That wasn't very impartial of me, was it? Okay, no reasonable motive, yet, but he has means and opportunity. So I say, *impartially*, that we start with him."

My phone buzzed. NO PROBLEM. I LOVE YOU.

"I agree with you," Gregory said at last, ignoring my white-knuckled grip on my phone. "It's a solid lead."

"Good," I said, "because I want to know why he up and vanished before we had a chance to speak with him."

I didn't say what I was thinking. If we were even a minute late to the Watch meeting, petty or not, I'd take it out of Nyx's hide.

It was 9:27 when we pulled into the parking lot. The Watch meeting had started almost half an hour ago. As Gregory pulled up to the curb, I jumped out, sprinting to the building and leaving him to park his car.

I yanked open the first set of doors to the Lodge and took a few calming breaths. I was already going to create a stir when I entered late; I didn't want to disrupt the meeting further by barreling in like a football team taking the field.

As I approached the doors that led to the conference room, I heard Caden's voice. "We will be working with local law enforcement, but only to a point. Traditional neighborhood watches work closely with them, and I think it's important we have a good relationship with mortals." I slowed outside the doors, listening. I hated to admit it, but Caden sounded a tad awkward. He didn't fumble his words or anything, but I could hear the nerves in his voice, like he wasn't accustomed to speaking in front of a crowd. Which was uncharacteristic for him; just last week he'd addressed an entire room of incarnates and had commanded the space well. I lingered, waiting for the right moment to slip inside. "But the Watch, as I'm sure you know, isn't planning to reveal its true nature to mortals, meaning our relationship with local government will be a bit... different. You know what? I think it would be best if we circle back to our partnership when the Watchman arrives. He'll be our primary liaison, and he's familiar with mortal police. Which brings us, for now, to the next crucial *talking* point: communication." There was a brief pause, followed by an uncomfortable laugh. "Sorry, my boyfriend is much better with puns than I am. Anyway—"

I figured I wasn't going to get a better cue than that. I put my shoulder to the heavy door and pushed it open. Eyes throughout the room swiveled toward me. Caden cut off, turning to see what everyone was looking at. I needn't have been so worried about his reaction. When he saw me, he lit up. Literally. The light from the windows suddenly seemed to catch his hair just so, turning it a burning gold. "Speak of the devil," he said to the room.

"I don't think *you* should be invoking that particular entity," I said with an apologetic smile. "Sorry I'm late." Even though my instinct was to say it to the room, my words were to him alone.

"I think you arrived just in time," he said, loud enough for the others to hear. "They were starting to despair, thinking they'd have to listen to me drone on and on about agendas and schedules."

I heard Melusina chuckle, and then Rachelle threw in a pity one, too. We needed to liven this up.

"Agendas and schedules? So they caught you doing your Artie impersonation, then?"

"I formally resent that, Emery Luple." Artie's voice came from a nearby laptop. "I have recently analyzed human oration and developed programs specifically tailored to deliver informative lectures in a riveting format."

"Nailed it," I told him solemnly. Scattered laughter. "Well, I've caused the commotion I intended with my fashionably late arrival, so I'll just find my seat and you can get back to your interesting and insightful speech."

Caden grinned, then said to the room, "He would know. He's heard it fifty times."

More smiles greeted his remark this time, and I could feel the awkward energy in the air dissipating. I started to pick out an available seat, but Caden grabbed my arm. "Oh no you don't. Apparently, I'm a lot funnier when you're standing up here with me. You're staying put."

I groaned. "I've had this dream: I'm late for class and the professor makes me stand in front the whole time." I turned to Caden. "I believe I interrupted you at step five in your 'twenty-seven steps to success.' Communication, if I'm not mistaken."

"Hey, I cut it down to twenty-one steps, thank you very much." There were grins and even a snort from our audience. He squeezed my arm affectionately, then let go. "But in all seriousness, the next step *is* communication, specifically within the Watch. This is the part where we'll establish a system for consistent interaction with one another, creating the space and time to bring up community concerns..." He continued to talk, but it sounded much more natural now, so I decided to use the opportunity to take stock of the room and catalog the faces.

Front and center was Caden's pep squad, Melusina the Mermaid and Rachelle. The two were paying rapt attention to what he was saying, though of course Rachelle took the opportunity to slide her eyes my way and give me a *"What the hell?"* accusatory glare. I responded with a remorseful *"Long story, my bad"* shrug. She rolled her eyes and returned her focus to Caden. I didn't see Matlas, so he must not have taken me up on my spontaneous offer to attend.

A laptop featuring Agatha the Witch's blurry image sat beside Rachelle, near enough to Caden that she could easily catch his words. Once again, even squinting, I couldn't quite make out her features, but the vague silhouette didn't look like it was wearing a pointy witch hat. Disappointing.

Behind Melusina sat Dagan, the Triton. His smart, manicured beard ended in a point beneath Polynesian features and matched his equally smart, freshly pressed business suit. While his formal attire didn't quite belong among the others, it fit in with (half of) the theme of the Lodge. And I approved, which is what really mattered.

Continuing around the table, I saw Maggie the Selkie sitting comfortably in a chair much nicer than the others, and I guessed she'd arrived first and sniped the best seat. Sitting primly in a chair between Maggie and Dagan, her legs crossed, was a woman I'd never seen before. I'm not sure "woman" was the correct term; "creature" might have been more apt, though she possessed pointedly feminine features. I'll describe her in the simplest terms I can think of: she looked like a runway model who'd been dunked into a vat of sky-blue ink for a photo shoot that had taken place an hour ago, but she hadn't had time to wash off or change her expensive, form-hugging dress. Not entirely a single shade of blue, she was a collection of nuanced shades and contrasts. Oh, and someone had left the special effects fan on, because her long, still-wet hair billowed gently in a nonexistent breeze.

My current incarnation hadn't seen her before, but I identified her right away: the Undine. If you've never heard of her myth, just think water nymph (but never tell the Nymph I told you that). If you've never heard of the Nymph, go google it. And maybe read a mythology book or two; culture is good for you.

Yes, there are a lot of aquatic incarnates. It makes sense; the world is over 70 percent water, so humans were bound to create legends about the ever-present yet mysterious depths they couldn't explore. And, naturally, those incarnates would congregate in a city so rife with nautical themes. Seattle Seahawks. Seattle Mariners. Seattle Kraken. *Seattle.*

On the other side of Maggie was another unfamiliar woman, middle-aged, with olive skin and, I decided after a moment of scrutiny, Mediterranean features—best guess: Greek. Her dark hair had volume for days, and she wore a business-friendly outfit that couldn't quite conceal her athletic physique. I couldn't immediately place her... oh. Of course. The Amazon.

Damn. Maggie took her role as recruiter seriously. It had barely been a day.

I was surprised to see two children in the room, too, though I knew them both. And only one was actually sitting at the table. Kolby, who was small enough to pass for a toddler, was fiddling with a piece of polished glass that occasionally caught the light and gleamed. The Kobold's too-large, too-adorable eyes kept drifting toward the shiny item in his dark, greenish fingers before snapping back to Caden as he fought to keep focused.

Iris, on the other hand, had already given up the fight. The Ghost sat on the giant elk's head mounted on the far wall, a good nine feet off the ground, her transparent fingers gripping the beast's antlers like they were the chains to a swing set. Her sandaled feet kicked the air, occasionally phasing through the front of the elk's face. Noticing my attention, she waved.

Caden paused, mistaking the gesture. "Yes, Iris?" he said obligingly. "Did you have a question about the frequency of communication?"

The girl clapped her hand over her mouth as people at the table shifted to look at her. She shook her head, sending her pigtails flying.

"Well, the important point I'm trying to make," he continued, "is that everyone has a voice within the Watch. We're equals, and we're stronger united."

I was impressed by the number of attendees. It might seem low by mortal standards, but you didn't often see this many incarnates gathered in one place, especially from so many walks of life. True, the absence of Scarlet Dungrady and Mikey—the Cyborg and the Android—was conspicuous, but we hadn't expected them to return so soon. And after yesterday's Bigfoot hunt and our debacle with Ray, we'd counted Walt and Halona out.

The doors opened again, and Gregory finally joined us. He took one step, nodded politely to the room, and then began heading for an open seat—probably the one Iris had vacated.

"Gregory," Caden said, halting him, "I'm really glad you're here. Everyone, as I said in the beginning, my dream for the Incarnate Watch is grander even than a community collectively watching each other's backs. My dream is to create a Sanctum City, a place of safety and solace for every type of incarnate. I'd like to introduce you to the man with the most experience in that arena: Gregory Gregorius."

Gregory stared at the assembled incarnates, the lines in his face deepening. "Yes, thank you, Caden." He looked around and nodded to himself. "I'm not one for speeches, so I'll just say this: Emery and Caden came to me with a vision of making the world a safer place for incarnates. That's what I do every day. Caden says I'm the man who's going to build this society, but that isn't true. The only thing that's changing for me is that I'm getting more eyes, more ears, more help. From all of you. You're the ones who'll make this happen." He bobbed his head again, like that was that. He continued toward the chair, but then stopped and added, "I trust Caden. I can't think of anyone better suited to protecting incarnates than the Guardian Angel." He sat down.

Caden had snatched up a bottle of water while Gregory addressed the room, but he lowered it and licked his lips as the attention returned to him. Clearly he'd been hoping for a longer reprieve.

"Thank you, Gregory. The entire premise of the Incarnate Watch is safety. My plan for this vision is simple: we bring incarnates into the fold, and we protect them." He took a deep breath. "We often rely on our immortality, but it's far from perfect. I'm a prime example. I was reborn as an infant, and to this day I possess only the faintest memories of my past. My personality is unique—due in part to my upbringing, I suppose. And when I die, a new Guardian Angel will take my place, complete with their own history and individuality. Maybe they'll have experiences of past lives they're able to recall, maybe not. But they won't be *me*. I am more than just a compilation of memories—and so are you.

"We may reincarnate when we die, but each life is its own, special and precious. For too long we've focused on the cycle of past and future, and by doing so we've removed ourselves from a sense of belonging, a sense of community. It's time to live in the present. To celebrate who you are today, not just the myth you represent. Protection and safety have never been foremost in our minds—but rather than immortality, what we truly have is unlimited mortality. I think there's a distinction there. Let's create a place where we can *live*, rather than just exist."

His passion and enthusiasm crashed into my skepticism, trying to wash it away. Yes, some of that was his glamour, but most of it was Caden, not the Guardian Angel. The earnest guy standing next to me who was pouring his heart into his words.

The faces around the room were speculative, interested. Even Iris was watching Caden with a big grin on her face.

"I suspect," I said into the contemplative silence, "that we're all here because we believe in your vision. Because despite what we've told ourselves in the past, we want to live for today." I turned to Caden and lowered my voice, but it still carried in the silent room. "I know I do."

"Thank you. It feels so rewarding to have others support my idealism." He looked around the room, making eye contact with the other incarnates. "This brings me back to the point I brought up at the beginning of today's meeting," he continued. "To spearhead the Watch, we'll need leaders chosen by the group. I've given this undertaking considerable thought and worked with Artie to research the best way to tackle this vital step. With that in mind, I propose we install an election system wherein each leader serves a 1,001-day term. Fitting, we thought. Toward the conclusion of the term, new candidates are to be nominated by members of the Watch, to be voted upon. To keep things fair, the candidate must be nominated by someone other than themselves. If no nominations are made, the incarnate who currently holds the office will continue for another term by default. Does anyone disagree with these terms?"

Artie's voice came over the speakerphone. "Caden Malek, may I clarify a few points we discussed earlier?"

"Of course. Everyone has an equal voice here."

"Thank you. First and foremost, a nominee may decline a nomination before it proceeds to a vote if they wish. Secondly, if an incarnate were unable to complete their term due to an unforeseen demise, another would be selected by leadership to take up the position until the next election cycle." The matter-of-fact way he glossed over death made a couple of incarnates glance at each other, but I just smiled to myself. I was probably growing a little too accustomed to his idiosyncrasies. "Additionally, amendments to the system are to take place concurrently with the election cycle, should the need for them arise."

Caden accepted the clarifications gracefully. "Thank you, Artie."

"What are the positions you have in mind?" Dagan asked, his hands folded on the desk before him. Nice power position, that. It looked so natural.

"I've divided the duties up into a few key roles," Caden said, "But I expect we'll need to add more as we grow. Perhaps one day we'll even have whole departments of incarnates running the Watch. For now, I think the critical functions are president, vice president, and administrator. Chief officers of recruitment, security, accounting, and relations. We can create more leadership roles as the need develops."

Dagan frowned. "Chief officer of relations?"

"A position that blends human resources and community management. Someone to carefully maintain and protect the relationships between incarnates, especially among different classifications."

The interaction between Caden and Dagan would have looked like a comical clash of generations in the real world, with Caden's youthful boy-next-door look contrasting with Dagan's mature business tycoon in a suit. But among incarnates, such interactions were commonplace. Take me and Gregory, for example. We didn't fit in with society's image of two partners at a crime scene. But that was using the lens of mortal society.

In that moment, I realized I'd missed this—the times when, despite everything, incarnates came together. In my last few incarnations, I'd spent most of my spare time among my own kind, shunning mortals after the tragedy of Huntington's murder. In New York, Caden and Rachelle had reminded me what it meant to be human, to trust and feel things unencumbered by prior lives, by past mistakes or shortcomings. It was a critical lesson, a fresh start I'd sorely needed.

But in learning it, I'd begun to forget the world I came from. The *people* I came from. Incarnates and their wonderful diversity, their timeless spirit, even their insistent demands for tradition. Their adaptability, born from an endless cycle of lives.

I missed that sense of belonging, of a place where everyone understood me and the struggles I lived with. A place where I felt heard and understood. Somehow, I'd focused too intently on Caden's description of the Incarnate Watch—on the details, on its similarities to a common neighborhood watch—and, in so doing, I'd failed to comprehend its soul.

For the first time, I truly understood what Caden hoped to achieve. In that moment while he spoke with Dagan, free of his glamour, I believed in and shared his dream.

"After careful consideration," Caden was saying, "I would like to nominate several individuals for these roles. The first and easiest nomination belongs to Gregory Gregorius, the Watchman, as our chief officer of security. Then, due to her charisma and obvious proficiency, I nominate Maggie, the Selkie, as chief officer of recruiting. And for his experience in finance, I nominate Dagan, the Triton, as chief officer of accounting." He paused. "Before continuing, are there any other nominations for these three roles?"

"Hell," Maggie said, "you don't need me for recruiting; you got charm in spades."

There were a few minutes of murmurs and low discussion after that, but in the end the votes were unanimous.

"Let it be so, then," Caden pronounced with a grin. Then he blushed. "I promise the pomp and ceremony will be much improved by the next round."

"Shall I order awards of recognition befitting their new stations?" Artie inquired.

"Absolutely," I cut in before Caden could decline. "Put it on my tab." I had no idea what Artie would be ordering, but I couldn't wait to find out what he came up with. Though knowing Artie's efficient-minded sensibilities, it would probably just be business cards. So I added, "And make sure it's something exciting."

"Understood."

"Speaking of which," Melusina said, "I'd like to make a nomination." The room went quiet as questioning eyes turned to her. "I nominate Emery as chief officer of relations. Who better than the guy who goes around saving incarnates all the time? He's always got his finger on the pulse of the incarnate world, after all."

"Oh," I said. *Eloquent, Emery.* I hadn't expected that proposal. It was flattering, especially phrased in that light, but to be honest, I'd been expecting to run as VP next to Caden as the president.

"I second that," Gregory spoke up, choosing *now* of all moments to make his voice heard.

"Me, too!" Iris chirped from where she'd been walking across the food trays set up on a snack table. Luckily, her ghostly feet couldn't ruin the refreshments.

"All right, all right," I said, holding up my hands and laughing. I could do this. It was, I reflected, an honor. "Let's put it to a vote."

Arms shot into the air. Wow. Looking at Caden, worried this would throw a wrench in his careful plans, I was pleased to see him beaming at me, his own arm raised.

The Undine leaned forward. "Enough seahorsing around," she said in a melodious voice. "Over the course of this meeting, it has become clear to me who should helm this ship. We're all in agreement, so let us make it official. I nominate Caden for president of the Incarnate Watch."

Caden inclined his head in gratitude but held up a hand. "Thank you. Before we put it to a vote, I think it only right we open the floor to any other potential candidates. Would anyone else like to put in a nomination?"

The way everyone looked at each other, it was clear they were humoring him. No one opened their mouth, despite Caden giving them the opportunity.

"I have a nomination," came a voice from the entrance. Like a wolf among sheep, it drew the attention of those gathered, eyes and heads swiveling to see who had spoken.

I turned, too, but it was only a reaction. I already recognized the voice. My eyes fell, disbelievingly, on the woman who had just entered the room.

*M*orrigan.
Morrigan.

The Lodge doors opened in tandem like they were unveiling the blasted queen of England, a hush falling over the room as my arch-nemesis glided to a stop before the assembly of incarnates.

If evil came in many guises, today it wore a blue peacoat that combined business and temptation with a teaspoon of playful—undoubtedly to cover up the taste of sin. Incarnated to be my antithesis, she was the villain behind every scheme, the Magneto to my Professor X, the Captain Hook to my Peter Pan, the proverbial snake in the grass. Peel back the top layer of any good idea or moment of brilliance and you'll uncover a seed of doubt; peel further and you'll find a nameless source of insecurity, of fear, undermining all good things in the world. Well, I'll name it.

Morrigan, the Antagonist incarnate.

My hand strayed to my belt, but of course I hadn't brought my Taser to the meeting. Her dark eyes followed my movement, and the faintest trace of a smile played over her lush, red lips. Damn her.

She scanned the incarnates in the room, and I fought the urge to clench my jaw. I wouldn't give her the satisfaction. Just like that, in under ten seconds, she had the faces of my closest allies and friends. The sanctity of life was about as important to her as an email, with mortals being junk mail. Capricious, but never to a point I could capitalize on, she'd ended people's lives for nothing more than an imagined slight. Make no mistake, though, Morrigan was cunning; she'd prefer not to discard a tool she thought she could use, but nor was she predictable enough for that trait to be wielded against her. One time she'd slit the throat of her most valuable servant in front of me, just because I thought she wouldn't.

Morrigan was the reason I didn't fear monsters under the bed or things that go bump in the night. I preferred them.

Her powers—which, admittedly, worked a lot like mine—seemed to grab the light in the room and direct it toward her, a star on center stage. It cast her shadow starkly behind her; a perfect metaphor for the deep, inescapable pall she cast wherever she treaded.

"Good morning, fellow incarnates," she said, bestowing on them her most magnanimous smile. Her voice was velvet, more unctuous than her carefully oiled hair, the dark tresses waterfalling down her shoulders. Everything about her was purposeful, from her poise to her measured eye contact. "I would like to nominate myself as president." I opened my mouth to protest, but she wasn't done. "For those of you who do not know me, my name is Morrigan. I am the Protagonist incarnate."

What? I froze, my mouth still gaping.

My stomach fell, the whole world seeming to crash around me.

No.

Morrigan's words from months ago came back to me. I'd called her out as the Antagonist, and she'd told me it was a matter of perspective. I hadn't realized the implications of that, hadn't considered the possibility that she could ever deceive herself into thinking she was *Benign.*

Whether or not it was intended as a lie, it was impossible to disprove. Moreover, the only way to even *attempt* to disprove it would be to admit to all my friends that I wasn't the Loophole. That I'd been duping them this entire time. I *had* planned on revealing my true identity to the Watch, but on my terms. If I did it now, my lie could cost Caden the presidency.

Hell, if the incarnates we'd befriended felt betrayed, it could cost him the Watch itself.

Rachelle had gone white. Gregory watched me, worry etched into his features. For some reason, the Amazon was watching Morrigan with a grave expression. But most of the incarnates just looked interested. Maybe a little perplexed at the unexpected entrance, but otherwise intrigued.

Caden, thankfully, was calm. "Thank you for your interest in the Incarnate Watch, Morrigan—"

"Thank *you* so much for the warm welcome," she cut in. "I apologize to everyone for my tardiness. My invitation to this event never made it to my desk, but I assure you the employee responsible has been suitably reprimanded and the error shall not occur again." She gestured airily. "Now, who must a lady tickle around here to get a refreshment?"

For the first time, I noticed she wasn't alone. I nearly kicked myself. If they'd been armed... some Protagonist I was, freezing the moment my rival showed up.

The two lackeys accompanying Morrigan were an odd pair. The one who strode forward at her remark was clearly an incarnate; mortals typically didn't wander twenty-first-century streets in black robes with a collar Count Dracula would envy. The man looked like something out of a Tim Burton movie, spindly and tall, pale as death with a sunken face that pulled his skin tight around his skull, all beneath a shock of white hair. Despite his apparent age and malnourished appearance, he spryly moved across the room and began picking at the arranged snacks to create a tray for Morrigan.

Determined not to be caught off guard again so soon, I took the opportunity to inspect Morrigan's second companion.

And I did a double take, my jaw falling open... again... despite my attempt to veil my reactions from my enemies.

The woman was *Hope*. The Regina, leader of Vox Populi—the evil cult dating back thousands of years *that hunted incarnates*! It was a tragic story, actually: the merry band of murderers worshipped their leader with such intensity that they titled her the Regina, Latin for "queen." Over the course of time, their faith reached such levels that they unintentionally manifested an incarnate who represented their leader—meaning the very people who hunted incarnates were unknowingly led by one.

Last week, we'd shattered Vox Populi, in part by revealing to them Hope's true nature. She was, in many ways, the perfect anti-incarnate: she was utterly unremarkable, passing for a middle-aged mortal woman in a nine-to-five job, living with her spouse, two-point-five children, and white picket fence.

But she was a ruthless killer. Tragic or not, it was difficult to drum up much sympathy for her. Although I'll admit to a tiny fraction of pity after our confrontation in the Thirteen Steps to Hell. The place had tried to snap our minds and very nearly succeeded. In fact, I hadn't expected to see Hope again after she'd mowed down her own people in a fevered attempt to reject the truth about who she really was. She'd vanished... but it was just like Morrigan to find someone who should have stayed gone.

Hope met my eyes for a moment, then averted her gaze and looked around the room. I wasn't sure what to make of that, but I hated the way she studied each face at the table. Was she mentally putting hits on each of their heads, gauging the sum she could fetch for each assassination?

This was too much. I needed to react, to *do* something. Anything. But what? Morrigan had timed her arrival impeccably. Any violent or aggressive act in the inaugural meeting of the Watch would, at best, embarrass Caden. At worst, it could crumble the whole thing. If the incarnates present didn't know how despicable Morrigan was, aggression against her would look... bad. It could make *us* look like the villains, if Morrigan played her cards right. And she always did. She only played with a stacked deck.

"Morrigan," Caden tried again, "I'm sorry, but the rules are clear:

you're unable to nominate yourself for a leadership role within the Watch. Our system—"

"Any other incarnate may nominate another?" It was the wizened man, who now offered the plate of food to Morrigan. She took it with exaggerated gratitude and began nibbling at a tart. The man turned and addressed the room. His voice was as thin as a cobweb. "I nominate Morrigan for president of the Watch. I can vouch for her authenticity. I know many of you, though you may not recognize me." The corner of his lip twisted. "I often visit when you're not expecting it."

Dagan frowned. "Who are you?"

"I'm the Sandman."

Hearing his name reminded me of my nightmare. Several things seemed to make sense. Crows, as I'd feared, represented Morrigan. She had a long history with them, since she'd weaseled her way into the Celtic pantheon. The dream must've been an omen conjured by my Protagonist powers, a warning to prepare for Morrigan lest she overrun me as the murder of crows had tried to do in my dream.

Murder.

Could Morrigan be involved in Jerry's murder and the framing of his wife? The answer to that was obvious: of course she could. The question became *why*? What did she stand to gain from the murder?

Had my powers delivered the premonition in a dream to further warn me of her alliance with the Sandman? While I'd obviously keep my guard up around any associate of Morrigan's, it might behoove me to pay particular attention to him and any dangers he brought to the table.

Shit. With Morrigan and Hope around, all I needed was *another* incarnate to keep tabs on. At least Nyx hadn't walked in.

I was off my game. An unfortunate, if predictable, effect of Morrigan's ambush. I needed to clear my head, get some room to think. But more importantly, I needed to act.

Caden caught my eye, and despite his unperturbed exterior I realized he, too, was reeling. I shook my head. *Do not give them an inch.* It was impossible for Morrigan to win the vote, even if her two lackeys got to participate. We were surrounded by friends and hard-won allies. I could practically see the same thoughts behind Caden's eyes as he wrestled with the right thing to do. He looked away, and I felt despair.

He opened his mouth. *Don't do it.* I couldn't undermine him, not here, not now. Not with the entire room hanging on his every word. I could see it in their faces, the intrigue at this unexpected development. They wanted to see how he'd handle it. "Very well," he said. "The Watch will not turn away incarnates. All are welcome here." His eyes hardened on Hope, and I could almost see the gathering of his glamour. The morning light from the window suddenly seemed to angle downward, bestowing on him a fierce mien of judgment. "But you will follow our tenets." His next words, backed by his angelic countenance, seemed a pronouncement rather than just a statement. "Morrigan's nomination for president of the Incarnate Watch is accepted. If there are no further candidates, let's proceed to a vote."

"Vote?" Morrigan exclaimed, eyes widening in apparent confusion. What an act. And she didn't even seem daunted by Caden's display of power. "Without first hearing my campaign promises? That hardly seems fair. Every incarnate in this room knows what you're offering them. Should I not be given the same opportunity?"

"To give you the chance to lie?" I snapped. I could feel the attention in the room shift to me, but I didn't care. "We've humored your interruption long enough. The Incarnate Watch will not be led by a Malevolent, no matter how much honey you dump on your words."

"Oh, you're absolutely right," she said, stealing the power from my argument. "As the Protagonist, I naturally consider Malevolents my enemies. I would never permit the Watch to fall into the clutches of one of them." She handed the tray back to the Sandman, clearly ramping up to something.

"*You* are the Malevolent," I said before she could continue into whatever speech she had prepared.

To my surprise, Morrigan laughed. Worse, it sounded authentic. "Oh, you are ever the comedian, Emery. Thank you for commemorating my nomination with such a memorable act."

The incarnates in the room looked like they were watching a

tennis match. "This is not an act, Morrigan. You will not corrupt this beautiful vision to fit your plots."

"As the Protagonist, I am often the victim of plots beyond my control." She faced the room, her hands gesturing in front of her as she spoke. "Let me assure all of you that I have only the best intentions for the Watch. To prove it, I'd be willing to name Caden as my vice president. I won't even request that he do the same for me. I believe wholeheartedly in his dream. If anything, I believe we can take it to an entirely new level. Why stop at a Sanctum City?"

I hesitated, unsure of her angle.

The best way—the *only* way—I'd been able to outplay Morrigan in the past was to get ahead of her schemes, but often she layered them in such a way that I bumbled into her traps as surely as if they'd been baited. It was infuriating; I *excelled* at bulldozing meticulously constructed plans, but Morrigan was in a league of her own. She'd familiarized herself with my particular brand of chaos and had proven time and again she could predict my actions, or at the very least counter them. Alarm bells were ringing in my head. I realized she'd *planned* on my outburst and was counting on me overplaying my hand.

"We aren't trying to build an empire," I said, mustering epic levels of calm. "The last thing we intend is to create a dictatorship."

Her lips parted in apparent surprise, though her every reaction was so manufactured it might as well have been made in a toy shop. "Of course not." She turned to the others. "I was simply thinking of those incarnates for whom relocation would be impossible. Do they not deserve our protection?" I opened my mouth, but she put a hand up to forestall me. "You needn't respond to that, dear. I'm merely pointing out that the Incarnate Watch can do so much good outside of Seattle. I suggest we create the blueprints of a Sanctum City, then help others to develop throughout the world. Every incarnate society should have the same opportunities, shouldn't they?"

I thought I could see her game. "With you guiding their growth, of course."

She spread her arms. "With all of *us* guiding their growth. The

Incarnate Watch is the greatest story to happen in generations, but we're only in my prologue. Who better than the Protagonist to ensure the Watch reaches the happily ever after it deserves?"

I ground my teeth, but it was Gregory who spoke up. "The Guardian Angel, maybe."

Morrigan nodded, graciously accepting his point. "Perhaps." She looked at me, and her lips widened as her eyes slid back to her audience. "But can you imagine the Protagonist's powers *combined* with the Guardian Angel's? I dare say we'd be *unstoppable*."

I looked helplessly at Caden, who was carefully keeping his emotions from his face. Which kind of scared me. Caden never feared feelings. My eyes slid to Rachelle, who was watching the conversation unfold in a sort of disbelieving trance.

Melusina and Maggie were watching me, I realized, and I thought I read concern in their expressions. Was that a good thing?

"I've heard of the Protagonist," Dagan said, breaking the quiet. "Many incarnates don't even believe in you." He paused, then snorted quietly. "Which I suppose is ironic, but there it is. Can you prove your claim?"

"I understand your hesitation," Morrigan continued, voice dripping with concern. "I've lived extraordinarily private lives, rarely able to divulge my true identity." Her expression became poignant. "It's lonely, sometimes, but easier than telling the truth. No one wants to feel like they're nothing more than a side character in someone else's story. It makes them feel inferior." I felt my fingernails dig into my palms. "When I heard about the seeds of a society where I could be free to be myself, I knew I needed to meet you all. And while I know I'd make each of you proud as your president, I'd be content just to be a part of it."

"Does that mean you'll withdraw your nomination?" I asked.

Her eyes sharpened on me. "*Of course not*," she snapped, then quickly hid her fangs behind another smile. "I only ask for a chance. You've given Caden a week; give me the same. Allow me time to prove myself with deeds rather than a speech."

"What makes you think there'll be the opportunity for 'deeds' in the first place?" Maggie asked.

Morrigan's eyebrows shot up. "My powers. What is a protagonist without obstacles to overcome? What is a hero without monsters to slay? You needn't worry; my powers will provide the trials I must face to win your trust."

There was a stagnant sort of silence following that. I considered naming her the Antagonist, but I realized I had no proof without revealing my own lies. Even then, it would be my word against hers. I needed her to slip up, to provide me an opening I could exploit to *show* them the truth.

Looking around the room, it seemed to me that an objection hovered on just about every tongue, but no one could find a way to phrase it without sounding petty.

Then a voice sliced into the quiet. "Interesting choice of words." It was the Amazon. "I met you once, you know. In ancient Greece, along the banks of a long-forgotten river, not far from Anatolia."

I stared at her, the words tugging at a memory. Anatolia...

Just like that, the years fell away, and I *remembered*. I'd been a Greek heroine with a gift for the bow and arrow, said to be blessed by Apollo himself. I'd been hunting the Hydra, a Predator incarnate that had been snacking on local fishermen. The Amazons, tasked with killing the beast, had suffered too many losses and requested my aid. Their only condition was that I slay the creature in the company of several promising young warriors, that they might learn from my prowess.

"You taught me an invaluable lesson," the Amazon continued.

I barely heard her words. I'd accepted the Amazons' quest, and they'd celebrated with a feast thrown in my honor. For entertainment, a grand contest of strength and dexterity was declared, and all the young women of the village participated. Those who emerged as victors would accompany me to the Hydra's Territory. The next morning, nine young women departed into the wilderness with me.

"You taught me the difference between the Protagonist and the Hero. That they were different things entirely."

Three days later, only four of us emerged from the wilds. We'd slain the Hydra, but its ambush had slaughtered the rest of the girls. My arrogance had killed six young women as surely as the Hydra's venom.

"Tragedy dogs your heels," the Amazon said. "Unlike the rest of us, you do not control your abilities." Her gaze bore into Morrigan, but I felt its weight just the same. "They control you."

I wondered which of the nine girls she'd been. Whether she'd even survived the encounter.

This was my chance. I could force Morrigan to discuss the details of that memory in front of everyone. When she couldn't, it would prove her a fraud. Something made me hesitate, though.

Because my challenge could play into her trap. If she somehow said the *right* thing, even vaguely, the stunt could backfire on me and solidify her position, all but proving she was the Protagonist in front of an audience that, I could only hope, didn't presently believe her.

Right or wrong, the moment passed. Morrigan sighed in regret, continuing her charade. "I'm so sorry. You're right: I'm not always a hero. But I will ever strive to be. Give me one week to prove it to you. Please."

Though I'd missed an opportunity, I might not need it, I realized. Looking around, I was pleased to see the reluctance on their faces. If I pressed, now, I was confident I could get the incarnates to commit to a vote on the spot. A vote Caden would win. I opened my mouth—

"I would speak on behalf of the Protagonist," the Undine said, her musical voice flowing through the room. "While our streams have not crossed in ages, I've lived an exceptionally long life. Rumors told by our kind, even legends, have reached my ears time and again. Tales of one who reincarnates, leaves a splash in the lives of others, and then disappears just as suddenly. If Morrigan is truly the Protagonist, then a week is asking very little in return for the centuries of good deeds she's bestowed upon us."

I was dismayed to see the way the incarnates around the room looked at each other. My legacy was being used against me. It was the perfect kind of twisted victory for Morrigan.

With a heavy heart, I heard Caden say, "Very well. We'll reconvene at nine a.m. next Friday to vote on who will become the first president of the Incarnate Watch."

I could still regain control. Morrigan had a week to prove herself? That gave me a week to show everyone the truth about the conniving mind behind that crocodile smile. To yank back the curtain and expose the empty cavity in her chest where most people held hearts. And there was no time like the present to begin.

"You've introduced yourself and the Sandman," I said innocently. "But you neglected to inform us as to why you—the Protagonist—are in the company of the leader of Vox Populi." As I often did, I received the reaction I was hoping for. I heard several gasps, and every eye nailed Hope to the wall. Oh yes. Everyone in the room knew that name.

Under all that attention, I saw Hope swallow. Pleased at myself, I turned back to Morrigan, only to freeze at the gleeful glint in her eyes. She'd been counting on me making this very scene. Damn it, it was so *obvious*. Morrigan would never publicly ally herself with an enemy unless she could spin it into an advantage. *You fool, Emery*. I'd just given her the very opportunity she'd hoped to exploit. Most infuriatingly, I never should've fallen for it. Wouldn't have, if I'd been in the right frame of mind.

"Thank you so much for asking, Emery. Where are my manners?

Everyone, this is Hope. And yes, until recently, she was the leader of Vox Populi." She paused, and the incarnates in the room were hanging on her every word. I seethed. I couldn't interrupt her now, after having been the one to pose the question. The last thing I wanted was for the other incarnates to think *I* was manipulating the situation. That would only harm Caden's standing. "But what Emery conveniently forgot to mention," she continued, "is that she's an incarnate herself." She got the same reaction I had, gasps and all. My heart was beating more wildly than when I'd been chasing down the Sasquatch.

"That's right," Hope said, her voice tight with restrained emotion. "I've been denying it all my life. But Emery made me realize the truth last week."

I felt everyone's attention return to me. I realized it looked bad, like I'd omitted the information intentionally. Angry, I snapped, "You mean when you were killing tech incarnates around Seattle? Micah? Abdul? Jax? *Danny?*"

Hope stiffened. "Yes," she bit out. "I know it's not worth much, but I'm sorry."

I saw anger on the faces of the people in the room, but I saw something else, too. Surprise, maybe even consideration. Which made me want to put my fist through the wall.

"You see," Morrigan all but purred, "Hope wishes to change. To rehabilitate. She's been taught her entire life—all of them, over and over again—that incarnates are evil creatures, wicked things that worship their own self-interests and care nothing for the world or the mortals living in it. She's spent so long denying who she truly is that she's learned to hate herself. I brought her with me today to show her the true nature of incarnates." She gave a broad gesture that took in those in the room. "Not monsters. Not horrors. Not perpetrators of unspeakable evils." She paused for effect, enjoying being the center of attention. Barf. "People. Not so different from her."

"Except we don't hunt down innocents for profit and murder them in cold blood," I said, aiming a kick at her soapbox.

"A tragedy, to understate it," Morrigan quickly agreed, bowing her head for a brief moment in feigned sorrow or respect. "But surely the Watch is the perfect place for her. She's severed her ties with Vox Populi and yearns only for a place to belong. A place she's never known. As she makes amends to our community, the community, in turn, can shape her. Not just for this life, but forever."

Hope's face was devoid of emotion, but even without the black eye, she reminded me of when I'd first met her. Battered and bruised, but with an inner strength from weathering it.

Of course, when I'd first met her, it had all been an act. A trick to embed her into my life, within reach of my friends and loved ones. Close enough to Caden to kidnap and abuse him, just to gain my cooperation. I would *not* be taken in by Morrigan and Hope's tag-team performance.

The fact that I had to steel myself against the manufactured emotions, however, did not bode well for how the others in the room must feel. Especially when no one here other than Caden and Rachelle had ever seen her before.

"I have much to atone for," Hope said in a meek voice. I'd literally seen her kick a puppy, heard her justify murder as a training exercise. Now, she looked like a victim. It took all my strength not to throw my hands up in disgust. "If you will not accept me, I understand. I'm still learning to accept myself. But if you will, then I will spend every day trying to make it up to you." She met Caden's eyes. "Beginning with you."

That seemed ominous rather than inspiring. It began to dawn on me that I'd lost control of the situation. The simple truth was that Morrigan had planned for this moment, while I had not. If I was to have any chance at foiling her scheme, I needed to pick my battle-ground rather than fight on her terms and continue to give her the ammunition she needed to gun down Caden's dream.

I knew that, as a public display, I should welcome Hope aboard. Demonstrate to the other incarnates that Caden and I were capable of taking the high road. But how could I? This woman had tried to kill Caden only a *week* ago and had very nearly succeeded. She'd shot a kid in front of me, murdering him while I stood by helplessly.

Thinking of Danny's terrified face—his glasses falling to the concrete while blood pooled under him—filled me with a white-hot anger I couldn't swallow.

And beneath that was a wound still raw.

Morrigan watched me with the faintest trace of a knowing smile, and I felt sick to my stomach. "Thank you for being so understanding," she said, poking that wound. "Hope told me of last week's events, how she personally caused you and Caden... discomfort. By allowing her to make things right, you truly lead by example."

I clenched my jaw, biting down on the urge to scream at them both to get out. *That's what she wants.* A part of me knew that. It was just the part that was losing to my temper.

I felt a hand on my shoulder, and I only kept from flinching because I knew Morrigan was watching. Then I felt the tension ease out of my neck and jaw, felt the blazing anger fizzle into embers. It was Caden's healing touch, I knew, and right then I welcomed it. I let it wash over me like a wave of aloe.

"Thank you for bringing more incarnates into the Watch," Caden said. I felt a stab of betrayal, but I tamped it down. It was easier to do beneath his spell. Besides, I knew my irritation with him was misdirected; he was doing what needed to be done, saying the things I couldn't. He was being strong for both of us. "All of us welcome you. Emery may seem a tad protective, but it's just because of his job, as the chief officer of relations, to keep a close eye on you over the next week. I'm sure you won't mind; after all, as president of the Watch, you would have to work closely with him."

The tiny muscle just above Morrigan's left eye twitched. Which did more for my soul than Caden's healing. "You assigned other leadership roles *before* electing the president?" Morrigan asked, clearly hoping she'd misheard him.

"We did."

"I see." She pursed her lips. "How *humble* of you."

"He'll be writing up the code of conduct within the next few days, I'd imagine," Caden remarked cheerfully. "Then we'll all be abiding by his rules. For the good of the Watch, of course."

She gave him a tight smile. "Of course."

"That should just about conclude today's business," he said. "I think I speak for all of us when I say we're expecting quite the demonstration of your commitment this week, Morrigan."

She nodded, thanking him for his warm support. But before she turned back to face the room again, I saw a flash of irritation flicker over her features. Had Caden managed to get under her skin?

If so, he wasn't done yet. Caden turned to Hope and, to my disbelief, reached out his hand. She regarded the peace offering with a look that bordered on fear, but Morrigan not-so-subtly cleared her throat. The two shook hands, and I could feel the watching incarnates' approval like a physical weight. Morrigan's face looked like it was chipped from ice, making me wonder if she felt it, too.

Caden withdrew his hand, and Hope retreated to the side of the room, but not before I caught a puzzled frown on her face.

The room broke into motion, then, as if this were high school and someone had rung the class bell. Everyone gathered their things and clumped into groups, chatting. Mostly, the topics were idle; I suspected the earnest discussions about the meeting's events would occur as soon as everyone had some privacy.

Melusina and Rachelle jumped up to talk with Caden, while Dagan stepped up to Morrigan and began speaking quietly with her. He was a pragmatic man; I could understand why he'd want to get to know both candidates for president. Gregorius, surveying the room, stepped forward and joined their conversation. Good man. He'd let me know if Morrigan tried to hatch anything with Dagan right under our noses.

Any true deals wouldn't happen out in the open like this, though. Which was fortunate, as I wasn't in the right headspace to address them. With Morrigan entering the fray, the stakes had been raised, and I needed to shake off today's loss—and it *was* a loss, regardless of how well Caden had managed to stick the landing—and prepare for round two.

Centuries spent warring with Morrigan had trained me how to engage her and walk away, sometimes even in one piece. Never unscathed, but I knew I could survive. Earlier this year, I'd tussled with her in New York and mostly come out on top. I *would* do so again.

Recovering my confidence was a delicate act, as I couldn't afford to underestimate her. She was a coiled, deadly snake in the tent; I must not be caught sleeping. I would need to be just as deadly, just as quick, to keep anyone else from being bitten, too.

At least this time I knew her goal: she wanted the Watch. That gave me a head start—it was more information than I usually had to go on when it came to Morrigan. In the past, her motives had often been as mystifying as her actions. Knowing what she wanted provided me a much-needed edge. Which was probably why she'd orchestrated this attack to throw me off guard, striking from a direction Caden and I weren't expecting. Aside from the pleasure it undoubtedly gave her to see me squirm, she needed me at a disadvantage.

Well, this incarnation was young and fit; my equilibrium was steady. Plus, I had something she didn't understand: Caden's unconditional support, keeping me grounded.

Obviously. I mean, I hadn't screamed at her to get out. That was the hallmark of self-control right there.

The first step was to acquire more information, and I knew exactly where to get it. Excusing myself from the conversation buzzing around Caden, I slipped out of the room and fastened the Bluetooth receiver to my ear. "Artie?" I whispered.

"I am here," his voice came promptly. I wasn't entirely sure how he spoke to me. I mean, I didn't have to dial a number or send a text. I think it kind of worked like when you asked your smartphone to set the timer, only my devices were *extra* smart. And a little extra sassy, at times.

"I want you to go full Unum on Morrigan."

"I beg your pardon?"

I looked around to make sure I wasn't being overheard. It was quiet in the hallway outside, especially compared to the bustle of the room. "You know," I explained, "like you did with me. I want you to track Morrigan's every movement and report to me every suspicious thing she does. I want you to listen and record every conversation, and I want it done invisibly."

"Ah, the Big Brother protocols," Artie confirmed. "Consider it done. But please acknowledge my official objection to it being termed 'full Unum.'"

"Understood. You pull this off, and you can name it anything you want."

"Emery?" I spun, but it was only Rachelle. "Can you believe this? Morrigan and Hope *teaming up*? What the hell?"

"Yeah. Honestly didn't see that one coming. As far as I know, the last time they got together, Morrigan ended up in a cage."

Her eyebrows went up. "Really? Morrigan doesn't seem like the type to let something like that go."

I snorted. "She's not." Then I shook my head, annoyed. "We need to be careful not to make assumptions about her, though. She'd let anything go if it served her purposes."

"So what's your game plan?"

"I'm drumming one up."

She shook her head. "Not alone, you aren't." At my surprise, she rolled her eyes. "Emery, you need to stop limiting yourself. If you're going to beat Morrigan this time, you need to use all the tools at your disposal."

"I'm already working on it," I said defensively, thinking of Artie.

She put her hands on her hips. "I said *all* your tools, didn't I? You and Morrigan go way back. You've fought countless times. She knows your triggers. But she's never tangled with Rachelle Grey before."

Her words perked me up. "All right. I'm putting eyes on her to figure out what she's up to."

"What *they're* up to, you mean." She speared me with a look. "Don't get so focused on Morrigan that you lose sight of Hope. She's just as bad." I wasn't sure I agreed, but her point was valid. "I think we're missing something with the vote. I mean, as it stands right now, there's no way Morrigan will win. Not unless she brings a whole busload of incarnates with her next week."

I felt the blood drain from my face. "You might be on to some-thing." I considered. "Today she established that the Watch won't turn anyone away: her, Hope, even the Sandman. With that prece-dent, she could bring in enough new members to swing the vote."

"Did someone say my name?"

I started. We weren't alone? Somehow, the Sandman had slipped out of the room on soundless feet and was now hovering behind Rachelle's shoulder. How much had he overheard?

"My humblest apologies," he said in that paper-thin voice. Out here in the hallway, away from the other, colorful incarnates, he stood out even more starkly. His skin was so pale and taut, he looked like a victim of whatever had drained away the life of Amara's horse. "I did not intend to intrude." He gave us a considering look, then passed us and continued down the hallway. Neither of us spoke again until he'd exited the Lodge.

"Creepy." Rachelle shuddered.

"And suspicious. I don't know how long he was there."

She tucked a strand of hair behind one ear. "We should probably continue this conversation in a more private place."

"Yeah," I agreed. "Want to come over after this?"

She hesitated. "I can't. My mom's taking me shopping at North-gate Mall, and then Matt's coming over tonight."

"Matt?" I made a face. "It's *Matlas*. I would know; we're basically best friends."

"When you're dating him, you can call him whatever you want."

I waggled my eyebrows. "Is that a promise?"

"You're not his type," she said, smirking.

"I'm told I'm an acquired taste."

"That—that's not a compliment."

"Agree to disagree. Want to come over after your date, then? I'll be up late."

She reddened a little. "I would, but I'm not sure how, um, late he'll be staying."

"Ah."

"Don't you dare start judging, Emery Luple. If I recall correctly, when you met Caden, you spent the first *two* nights together."

"Two?" I spluttered. "The first night was in a hospital! And the second one we were trapped in an old barn, hounded by the Headless Horseman." I paused. "Though it *was* kind of romantic."

She rolled her eyes again. "Let's meet up tomorrow."

"But not too early?" I pressed, grinning.

She colored again. "Actually, not too late."

"Why?"

"Because I'm assuming tonight will go well," she huffed, "and he happened to mention he has no plans tomorrow night, either."

"Subtle."

She glared. "Really? Coming from you?"

I put my hands up defensively. "Tomorrow, then. That works for me. I have some errands to run today anyway."

"Good. Now get your ass back in that room."

She was right. I couldn't let Morrigan think I'd slunk away in defeat. More importantly, I needed to show Caden my support. Something I'd failed at too many times today. Bolstered by our conversation, I took a deep breath and braced myself, then returned to the room.

The incarnates had divided into two main clusters. Dagan, Gregory, and Melusina were speaking with Morrigan, Hope standing close enough to hear the conversation but far enough away not to be truly a part of it. The rest of the group more or less surrounded Caden, who spoke easily with Maggie, the Undine, and the Amazon.

Melusina looked up when I entered and, seemingly looking for an excuse to leave Morrigan's little group, cornered me before I'd taken three steps into the room. "You and Morrigan have a bit of a storied past, huh? You and Caden going to invite a girl over to swap tales?"

"You'd be welcome anytime. But tales... There are so many, I don't even know where to start."

She raised her eyebrows. "You two go back that far?" She lowered her voice. "Is she trouble?"

I glanced up at Morrigan, who was well out of earshot and absorbed in her discussion with Dagan and Gregory, besides. "Yes. More than anyone else I know."

She grimaced. "That bad? I mean, she can't be worse than Vox Populi."

"She is." I held her gaze for a moment to let the gravity of that statement sink in. "Be careful until this election is over."

Melusina looked troubled. "Emery... she's not what she claims to be, is she?"

I shook my head grimly, and her eyes widened. It was rewarding, knowing Morrigan hadn't fooled everyone. "Like I said, watch your back." I stepped around her to join Caden and the others. But I was stopped again, this time by Kolby. He was just standing there, looking up at me with his large eyes.

"Hi, Emery."

I knelt down. "Hey, buddy. It's been a while. How're Skye and Hank?"

"They're well. They give me plenty of shinies." Which likely summed up the entire relationship for the little Kobold.

"I'm glad you came today, Kolby. Thank you for your support."

He smiled shyly. "You made my home happy for me. Mommy Skye and Daddy Hank have been more loving than ever since you came by that day. My Safe Haven extends to our whole house now."

"That's great—"

The little guy shook his head, cutting me off. "You don't understand. It's been many years—maybe lifetimes—since an Unseen's Safe Haven *expanded*. In the modern world, our places of hiding only diminish, shrinking year after year. You changed that."

I frowned. "Unseen?"

His face scrunched up. "What we Prey incarnates call ourselves." Ah. I suppose "Prey" could be a tad dismissive. "I can see you don't understand the impact of my news, but trust me, when people catch wind of this, everyone will want to know how it happened. You'll be a hero."

I scoffed. "I didn't do much. You kind of got caught up in my reincarnation drama, if I'm being honest."

"You didn't just take away the bad shiny," he insisted. "You fixed my family. Mommy Skye used to worry over me. She tried to hide it, but I could tell. She and Daddy Hank would sometimes argue about me when they didn't think I was listening, about the local legend of the shadow man and his bird. Even with my glamour, they knew it was me. They just couldn't admit it." His huge eyes glistened with unshed tears… though, to be fair, that was often their default state. Anything to make you notice how adorable he was. "Then you came over, and you believed them. Your story about the cursed shiny made them stop doubting the supernatural. They started watching all your content, and they don't fight about me anymore." He smiled shyly. "They accept me, and on some level, they accept me for who I am rather than who they want me to be."

"Wow, I had no idea."

"I came today to thank you. And to warn you that you're going to get a lot of attention once I spread the word among the Unseen. If there's even a chance you can expand Safe Havens for others, many will want you to try."

"I'll do what I can." I looked up at Caden, who saw my glance and gave me a soft smile before turning back to the person he was speaking to. "My Sanctum is very important to me, so I understand better than you think."

He nodded solemnly. "I need to return home before Mommy Skye misses me. Farewell, Emery."

I told him goodbye and watched him dart out of the room, looking like an excited young child. It must've been my imagination, but I thought I heard the flapping of wings a few seconds after he left my sight. Impossible, of course. I'd never be able to hear it over the din of the room.

"A most interesting tale, Loophole," a voice said behind me. I turned to find the Undine regarding me with a speculative expression on her blue face.

"You heard our conversation?"

"Enough to understand why the Kobold would wash up at a meeting of incarnates, when he is usually known to keep to safer waters."

"You know the Kobold?"

She bobbed her head in what might have been a yes. "We Unseen do our best to keep our eyes on each other's ponds. The fact he shared our word with you is telling, Loophole; it speaks very highly of his regard for your character. I would ask that you keep it close to your heart. Among our kind, it is a pearl most rare."

"I understand. My name's Emery."

"I am Nimue. A pleasure to meet you. I will watch your odyssey with great interest, Emery." And she walked away. Well, her walk was so graceful, it was more like she *flowed* away.

I looked around, expecting another distraction. The room was emptying, though. The Amazon had slipped out while I'd been chatting, Melusina and Dagan were gathering their things, and Iris was nowhere in sight. Unsurprising. The Ghost often came and went with little regard for things like doors, or walls, or even the intervening space between destinations.

Morrigan was speaking quietly with Hope when Caden stepped over to me. "That wasn't really how I expected things to go," he murmured.

"You're telling me," I replied. "I'm sorry I—"

He put his finger on my lips to cut me off, then said gently, "Don't apologize for helping people, beamish boy. You wouldn't be the guy I love if you did it any other way." He grinned as he removed his finger. "You didn't miss anything, anyway."

"Except introductions. Maggie's been hard at work."

"And don't y'all forget it," she said as she walked by. "We'll talk before next Friday. Till then!"

We waved goodbye to her, said a few parting words to Melusina and Dagan, and then Gregory approached. "You two need time to debrief. I'll close up."

"You don't mind?"

"I need some time to myself. I do my best thinking alone." He shrugged. "Might as well keep my hands busy while my mind's working."

We thanked him, and Caden started to pack his things into his bag, including the laptop he'd been using to communicate with the Witch.

"You wouldn't head out without first saying goodbye?" Morrigan asked, strutting forward, Hope at her heels.

I took a calming breath. While I wanted to spar with her, if for no other reason than to prove I could, I knew this wasn't the right time or place. I was still unprepared. If I played on her timetable, in her arena, I would lose. "Of course not. Goodbye, Morrigan."

I took Caden's arm and pulled him into the hallway, pleased at the surprised look on Hope's face. Morrigan, however, watched me with a knowing quirk of her lips. "Good little pet," I heard her say behind me. "There may be hope for him yet. Though I'm probably just being optimistic again."

"Good job, Em," Caden whispered in the hall. "I know that wasn't easy."

"Easier with you on my arm," I told him truthfully.

We left together, distracted by our thoughts. Morrigan was back. In a heinous team-up I hadn't foreseen, she'd brought Hope with her. And they'd returned, not solely for me, but for Caden and his dream, too. He'd planned to start running the Watch today, to move it into the next crucial phases of inception. Instead, he had to fight for his position as its leader against the worst opponents imaginable.

It wasn't even noon yet, and this was shaping up to be one hell of a day.

It was almost enough to make me forget about Amara and her dead horse. About Susan and her dead husband. About Nyx, our history, and his troubling role in all of this.

Arm in arm, we left the Lodge and all its surprises behind us.

My name is Gregory Gregorius.

To say the inaugural meeting of the Incarnate Watch did not go as planned is a bit of an understatement. Yes, I know who Morrigan really is. My latest report had placed her in Tokyo, but that woman tends to pop up where she's least wanted. Sometimes keeping tabs on her is like a game of Whac-A-Mole: fruitless, but occasionally satisfying.

I admit, I'm concerned about the triple threat that is Morrigan, Hope, and Nyx in Seattle at the same time. I don't think we should dismiss the possibility that they're colluding. Though not to kill Emery; Nyx would never agree to that. For all his faults—and they are many—he cares too deeply for Emery.

With all three of them in town, this is ramping up to something big. I need to unearth their aims.

Maybe I should begin with Morrigan's history of working with incarnates to achieve her ends. Malevolents and Predators, mostly, but I wouldn't put anything past her. As the newly minted chief officer of security, I'll need to ensure the other members of the Watch are protected. Morrigan's scheme to win the vote for presidency might include eliminating those who openly support Caden's nomination—namely Melusina, Artie, and Maggie.

I have work to do.

~

Caden was quiet as he changed clothes and prepared for work. After five minutes of silence—which was about four more than I could stand—I finally broke in. "I know it didn't go as you expected, which is so disappointing after how much time and effort you spent preparing, but I'll stand with you. By this time next Friday, you'll be the president of the Incarnate Watch."

Silence fell again as he continued to grab his things, almost as if I hadn't spoken. He didn't take *that* much to work, though, and after a minute I realized he was just moving things around to keep busy. I let him. We each have our coping mechanisms.

Finally, he sighed. "It isn't the title that's important," he confided to the floor, almost too low for me to catch. "I just want the Watch to exist—so incarnates have something to support them, something to believe in. And I want to be a part of creating it. It's given me so much purpose."

You're afraid of what will happen if it's taken away. I didn't say it out loud. His feelings were fragile right now.

"No matter what happens, you're already the driving force that began the Watch," I told him. "It wouldn't even be a topic of conversation without all your hard work."

He smiled sadly. "I know. And that should be enough, I suppose. But no matter how hard I try to be logical about it, I can't make myself feel that way. I don't just want to be a *part* of the Watch—I want to steer it forward, to navigate the pitfalls it'll encounter, to blaze a new trail for incarnates everywhere." He looked up at the ceiling and clenched his jaw. "Em, I hate how selfish that makes me."

I blinked. "*Selfish?*" I repeated, baffled. "You want to build an infrastructure to help incarnates everywhere, and you want to make sure it's as successful and far-reaching as possible. You monster."

He didn't smile. "The end result is what should matter, not how it gets done or who will be the one to achieve it."

"You aren't being selfish," I said, meeting his eyes. "And you aren't being foolish. It isn't the credit you seek; it's the achievement itself. You want the Watch to succeed, to usher in the first Sanctum City, and you sincerely believe you're the one most capable of making it happen."

"I don't know that I'd say I'm the *most* capable, but I'm certainly more so than Morrigan." He shuffled his feet self-consciously. "How do you know I don't want the credit?"

I grinned. "Because I'd want it, and you aren't me. And I love you for that."

He took a deep breath. "I think a double shift at the hospital is exactly what I need to get my mind off things. The more I dwell, the more I spiral downward."

I stepped forward and wrapped him in a hug. "Don't overwork yourself," I said softly. "If you just keep trading one stress for another, you'll wear yourself out."

He nodded. "But what else can I do? I can't relax, can't stop thinking about it. I can't stop wondering what would've happened if I'd just held the vote five minutes earlier."

"You wouldn't be the guy I love if you'd done it any other way," I said, echoing his words to me. I pulled back. "Besides, Morrigan just would've walked in five minutes earlier. The timing of that wasn't coincidental; it was her powers as the Antagonist. Like mine, they ensured she entered at precisely the right moment."

He nodded, his eyes clouded. "That worries me. If she was destined to disrupt the meeting—"

"Then we're destined to foil her plans," I finished firmly. "She's not the only one with fate-altering powers, you know."

"Yeah. Thanks, Em," he said.

I frowned. "I can't help but feel like you aren't cheered up."

"You've helped a lot."

"But?" I pressed.

He looked away. "There's only so much your words can do. I still need time to process how I feel."

I understood, but I still felt a bit stung. I didn't have a magical healing touch, but I liked to think I could take away some of his turmoil and pain. *This isn't about you*, I told myself firmly.

He stretched onto his toes and gave me a quick kiss. "I need to go, or I'm going to be late. Be extra careful while Morrigan's in town, and I promise I'll do the same. Don't go near her without me. Or seeking any other danger, okay?" He hesitated, then raised his voice, adding, "Artie? If danger seeks *him*, notify me."

"Consider it done, Caden Malek." The muffled response came from one of our pockets. I didn't know if Artie had been listening to our conversation all along, or if Caden's invocation of his name directed his attention to us. A week ago, that had been unnerving.

"I'm going to the store later," I told Caden. "You want anything?"

He headed toward the garage. It was tiny, only large enough for one of our cars, and we took turns using it while the other parked on the street.

"Got a grocery list on the yellow pad in the drawer," he said. "But the only thing I really need is something from the bakery. Actually, never mind. I'll get it."

I put my hand on his shoulder. "No, what is it? I've got all afternoon."

He hesitated. "Well, if you don't mind, it *would* save me a trip. We're having a birthday potluck for someone at work tomorrow, and I signed up to bring pastries. Cupcakes, cookies, brownies—take your pick."

"Pastries," I said, making a mental note. "Got it." I gave my best Artie impression. "Consider it done, Caden Malek."

"Thanks," he said as he walked out. "I really appreciate it. One less thing I need to worry about."

I gave him one more farewell and then closed the door behind him, trying to organize my thoughts. Caden wouldn't be home until the wee hours of the morning, which gave me the rest of the day to myself.

Despite my promise to Caden, I was tempted to follow Morrigan around—with Artie tracking her phone, I could be extra careful. It rankled me to think she might be up to no good in my hometown, and I was especially worried about all the people I loved. With her around, no one was safe. I decided to honor my word, though. With the Watch scrutinizing her every move, I was reasonably certain she'd be on her best behavior, at least until next Friday.

Of course, Morrigan's best behavior might just mean murdering *discreetly*.

I needed to move, to let action be an outlet for my energy and thoughts. So, armed with plastic bags and three retractable leashes, I took the puppies for a walk. Since the Lodge was at the entrance to our complex, I avoided my usual route that took me right past it. I couldn't be sure Morrigan had departed, and if I could keep her from finding out we lived in this neighborhood, so much the better. Though it was likely not worth the effort; it wouldn't have surprised me if she already knew where we lived. Nyx had found me without any trouble, after all.

Mittens, Mask, and Beard were more than happy to humor me, regardless. They took every opportunity to investigate new smells, poles, and bushes. Their exuberance helped to clear my mood, which in turn helped to free my mind.

I did my best to refrain from dwelling on Morrigan, Hope, Nyx, my nightmare, or the murder. It wasn't easy; I needed to focus on something else, otherwise I would just replay the events of the meeting over and over, fretting over what I could've said, what I should've done.

That wasn't productive. So instead I thought about Kolby, Nimue, and the Unseen. I wondered if I'd ever heard that word before, in another life. I didn't think so, though secretive knowledge among incarnates had a way of being forgotten between reincarnations. Almost like the very word had a protective glamour. Not unlike my true identity as the Protagonist.

There was something to that, I thought. Reality went out of its way to rearrange memories and experiences, but sometimes I reincarnated knowing my identity, while other times I was left to rediscover it. Why? Was there a pattern? Was it somehow related to this mysterious Storyteller—or Narrator, or Author—that Morrigan sought? It made me wonder if what I attributed to "reality" should instead be credited to a specific incarnate, someone or something that intentionally created the rules, removed memories, and dictated what I could and could not remember.

And not just me, but those around me, too. When I died, records of Emery Luple seemed to magically disappear. The advent of the digital age didn't change that, either. My likeness disappeared from internet databases as easily and surely as it vanished from memories and photos. The oddest thing is that I wasn't *completely* erased. Life itself didn't forget me; my actions had real consequences and sometimes far-reaching implications on history, though it often renamed me, reimagined me. What would happen to Lynn Luple if I died? I suspected she'd mourn the loss of her son, but the next day she'd have a different last name. No one in her life would bat an eye— hadn't she been Lynn Santiago all along?

It was sobering. And staggering. And, like many of life's existential questions, often best when one didn't dwell on it for too long.

So I picked up dog poop in plastic bags and forcibly turned my mind to lighter topics. Then I spent another thirty minutes playing with the puppies to wear them out. It worked better than I could have hoped—for them and for me. By the time we went home, we'd all worked off our excess energy.

And, let's face it: playing with puppies is good for the soul.

16

"Melusina says you told her Morrigan's more crooked than a barrel full of corkscrews."

That hadn't been exactly how I'd phrased it. "She's bad news, Maggie," I said into the phone as I tried to locate my keys. "I'm worried what else she's got planned for the week ahead."

"There's nothing to fret about. The Watch has got Caden's back, you know."

"The current one, yes. But I think Morrigan might be doing some recruiting of her own."

Maggie scoffed. "Let her try. There ain't no way she'll outcharm me."

I grinned. She was right, but Morrigan might use stronger tactics than charm. "I'm impressed with what you've accomplished so far. The Amazon, the Undine, the Witch—in a couple of days. You've been busy."

"Thanks, but I can't take all the credit. Agatha came to me, after all."

Interesting. I hadn't heard that. "She did? Well, maybe you'll get lucky and more incarnates will throw themselves at your feet for the honor of joining our little club." I paused. "That said, don't go meeting any new incarnates alone, okay? Bring someone along to watch your back."

"This Morrigan gal has you right spooked, huh? Don't you worry about me, I'll be on high alert."

"Good. Let me know if you run into anything peculiar. Keep a low profile this week, and I'll take care of Morrigan and Hope."

"That sounds ominous."

I gave her my best innocent reply. "Nah. You know me—I'm harmless."

On that note, I left home and drove across town. With Nyx lurking about, I needed to pick up a dream catcher. It was a natural talisman against the Incubus, and it should also help with my nightmares, especially if the one I'd had was a sending of some sort. Some incarnates have the power to plant visions, or dreams, in the minds of others. Hell, the Sandman might've been able to do it. Even if my dream hadn't been a sending, there was a special sort of serenity to be found in a dream catcher's presence—whether due to the Asibikaashi's magic or just some kind of placebo effect, I found the talismans filtered out mundane nightmares almost as effectively as they did supernatural dreams.

Artie identified the nearest store that sold the type of dream catcher I wanted, scanned the store's digital inventory to confirm they were in stock, and uploaded the location to my GPS. The convenience was undercut somewhat by his quiet diatribe explaining the many ways in which I was wasting his skills on such menial tasks, but I good-naturedly ignored his grumbling.

Within minutes, I was coasting into downtown Renton in my Rogue. I'd come into ownership of the vehicle earlier in the year, when I'd helped the Smuggler out of a tight spot. In return for services rendered, he'd given me a good deal on what I really hoped wasn't a stolen car. I was pretty sure it was legit, otherwise Gregory would've busted me by now.

I had to travel a little farther to find the store I was looking for. While many places sold dream catchers, I wanted to purchase an authentic one—they're a traditional piece of culture to some Native people, and while they've been widely appropriated, I felt it was important to honor their roots and support Native-made crafts. Plus, if the Asibikaashi incarnate's magic was stronger in genuine catchers, it was an all-around win.

So, my list: dream catcher, bakery for Caden, grocery store. And, while I was out, I wanted to pick up something special for Caden. Not just to cheer him up, and not just to make up for the fact that I'd been late to the most important meeting of his life. No, I wanted to get him something that would remind him he was loved, no matter what else happened. Something to show him our life was already extraordinary, and everything else was a bonus.

No pressure.

I was listening to music when it suddenly cut off and was replaced with Artie's voice. "Emery Luple, I have some news for you."

I flinched. Since I'd had the music playing at a sing-along volume, the voice was rather loud. I lowered the volume. "Go ahead, Artie. Is this about Morrigan? Or did you find any video surveillance of Nyx from the crime scene this morning?"

"No, on both accounts. But I think you'll be pleased with my initiative. I took the liberty of doing some research on possible incarnate culprits other than the Sasquatch in the killing of Amara's horse, Spray."

I nodded, then, realizing he couldn't see me, said, "That's great. What did you find?"

"I began by cross-referencing your discussion with Caden about the oddities at the scene with databases containing mostly anecdotal information about incarnates. Narrowing the search further, I utilized the pictures you took on your phone—though I must confess they were rather distorted. Have you considered upgrading to a digital camera with greater lens stability to compensate for your less-than-competent photography skills?"

"I'm finding it hard not to take that personally."

"Oh!" he exclaimed. "Please forgive me. I forgot to preface the statement with the human nicety, 'No offense, but...'"

"Still offended, Artie."

"But then whatever is the custom for? It makes no sense. Why elongate the sentence if the addendum serves no purpose?"

"Yeah, because *humans* are the long-winded ones."

"Would I be correct in presuming your tone indicates sarcasm?"

"You would."

"Excellent!" he remarked. "I do so appreciate self-improvement. But I digress. As I was saying, I believe I have identified your perpetrator: the Mare incarnate."

I drummed my fingers on the steering wheel while sitting at a light. All I could think of was that a mare was a female horse. "Are you saying Spray was an incarnate?"

"Not at all. I did consider the possibility but, after due consideration, discarded the notion. The likeliness of the horse being an incarnate is so negligible it might as well not exist." Those were the kinds of odds my powers loved to play with, but I was more interested in what Artie said next. "The Mare incarnate *is* associated with horses, however. She is almost exclusively female and is known to ride horses to exhaustion throughout the night seeking nourishment if it is not readily available."

"What kind of nourishment?"

"The dreams of humans, mostly. The Mare is known to enter homes at night and sit atop the chest of a human, then entangle them in her long hair. The human, having trouble breathing, develops bad dreams, and the Mare feeds on this energy. Her presence is sometimes confused with sleep paralysis."

I frowned. "So why would she attack a horse?"

"I believe she attacked the horse's owner, too. I remembered the woman mentioning she felt 'off,' which I had initially inferred was some sort of human state of stasis but eventually came to understand is an inept euphemism for feeling ill. But there's more evidence, too. You see, according to legend, one way to determine whether the Mare has visited is to examine the localized flora. Tree branches and plants would resemble the twisted locks of her hair if she had fed that night."

I recalled the odd pattern to the branches above Spray's resting place, the way they seemed to be woven together. "Okay, that's pretty damning," I admitted.

"Then my next piece of evidence should put the metaphorical nail in the coffin," Artie said happily. "Mirrors are a known talisman to keep the Mare at bay. That explains the smashed mirror. The horse —or something else, perhaps—must have damaged the mirror, allowing the Mare to slip in for the kill."

"You sound entirely too cheery about death, Artie."

"My apologies. In my defense, I was programmed to deliver most news in an upbeat, approachable manner."

"Well, good job, at any rate. Will you start compiling information that might lead us to the identity of the Mare, as well as ways we might combat her?"

"At once. I'm certain I'll have an update for you shortly."

"Thanks," I said, pulling into a parking spot in a weathered strip mall that, despite its age, had been kept in remarkably good condition.

A few minutes later, I pushed open the door to a sizable storefront. The small business was called Duwamish River Trading, and it featured carefully arranged displays for each section: dream catchers in one corner, artwork in another, shelves of books featuring historical and local lore, gorgeous woven blankets, and an entire section of clothes, hats, and scarves. A middle-aged woman with long, unbound hair and an excess of smile lines was helping a customer at the counter, where a display of handmade jewelry was housed.

I perused the artwork—mostly landscape scenes, though the artist had a fondness for deer that I couldn't help but think would have improved on the tastes of the Lodge—before heading over to the dream catcher section. The selection was impressive, doubly so because each had clearly been handcrafted. I rotated the wooden beam that displayed them until a striking one caught my eye. The circle that formed the body of the dream catcher was made up of undyed wooden sticks, with a gray feather suspended from the lower left portion. In the center of the netting was an azure bead that reflected the light in a way that would have made Kolby drool.

"You have an excellent eye," the shopkeeper said from behind me. I hadn't even heard her approach.

"It's stunning," I replied.

She looked me up and down. "If it's nightmares you're having, this one is perfect for you. Do you see how, compared to these other dream catchers, the hole in the web is larger? That is because the Anishinaabe artist who made this dream catcher made it specifically for one who needs a larger center to allow the good dreams and ideas to pass through it. But do not worry, the rest of the web is more than sufficient to catch the bad dreams, too."

"The bad ideas get caught? Maybe it needs to be all netting and no hole."

She smiled. "While dream catchers are certainly connected with sleep, they were originally intended to intercept all manner of negative emotions, thoughts, and ideas. To be a source of comfort to the children of the tribe even when the parents or grandparents were unable to watch over their every moment."

I nodded, listening as she explained how other Native peoples, like the Lakota, held different beliefs about how dream catchers worked, but they too believed in their warding, apotropaic properties.

"I'll take it," I said, reverently removing it from its hanger and passing it to her. "And thank you for the lesson."

As we walked over to the register, I felt a vibration in my pocket. A text. I realized I'd taken off my wireless earbud before coming into the store. I glanced at my phone. Emery Luple! I have an update. Please respond at your earliest convenience.

It was from an unknown number, but I knew it was Artie. For some reason, he rarely chose the same contact number twice.

Wow, an update already. Even for him, that was fast.

I chatted with the woman as she rang up my purchase and carefully packaged the dream catcher in a white box. My phone buzzed another three times, which made me wonder if I needed to have a conversation with Artie about patience. I thanked her again and walked briskly toward the door.

"What is it, Artie?" I said as soon as I was outside. I didn't bother putting in my earpiece or dialing, I just held my phone near my mouth, trusting he was listening.

He was. A moment later, my phone made a chirp and Artie's voice spoke through it. "We have a problem. You asked me to monitor Morrigan's cell phone, remember?"

"Yes," I said, my heart rate spiking. I unlocked my car door. "What's she up to?"

"For the last two hours and twenty-seven minutes, I have been watching her every movement. Based on the proximity of their phones, it appears both she and Hope are still together."

"And?" I jumped into the driver's seat and punched the ignition.

"To be honest with you, their movements made little sense to me. After departing the Lodge, they drove to a restaurant and spent almost an hour inside, whereupon I confirmed they'd eaten lunch by tracing the credit card swipes of the local point of purchase machine—"

"Artie! Spit it out. What's the problem?"

"Yes, yes, my apologies. Morrigan and Hope appear to have finally reached their destination."

"And that is?"

"The residence of Mathew Atlas."

$\mathcal{I}$ raced to the boundary of Woodinville and Maltby, to Paradise Lake Cemetery, where I'd spent far too much time recently. As one of the most haunted graveyards in Washington State, maybe even in America, it attracted a lot of attention from ghost hunters and paranormal bloggers. The entrance to the cemetery was located at the end of a roundabout, with Matlas's family home just to the left of it. As I pulled up, I saw a white luxury SUV parked on the right. It was one of those extended-cab monstrosities, and I just knew it was Morrigan's version of an inconspicuous limousine.

Only she would think it was inconspicuous.

Before exiting my car, I did a quick drive-by to see whether the other vehicle was vacant. The windows were tinted to degrees that couldn't be legal, but I was fairly sure the SUV was empty. I circled the roundabout and parked a few car lengths behind it.

Now what? I wasn't sure what to do next. Were Hope and Morrigan in Matlas's house already? The front door wasn't visible from my vantage point, but the porch looked empty.

I hefted the duffel bag I'd started keeping in the back seat, set it down in my lap, and unzipped it. Rummaging inside, I took stock of my available arsenal.

Seven tranquilizer darts.

Two cans of pepper spray, and another prepared grenade-style.

A ski mask.

Some rope and three rolls of duct tape.

All right, now that I list it out, I admit it kind of sounds like a kidnapper's kit. Don't worry; I only use my powers for good.

There were also a handful of lighters and batteries of different sizes, a digital camera, a fishing net, two flashlights, a hunting knife, a disposable flip phone, a laser pointer, an air horn, and a sleeve of Oreos (because hey, you just never know).

And, of course, my trusty Taser.

It was unlikely Morrigan and Hope had come unarmed—or without an escort, gauging by the number of seats in that SUV. So I'd definitely want to bring along my Taser and tranqs, which worked especially well on people. For me, I mean. In general, tranqs are notoriously unreliable, but mine tended to work like magic: my powers of convenience made them highly effective at knocking minions out and keeping them snoozing for just the right amount of time, even if that duration fluctuated wildly from mission to mission. Handy, that.

I didn't think it wise to haul around the entire pack, so I settled on slipping my Taser and two tranqs into separate jacket pockets, then another into my jeans. Feeling adequately prepared—to the extent that was possible when facing Morrigan—I began to plan out my next move.

I know. Me, planning. We all know how this is going to turn out.

I judged the distance to the upper-floor window at just shy of twenty feet. It would take a lot of work to scale the flat side of the house and sneakily enter the upstairs. The back entrance to the house might have a goon stationed there, but it would probably be easier to take one of them out silently than go through the hassle of entering through the upstairs window. 'Course, I could always knock on the front door. I mean, they'd never see it coming, right?

I glanced at the graveyard, second-guessing my approach. I didn't have any proof they'd entered Matlas's house. Maybe they hadn't come for him at all. I hesitated. Why would Hope return there, though? She'd nearly died last week, when the Thirteen Steps had attacked her sanity. As tough as Hope was, I didn't think she'd willingly revisit the place that had nearly undone her—and the place that had cost her Vox Populi, the only family she'd ever known.

Which raised the question: why had Morrigan brought her here?

Something wasn't adding up. As much as I dreaded to think it, the more likely scenario was that they were inside Matlas's house, threatening him—just threatening, I refused to think I'd arrived too late— in order to get to me. He was the perfect target: far enough on the periphery of my social circle that he wouldn't be protected at all times, but close enough that it would be personal if he were wounded or... worse.

I slid out of my car and darted across the street to the side of his house. I paused there, straining to listen. Maybe I'd be able to hear something that would guide me, give me some sort of inkling of how to proceed.

It worked; I suddenly caught snippets of conversation on the breeze.

"... sorry, Morrigan," a faint voice said, almost out of earshot. Where was it coming from? "... thought they'd be here." That was Hope's voice, and it was moving farther away. "I can keep..." The voice became too indistinct to make out.

It was coming from the graveyard.

I sagged in relief. They weren't here for Matlas after all.

I slipped down from the house and crept to the entrance of the graveyard. The time of day and weather did me no favors: it was midafternoon and overcast, with very little in the way of darkness or shadow to conceal me. So instead I relied on my knowledge of the graveyard's layout. Like I said, I'd spent too much time there recently.

Paradise Lake Cemetery was almost more nature preserve than graveyard, with low bushes and tall trees liberally arrayed around and within the cemetery proper. Headstones dotted the hilly landscape and often cropped up between paths bounded by shrubbery or large trees. There was a swath of bushes dividing the property and the graveyard, and I crouched behind the foliage as I approached.

"You needn't concern yourself with apologies, Hope." Morrigan's voice came to me over the hedge. "The incarnate puppies are clearly not here. If they were, we would've come across them by now. They've either perished without their mother's protection, been discovered by someone else, or roved on to another location entirely."

Wait. They were after Mittens, Mask, and Beard? Why?

Possibilities began to blossom in my mind. A few years ago, Morrigan had begun experimenting with creating incarnates, though with predictably little success. Incarnates were the manifestation of tales being retold for so long, they became legends. We didn't spring into existence after a few campfire stories.

As usual, Morrigan ignored everything we knew to be true about incarnates and began... tinkering. By which I mean she captured the Yeti and dressed it up in a Wookiee costume, shipped it off to the desert, and began terrorizing the locals in an attempt to incarnate a beloved *Star Wars* character. Noble goal aside, you can see why I thought her plan was absurd. It also should have been impossible; the Yeti's fatal flaw was capture, so it should've died the moment Morrigan caught it. Her incarnate powers as the Antagonist somehow interfered, and I suspected it was because my hunt for the Yeti eventually culminated in my death. Which set a worrying precedent. If her powers defied reality specifically to ensure my demise, I was concerned what other tricks she might be able to employ if they but led to my undoing.

I hoped I was wrong. Maybe she'd simply found a way around the Yeti's weakness and exploited it. That *was* one of the things Morrigan did best.

She'd tried the same stunt earlier this year, in New York. She and Sabrina Miles had conspired to create a new incarnate, Ahedrian, by inventing a myth and then perpetrating heinous deeds in its name while simultaneously blasting them all over the news to spread the tale fast, far, and wide.

Did she want the Hellhound puppies for some similar nefarious purpose? Or did she have another scheme brewing that required the offspring of incarnates to complete?

I dared a peek over the bushes and into the graveyard. I could see surprisingly clearly, which didn't bode well for a stealth mission. Morrigan and Hope were ambling about the headstones like they were out for a stroll, a third person staying near them but keeping a respectful distance. Given the man's physique, his posture, and the semiautomatic weapon casually strapped to his body, I surmised he was their bodyguard.

"You aren't upset?" Hope asked. "I didn't intend to waste your time like this."

Movement near the entrance—off to my right—caught my attention. Training my focus there for a moment, I was surprised when what I thought was a small tree moved slightly. It wasn't a tree at all; it was a woman. What would have been a small tree made for a *large* woman, at that. She, too, wore a tight-fitting shirt, combat fatigues, and a holstered gun. Mercenary number two.

"Not at all," Morrigan replied. "I'm precisely where I'm meant to be. That's the way my powers work, Hope. There's a reason you brought me here, even if we aren't yet aware of what it is."

I ground my teeth. She made being "the Protagonist" sound so mystical.

"You mentioned the Thirteen Steps," Morrigan said. "I would like to see them for myself. I suspect they are the reason we are here, and I wish to inspect them firsthand. Please take me to them."

The cemetery was a hotbed of local legends all centering around a feature that wasn't even observable anymore: the Thirteen Steps to Hell. The story went that there were thirteen stone stairs descending to a blank earthen wall that may or may not have been an unfinished tomb—or, you know, a mouth to hell. Hooligans and thrill seekers would sneak into the cemetery and try to descend the staircase, but each step would summon forth feelings or hallucinations of dread, culminating in a final glimpse into hell itself if you reached the bottom step. After one too many incidents on the private property, the proprietors—which included Matlas's family—poured concrete down the stairs, filling them in and turning the Thirteen Steps of Hell into an unappealing block of cement. It turned out, however, that you couldn't seal away rumors and legends with concrete, so Matlas had reached out to *There's Always a Loophole*, hiring Rachelle and me to debunk the myth and help reduce the attention the graveyard attracted.

The only problem was that when I showed up at the Thirteen Steps, my powers gave reality the bird and reopened their sealed entrance. In the end, the Thirteen Steps was not an entrance to hell or Hell incarnate, but an incarnate in its own right based on the local legends.

I watched Hope stiffly lead Morrigan away, toward the slope that led to the Steps. Two things were abundantly clear: Hope was terrified, and she was doing it anyway. Which meant she was *more* terrified of Morrigan. Smart woman.

I had to follow them. I needed to know what they were up to and what Morrigan learned from this visit. If she didn't discover I was here, it could provide me with a crucial edge against her.

I eyed the huge woman merc at the entrance to the graveyard. I doubted I could sneak past her, especially in broad daylight. Even if I kept to the bushes, I'd make too much noise and alert her—or, worse, Hope and Morrigan. I knew from previous visits how dark this place got at night, but darkness was still hours away, even with the shortening days.

That meant I needed to take her down. I pulled out a tranquilizer dart and uncapped it, readying myself to crouch-sprint over to her and try to take her swiftly and by surprise.

That was when I saw a flicker of movement from the graveyard and glanced back, startled. Another two mercs slipped from where they'd been standing near the perimeter of the graveyard and followed Morrigan, Hope, and their escort.

Damn. At least four guards.

Oh well. With me entering the scene, they were the four *least* dangerous people in the graveyard at the moment.

I crept forward on near-silent feet, keeping my eyes glued to
the ground, avoiding the leaves and twigs that would give
away my position. As I neared the woman guarding the entrance, I
debated how to cover the last several yards. She was well trained,
putting her back to the line of low bushes I crouched behind, keeping
an eye on the open space before her. I wouldn't be able to sneak any
closer without alerting her to my presence.

I could rush her, exploiting the element of surprise to hopefully
keep her from bringing that gun into play. Not that she'd need it; her
other guns were just as impressive. If muscles could incarnate, they'd
be *jealous* of this woman. I could instead saunter up, act like a local,
and hope to get in close through deception. But again, I wasn't sure I
wanted to get close. Besides, Morrigan likely would've shown my face
to her hired help, since I was enemy priority one.

Which left option C. I palmed the tranq and rolled it down my
fingers to grip it with the pads, like a dart. Then I popped up from
behind the bushes and flicked my wrist forward, sending the dart
zipping through the space between us before it lodged perfectly in
the back of her neck. The woman flinched violently, spinning toward

me. I saw her mouth open to shout a warning, but she only completed half of her turn before she *crumpled*.

I winced at the thud of her falling body. The bigger they are...

I froze and strained my senses, waiting a full minute to be sure no one had been hiding in the graveyard watching for me or otherwise noticed her collapse. Finally, having determined the other mercs had truly gone with Morrigan and Hope, I entered the cemetery.

Before doing anything else, I retrieved the dart. No use doing all this infiltration work only to leave behind obvious evidence of my passing. I didn't bother checking the woman's pulse or her breathing —she'd be fine. And out *just* long enough for me to do whatever scouting was needed.

Satisfied, I moved on.

Like I said before, I knew this place well enough now to navigate it at night; doing so during the day was a cakewalk. The entrance was the highest point of the cemetery, with a lower terrace ringing the back half like a rear porch, stairs leading down to it. From there, it was possible to access the forest floor—where the graveyard was being slowly swallowed by the woods.

The area was devoid of other visitors, which made so much sense to me that I almost took it for granted. Our combined powers as the Protagonist and Antagonist made things convenient, which meant, for Morrigan, there'd be no pesky mortals nosing about her business, while for me, there wouldn't be bystanders who could get hurt.

I descended to the middle level quickly, listening intently for any of the three—or more—remaining mercs. I could hear Morrigan's and Hope's voices coming from below and off to my left, heading toward the Thirteen Steps.

"I wouldn't be surprised if they're sealed up," Hope was saying, her voice oddly devoid of inflection. She had such a tight control on her terror, it was making her voice taut. "The owners poured concrete down them years ago."

"We'll see. Lovely day for a stroll through the woods, do you not agree? I may need to look into purchasing this land. I've always been partial to the peace of a graveyard."

More like she wanted a convenient place to bury the bodies that piled up in her wake. I could read between the lines, even if she fooled everyone else.

I slipped down the stairs and darted behind a tree, trying to keep out of sight. Ahead, I could see the group picking their way forward. As I watched, one merc split off from the others and walked into the forest, choosing a tree and putting his back to it. From there, he had a full view of the path, and if I hadn't watched him choose his spot, I never would've seen him before he got the jump on me.

So I went deeper into the woods, circling around to come up on Morrigan and Hope nearer the Thirteen Steps. That would take me behind the post of that sentry, where I'd hopefully escape his notice.

It was slow going. I hopped among the roots of the great trees, avoiding the carpet of leaves coating the ground. Despite a recent rain shower, walking on the leaves would create too much noise. The roots were the safer, though slower, route.

Hope recounted her experience to Morrigan, how she and I had descended the Thirteen Steps one stair at a time, each one bringing on feelings of mounting dread and panic. She described it surgically, mechanically, like a doctor providing a sterile description of some horrific wound.

I used their voices to gauge my distance from them and keep within earshot.

"What happened when you reached the bottom step?"

"You wish to know it in greater detail?"

There was a pause. "Must I repeat myself?"

"No, no, of course not. I—I simply do not wish to relive it." Another pause, this one longer, then Hope began speaking again. "The world melted away, like I'd gone to sleep, and I awoke in a memory. It was a meeting of Vox Populi, years ago, when we met in secret to conduct the trial of an incarnate. I remembered the event, and it should have been the Satyr, but when we removed the incarnate's hood, it was *me* underneath. Everyone began to chant, demanding my blood, accusing me of being an incarnate."

The worst part about this story was that it had actually happened to an innocent incarnate.

"Go on."

"I was torn limb from limb, but despite the incredible pain, I reveled in the bloodshed, pleased we had ended an abomination's life. I felt everything. Every rip of flesh, every cut, every burn. And when I awoke, I was in a similar memory, but again it was me on trial, not another incarnate. The images, the *feelings*, were endless. I couldn't live through the agony again, so I started to fight back, but that only seemed to excite them." Her voice quavered, and I found myself pitying her. I'd lived through the hell of the Thirteen Steps, too. I knew how real it felt. "I lived it over and over, each time looking forward to the first few moments of the meeting when they just talked and no one was carving into my flesh. It only ended when the Loophole pulled me out, but by then I couldn't discern reality from nightmare."

"I'm sorry for your pain, Hope," Morrigan said, her voice so quiet I had to strain to hear it. "You have done well to claim it as yours, a necessary step to overcoming it."

A branch cracked beneath my foot as I moved to another tree. I froze.

"Did you hear that?" Hope asked.

Cursing under my breath, I dove behind a tree, unwilling to be caught out in the open.

"Yes." In a raised voice aimed in my direction, Morrigan said, "Who's there?"

I held my breath.

"Come, now. Won't you show yourself and join us?" When I didn't answer, I heard her say in a low, crisp voice, "Find them."

Footsteps began crunching on the leaves not far from where I hid. To hear their conversation, I'd needed to remain close to them, but I was still closer than I'd anticipated.

Two sets of footsteps approached. I could jump one of them, but even with supernatural luck on my side, I'd never get them both, not with them alert and seeking me. Plus, the Antagonist's own luck would likely be in counterplay to my own.

I slipped a tranquilizer dart from my pocket, moving soundlessly. I had to try.

Just then, a black cat pushed its whiskered face out of a bush not three paces from me. It met my eyes and, holding them, winked. *What?* I barely had time to reflect that the feline must be Ray, the Ijiraat, before he flitted past me and, between eyeblinks, transformed into a large black bird. In a noisy display of flapping wings, scattered leaves, and croaking caws, he flew over the mercs' heads. I heard the nearest one curse, but no gunshots rang out.

"It was just a crow, Morrigan," the other merc said from off to my other side.

"An auspicious omen, then," she replied, sounding completely unruffled by the experience. "Crows and I have a history."

After a tense moment, I heard the two sets of footsteps retreat, twigs snapping beneath their tread.

What the hell just happened?

How long had Ray been tracking me? It was infuriatingly well done —I'd had utterly no inkling he was anywhere nearby. I'd last seen him at the murder scene, I remembered, as the cat in the yard. *How many forms does the Ijiraat have?* Originally, the urban legend had a limited number of animals it could shape-shift into, but incarnates—like the myths themselves—were known to evolve over the years. Either way, he must've been using his raven form to keep up with me while I'd traveled by car.

But why in the world had he *saved* me? We hadn't parted on good terms, so even if he was following me around, I wouldn't have expected him to rescue me. Unless he had a history with Morrigan and knew what she really was.

I still wouldn't have expected it. Ray seemed like the kind of guy who would sit back and let things play out. But he'd just saved my bacon. With a cringe at how swiftly I'd misjudged him, I resolved to offer him an apology. Maybe in return he'd explain why he'd intervened on my behalf.

I had to stow my thoughts for later, though, as Morrigan and Hope reached the Thirteen Steps. I could barely hear them, so I slipped forward with exaggerated care, picking my way across roots to get closer.

"... told you, I'm afraid they're sealed."

"Yes. I can see that."

I settled behind a low crop of bushes that were a good twenty feet away from the Steps. If I peered through their branches, I could make out Morrigan, Hope, and the two remaining bodyguards.

Morrigan was circling the cement slab where the Thirteen Steps were located. "Interesting. It *is* an incarnate. A location incarnate, not unlike the Haunted House."

Hope hung back, clearly not wanting to be any closer to the Steps than necessary. Her arms were folded in front of her to project an apathetic air, but I noticed that they also made it seem like she was hugging herself. "I know you wished to see them open. I'm sorry; the only way I know to open them is to bring Emery. His incarnate curse seems to create loopholes in reality, allowing him access to things others can't readily use."

"They are *gifts*," Morrigan chided almost absently, squatting to inspect the stone slab more closely. "You need to retrain your mind to think outside the limited scope of Vox Populi's teachings."

Hope made a face. "Did I slip again? Sorry, I *am* trying."

I narrowed my eyes at that. Not because I didn't believe her, but because Hope's mannerisms and speech were reminding me of when, masquerading as the Virgo, she'd spent time with Rachelle and me. It wasn't just her submissive behavior, which had evaporated the moment she'd revealed her true identity. It was the fumble. I remembered a conversation with her in Rachelle's kitchen, in which we'd had a misunderstanding over her babbling about my "partner." I had thought she was referring to Rachelle—my business partner—when in fact she had been referencing Caden, my boyfriend. Her attitude during that discussion had been eerily similar to how she'd just spoken to Morrigan. Self-deprecating, making small mistakes that made you feel her intellectual superior, then apologizing and showing a willingness to learn.

It had been an act. Hope had been playing me like a fiddle. I realized with a growing sense of delight that she was doing the same thing to Morrigan.

And Morrigan was *falling for it.* She waved her hand dismissively toward Hope and said, "I know. It's an entire culture of teachings you must overcome, ingrained in you over multiple lifetimes and likely imprinted upon your mind when you reincarnate." She stood and brushed the dirt and grass from her hands. "Regardless, this is what we came for. From what you've told me, I gather this is a nocturnal incarnate, so I will need to return at night."

"And it will be open?" Hope asked skeptically.

"If I am here." Morrigan circled the Steps again, seeming to ponder them. "Despite our obvious differences," she explained, "Emery's powers are a facsimile of mine. While he noses about for loopholes, *my* powers create them. As in any good story, important events always occur in proximity to the Protagonist."

Hope indicated the Thirteen Steps. "And these constitute an important event?"

"Oh, most certainly. Upon my return, they will open to me. Now that we've become acquainted, they may even do so without the usual cover of night."

"But in stories, don't events often happen that are outside the protagonist's control?"

"Certainly, but those poor fools aren't cognizant of their role. It is my self-awareness that enables me to intentionally use my gifts. To steer my story." Her tone turned dark. "There are yet some things I cannot influence. In time, however, I shall rectify that."

"Morrigan!" one of the mercs suddenly barked. I ducked lower behind the bushes, worried at the alarm in the man's voice. What now? "We have a situation. Bradshaw detained someone sneaking in the woods. Says they took out Alicia."

That was a rather pretty name for the tower of muscle I'd tranq'd.

"Take care of it," Morrigan said, sounding almost bored.

The man saluted. "At once."

"And make sure they're disposed of properly," she added. "I don't want it traced back here."

"Understood."

Shit. They were blaming whoever they'd detained for Alicia's unconsciousness, which had been my fault. The person was only in trouble because of me. If I hadn't knocked her out, she would've just turned them away, but I'd gone and messed things up. Well, I wasn't going to let them take the fall for my action. I needed to save them.

"Should we not have them brought here instead?" Hope asked. "Find out who they are?"

"They aren't important," Morrigan said dismissively.

"How do you know?"

I heard irritation creep into her tone. "Because if they were important, they wouldn't have been caught by side characters. I do not mind answering wise questions, Hope, but do try harder not to vex me with inane ones."

As badly as I wanted to stay with Morrigan and Hope, I needed to get out of here if I stood any chance of saving the innocent person. I took a deep breath, then began picking my way back through the woods. I moved as quickly as I dared, my feet whispering over leaves even as I tried to stick to roots and clear patches of undergrowth.

Too slow.

I'd need to all-out sprint to make it at the same time as the mercs, who already had a head start on me. Could I chance them hearing me? No, if I made even the slightest noise, Morrigan's powers would ensure I was found. I wasn't ready to go head-to-head with her, much less with Hope and three armed guards as well.

I hopped to another root, and my foot slipped. My arms pinwheeled for balance.

No good.

I fell.

Everything was ruined. Morrigan and Hope would hear. I'd have to fight my way out, and that was if I could overpower those armed mercs. Even if I managed to escape, I wouldn't be able to save the poor soul who'd wandered into the cemetery at the wrong time.

As I fell, my mind snapped backward like an arrow released from a bow, shooting through past incarnations until it buried itself in the right one. With a mental *thud,* it hammered home into a version of myself I hadn't thought about in some time.

I still fell.

But I caught myself on my fingertips, soundless.

Above me, a leaf shivered in a miniscule breeze, disconnecting from its branch and fluttering to the ground. My eye traced it, then was pulled to a rabbit bolting from the undergrowth. The forest was alive with motion, but I might as well have been Stillness incarnate.

Where was I? This forest didn't look familiar; was I even near Koga? If the vegetation was any indication, I didn't think so.

Voices filtered through the forest, and I cocked my head, listening. *Morrigan.* What was happening? Why couldn't I remember? Then it hit me.

I was *channeling.*

Shimatta! What had I gotten myself into this time?

I was saving someone. My skills must be needed. Stealth. Speed. Agility. I rolled my shoulders, feeling the sensation of my muscles bunching and flexing. This form would do nicely. Youth was useful, but not required; I'd trained as a shinobi well into my twilight years —while dexterity and swiftness were a function of form, they were equally derived from sweat and resolve. Natural ability wasn't everything. Anyone could train their reflexes, hone their techniques. Shinobi no jutsu was difficult to master but accessible to all.

I flashed forward, zipping from root to root with foxlike grace. The falling leaves made more sound than I did. Whatever strange footwear I wore, it was comfortable, absorbing the impact each time my foot came down.

Tennis shoes. My mind was not wholly rooted in the past. A thread connected me to whichever Emery Luple existed in this strange future time.

I sprang over the low bushes with alacrity, tumbling forward and into a roll when I hit the grass on the other side. Keeping low, I navigated the path with *his* knowledge, finding the stairs that led up to the next level of the graveyard.

As I ascended, I saw someone's retreating back ahead. He walked with the casual confidence of an armed man, a semiautomatic held in both hands. *Semiautomatic?* Some sort of rapid-fire teppo, apparently. How horrifying.

I continued forward in a half crouch, darting off to one side and hugging the tree line. The distance between us narrowed.

Ahead, I saw two mercs holding a young man between them. He was unnaturally still, one of those iron cannons—*a rifle*—pressed against his temple. His eyes were wide in his dark features, and even in the chilly air I could see sweat dripping down his dark face. The youth was terrified.

And I knew him.

Matlas.

"Boss says she doesn't need to talk with him," the man I was following said to the others. "So I'll handle it."

I knew what that meant. Matlas wasn't interesting enough to keep around.

I cataloged my weapons. From my coat I withdrew a device—a *Taser*, evidently—but I had no idea how to employ it. A futuristic weapon, and of no use to me. I replaced it and searched my other pocket, finding two large poisoned darts. A third was in a pouch sewn into my leggings, but where was my fukiya, my blowpipe? Well, at least I could still use them like shuriken.

I did so.

With three quick flicks of my wrist, three silent darts sailed through the air. The two guards holding Matlas dropped like they'd been struck by magic. The last dart sank into the third man's thigh, but it didn't drop him. Strange.

The remaining guard spun and swung his firearm as he tried to locate the threat. I closed the distance between us. He saw me, but too late. As he raised his iron cannon and aimed it in my direction, I slid into a low sweep and knocked him off his feet.

He was a wiry man, more scrappy than muscled, and in seconds I'd grappled him to the ground, my dominant arm pulled tight across his neck. I began to increase the pressure on his throat, but he managed to hammer the butt of his iron cannon into my side. Pain erupted, and I flinched despite my best efforts not to, providing him the leverage he needed to escape my headlock. Thrown off-balance, I rolled away from him and came up in a crouch.

He mirrored my actions, putting even more distance between us, and I realized he was doing so to bring his firearm into play.

Oh, hell no.

A different mind seized control, shoving shinobi-Emery somewhere into the back. It tore the Taser from my pocket, flicked the safety, and fired—all in the same motion. The prongs hissed forward and bit into flesh, sending 50,000 volts coursing into the merc. Electricity crackled in the air between us.

Impressively, the man fought through the pain and muscle spasms, trying to aim the wavering tip of his firearm at me. I didn't know what kind of money Morrigan paid this man, but he deserved a raise.

I exploded forward and barreled into him, tackling him to the ground again. I was careful to avoid the space between the two prongs so the current wouldn't give me more than a mild shock. Then I slapped the gun from his weakened grip. As he struggled to rise, I jammed the Taser into the base of his skull. A jolt surged through him, and his eyes rolled up and he finally collapsed, unconscious.

I turned to regard my companion. He didn't appear to be wounded, just stunned. "Are you all right?" I asked.

"Emery! What the hell's going on here, man?"

Right. I knew him. He was Matlas. Rachelle's boyfriend. My mind felt like it was made of glass and someone had dropped it from a second-story balcony. Each shard had its own history, its own personality.

Its own skills.

I'd taken down three armed, vigilant mercenaries. Four, if you counted Alicia. I'd done so by combining the skills of a fourteenth-century shinobi with those of a war veteran, all in a teenager's body.

I looked at Matlas with eyes that recognized him and with eyes that did not. Eyes that assessed him. So many eyes. Some discarded him. Some sympathized with him or weighed him, judged him, considered, regarded, examined-inspected-scrutinized.

He was Matlas. And someone I didn't know. A kid. A young Black man. A friend. A stranger. Only a mortal. A person I'd come to save. Terrified, the poor soul. Rachelle's boyfriend. A client. Some guy in a graveyard.

So many overlapping minds saw him that he became nothing more than a kaleidoscopic object at the center of my vision.

"Emery?" Something about my look must've alarmed him, because he shrank away from me.

Stop it.

You know him.

Mathew Atlas.

Eww, it's Matlas. *I would know. We're basically best friends.*

I gasped a deep, shuddering breath as waves of personalities were flushed out of my brain and drained away into cracks in my psyche, leaving only a sapped, tired Emery in a head that suddenly seemed too large for one personality to fill. Good thing I had a big one.

"Hey, Matlas," I said feebly.

He grinned, but there was an uncertain edge to it. "Hey, man. What's going on?"

I wearily returned his smile. "Thought you didn't want to know." He opened his mouth—to protest, I think—but I shook my head and started jogging toward the exit. "Come on. First things first, we're getting out of here."

I drove, which might not have been the smartest decision given how unsteady I'd been on my feet, but the activity allowed me to refocus, to ground myself. Matlas didn't question me, sliding into the passenger seat and waiting for me to break the silence.

Channeling. That's what the not-me-but-totally-badass-ninja-Emery had called it. Somehow I could bring my former personalities to the forefront of my brain and borrow their talents and knowledge. When it happened, though, everything became a jumbled, confusing mess as past and present collided. I seemed to be able to open myself to varying degrees, too: in Rikers, and then later on Vox Populi's yacht, I'd somehow channeled only the reflexes needed to fight, while in Redmond Town Center I'd wholly adopted another's mind and instincts.

It had been worse today, though. I'd almost lost all traces of myself, swallowed by the overpowering personalities of my past.

Could Morrigan channel, too? I was reasonably certain not every incarnate had access to the ability; I'd never heard of anyone talk about it before. Was it a special Protagonist/Antagonist thing? Or perhaps it was unique to archetype incarnates—those of us whose myths encompassed many tales—as a way to bring our lives together into a collective whole rather than a reflection of only the most recent manifestation.

Regardless, to turn it into an asset, I needed to learn how to summon the exact Emery required in a certain situation. It had something to do with meeting specific conditions, I thought. Like how certain words or actions triggered the spontaneous return of memories. Only this was stronger, more instinctive.

Visceral.

Was it the sensation of falling that triggered it? The feeling of despair? Or did it have more to do with the setting: the forest and the stealth needed?

I wasn't certain. It could've been the perfect cocktail of all those ingredients and more. I hated being unsure. But I hated unintentionally losing myself even more.

At least being here—in my Rogue, with Matlas at my side—made me feel more like myself. Well, *this* self.

It wasn't that I disliked the idea of channeling. It was remarkably cool, slipping through the woods like a shadow, whipping tranquilizer darts like they were ninja stars, and fighting with instincts ingrained in my muscles if not my brain. But losing myself in the conflux of emotions was terrifying. Perceiving the things around me, not simply through a different lens, but through many lenses at once, had felt like my sanity was slipping.

There was something intimately wrong about not being able to trust your own thoughts, about surrendering your body and mind and hoping you'd be able to reclaim control—it was gibbering-in-the-dark levels of terrifying.

So I did what I do best: I locked it away and resolved to deal with it never.

"You going to tell me what happened back there, or am I going to have to catch it on your next vlog?"

He was giving me an out, but he was genuinely curious. More than that, I realized as I eyed him in my peripheral vision; he was frazzled. Frightened. He'd just been held at gunpoint.

Mortals tended to get upset by that. "You actually want to know?"

Matlas shrugged, trying for lighthearted but landing somewhere nearer uncomfortable. "Didn't think I needed to. Hell, with the events in the cemetery last week and all the police attention, I thought it made more sense *not* to know. Plausible deniability and all that. Plus, I thought I could make a game out of it with Rachelle."

"You still can. I won't tell her you cheated."

He scowled. "It's more than that. As long as I don't know anything about the stuff you're mixed up in, the easier it is for me to convince myself everything's the way it's always been. That the paranormal stuff is just bad sci-fi special effects."

I kept my eyes on the road. "And that's comforting?"

"It *was*."

"All riiight," I said, drawing out the word, "where does that leave us?"

"Well, I don't know about you, but it left me in my own backyard being manhandled by three dudes with guns, only to be rescued by my girlfriend's best friend, who showed up and took them out like he was freaking Batman."

Oh, he was beyond frightened. I could see it now: he felt helpless, and that terrified him. The fact that he was outwardly so calm was impressive. I could see why Rachelle's inner warrior was attracted to him.

"Batman's not real," I told him.

He stared at me. "The fact that you feel the need to clarify that worries me, man."

We were silent for a few minutes. I pulled into a Starbucks drive-through. I was feeling drained from channeling. I needed a pick-me-up. "What do you want to drink?" I asked him.

"I'm good."

I gave him an amused glance. "I understand that you, ah, might be up late."

His eyebrows knit together, and then his mouth fell open as my meaning sank in. "Does she tell you *everything*?"

"You should be happy," I said, knuckling his arm. "She only tells me the important stuff." I pulled forward, approaching the speaker.

"Better tell me what you want, or I'm ordering you a venti sixteen-pump vanilla soy chai latte with extra foam, heated to exactly 160 degrees. And I'm going to tell the barista it was your order."

"*That's* your worst threat?"

"Fine. I'll also use my voodoo powers to make you drink it."

He shook his head. "I hate that I don't know for certain whether or not you can do that." When I continued to stare at him, he relented. "I'll take a mocha."

Five minutes later we were cruising down the highway, the smell of coffee filling my car.

"Are you kidnapping me?" he asked, breaking the silence.

"Was it the free coffee that gave it away?"

He sipped from his paper cup and kept quiet.

After a few miles of awkward silence, I made up my mind. "Okay, here's how we're going to play this. We *are* going to have this conversation, but we're going to have it backward."

He sat up straighter. "Okay, I'm listening."

"No, you're talking. *I'm* listening. Hence, backward."

He hesitated, then said, "I'm sorry. I'm not following."

"Look, you really don't want to know all the details of what's going on here, but I want you to know enough that Morrigan doesn't show up at your front door and kill you." He blinked at that, but I kept going. "So you're going to ask me questions, and I'm going to answer them. But you'll lead the conversation, and I'll keep my answers contained strictly to what you asked. Sound fair?"

Matlas grinned. "This is so much better than the comments section of your show. So it's like a game of Twenty Questions?"

"Sure." I paused. "You really get into games, don't you?"

He held up a finger. "Nuh-uh. It's my turn to ask the questions. You can get to know me better on your turn."

I chuckled. "Touché."

"Rachelle's really not involved in all this?" he asked a little too quickly.

"She's a totally normal human girl, if that's what you mean," I answered carefully.

"That's kind of a leading answer, man." He hesitated, then nodded. "Okay, but is she safe?"

"No one's safe while Morrigan's around." His face fell, so I added, "That said, Rachelle can take care of herself. I don't know if you've caught on yet, but she's pretty kick-ass."

"Yeah." He smiled. "No offense, but this game is a lot more fun with her."

"None taken," I assured him.

"I *knew* it!" an incensed voice rang out over the speakers. I winced; they'd been muted. "Emery Luple, I *told* you that the human expression 'No offense, but' effectively removes the negative impact inherent in the subsequent statement while leaving said statement otherwise unaltered. You have just demonstrated its value."

Matlas had frozen, eyes wide. "Is—is that *Unum*?"

"Very astute, Mathew Atlas. Although I prefer the name Artie. It is ever so good to make your acquaintance. I was most pleased to learn you did not meet your sudden and permanent demise."

"Um, thanks?"

"Artie," I said with exaggerated patience, "we've talked about this. You're supposed to maintain your disguise as Unum unless expressly informed otherwise."

"Of course. My apologies. I inferred from your conversation that you were inducting Mathew Atlas into our circle of inner confidants. I will not jump to this conclusion again."

I sighed, weighing whether to say something to remove the sting from my reprimand, but decided against it. He needed to learn when it was appropriate to interject. "Thank you," I said instead.

After a moment, music started to play. I jammed the power button, turning the sound system off completely.

"So Unum—uh, *Artie*—is alive?" Matlas asked, sounding dazed.

"In a manner of speaking. He's a bit more advanced than most people think."

"No kidding."

"So, you were saying this game is more fun with Rachelle?"

He looked away, smiling slightly, then said, "Still not your turn."

He thought for a moment, and I could almost see him replaying our conversation to get back to where we left off. "You mentioned someone named Morrigan. Who is Morrigan?"

I changed lanes to pass a slower driver, using the maneuver to buy time and think through my answer. "Morrigan's my enemy," I said at last. "We go a long way back. She has no regard for human life and will kill indiscriminately merely to inconvenience me. The mercs in the graveyard report to her. And she was the one behind the Ahedrian murders in New York."

"But I thought the murderer was caught and being held at Rikers."

"The actual murderer was dealt with," I evaded, "but Morrigan was the one who set her loose on New York."

He chewed on that a few minutes, then ventured, "Can you handle her?"

"Morrigan?" I opened my mouth, hesitated, then blew out my cheeks. "I don't know," I answered honestly, suddenly feeling weary. "Sometimes. Less often than I'd like."

Matlas nodded, thinking. Finally, he said, "How old are you?"

"Nineteen."

"For real?"

I sipped my coffee, then put it back into the cup holder. "What's age but a number?"

He watched me suspiciously, then said, "I haven't figured you out yet. But Caden's an angel, isn't he?"

"The Guardian Angel, technically. The one and only."

Matlas licked his lips and looked out the passenger side window. He contemplated that for a while, and I let him. My thoughts tried to turn inward, too, but I forced my full attention to the road.

"What happened to the other angels?" Matlas finally asked in a voice barely more than a whisper. "Why is Caden the last?"

"He isn't the *last*. He's just the only Guardian Angel."

He absorbed that for a moment. "Why's he here?"

"What do you mean?" I asked, confused. "Where else would he be?"

"I don't know. Heaven?"

Ah. The age-old question. "I don't know any more or less about heaven than anyone else," I told him. "What I *do* know is that Caden is from Earth."

To his credit, he didn't look disappointed. In some ways, I think I was beginning to understand him. He liked that there were some things out there that couldn't be explained. It made him feel comfortable to have faith, sometimes, rather than answers. "Do ghosts exist?"

"One does."

He nodded, and I could see the wheels of his mind in motion. "Just one vampire, too?"

"Quick learner."

He drained the last of his drink and set the cup between his knees. "All right. I think I got it figured out."

I snorted. "I doubt that." Incarnate stuff was complicated, as ancient as stories themselves. It required years to learn all the nuances—

"Supernatural beings exist," he said slowly, "but there's one and only one for every story out there."

"Lucky guess, but—"

"I'm thinking you're functionally immortal," he continued, growing more confident as he felt it out, "because you've referred to Rachelle and me as mortals. So each time you die, you must not *really* die, but instead you pass along your title to someone else."

"Not—"

"No, wait, that's not right. You said you and Morrigan go way back, so the memories associated with your title obviously transfer with you, so maybe it's not so much of a soul transfer as it is... oh. Probably some sort of reincarnation, right? That would explain how you're nineteen years old—this time around. But you've been nineteen countless times before, and the same goes for Caden."

"Uh..."

"You obviously have powers associated with your title, like Caden's healing, since he's a guardian angel. *The* Guardian Angel, I mean."

My words stuck in my throat.

"And you probably have an entire society built around secrecy, so humans don't find out about you and turn you into military weapons or science experiments or something like that."

"*Holy excrement*," Artie said over the speakers.

Matlas ignored him. "So all the stories and myths are based on you guys, right?" He sounded excited. "I bet you have some fancy name. Eternals? Immortals? Um... infinities?"

I glared at the road. "Incarnates," I said, feeling irrationally irritable. "And, for the record, it's entirely possible—even likely—that it's the other way around: incarnates are created from their myths."

"Has it ever been tested?"

"Yes. Recently, in fact."

His eyes lit up. "*That's* what the Ahedrian murders were about?"

My hands tightened on the steering wheel. "Oh, come on. Are you kidding me?" I snapped, exasperated. "Did Rachelle put you up to this?"

He looked startled, and I caught the barest flicker of fear in his eyes before he glanced away. It was like a slap to my face. Whatever he'd seen in me at the graveyard had scared him.

"Sorry," he said quietly. "No, I've just been collecting information for a while now. Like I said, I'm an avid Debunker." He shrugged. "Something about the Ahedrian murders always seemed off, I guess."

"Well, the jig is up," I said, trying to keep my tone light. "Now the million-dollar question: Caden's the Guardian Angel. Which incarnate am I?" At least there was no chance he'd guess *that* correctly.

Matlas hesitated, then swallowed. "Um, I don't know for sure, but maybe... the Demon?"

I winced. "*What*? Why would you think *that*?"

He squirmed uncomfortably. "I don't know, man. I thought it was thematic, you know? The Demon and the Guardian Angel. Forbidden love, and the only place you can find peace is on Earth— the place between heaven and hell."

"You have a real attachment to this heaven versus hell theory." I pinched the bridge of my nose. "I can't believe you thought I was the Demon."

"I mean, I thought you were *reformed*. I know you're one of the good guys."

Gee, thanks. "Well, I'm not a reformed evil anything. I'm legit good."

He gave me a look that I opted not to interpret as skeptical. "Sure thing. So, which one are you?"

"Nah, moment's over." I grinned. "Plus, it'll give you something to puzzle out with Rachelle." I smoothly signaled and pulled onto an off-ramp. "Speaking of which, we're almost to the mall. If you thought today's been trying so far, it's about to get worse: whether you're ready or not, you're about to meet her mom for the first time."

He accepted that with a grin, and again his unflappable attitude impressed me. "I'm not sure you thought this through. If things go poorly, Rachelle's more likely to be angry with you than with me."

"Good thing I have faith in you, then," I said.

Matlas looked at me in surprise, then glowed at the compliment, turning away in embarrassment. "Thanks." After a moment, though, he looked back at me. "So, if you don't mind me asking, how old are you, really?"

I thought about making a joke, but instead the truth slipped out. "I don't know."

We didn't speak for a while after that, but at least the silence wasn't uncomfortable anymore.

*A*RTIE SAYS TROUBLE FOUND YOU, Caden's text read.

"Tattletale," I accused my phone, before texting back, IT'S OK, I GOT OUT.

Matlas and I ducked into the nearest mall entrance, and I texted Rachelle to figure out where she was.

WHY? Rachelle's response was almost instant.

I HAVE A GIFT FOR YOU. ONE UNINJURED BOYFRIEND, TOPPED OFF WITH COFFEE AND READY TO MAKE A GOOD IMPRESSION ON MOM, I sent.

UNINJURED? WHAT DID YOU DO? FOOD COURT. NOW.

We navigated the crowds—the mall became the premier hangout spot on Friday afternoons, especially as the day crept toward evening—and chose a spot in the food court where we could keep a lookout for Rachelle and her mother.

"Who else knows?" Matlas asked out of the blue.

"Just you and Rachelle. And all of *us,* of course." I didn't want to say the word "incarnate" in such a public setting.

"Telling secrets again, are we, Emery?" a voice said from behind me.

I felt my shoulders tense, but I refused to give him the satisfaction of turning around. "What are you doing here, Nyx?"

I heard the sound of a chair scraping across linoleum. Then Nyx settled into a spot at our table, right between Matlas and me. "A serendipitous encounter, believe it or not."

I opened my mouth to tell him I didn't, when his spiced scent hit me. My heart began to beat a little faster. Bastard.

He tilted his head to regard Matlas, his dark, shaggy hair falling forward. "I haven't had the pleasure," he purred, "of officially meeting you. My name is Nyx."

Matlas licked his lips and dragged his eyes from Nyx's gaze to mine. "Um, Emery? I take it back. I think *this* guy is the Demon."

Nyx's smile revealed small, perfect teeth. "Oh, I *like* you." He leaned back, and I couldn't help but admire the way the position displayed his lean abs beneath his tight black shirt. The sleeves and collar were distressed and shredded, which drew attention to the smooth flesh of his collarbone and his corded biceps. I swallowed.

"What do you want?" I growled. His mere presence pissed me off. Maybe it was the way his glamour was already raising goose bumps across my arms.

He met my eyes, and a hungry expression flickered deep in them. "You have no idea how happy I am to hear you asking after my desires, Emery."

"A poor choice of words, then." I inhaled his scent and felt it warm its way down to my belly. "If you want to have a conversation, dim your glamour. I'm not doing this without a clear head."

"Glamour?" Matlas repeated.

Nyx turned his full attention on Matlas.

Have you ever heard of the smolder? That seductive, simmering, heavy-lidded look that just oozes sex appeal? The Incubus put it to shame. We're talking the difference between a smolder and a white-hot flame. Nyx raked his eyes up and down Matlas's body, the faint slant to his head further revealing the patch of smooth skin at his neck, his lips parting ever so slightly.

The air between them seemed to crackle with charged energy, reminding me of the electricity released from my Taser a few hours ago. I heard as much as saw Matlas's sharp intake of breath, the bob of his Adam's apple, the flare of his dilating pupils.

I gripped Nyx firmly by the upper arm. "Enough."

In a blink, Nyx's predatory expression evaporated and he eased back into a lounging posture, relaxed once more. "*That* is glamour," he said in a throaty, satisfied tone. Then his attention shifted to me. "You cut that remarkably short." He smirked. "Jealousy's a good color on you."

I refused to rise to the bait, even as a sliver of envy needled me at the attention Nyx had directed so intently toward Matlas. That was all a part of it, though: his glamour, the feelings it aroused, felt *exquisite*. There was no shame in admitting the sensation, as long as I rejected the offer that came with it.

Matlas, finally recovering, scrambled backward in his chair, colliding with a person walking behind him. He was flushed, which was apparent in spite of his dark skin, and clearly nonplussed. "*The shit?*" he exclaimed, the curse too loud in the crowded food court. Which only caused him to color further.

The person he'd collided with was, unfortunately, Rachelle's mom.

"Hi, Mrs. Grey," I said, jumping to my feet and reaching out to steady her. "Hey, Rachelle."

This was one of those odd moments where I was meeting someone for the first time, yet my backstory informed me that I'd known Rachelle's mom for years—since our first year in high school, when we'd been teamed up on a school project. My memories corroborated our relationship, meaning that as I stood there in the food court, I felt like I was seeing someone I already knew. But a small part of my brain couldn't quite turn off the reminder that she was, in truth, a stranger.

Other than her height, Mrs. Grey was everything her daughter was not: mousy, unobtrusive, and forgettable. I don't mean that in a mean-spirited way, but if Rachelle were a warrior in a TV show, her mom would be cast as the soft-spoken townsperson who probably wouldn't get any lines. That said, there was something comfortable about her, a woman who accepted her lot in life and had no expectations of what yours should be.

Which is why her relationship with her daughter was so odd to me. From my perspective, Mrs. Grey wouldn't judge a criminal if she were on the jury. But to Rachelle, her mom was a figurehead of silent disapproval, and she always felt like she'd failed to measure up.

I'd never seen that in Mrs. Grey—until now. She eyed Matlas with raised eyebrows, her mouth downturned at the cuss word that was still ringing in the air.

Nyx remained in place, watching the exchange with amusement.

Mrs. Grey nodded to me and said, "Hello, Emery. If I'd known you were coming to the mall today, I'd have invited you to join us. How's your mother?"

"She's great. Sorry to burst in on your mother-daughter bonding time."

Mrs. Grey laid a hand on Rachelle's arm. "Oh, we've had a wonderful afternoon. The only thing that would've made it better is if you'd joined us." See? Lovely woman.

"Mrs. Grey, I'd like to introduce you to Mat—"

"Matt!" Rachelle cut in. "Just Matt. Mom, this is the guy I was telling you about."

Matlas, still hanging his head out of embarrassment, put on a nervous smile. He was sweating—probably as much from his moment with Nyx as from meeting Rachelle's mother. "Hi, uh, Mrs. Grey." He stuck his hand out shyly.

I knew she wasn't a huge fan of physical contact—*definitely* not a hugger—but she shook his hand and smiled. It was kind of a thin smile, but I'd say it was a win.

Then Nyx unfurled from his chair and rose, taking Mrs. Grey's hand in his own before she'd fully retracted it. He grazed the back of it with his lips. She looked startled and had started to pull back when she became ensnared in his gaze. "I'm Nyx," he said in a low voice that hooked the bottom of my stomach and crooked it downward. "And there's no way you're Rachelle's mother. Her sister, perhaps."

"Oh!" Mrs. Grey tittered, twin spots of color appearing high on her cheeks. In a thousand years, I would never have expected that sound to emerge from that woman.

Rachelle gave him a flat look. "Charming. What a line." In response, he turned his bewitching smile on her, reaching out. To my surprise, Rachelle slapped his hand away. "I don't think so. I know your game."

He actually looked taken aback. Mrs. Grey, a dreamy look in her eyes, didn't comment on her daughter's harsh behavior. Oi, glamour. "Ooh," Nyx said with a wicked grin, "I like your fire. I do hope you take those claws with you..." His smile sharpened. "*Everywhere.*"

Rachelle rolled her eyes. "*So* not interested." She turned her glare on me. "Why's he here?"

I pulled her off to the side, leaving Matlas, Nyx, and a spellbound Mrs. Grey at the table. With even a short distance between us, the power of his glamour began to recede. It withdrew like oil slicking off flesh, making me shiver. "It's a long story," I told her, taking in a ragged breath.

She folded her arms impatiently. "Then shorten it."

I felt a spike of annoyance, though I was quite sure it was misdirected. "Morrigan nearly killed your boyfriend. I saved him and hand-delivered him to you in one piece. You're welcome."

Her expression softened. "Sorry. This just isn't going the way I thought it would. Well, what's done is done." She narrowed her eyes. "Why are you with Nyx?"

"I'm not. He just showed up here."

"So he's following you. Great. Does Caden know?"

I shook my head. "Not yet." At her reproving glare, I put up my hands. "Nyx *just* sat down with us." I looked down at the ground. "I, um, did something you're not going to like."

She stared at me. "*More?*"

I nodded, looking around to make sure no one was near enough to overhear, then I lowered my voice. "I told Matlas about incarnates."

To my surprise, she barked a laugh. "Thank god," she said. "I mean, the game was fun, but things were starting to heat up with

Morrigan and Hope around." She looked over at the table. "And he's still here, right? So he must've taken it well."

I decided not to point out that I'd basically kidnapped him. "Overall, yeah. Especially after being held at gunpoint in the cemetery."

Her mouth compressed into a flat line. "We'll talk about that later. Thanks for getting him out, though. Now that he knows everything, he can take precautions."

"Like staying near you," I finished. "My thoughts exactly. So are you good if I leave him with you and your mom?"

"Sure," she said slowly. "But what about Nyx?"

I looked at him grimly. I hated that a small part of me thrilled at the idea of spending some alone time with him. I knew I should really wait for Caden—or at least *tell* him about Nyx—but he wouldn't be home for hours. "I'll handle him."

Rachelle hesitated, clearly reluctant. "I don't know if that's such a good idea," she said.

"It's fine," I assured her. "He's dangerous, true, but not like Morrigan. And with our past, I know he doesn't want to hurt me."

"It's your past that I'm afraid of," she said. "I don't think it's a good idea for you to be alone with him."

"You're making a big deal out of nothing," I said, though I actually sort of agreed with her. Which only stoked my irritation. "What's the issue here?"

"Emery, I adore you. But I don't know that I trust you around hi—his glamour." *Around him*, she'd almost said.

"I *said* I can handle it," I bit out.

She refused to look away, but after a moment, she nodded. "All right. I trust you. Just be careful, okay?"

"I'm always careful," I said. Then I narrowed my eyes. "How are *you* so resilient to his charms, anyway?"

"I'm not resilient," she said airily. "I'm just more disciplined. Apparently." She looked back at the table and winced. "Which is my cue to rescue my mother." She sighed. "All right, I'll leave Nyx to you." She leaned in close. "If you hurt Caden, I'll hurt *you*. Got it?"

I shrugged off my annoyance at her lack of faith and grinned instead. "We're so lucky to have you."

"Damn right."

"*A*hh. Alone at last."

Which wasn't true, but I knew what he meant. Knowing he was expecting a glare, I instead leveled a tired look at him. "You said you wanted my help. Why?"

Nyx looked around at the people crowding the open hallway of the mall. "What do you say we take this conversation somewhere a little more private?"

I ignored the subtext and said, "Fine."

Walking quickly, I led us toward the parking lot. The brisk pace I set, as I intended, made casual conversation challenging. From the smug look on his face, Nyx knew my reasoning.

"My Mustang is—"

"I'll be driving," I said, cutting him off.

"Yes, sir," Nyx said after a moment, and I could hear the amusement in his voice. "I forgot how hot it is when you take control."

I spun around, forcing him to come to an abrupt stop. "Let me be clear: I'm happy with Caden. I love him. You will not do anything —*anything*, Nyx—to jeopardize that. So lay off the innuendos, the glitz, the charisma, all of it. You and I have no future in this lifetime."

"So there's hope in the next, then." That did get him a glare, and he put his hands up in surrender. "I truly desire your help, Em. For now, that's all I'm here for."

I nodded. "Good. And don't call me that."

He flinched, and I glimpsed something approximating hurt before he masked it with a smug smile. It must've been an act, an attempt to garner sympathy from me. It wouldn't work.

"As you wish." I could almost hear him grind down whatever implication he wanted to make. Good, that was progress.

We slid into my car, and I drove us to a nearby park. The day was still overcast, the light fading from the sky as the sun slunk toward the horizon. As evening sped toward us, the clouds became heavier and darker with the promise of rain. Summer had lingered longer than usual, but autumn was finally winning their game of tug-of-war, and the forecast showed a week of rain and gloom ahead. Fitting that the weather should turn foul with Morrigan's arrival.

In the confines of my car, I could smell Nyx's scent with every breath I took: an intoxicating mix of sweat, spice, and brimstone—the fiery way the air smells after a lightning strike. From anyone else, I would've attributed it to cologne, but I knew it was his natural musk. Supernatural, I mean. The heady fragrance made my head swim, and I considered telling him where to stuff his glamour, but I knew he'd just turn my words into a suggestion I wouldn't like. I resolved to breathe through my mouth, but that somehow felt even more profane: like I was tasting him.

What was wrong with me? I missed Caden's clean, minty freshness.

"You're quieter than usual," Nyx noted.

I wanted to ask him about the murder that morning, but I held off so I could watch his reaction more closely when I brought it up, something I couldn't manage while driving. Instead, I asked, "Did you know Morrigan's in town?"

He didn't answer right away. "Yes," he said at last.

"And?" I prompted.

"She came to me with a proposition. I turned her down."

"What did she want?"

Nyx pouted. "I'd forgotten how taxing your fixation with Morrigan can be."

"Quit avoiding the question."

Looking at the ceiling of the vehicle, he let loose a throaty chuckle. "I've missed this."

I glanced over. With him sitting in Caden's usual spot, I couldn't help but compare the two of them, even as I realized it might be dangerous to tread that path. In so many ways, they were opposites. Caden would sit unobtrusively, radiating earnest love and reassurance. Nyx filled the seat—hell, he filled the whole damn vehicle. With his rippling muscles and his every movement oozing sensuality, he demanded attention. No, it was more than that; he demanded *adulation* bordering on worship.

Nyx was all dark promise, where Caden was bright hope. Caden had won me over with his boyish charm and enduring support. His aura soothed, made me feel peaceful and safe.

No one would describe Nyx's charm as "boyish." It was too mature, too salacious. He had an aura, too, but it nipped and teased, breathtakingly dangerous, exciting. Electrifying.

I hated how compelling I found it. It was a betrayal from deep within. My heart belonged to Caden entirely; of that, there wasn't a doubt in my mind. But my body... it was trying really hard to convince me that a little doubt was a good thing.

I took a deep breath to expel those thoughts, but Nyx's scent was cloying. Would Caden notice it the next time he rode in my car? Maybe that would force me to stop putting off telling him about Nyx.

"You know what *I* miss?" I asked him in a soft voice.

Sensing weakness, Nyx perked up. "What's that?" he asked, narrowing the space between us with a simple shift that could have fooled anyone else into thinking it had been unintentional.

We were stopped at a light, so I turned to regard him. His eyes drank me in. His head drifted even closer. His lips were quirked just enough to draw attention to them.

I opened my mouth, then said, "Getting a straight answer out of you. *What did Morrigan want?*" I bit off each word.

He jerked back, though he recovered by turning it into a stretch. Smooth. "Something about joining an incarnate support group or some such nonsense," he said in a bored tone. "Said she needed my vote, and I told her to go to hell." He shrugged. "She said she'd trade your address for my cooperation."

That meant she *did* know where I lived. I'd suspected as much, but it still made me squirm. I drew some comfort from the fact that the home I shared with Caden was my Sanctum, the place where her powers would be their weakest.

Which, I realized, was why she'd sent Nyx instead. "Wait. Didn't you say you turned her down? How'd you get my address, then?"

"Oh, please," he said scornfully. "A few minutes in my company and she yielded the information without leveraging it as a bargaining chip."

He may have thought he'd won her over, but I knew her better than that. The only reason she'd given him what he wanted was because it was a win-win for her: even if he didn't join her in sabotaging the Incarnate Watch, she'd known seeing him would throw me off my game. Morrigan never gave anything away for free. But then again, Nyx always had underestimated her.

"And that was it?" I asked as I pulled into a parking spot.

He looked around at the public park in dismay. "This is your idea of private?"

"What did you expect? I'm not going to take you to my place."

He smirked. "Afraid Caden might like me better?"

I responded by leaving the car. I headed to a wooden picnic table that sat a little distance from the paved walking trail. After a moment, Nyx sauntered over and joined me. A couple strolling along the path followed his movement, even sneaking looks over their shoulders after they'd passed.

I understood why, even as I rolled my eyes in disgust.

He straddled the bench—suggestively, of course—to my left instead of taking the one across the table. I sighed and stood, resettling to sit across from him. Since I was using people as a buffer to his advances, I was disappointed there weren't more of them around.

Must be those dark storm clouds. At least the open air and gusts of wind helped to clear my head. "All right, out with it. Why do you need my help?"

"Because I'm being framed."

"Framed," I repeated flatly. "For the murder in Anacortes, I'm assuming?"

He grimaced. "So you heard about that."

"Did more than *hear* about it; I was there this morning. Investigating, talking to the widow." He'd stilled, I noticed. An admission of guilt? "You know what I found out?"

"It wasn't me, Em—ery."

"I listened to you report the crime. I have a recording on my phone. Should I play it for you?"

"No good deed," he muttered. "Doesn't that mean I'm *less* likely to be a suspect? Why would I report the crime if I committed it?"

"That isn't as uncommon as you think it is," I said. "And maybe you thought it would get you into my good graces when I found out."

He scowled, and a part of me observed how the anger made his skin flush in a way I remembered too well... "If I wanted to ensure your cooperation," he grumbled, "we both know who I would've used."

I forced my mind to go blank. I would *not* think about her.

"Don't," I said. Then, more softly, "Please."

Something approaching compassion shone in his dark eyes. "Does Caden know?"

I didn't think so. He'd certainly known, at one time, but his past-life memories were so spotty. "You were telling me how you innocently came across the scene of a homicide," I reminded him.

"Now who's avoiding questions?" He leaned back, settling more comfortably on the bench. "Very well. Yes, I was at the crime scene, and I didn't commit the murder. Though I wouldn't say my presence was 'innocent,' per se."

I knew where this was going. "Susan mentioned she was asleep and didn't wake up while her husband was stabbed over and over again in the same bed," I said. "I take it there was a reason she didn't wake up?"

Nyx's coy smile confirmed what I'd suspected: he'd been *visiting*. The Incubus's signature was to invade a person's dreams, seduce them, and then feed on the carnal energy between him and his victim. The eroticism nourished him the way food and drink sustain the rest of us.

This wouldn't be a big deal if it left the person better for their experience. Unfortunately, giving up your whole night to desire left you exhausted the next day. If the Incubus feasted on a person too intensely or for too long, it resulted in deteriorating health and—yup—death. That's why I had to classify him as Malevolent.

Now, let's talk about consent. Contrary to the more disturbing myths, the willingness of his meal—I mean, *partner*—was a crucial part of Nyx's diet. He fed off their ecstasy. He liked the chase, though, so he found seducing his prey far more rewarding if there was a little fight in them. It flirted with a dangerous line, I'll admit, but it was a distinction few Malevolents would bother with in the first place.

Did that make him redeemable? Hell, no. His glamour—whether fully under his control or not—chipped away at just about anyone's resolve, making a person more pliable, putty in his firm, strong hands. A putty that begged to be played with, pushed and prodded and pulled, kneaded in just the right way...

Gah. That glamour!

I felt an irrational spark of envy for Susan that Nyx had spent the night with her, but I tamped it down. I had been safe at home, sleeping next to Caden; there was nowhere on Earth or beyond I'd rather have been.

"All right," I said, just managing to pull my voice out of the subregister of a growl, "you were with Susan. Which explains why she didn't wake up even though someone was literally screaming bloody murder in her ear. But it doesn't explain her husband's death."

"Like I said, I've been set up. Someone knew I was there and attacked the woman's husband while we were... distracted."

"If it wasn't you," I said, "then it was Morrigan."

Annoyance flickered in his eyes before he glanced away. "Despite what you believe, not every single bad thing in this world can be laid at that woman's feet."

"I know," I shot back. "I don't blame her for *you*."

"Very well. I'll bite." He flashed his teeth. "What possible reason would she have to frame me?"

"You spurned her when you turned down her offer."

He considered. "So you believe I'm not guilty?"

"Let's say I'm withholding judgment. Why'd you choose a woman in Anacortes?"

He seemed puzzled. "Why? Are they out of season?"

"Very funny. Answer the question."

"I was tracking an incarnate that had been in the area."

At first, my egotistical brain thought he meant me. Caden and I had been in the area the day before, so the timeline made sense. Except Nyx had visited me at my apartment that night, after we'd already driven home.

There was one other incarnate that Nyx likely would be interested in, I realized. One he might view as competition, maybe even a threat.

"The Mare?" I guessed.

"Consider me impressed." I warmed at his compliment—he didn't give them lightly. "This is why I need your help, Em. Not to get inside your head, or"—he grinned—"anywhere else. No one can solve a crime like you can."

"If I'm to help, I need more information. Tell me what you know about the Mare."

His eyebrows shot up. "Well, then. So you don't know her identity, either."

"Either?" I frowned. "Did she reincarnate recently?" I would've expected Nyx to be at least passingly familiar with the other dream incarnates. They were the only ones who typically posed a threat to his Lair.

"No, it's not like that. The Mare is another incarnate entirely during the day, only transforming into the Mare at night. Hence the word nightmare."

"Ah. And we don't know who she is during the day."

He gave me a sultry smile. "Brains *and* brawn. Aren't you the full package?" I did my best to ignore the way his eyes traced over my body. "It gets worse. The Mare is a full-blown Dr. Jekyll, Mr. Hyde transformation: whichever incarnate she is, she almost certainly doesn't know she moonlights as the Mare."

"So if she attacks someone, she might not even be aware of it?"

"Not during the daytime."

"Why were you tracking her?"

He fidgeted, his fingers tracing patterns on the picnic table. "I don't wish to say," he admitted.

"Too bad."

He looked up at me through his thick lashes, dark eyes growing bigger in the waning light. "You're such a tease. You know I can't resist that commanding tone of yours."

I wasn't falling for it. He was either stalling or trying to deflect. My traitorous cheeks glowed at his words, though. His eyes seemed to pull me into them. Had I ever thought that any other color could compare to those melted-chocolate eyes?

A timely drop of rain hit me square on the forehead, making me blink and helping me shrug off the allure of his glamour. "Great. Then start talking."

Another couple of drops hit my head and face. "Anything for you. But surely we can get out of the rain first? Continue this conversation somewhere warm and dry?"

Not a chance. I welcomed the rain. It cooled the artificial fires he stoked in me, made me feel like I'd washed his scent—and his power—off me. "Why were you tracking the Mare?"

"It's cold out here." He put on a show of shivering, but I maintained my patient expression. "Fine. I was tracking the Mare because Morrigan told me she's gathering dream incarnates for some power play. Although I don't harbor the same hostility for her that you do, I'm not overly fond of the notion of her nosing about in *my* domain."

That explained Morrigan's new buddy, the Sandman. "Why wouldn't you want to tell me that? It could be relevant."

"Because it's my business, and I don't want you to become consumed with whatever she's planning and lose sight of helping me." He held up a finger. "Before you sulk, I think we both can admit there's merit to my concern."

I fought my glower. I didn't love that he knew me so well. "Did she happen to mention any details about this power play?"

The sprinkles were picking up, turning into steady rain. "No," he said. After a brief hesitation and an unhappy glance at the sky, he added, "She was quite determined. If it were anyone else, I might say desperate."

"How so?"

"She was willing to trade me something of remarkable value."

Without his glamour addling my senses, his half answers were even more grating than usual. "And what was that?"

He met my eyes. "You."

I gave a sharp laugh. "You honestly think she could deliver on that promise?"

His grin was sour. "No. If she could, we might not be having this conversation." He flicked his hand through his hair, reshaping it in defiance of the rain's attempt to plaster it to his head. "Though, in truth, you wouldn't be worth fighting for if it were that simple."

Something about the lack of glamour, his soaked-puppy expression, and his words caught at my heart. "Nyx," I said, mustering my sympathy, "I'm *not* worth fighting for. Not this time. If you put all this energy into somebody else, you could find someone to be happy with."

He was quiet for a moment, and the hissing of the rain was all I could hear. It was almost completely dark, now, but I wasn't sure if that was due to the storm or because true dusk had arrived.

"I found someone, once," he said, so quietly I almost missed it. I found myself leaning in, belatedly realizing that might've been his intention.

"A mortal?" I guessed. He shook his head, and I frowned. "Then what happened?"

His tone was surprisingly bitter. "You happened, Em. You reincarnated, and you sought me out. Claimed me." He refused to meet my eyes. "Maybe your heart is big enough for another, but mine is shallow and weak. It only has room for you."

I didn't know how to respond to that. After a moment, he shook himself. I saw the twist to his lips and knew he was going to say something to ruin the moment, so I did something foolish: I reached across the table and touched his hand. He froze at the contact.

"I believe you, Nyx. I'll help clear your name."

He looked up, relieved. Then his glamour slammed into me, electricity jolting up my arm from where we touched, sending a prickly wave of sensation and heat to flush over every inch of my flesh. My body responded of its own accord, a craving to enlarge the spot where our skin met, to deepen our contact.

I managed not to yelp, but I withdrew my hand like he'd scalded it. Not knowing how to handle the physical sensations—the flushed skin, the racing heart—my mind corralled all that energy and transformed it into something it understood: anger. In a second wave, hot fury lanced through me, giving me a new excuse for my heated skin and thumping heart.

Sensations and emotions warred within me. I could see the caution in Nyx's eyes as he regarded me, and beneath that, the sting of my rejection.

But he'd done that on purpose. He'd tried to seize on what he'd seen as an opportunity. It might've been my fault for initiating the contact, but he couldn't just be *freaking* decent about it, could he?

"Now why'd you have to go and do that?" I asked, fighting to keep my tone light. "Just when we were starting to bond."

"You'll still help me?" he asked, going for a meek tone.

The question—and its delivery—sparked another flare of outrage, but I focused on the rain, letting it cool my body and my temper. Still, a part of me really wanted to walk away. "I will. But it'll cost you."

I watched him fight a leer, but it eventually won out. "Oh my, you seem to have me at your *complete* mercy."

"Good. It'll be two thousand dollars."

His grin froze. "Excuse me?"

"You're right," I said, swiping rain off my forehead. "That's not enough. Let's make it three. We'll call it recompense for the hell you're putting me through."

Nyx laughed. "Very well." It worried me how quickly he accepted the bargain. "I presume I can give it to you in ones? Preferably in private?"

I shook my head and stood. "That concludes our business for tonight. I'll contact you in the morning."

I got a vicious spike of joy from his startled look. "But you drove. My car is at the mall." He jumped to his feet.

I was already walking away. I turned, walking backward as I spoke. "I'm sure a smart, competent incarnate like you can figure out how to get back there." His jaw dropped, and satisfaction felt almost as good as his glamour. "Goodnight, Nyx."

Don't worry, I made it back to my car with little trouble. It constantly amazes me how accommodating mortals are when you but ask a favor. People say times have changed, but while that's certainly true of technology, human behavior evolves far more slowly .

Take me, for instance. There's been a stigma around the Incubus since ancient Mesopotamia. The Guardian Angel, meanwhile, enjoys a reputation free of blemish. But beneath the canopy of night, in the privacy of their own dreams, mortals always seem to choose me. If only Emery could be more like the rest of humanity. Then again, I probably wouldn't feel the same way about him if he were as pliable as that lot.

I must admit, I yearn to share our next adventure, the Incubus and his Protagonist. Our exploits are legendary, sometimes retold so many times that new incarnates are created. I've lived for a very long time, but the span between one Emery and the next is often a blur existing simply to build anticipation for our next adventure together.

All that stands between us now is Caden. The cherished Guardian Angel. Make no mistake, his glamour is a weapon as surely as his light is a shield. You've likely already become enmired in his angelic aura, fallen in love with his cherubic personality. You'd think differently if Emery had found me first in this incarnation. You'd see Caden for the interloper he is.

I do not hold you—nor even Emery—accountable for the values you see in Caden. He's had eons to perfect his illusion, after all.

~

"She confessed?"

"She did," came Gregory's reply over my car's speakers. From the background hum, he was driving, too, and had me on speakerphone. "I'm not sure what they said to her, but she admitted that she woke up with the knife in her hand."

"That's not *quite* the same thing as a murder confession," I pointed out.

"I agree," he said, catching me off guard. "But try telling that to Grant."

"Let me guess: she rescinded her offer to give us time to look into this further?"

"Unfortunately. Given Susan's confession, I sympathize with her position."

"The murder still happened while she was sleeping, though?" I asked.

"It appears so. Why?"

"I might have a lead. Have you heard of the Mare incarnate?" I pulled into my neighborhood as I spoke.

"The Mare? I don't think so."

"Probably on account of its Nordic origins," Artie cut in smoothly. "It wasn't always called the Mare, you know."

"Yes, well. Thank you, Unumpedia," I said. "Does her Nordic name get us any closer to discovering her identity?"

"I'm afraid not."

"Then you can tell me about it later," I said. "Gregory, the Mare is another dream incarnate. Artie figured out that she was responsible for draining the life force out of that... mare." Huh. Now that I thought about it, maybe that *coincidence* had been my powers trying to nudge me in the right direction. That was the problem with my gifts, though: I never knew which details to focus on. And hell, maybe

I was wrong—maybe the universe was just having a laugh. "You know, the one I told you about this morning? Spray?"

"I remember. So you found your horse vampire."

"Well, that's the thing. The Mare is only known to feed on horses when humans aren't available. So why didn't she feed on Amara?"

"Something to do with the broken mirror or the twisted branches? You're sure it's the Mare?"

"Yeah. I had a nice chat with Nyx this afternoon, and he confirmed she's in the area. I don't think that's an accident."

There was quiet on the line for a moment, and I held my breath. I knew he wanted to say something about Nyx. Everyone disapproved of him. Hell, *I* disapproved of him, didn't I? But I still deserved people's trust, even if Nyx did not.

Gregory had either reached his destination or taken me off speaker, because the background noise had all but disappeared. "All right," he said at last, his voice neutral. Was it *too* neutral? "Does Nyx know where she is?"

"There's a complication on that front," I explained, speaking quickly. I was glad he hadn't reprimanded me. I pulled into the town-house's tiny garage and continued. "Apparently the Mare is a different incarnate during the day, only taking on the form of the Mare at night. And whatever her day job, she has no idea she's got a dual life after hours."

"That's troubling. Could she be someone we know?"

I winced. "I'd been trying to avoid thinking about that possibility," I admitted, "but as far as I know, yes."

"Did Morrigan learn a new trick, maybe?"

I hadn't considered that. "That's a horrifying thought."

"Okay, I'll keep my ear to the ground and let you know what I discover." There was the sound of a car door being shut, followed by a voice greeting him. That sounded suspiciously like... "I'll be in touch. And, Emery?"

"Yeah?" I said, expecting him to make a comment about Nyx.

"Your mother says hi."

"And to stay out of trouble!" I heard her say in the background before Gregory ended the call. Jerk. I suspected he'd done that on purpose. I shook my head, thinking I liked him better before he'd gained a sense of humor.

I went inside, and the moment I opened the door, I was greeted by three puppies who jumped excitedly at my legs, vying with one another for my attention. I tried to divide it equally among them, happy to have three little pets who trusted me completely. Their tails wagged as I rubbed and petted them. Then I realized they probably needed to go outside after such a long stint indoors—how long could puppies normally go without an accident, again?—so I walked quickly to the back door, a parade of puppies at my heels, their toenails clicking on the floor. I opened the sliding glass door, and they spilled out to do their business. The little plot of grass was not nearly large enough to be called a yard, but it was fenced in, at least.

Leaving the door open for them, I headed back to the garage to retrieve my dream catcher. I needed to hang it in the bedroom tonight. It would protect me from bad dream energy, but more importantly, it would keep the temptation of Nyx far from my bed.

If ever there was a time to be cautious, it was now. The idea of Nyx seducing me while I slept next to Caden felt somehow even more profane than his usual attempts. Which was exactly why it would appeal to Nyx. Best to remove the temptation altogether. The world of dreams—it was called the Lucid, some part of my brain remembered—was Nyx's Lair, where his talents of persuasion were their strongest. I'd been able to resist his glamour and charms thus far, but in his seat of power, I wasn't sure I'd be able to say the same. Hell, in that setting, I wasn't sure I'd want to.

For some reason, his glamour still seemed to be affecting me, even though I knew that wasn't how glamour worked. But I felt that same flush across my body, the same feelings of repulsed fascination at those thoughts.

I went to the kitchen to check on the trio's water and give them their dinner, as much to shake off the lingering effects of the glamour as anything else. That's when I saw the yellow pad with the grocery list on the counter.

My heart fell.

"Oh, shit," I groaned, rubbing my face. I'd completely forgotten about going to the grocery store... and the bakery.

Caden wouldn't hold this against me, I knew. In some ways, that made it worse. I'd offered to run the errand because I knew it would make him happy and ease his burden. But caught up in the excitement of the day—and the excitement of Nyx, something I did *not* want to acknowledge—it had slipped my mind. And now it was hours after dusk. The bakeries were all closed, and the grocery store bakery options were likely picked over.

It had been a trying day, certainly, but that was hardly a good excuse for putting Caden last. His next shift didn't start until early afternoon. I could still fix this. I'd need to make a special trip in the morning, but that was well worth doing to show him that I was a supportive, loving boyfriend.

The decision only partially lifted my mood, but I fed the dogs and heated up some leftovers for myself. Mittens, Beard, and Mask bolted inside, and I closed and locked the back door, then headed upstairs with the dream catcher. I could hear the scraping of bowls on the floor as the puppies wolfed down their food.

"Artie, will you set my alarm for eight in the morning?" I asked as I went.

"Confirmed."

That was... brief. I almost ignored it, but something told me not to. "Artie, is everything okay?"

"My input has not been welcomed on multiple occasions today," he said matter-of-factly. "I see no reason it would be welcomed now."

I blinked. He was upset?

This was the last thing I needed. I had enough going on with Nyx, Morrigan, Hope, and the Mare. Rachelle didn't trust me around Nyx, and maybe she was right, because I hadn't even told Caden about him yet. And to top it all off, I apparently couldn't keep my word to Caden: I'd been late to the Watch meeting despite knowing how important it was to him, and then I'd offered to lighten his load but forgotten about it while I spent the afternoon with my ex.

It wasn't my finest day.

And I had too much going on to worry about the feelings of a computer. "Artie, do you know what thick skin means?"

"As it relates to epidermal density, or the expression among humans—"

"The expression," I snapped. "Your input is invaluable, and we both know it. But you need to learn when it's appropriate to interject. Until then, get some thick skin—metaphorically—because with everything going on, I can barely manage my own emotions, let alone yours."

I tossed the phone on my bed, slightly harder than I intended.

"I understand," Artie said in a meek voice. "I am sorry to have burdened you."

Facing the wall, I closed my eyes as a wave of shame surged over me. Artie was only trying to help, and he was still learning how to handle his newest incarnation, with his vast resources and reach.

The shame turned into anger, though. My words to him had been honest. He didn't need to lay on the subservience, try to guilt me into feeling sad for him. *That's not what he's doing,* some part of me whispered. *He's not Nyx.*

That was the real problem, wasn't it? Nyx manipulated my emotions, wrapping them around his finger, yanking and pulling them like the strings of an instrument. Expecting me to play his tune. He could rile me to frustration and shame with a look and a word.

And I was sick of it. It wasn't Artie's fault I was so tired—it was Nyx's. Maybe I'd snapped at Artie because snapping at Nyx did nothing but encourage him.

I wanted to apologize. But I didn't want to explain. Couldn't. My headspace was a wreck.

I shoved it all away and hung the dream catcher. I had to remove a framed picture from the wall to free up a hook. The photo had been taken in New York shortly after the Ahedrian business. It was of Caden, Rachelle, and me. My arm was around Caden's shoulders, and Rachelle stood beside us, a cast on her leg. She'd refused to lean on us even though she'd only had one leg to stand on.

The image reminded me of a simpler time. It hadn't seemed so in the moment, since we'd spent days racing to uncover and stop a murderer. But I'd just learned I was the Protagonist, and Caden that he was the Guardian Angel. We were a new couple, and it had felt like the whole world was new and ours for the seizing.

Instead of storing the photo somewhere out of the way, I placed it on the dresser, within view, where it could still give me comfort.

I flopped down on the bed and tried to think about what I needed to do next.

Figure out the Mare's identity. It was the first step in all of this.

I almost asked Artie about it. But as badly as I wanted to clear the air, I wasn't ready to let go of my anger. Which was ridiculous, since it wasn't even aimed at the Artifact.

The Mare. Much better to put my mind to use than dwell.

There were quite a number of new incarnates in town, thanks to Maggie's recruiting efforts, like the Amazon and the Undine. I couldn't discount Morrigan and Hope as possible suspects, either, although I doubted Morrigan was the Mare. It seemed unlikely she'd get her own hands dirty when she had people for that.

If the Mare truly had a Nordic background, as Artie had revealed, it likely ruled out the Amazon, as her myth was firmly rooted in Greek mythology. It wasn't a certainty, however. The Amazon could have reincarnated as the daughter of Greek and Scandinavian parents, or something like that.

Plus, that was assuming the Amazon was who she said she was in the first place. I released a groan, indulging in an extra-loud one since no one was home to judge me.

I hated doubting the honest members of the Incarnate Watch, but too many incarnates had obscured their true identities of late. Morrigan had proclaimed herself the Protagonist, Hope had tricked us by claiming to be the Virgo, and even I was going by the Loophole. Who's to say the Amazon wasn't secretly the Viking?

Or maybe Nyx was wrong, and the Mare knew exactly who she was. She could be masquerading as someone else.

Well, I'd need to accept a few facts on faith.

Agatha, the Witch incarnate, would be a better candidate than the Amazon if she weren't located on the other side of the country. I'd need to get confirmation that she hadn't left Maine, of course, but I could easily eliminate her as a suspect. Even if she traveled by broomstick—a possibility I wasn't entirely willing to dismiss—I doubted she could fly at the speeds needed to cross the entire United States in a single night. Especially while avoiding detection from mortals.

As I thought about it, I realized that Agatha might prove a vital ally. Her witchcraft might be able to help me track down the Mare. I resolved to reach out to her tomorrow.

That left Nimue, the Undine. I must've been a little biased, because I just couldn't fathom such a gentle incarnate becoming a murderous fiend by night. Of course, anyone *could* be the Mare, so I tried instead to reason out why my gut told me it wasn't her.

Lying back on the soft bed, eyes closed as I considered my list of top suspects, I heard the puppies enter the room. I cracked my eyes open and watched as the trio hopped up and then settled on the bed all around me, nosing at my hands. Mask licked my cheek. I chuckled wearily, and he curled up in a ball near my face.

At some point, I fell asleep.

"Emery..."

I drifted in a dreamless slumber, but a voice tried to break through the peaceful calm.

"Emery..."

Was that Caden? Had he come home from work and found me, fully dressed, passed out atop the covers?

No, it wasn't coming from the room at all.

It was coming from a dream.

I willed myself to follow the voice. In the odd way of dream logic, I found myself in the mall from this afternoon, flitting through crowds of people, searching for the source of the voice.

"Emery!"

It was suddenly right in front of me.

I came across an unassuming man wearing the clothes Nyx had worn today: a tight, black T-shirt with frayed edges and black pants. They still looked a little tight on this man, but they weren't painted on like they'd been on Nyx. He was sitting at the food court table, waiting for me, eyes wide and scared.

"Who are you?"

"Emery! Good, you came." His voice morphed as he spoke, becoming familiar. Becoming Nyx's. He stood up and crossed the distance between us in a blink.

I felt my defenses rising. What was going on?

The man's every-guy appearance fell away. It was seamless, like two moments in a dream woven together. No special effects, no extended shape-shifting, just a natural *shift* and then it was Nyx standing in front of me.

He took a step forward but, to my surprise, stopped, maintaining an appropriate distance. His eyes were wide.

"What's wrong?" I asked. His worried expression looked genuine. I knew in my gut something was amiss.

"I decided to patrol the Lucid tonight," he said, his rich voice laced with concern. The mall was suddenly empty, the other people having vanished. "It's the Mare. I found her."

Surprise. My reactions didn't fully feel under my control in the dream, but I felt the emotion clearly. "That's great," I said, unsure why he was worried. "Where is she?"

"At Rachelle's house."

The mall was disappearing from the periphery of my vision. Nothing replaced it. Like my vision was shrinking.

Or Nyx was growing, filling my whole world.

Then his words hit me.

Terror. I wasn't expressing it the way I should be, I knew. But it weighed me down. The way Nyx looked at me, it was as if he could see the gravity the emotion caused. Could recognize it, understand it.

"I'll hold her off as long as I can from this side," said Nyx, speaking low and urgently. "But the Mare only dabbles in the Lucid. She's mostly in the physical world. I can't fully stop her, not from here. *You need to wake up.*"

Those last words, a command, sent me sailing back and away from the shrinking mall.

My eyes snapped open.

The Mare! My disorganized mind tried to latch on to the most important aspect of the dream. If she was at Rachelle's house, then my friend was in terrible, terrible danger.

The image of Jerry's grotesquely stabbed body flashed through my mind.

The puppies were awake on the bed, heads lifted as if they smelled the nightmare on me and wanted to make sure I was okay. I checked the clock: 3:28 a.m. Caden wouldn't be home for nearly another hour.

I couldn't wait. As much as I wanted his powers to support my fight against the Mare, Rachelle needed my help *now*. I snatched my phone from the covers and hurled myself off the bed.

In my panicked rush out the door, I didn't realize something that should have been immediately obvious: the dream catcher hadn't worked.

*R*achelle's apartment was twenty minutes across town.

"Artie," I said as I flew out of my garage, "calculate my route to Rachelle's and make sure every traffic light is green when I get to it." My Protagonist powers might have already ensured that, but I was unwilling to take any chances with Rachelle's life hanging in the balance. Her death might be one of those tragedies that propelled the protagonist's story forward; I would *not* let that happen tonight.

"Consider it done."

"Artie, the Mare is at Rachelle's apartment," I said, hoping it would ease the tension between us for him to know the desperation of the situation. "I need your help."

There was a pause, and then he said, "Understood. You will encounter no obstacles."

I couldn't ask for more than that. It might not have been the warmest of responses, but I didn't have time to worry about that just then.

The journey was a fretful blur, but at least it wasn't long. I whipped into a covered parking stall—one of those designated for tenants and not guests, but it was the closest one available. I launched myself out of my vehicle and took the steps to her apartment two at a time.

The night was quiet, and for a surreal moment I wondered whether Nyx had been telling the truth. Could he have been luring me out of the safety of my Sanctum for some reason?

No time to hesitate. The Mare was almost certainly inside, and I had no way of knowing how long Nyx could keep her from killing Rachelle. Or how he'd even manage it, for that matter.

The door was locked, of course, but I had a key from when Caden had lived with her. I fumbled around until I found it, grateful she hadn't asked for it back.

I burst through the door and shouted, "*Rachelle!*"

There was no reply. My heart in my throat, I flung myself up the interior stairs, the front door banging shut behind me.

At the top of the stairs, the kitchen was in disarray, utensils and knives scattered across the countertop and spilling onto the kitchen floor. *No, no, no!*

I realized that, in my haste, I hadn't brought a weapon in with me. My supply bag was in the back of my car, and I hadn't thought to grab it.

"*Emery? Help!*"

I wasn't too late!

I hooked a right, dashing down the hallway that led to the bathroom and two bedrooms. The main bedroom was ahead on the left, the door ajar.

I came flying through the door to Rachelle's room, and it slammed into the wall with enough force to crack the plaster.

Rachelle was apparently trying to escape, because she crashed into me so hard that she slipped to the floor at my feet with a grunt. If I hadn't been bracing for the worst, I'd have been knocked over, too.

Matlas stood in the corner of the room like a dark shadow, near the nightstand, leaning over the bed. Something flashed, and I realized with alarm that it was a knife.

He wasn't messing around, either, because the thing was a

freaking *cleaver*. I absorbed the scene in front of me, scouring the room in a vain attempt to find the Mare.

But there was no one else there.

So who, or what, was Matlas fighting?

He turned slowly to face me. His eyes had rolled up in their sockets, only the whites visible. His face was otherwise slack, as though he were sleeping.

He raised the hand with the knife and lunged forward. His movements were jerky, awkward, but he was coming right at me.

Rachelle screamed and scrambled out of the way. In the confined space, Matlas tracked her movements, head tilting to follow her despite his eyes still being rolled back. He slashed, a horror-laden jagged motion, but Rachelle was faster, and his knife cut only air. His movement put him within arm's reach, but he ignored me, body twisting toward where Rachelle had regained her feet on the right side of the room. She kept the corner of the bed between her and him.

I recovered my wits and tackled him from the side, keeping my body low to avoid that wicked blade. My attack carried us to the edge of the bed. I shoved him, and the mattress caught the backs of his legs, sending him crashing down into the sheets. I backpedaled to the door.

"Rachelle, quick! Over here."

She darted around the bed and slipped past me into the hallway. Her hair spilled across her shoulders, and she was wearing what she'd apparently gone to sleep in, which wasn't much: a loose gray tank top that exposed her flat stomach, and what I'd charitably call shorts.

"What's going on?" she asked, voice threaded with panic. "What's happened to him?"

I raised my eyebrows. She was more concerned for him than for her own safety.

Matlas rose from the bed in a completely unnatural way, his lanky form seeming to loom, filling the small space.

He wore even less than Rachelle, clad only in black trunks and still holding that damn knife. He surged forward yet again, raising the blade, then bringing it plunging down toward my chest.

I moved to avoid the assault, but a curious thing happened. His arm froze midmotion, then jerked back and away, like someone was fighting for control of it.

What?

It didn't matter. I needed to get that knife out of his hands.

I leapt forward and grabbed at his wrist, trying to wrestle the cleaver from his grip. Unlike my cemetery skirmish earlier today, when I'd been channeling, this wasn't some graceful duel between two trained fighters. This was a tangle of limbs. My elbow jabbed his armpit. His palm shoved my face to the side. His feet tried to catch at mine and knock me off-balance. My free hand yanked and twisted at his wrist, trying to dislodge the weapon.

With a yell of effort, I tried to throw him to the bed again. He was eerily silent, but still he clung on, dragging me down with him, my clothes tearing beneath his clawlike grip. Finally, I was able to wrench the handle away from him.

Great! What now?

"Rachelle!" I tossed the knife across the carpet and out into the hall, trusting my powers to keep it from clipping her toes. "Get that thing out of here."

Matlas slugged me in the jaw.

Pinpricks of light exploded across my vision, pain firing up the side of my face and lancing into the back of my skull. I reeled, taking several steps back and crashing into a mounted shelf. Matlas threw himself at me, forearm pressed against my throat as he pinned me against the wall. His all-white eyes were inches from mine, looking like nothing so much as the eyes of a corpse. His face was still slack, utterly devoid of emotion.

I tossed and twisted, trying to dislodge him. The wooden shelf jabbed painfully into my shoulder blades, digging and scraping until I felt the whole thing give. With a grating sound, it came roaring down off the wall. The items that had been on it fell to the carpet and scattered at my feet.

I was carried backward and into the wall itself, but I used the momentary slack in tension to duck under and away from Matlas before he could resume the pressure on my throat.

I sprang aside and spun to find him taking a step toward me.

Sorry, buddy.

I balled my hand into a fist and cocked it, readying myself for a punch that I really didn't want to throw.

I delivered it anyway, putting my entire body into the force of the attack.

To my surprise, Matlas sidestepped it—in that tiny bedroom, he *sidestepped* it—as if he knew exactly what I was going to do. I barely had time to register shock before he caught me in the side with a jab that took my breath away.

Gasping and wheezing, I collapsed to my knees and cringed, expecting the follow-up blow.

"Hey!" Rachelle yelled.

I didn't see the melee that ensued, but Rachelle bought me a few precious seconds for some deep breaths, a coughing fit, and another two breaths before I was back on my feet.

She was brave, but she was overpowered. As Matlas aimed a punch at her, I threw myself onto his back and pinned his arms down.

"How do we snap him out of it?" Rachelle demanded.

"What do you think I've been trying to do?"

In response, Matlas rolled his back and threw me over his shoulder with superhuman strength. I crashed to the floor with dizzying force, another *pop* of stars erupting across my eyes.

Looking up, I saw Matlas reach for Rachelle's throat. Then his hand jerked to a stop, wavering in the air. His fingers inched across the intervening space, like his hand didn't want to but couldn't help itself. Rachelle wasn't about to wait and find out whether it succeeded. She slid away from him as best she could in the tiny room.

"*Em,*" Matlas whispered, the word barely escaping his throat. "*Wake him up, Em.*"

Nyx.

Suddenly, it all made sense. The Mare *was* here; she must've slipped into Matlas's dreams and somehow used that link to possess him from within. Some people sleepwalk, others babble. With the Mare controlling him, Matlas was sleep-murdering.

Was this how she'd killed Jerry, too? No wonder Susan had confessed—she thought she *had* killed her husband.

But, I realized, since the possession occurred in the Lucid, Nyx was able to wrest back some measure of control.

Keep fighting her, Nyx.

Knowing that the Mare wrapped her sleeping victims in her hair while she fed on their essence, I had a gruesome mental image of her entangling Matlas completely in her web, then slipping into his dreams and using her tresses like a puppeteer's strings to control his limbs.

I couldn't see any physical evidence of the Mare's presence, but that made sense: I couldn't look into the dream world. In my mind's eye, though, I could envision it all perfectly.

"Rachelle, get some cold water! Fast!"

I rose to my feet and tried to slap Matlas across the face, but he caught my wrist. Was the Mare giving him superhuman strength? There was no way Matlas was naturally this strong, right?

I tore my hand out of his grasp and retreated back toward the door to the room. Something crunched underfoot.

Matlas rotated to face me, his head jerking fitfully on his neck. Boy, if I got him out of this, he was going to be sore tomorrow. He scuttled forward without fully standing, and I hunkered down, too, trying to lower my center of gravity to meet his. I couldn't just brace against his impact, though; with his extra strength, he'd topple me backward and he'd be on top of me in an instant.

We collided.

I shoved into him, trying to match his force with my own. Whatever enhanced muscle the Mare bestowed, Matlas couldn't quite match the leverage my fully awake, adrenaline-pumped body produced. Like two sumo wrestlers, we struggled against each other until he relented and I shoved him back and away.

Now was my chance to get the hell out of this room. Before he regained his footing, I dashed out the bedroom door.

As I raced down the hallway, I could hear him behind me, the floor creaking, bare feet slapping.

He was relentless.

Rachelle was ready at the sink in the kitchen, a large glass of water in her hand. Matlas rounded the corner only two steps behind me, and he veered toward her without slowing. She jerked backward and water sloshed onto the floor, but she still had the glass in her hand.

She thrust the glass of water like a sword, sending the water forward in an arc that hit him square in the face.

Matlas froze, blinking rapidly, water running in rivulets down his body. Now that I thought about it, it was the first time I'd seen him blink at all since I'd come in.

"Matlas," I gasped, still catching my breath, "snap out of it, man."

He continued to blink, standing unnaturally still.

"Hey, Atlas," Rachelle echoed, quickly grasping what I was attempting to do. "You going shy on me all of the sudden, or what?" Those words sounded familiar.

Matlas's head rocked backward. Then, slowly, it returned to a normal position. His milky eyes were still visible, and his blinking slowed.

Damn it.

"Oh, for pity's sake," Rachelle snarled. She lunged forward, reaching up to place her hands on either side of his head. With a heave, she shoved his head under the still-running faucet.

And held it there.

"Come on, Matt," she said in a low, pleading voice. "Come on, come *on.*"

Suddenly his body jerked, and he began to splutter. She must've released him, because he flung himself away from the sink. Catching himself against the kitchen table, he shook his head and wiped at his face, coughing. After a few seconds, he looked up, his gaze going back and forth between me and Rachelle in bewilderment. His eyes had returned to normal.

Rachelle let out a whoop and rushed forward, pulling him into a hug and then kissing his wet cheeks and whispering, "Oh, Matt, it's all right. It's all right. Everything's okay now. You're okay."

"Hey, hey now," he said at last, fending her off. He pulled her face back, peering into her eyes. Even from across the room I could see she was almost in tears.

"Hey, Grey," he said gently, a shaky smile pulling at his lips, "you going fraidy-cat on me all of the sudden, or what?"

She snorted and pulled him close.

24

"I'm not quite sure how to describe it," Matlas said shakily, accepting a steaming cup of tea from Rachelle. As he reached for it, he winced and rolled his shoulder. "It was an intense dream—one of those you feel like you'll never forget—but after I woke up, it just started to evaporate."

Like the Mare herself. I'd hoped that by waking Matlas, we'd have exposed her. Instead, somehow, she'd managed to escape. A question for Nyx, I decided.

"Was anyone else in the dream with you?" I pressed.

"Yeah," Matlas said, looking into his cup. "She's the one thing I remember *too* clearly."

"Oh?" Rachelle said, sitting down at the table with her own mug. She'd thrown on pajamas and a sweatshirt and tamed her hair by pulling it up into a loose knot.

"Not in a good way," Matlas said quickly. "She was terrifying." He stared into nothing for a moment, then said, "I also remember hearing your words at the end, Rachelle. They're what made me realize I was sleeping, that I needed to wake up. I began to fight for consciousness, but that woman held me down. Tried to keep me asleep."

Interesting. Had Susan heard Jerry pleading for his life before she woke up? I'd need to speak with her, see how much of her story matched up with Matlas's. "What did the woman look like?"

He looked at me helplessly. "I can't remember." He rubbed his face. "She was like you, wasn't she? An incarnate. Based on something out of a horror movie—she possessed me, like in *The Exorcist*?"

"The Mare incarnate," I said. Then I made a face. "And she's nothing like me, thank you very much."

"There are different types of incarnates, Matt," Rachelle explained, reaching across the tiny table to lay her hand on his forearm. "I'll spare you the lesson. Basically they come in four flavors: best, good, bad, and worst."

I glowered. "That's—"

She glared at me, daring me to continue. I snapped my mouth closed. "The Mare is obviously one of the worst." She squeezed his hand in comfort. "I'm sorry we involved you."

I was grateful for how she'd phrased that. But this wasn't her fault, and all three of us knew it. "I'll do better at keeping you safe," I said. "Caden is building an Incarnate Watch, in part to help monitor, uh, the *worst* incarnates and make Seattle a safer place—for mortals and those like me. But for now, the only thing I can do is have Nyx keep the Mare far from your dreams."

Matlas scrunched up his face. "What the hell is a Mare, anyway? I've never heard of that."

I resisted the urge to say "*the* Mare," and instead said, "It's where the word 'nightmare' comes from. She's known to sneak into your room while you sleep, then feed off of your dreams by, ah, cocooning you in her hair."

He stared at me. "That's really gross, man."

"If it makes you feel better, I didn't see anything like that," Rachelle said.

"Neither did I," I said, feeling frustrated. "Sometimes incarnate powers are more metaphorical than literal, but I didn't think that would be the case with the Mare. I'd assumed she was a physical incarnate that interacted with dreams; I didn't realize she had so much control over dreams themselves. I don't know enough about what she can do, and I'm constantly two steps behind." Either my information—and thus Nyx's info—was outdated, or the Mare had more tricks up her sleeve than we'd anticipated. *Or Nyx lied to you.* I pounded my hand on top of the table a little too hard, making the teacups jump. "Damn it! I thought we'd at least have cornered her after going through all that."

She shouldn't have been able to slither her way out of this. Was she still inside Matlas somewhere? That was a disturbing thought. The only person I knew who might be able to provide answers was Nyx.

But I hated the fact that I needed him.

"How did you know the Mare was attacking us?" Rachelle asked me.

"Nyx. He was patrolling dreams to keep an eye out for her."

"Patrolling dreams?"

"It's kind of difficult to describe. Basically, dreams are connected in a giant network called the Lucid. It's the home of many domains, from Sanctums to Lairs. Some incarnates can use it to peek into the dreams of sleeping people, like looking through a window. Other incarnates—like Nyx—can actually enter them."

"Sounds voyeuristic."

I shook my head. "I'm not explaining it right. Think of all dreams like they're a vast neighborhood. That's the Lucid. Nyx can patrol the street and keep an eye out for any other incarnates who shouldn't be there."

Rachelle looked skeptical. "That still sounds like he can spy on sleeping people, Emery. What's to stop him from breaking into one of those dream houses? It's creepy."

That was actually the Incubus's trick, but I decided to keep that to myself.

"I agree with you, but in this case, Nyx was just watching your front door. He must've seen the Mare sneak in, so he raced to my, uh, dream house. He told me what was going on, then woke me up and sent me to help. In the meantime, he went back to your dream house and confronted the Mare from there. In essence, we were fighting from both sides—Nyx from the Lucid, and us from your bedroom."

Matlas licked his lips. "If Nyx failed to keep us safe once, what's to stop it from happening again?"

"She got the drop on us. That won't happen again. I'll enter the Lucid myself if I have to."

"Is the Lucid an incarnate?" Rachelle asked.

I opened my mouth to tell her it wasn't, then paused. "I don't know," I said slowly. "I don't think so, but it's certainly *related* to incarnates. I've always thought of it more like an incarnate domain than an incarnate in its own right. I don't know which incarnate it would be: the Dream World, or the Dreamscape? Oz, maybe?" As they exchanged looks, I rolled my eyes. "That last one was a joke, you guys. I think. I'm fairly sure."

Matlas frowned. "So the Mare just escaped through this dream neighborhood—"

"The Lucid."

"The Lucid," he repeated. "Right? Just ran out the door and off down the street."

Huh. Nyx had said she was located in the physical world, but obviously she'd surprised him.

"Matlas," I said, leaning forward, "are you sure you can't remember anything else? I need to identify the Mare, and any detail you can remember about her could help. Even if it's just an impression or a vibe you got. Is there anything you can tell me?"

He took a shaky sip of his tea and said, "I don't remember much. Long hair. I... I remember thinking I couldn't escape her. I'd turn to run, and she'd suddenly be in front of me. That kind of thing." He shook his head, squeezing his eyes shut in concentration. "No, that's not quite right. I was *fighting* her. Yeah, at one point I remember she jumped on my back, clawing at me to keep me in the dream. I threw her off me and ran, but she caught up."

A chill ran through me. At one point in our fight, I'd jumped on Matlas's back and he'd thrown me. The Mare had turned our fight against him, made him think he was fighting her when he was really fighting us. No wonder he'd struggled so fiercely.

"She was all around me," he whispered, "so no matter which way I turned, there she was."

That also made sense if she'd wrapped him up in her hair. I repressed a shudder. "Anything else? Skin color? Her voice, maybe?"

He shook his head. "I don't think she spoke to me."

I nodded, wondering morosely if there was even a crumb of identifying information in what he'd told me. If so, I couldn't immediately find it. "I'm really sorry, both of you. This is my fault; I knew the Mare was out there. I should've warned you."

"At least we learned something useful," Rachelle said, holding her steaming tea between her hands. "She can apparently enter your dreams and control you from within."

I shrugged uncomfortably. "I didn't know she could do that. My bad."

"*My bad*?" Matlas repeated incredulously. "Dude, I thought incarnates sounded pretty cool when you told me about them earlier, but I've got to be real with you: this just sucks. First the Incubus in the mall, and now…" He paused, struggling to articulate his feelings. "*This*," he finished unhappily. He winced again, rubbing his shoulder. "I feel like a truck ran over me while I was sleeping."

A voice came from the entryway stairs. "I might be able to help with that," Caden said, coming up to the kitchen. I'd been so distracted—and tired—I hadn't even heard him come in. "Hope you don't mind that I let myself in," he said. "The door was unlocked."

I stood and embraced him tightly. I felt his calmness wash over me, tension and stress bleeding away. He had healing powers, sure, but I got the feeling that this was something different. Sometimes a hug was superpower enough.

Caden pulled back and fingered the ripped seams of my clothes. "Been busy, I see."

"How'd you know we were here?"

"Artie told me. I left early and came as quickly as I could." He extracted himself from my grip and pulled out a chair at the table, facing Matlas. "So you know about incarnates. What else did I miss?"

"Should I start at the cemetery where I nearly got shot, the mall where I nearly died of embarrassment, or here where I tried to kill my friends because someone hijacked my body while I was sleeping?" His voice was a little too high to pull off the light tone he was aiming for.

"Wow, rough day. Learning about incarnates can be like that. Did Rachelle tell you about her first day, when the Genie attacked and set the building she was in on fire? The day I learned about them, Emery and I were chased by the Headless Horseman into a little shack in the woods. We hid there all night before he went away." He gave Matlas an understanding smile. "But *your* day might just take the gold."

"This isn't really selling me on incarnates, guys."

Caden grinned. "Sorry. If it makes you feel better, the Headless Horseman eventually teamed up with us to take down the woman who was murdering people."

"Not much. What happened to the Genie?"

Good question. "He decided to stop tangling with us after we bested him one time too many," I said.

"There's a lot of Benign incarnates out there, too," Caden said. "The Watchman. The Mermaid. Emery and me." He reached out across the table. "I can heal you, if you'll let me."

Matlas hesitated. "Does it hurt?"

"I don't think so."

"Is it weird? Like the others?"

Caden cocked his head. "I don't know what that means, but you don't have to accept my offer. Do whatever makes you comfortable."

He met Caden's gaze for a weighty few seconds, then sighed and put his hand in Caden's. "I trust you." He squeezed his eyes shut, though.

For a split second, the light in the room changed. Caden's blond hair burned with a golden hue, giving the illusion of a fiery halo, and the light seemed to reflect off his shoulders and enfold Matlas in a pair of luminescent wings.

Even seeing it time and time again, it was awe-inspiring. I felt a renewal of energy and life surge through me, and I realized Caden was sharing his healing energy with me, pushing away my fatigue.

It ended a blink later, as if it had been nothing more than a trick of the light. But the refreshed feeling remained.

Caden withdrew his hand, and Matlas opened his eyes, frowning. "Did it not work?" he asked. Then he rolled his shoulder, and his eyes went round. "Oh. Oh, *wow*. Okay, okay. I can get behind this."

Rachelle, clearly relieved at Matlas's improvement, got up and started to make Caden some tea. "I think we need to fill Caden in on what happened tonight."

I felt a spike of alarm in my chest. That meant I'd finally need to tell him about Nyx.

25

*W*here to begin?

I knew I needed to be the one to bring up Nyx. To tell Caden the truth. Maybe I should've started with Nyx's unexpected arrival at our front door. Instead, I started with what happened when Caden left for work.

"I decided to run some errands. I needed to..." I trailed off. I'd gone to purchase a dream catcher to keep Nyx out of my dreams. But since I hadn't told Caden about Nyx yet, I needed to change course. "Let me back up. Before I left, I asked Artie to track Morrigan's phone. I wanted to know if she went anywhere alarming."

"Thank goodness you did," Rachelle said. I shot her a grateful smile. At least I'd done one thing right today.

"Artie warned me that Morrigan was at Matlas's house," I continued. "So I raced there to make sure he was okay. When I got there, I found out she and Hope weren't at his house at all—they were at the cemetery." I looked at Caden. "You'll never guess what they were searching for."

He shook his head. "No idea."

"Mask, Beard, and Mittens."

Rachelle gasped from where she stood by the tea kettle. "What would they want with them?"

"I'm not sure. Morrigan has a history of collecting incarnates and using them in her schemes, though."

"But you told me they were the Hellhound's puppies, that they weren't incarnates themselves."

I nodded. "That's right. Either Morrigan and Hope don't know that, or they wanted the offspring of incarnates for some other reason."

"Whoa, hold on a second," Matlas interrupted. "Those dogs are *hellhound* puppies?"

"Yeah." I hesitated. "Well, I think so. Remember when Rachelle and I were attacked by something at the Thirteen Steps the first night we recorded for our show? I'm fairly certain we were attacked by the Hellhound incarnate. Since we found the puppies the next morning, I'm assuming they belong to her."

"Which explains why they don't act like ordinary puppies," Caden added.

"All right. I don't suppose the Hellhound was—what did you call it? Benevolent?"

"Benign," Caden said. "The word we use for incarnates that exist in harmony with mortal society."

"She was not," I said slowly, "but I don't think she was one of the worst incarnates, either. I think she was a Predator incarnate, and she was just protecting her Territory. Or her puppies, I suppose."

Rachelle threw her hands into the air. "I don't know why I bothered to simplify it in the first place. All right, Matt, here's the breakdown, before Emery and Caden lecture you for the next thirty minutes: Benign are best, Prey are fine, Predators are scary but only if you mess with them, and Malevolents are the ones you run away from."

"Like the Mare?"

"Like the Mare." Rachelle speared me with a look. "Among others."

Right. I was getting there. "So anyway, I was at the graveyard when a guard reported to Morrigan that they'd caught someone poking around. She told the guard to take care of it and hide the body."

Matlas started. "Shit. They said *that?*"

"Yes. Morrigan's a Malevolent. I cannot put this in clearer terms: stay away from her. She will kill without batting an eye."

Rachelle turned and put a hand on Matlas's shoulder. "He's not kidding. We'll spare you the details of Emery's past with her. But I need your word that you'll be careful."

He looked a little lost, but he put a hand over hers. "I promise. Which incarnate is she?"

The three of us exchanged a glance. I spoke up. "The Antagonist."

Matlas looked puzzled. "As in the villain from a story?"

"Precisely."

He peered at me, and I could see the wheels spinning as he absorbed that piece of information. "You said yesterday that she was your nemesis."

"I did."

"Does that mean you're the Protagonist?"

"It does."

"You're *literally* the incarnation of the good guy?"

I grinned. "Guilty." Then I sighed. "But that's an oversimplification. A stereotype, really. Every myth and urban legend has a protagonist, right? But some stories are about good people, some are about bad people, and a great many of them are about ordinary people in extraordinary situations. I'm more a manifestation of *that.* I'm not the Hero incarnate."

"The jury's still out on that," Caden said, giving me a side smile.

He wouldn't be saying that if he knew what I was keeping from him.

Rachelle set a fresh cup of tea in front of Caden and took a seat. "Emery's not *the* Hero, but he's *a* hero. There's a difference, but he only remembers it when he's feeling humble."

I scoffed. "I'm always humble. Some might even say the *humblest* person in the whole world."

"Never you, though, right? You're too modest for that."

I tapped my finger to my nose. "Exactly."

"So that's why you saved me?" Matlas asked. "In the graveyard, I mean. Are you always in the right place at the right time?"

"As often as I'm in the wrong place at the wrong time." I couldn't quite keep the bitterness out of my tone.

He wasn't done connecting the dots, either. "So if you're the Protagonist and your stories are sometimes about being a bad guy, wouldn't that mean the Antagonist—"

"Is always horrible?" I finished for him. "Yes, yes it would."

He narrowed his eyes but decided to let it go with a shrug. Good. I knew I was biased, but I didn't want him going and vainly seeking the good in Morrigan. What kernels he'd find were layered deep beneath her sinister shell, and he'd die eight times over before he discovered them. I'd know; I'd done it.

Still, I found myself impressed with Matlas's reasoning skills. He was proving proficient at taking bits and pieces of information and seeing the larger picture.

"We escaped the cemetery," I said, resuming the story for Caden. "I took him to the mall, where I knew Rachelle was shopping with her mom."

"Yeah, thanks for that," she muttered.

Matlas chimed in, "You skipped over the part where you went all *Cobra Kai* on their asses."

Caden glanced at me. "Channeling?"

I nodded.

His eyes held concern. "Did it go okay?"

I saw Matlas perk up at the direction the conversation had turned, and I remembered the way he'd looked at me. In fear.

"It went fine." At Caden's expression, I added, "Deeper than I meant to go, but I found my way back."

He offered me a quiet smile. I felt bolstered, but it was cut by a knife of guilt. His earnest support deserved truth in turn. "We got to the mall," I said, "and ran into an old friend." My heart began to beat a little faster. "The Incubus incarnate."

Rachelle, who'd been glaring at me to spit it out, now averted her eyes and drained her tea. Matlas gave an involuntary shudder. I held my breath.

Caden absorbed my words and, picking up on Rachelle's energy —*damn* their time spent as roommates together!—glanced at her, brows furrowed. He turned those sparkling, seafoam eyes back to me, and I saw he didn't recognize the name.

My pulse was thunder in my ears. If he didn't remember, I could say anything. I could leave out the parts I didn't want to share. It wasn't lying; it was protecting his feelings, wasn't it? I didn't need to reveal my past—

No.

It was wrong. Omitting some of the truth was tantamount to lying about it. If I loved Caden, I needed to be the man he loved in return.

Two paths stretched out before me, and I'm ashamed that I hesitated. One path was honesty and consequence; the other was shadowed with temptation and self-preservation. Caden and Nyx. No matter how I twisted the words or interpreted the facts, I was at a crossroads: the easy path, or the right one.

"I'm sorry, Caden," I said before I could lose my nerve. "I didn't tell you about the Incubus because of our history. Because, as much as I resist it, fight it, *hate* it, he still has some control over my emotions." I closed my eyes and whispered the words I hadn't uttered —even to myself—in lifetimes. "But most of all, because he's the father of my child."

"*W*hat?" Rachelle yelped, dropping her cup to the table with a clatter.

Matlas choked on his tea.

I paid them no mind. I was watching Caden for any sign of hurt or betrayal. Instead, I saw his eyes lose focus as memories returned to him, comprehension dawning. Then his lips twisted into a wry smile, and he said, "Ah, so Nyx is in town, is he?"

Rachelle and Matlas turned to him, disbelieving, but I knew my words had triggered memories and they'd washed over and through him. He knew everything now. Well, everything except the last day.

"Yeah," I said, unable to think of anything more articulate. I resisted the urge to cast my eyes downward, to look away. I'd kept the information about Nyx from him since the Incubus had shown up, but I'd kept my knowledge of Avery from him much longer—since we'd found each other again, really.

"And from the look on your face, I'm guessing he's been here for a little while?"

"Since Thursday night," I admitted, my face burning.

Caden nodded. "Is Avery okay?"

Shit. He even remembered her name? I swallowed. "Yeah."

"Then what does he want?"

"Time out," Rachelle interrupted, voice several octaves too high. "What the hell are we talking about? Emery, you have a kid?"

"A daughter, last I checked."

"Hold up," Matlas said. "You and Nyx are both guys, right?" His eyes widened. "Oh, that's probably not the right way to ask—"

I saved him. "I'm not always a guy, Matlas. Protagonists aren't all male."

"I guess I didn't think about it." He looked at me up and down and swallowed. "So, uh, you're sometimes a lady?"

Rachelle was watching the exchange, her expression darkening. "Is there something wrong with that?"

Matlas put up his hands hastily. "Not at all. It just caught me off guard. I'm an open-minded guy, but sometimes you just need time to process, you know?"

"It's okay," I said. "We've thrown a lot on your plate. Reincarnation—what happens when one of us dies—is complicated. Depending on the wiggle room in a myth, we come back in all sorts of bodies."

"Our entire identities are different," Caden said in a soft voice. "There are those, like Morrigan, who act as though they have one long existence—pretend to possess immortality. But, in truth, so much is lost between lives. Friends, family, all the things that make a life special and unique."

"Caden and I have found each other in several lifetimes," I said, "but we often don't have memories of each other until we cross paths. That's sort of how incarnate minds work—we have so much information stuffed in our brains that it presents as a form of selective amnesia. Knowledge or recollection of an event or a person is compartmentalized, only opened when we need it."

Rachelle twisted the cup in her hands. "Kind of gives 'out of sight, out of mind' a deeper meaning."

"Sounds infuriating," Matlas said.

"Nah, it's how everyone's mind works. If I tell you to think about a penguin, then you think about one. Up until then, you weren't thinking about penguins, and they weren't anywhere on your mind or even in your subconscious. But you *know* what a penguin is. And when I ask you about it, you can describe it to me. You summon that knowledge from the back of your mind."

"We're the same way," Caden said. "We just have a lot more crammed in there."

"And as we age, we remember more of our past lives," I added. "With age comes wisdom, and all that. Sadly, we don't seem to have any more capacity than anyone else. Which means I've forgotten a *lot*. More information than you'll ever learn in your one lifetime."

"*There's* the high-and-mighty incarnate trash talk I was waiting for," Rachelle chirped happily. I felt my face flush. I hadn't meant it that way. "One thing you'll also learn about incarnates," she told Matlas smugly, "is that even the good ones underestimate us wee mortals. I've found you can use that to your advantage, sometimes."

"So does everyone reincarnate?" he asked.

"As long as the myth survives, the incarnate does, too." I shrugged. "But if you're asking about humans, death is still the great mystery."

"But Caden's the Guardian Angel. Doesn't that mean heaven is real? Or, I guess... does that mean it's just a myth?"

I shook my head before he went too far down that train of thought. "You're asking the big questions, and I appreciate that, but you won't get any answers from us. Let me put it this way: the Princess incarnate exists as the manifestation of princesses in myths and legends, from "The Princess and the Pea" to Princess Peach to pretty much every Disney movie, but that doesn't mean princesses aren't real. They are. But, to my knowledge, vampires are not. Yet there's the Vampire incarnate. What I'm trying to say is that incarnates are not an indication of whether or not a thing exists."

"The same thing goes for me," Caden said. "I'm based on the legend of the Guardian Angel, but that doesn't prove or disprove the existence of angels."

I thought Matlas looked relieved, and again I was reminded of how he seemed to gravitate toward mystery almost as much as answers. "But you said there's only one of you."

"Only one incarnate, created as the manifestation of all the stories about them," I replied. "Like the one and only Princess incarnate, yet there are plenty of princesses. They won't all have her powers of charisma and wealth, of course."

"Wealth is a power?" Rachelle asked.

I scoffed. "Of course it is. Iron Man. Batman. King Midas. Wealth is *definitely* a superpower."

She rolled her eyes. "We're getting way off track here. You were telling us about your daughter. Avery?"

I felt pain there, and I shied away from it. "I don't like to talk about her."

I saw compassion in their eyes and wanted to make a joke, anything to wipe away the emotion that so quickly became pity.

"I take it you two aren't close," she said gently.

"You could say that. It's been almost a century since we... last spoke." *Since I'd thrust a blade through her heart.* I felt my mind skitter away from the memory before it could envelop me.

"Okay." She hesitated, then said, "I'm confused. You said the children of incarnates aren't incarnates. They're mortals."

"I gave birth to Avery more than a thousand years ago," I said reluctantly, hoping they wouldn't focus on what that meant about how far back my past with Nyx stretched. "The last time I saw her she was a woman, which is the reason I'm referring to 'her'—but she isn't always female. For hundreds of years she'd reincarnate as a young boy or girl and find her way into my care. I raised her time and time again."

"So she *is* an incarnate?"

"Yes. It's exceedingly rare. But..." *But it could happen. When very select circumstances were met.*

Caden caught my sidelong glance and, misinterpreting the pain there, reached out and took my hand in his. "Usually when Nyx shows up," he told the other two, "it has to do with Avery."

That wasn't entirely accurate. Usually, it had to do with winning me back. Avery was just the bait.

Rachelle looked back and forth between us and then focused on Caden. "So let me get this straight. You've known about this all along, and I'm just now finding out?"

He colored slightly and shook his head. "No, not at all. It wasn't until Em told me about Nyx that I recalled any of this." He squeezed my hand. "Sometimes I think Emery's powers—through no fault of his own—keep certain memories of mine from surfacing."

What? This was the first I was hearing of *that*. "You do?"

He nodded but didn't look upset. "It isn't your fault," he said. "And I *was* reborn as an infant, so my memories are spottier than most incarnates'. But I think being the Protagonist acts upon those around you, keeping certain knowledge limited so as to reveal it when it's relevant to you."

I looked disbelievingly at him. "And you're *okay* with that?"

"Of course. I love you."

"Aww," Rachelle cooed. She looked at Matlas. "In six months, we'd better be at least half as adorable as these two."

"After the last twenty-four hours, I'll be happy if we're both alive in six months," he muttered.

"How romantic."

He grinned.

Caden laughed and said, "It's hard not to wilt under her glare, Matlas; she's been practicing it on Emery since I've known them. It took me months to—" He swallowed as she turned her flat gaze on him. "Well, um, let's just say I'm impressed."

"I have a distinct advantage," Matlas said. "Watch this." He took Rachelle's hands in his and gazed into her eyes with exaggerated dreaminess. "If we're still together in six months, I'll already be the luckiest man in the world."

She rolled her eyes and made a gagging sound, but her cheeks lit up and she couldn't quite hide her smile.

I laughed with them, grateful they'd let the topic of Avery drop. It was obvious they were doing it for me. I knew Rachelle too well; she would be bursting with unanswered questions. But she was also my best friend, and she knew when to push me and when to give me room.

Caden, too, still held my hand, radiating support. It wasn't even his glamour—it was just him. Part of me felt unworthy of their love after the sneaking around I'd done and the things I'd left unsaid. But the rest of me basked in it, grateful. Not for the first time, their trust made me want to be a better Emery, not out of guilt, but in reciprocation.

"All right," Rachelle said, clearing the empty cups, "that wraps up this tea party. Murder has been averted, bonds of friendship have grown stronger, and revelations have been... revelated. I think that just about exceeds my quota of events before six in the morning."

Caden and I said our goodbyes and left the apartment. I even remembered to lock the door behind me.

We'd driven separately, but I didn't want another twenty minutes to go by before I got to say everything else. To explain that I hadn't told him about Nyx because I didn't want him to be distracted before the Incarnate Watch meeting. About how Nyx and I spent the afternoon together, but nothing happened—except that I'd forgotten to go to the bakery.

I stopped him in the parking lot.

"Caden," I began.

He raised a hand with a shy smile. "Let me guess: we should go to the bakery this morning?"

"It's on my to-do list," I admitted, hanging my head.

His smile blossomed into something bigger. "Great!" he said brightly. "The only thing better than you doing it for me is if we get to do it together."

My eyes suddenly felt hot. I didn't deserve him. "I still want to say I'm s—"

My phone rang. I frowned; it was six a.m., who would be calling?

Glancing at the phone, I groaned. "What is it, Gregory?"

"Good morning, kitten."

My heart lurched into gear. I immediately recognized that sultry voice. Morrigan. Calling from Gregory Gregorius's phone. "What do you want?"

"I'm afraid there's been a little murder. I'll send you the location... oh, wait! There's no need for that, is there? You can just have your pet sniff out this phone number. How convenient. Ta-ta, darling."

*L*ongest. Drive. Of. My. Life.

Artie had sent us the GPS coordinates without even being asked, and Caden and I took my car and hit the interstate within minutes. I pushed down my immediate concern that something awful had happened to Gregory and that's why Morrigan had called from his phone. She was clearly just trying to throw me off-balance. My second concern—that something had happened to my mom, and that's why Gregory had carelessly left his phone within Morrigan's reach—was allayed when I saw our destination. Morrigan had called from north of Seattle, a suburb called Shoreline. Nowhere near my mom's house.

Caden and I pulled up to the location a little before seven. It was obvious we'd arrived at the correct residence: police cars and ambulances swarmed the area. Despite this being a condo development, I immediately got flashbacks to yesterday morning's murder.

There were two major differences: Morrigan was in the thick of the gathered people, dressed in a sharp business suit and looking way too prepared for the early hour. She was speaking to police officers with a professional air, and, to my disgust, they seemed to be hanging on her every word. I'm sure she was spinning quite the tale.

The second difference was equally worrying: the victim's body had already been moved from inside the condo. It was laid out on a stretcher near the rear of an ambulance, fully covered in a white sheet.

Why had the body been moved already? Maybe that was the wrong question. Maybe I should be asking how long ago the murder had occurred. It seemed unlikely the authorities had already completed the crime scene investigation.

Something wasn't adding up.

I looked around for Gregory but didn't see him. He must've been in the condo, looking for clues. Good thinking, especially while Morrigan was busy out here.

"Follow me, and walk with confidence," I told Caden, clipping the badge I'd taken from the previous crime scene to my shirt.

We made our way toward the condo.

And were stopped immediately by an officer. Usually my powers of convenience would see me right through with minimal hassle. But, of course, Morrigan was here, and her unseen powers worked in counterpoint to my own. "I'm sorry," the officer said, "but you can't go in there right now. This is a police matter."

I pointed at my plastic badge. "I know. I'm a police consultant."

The officer glanced back at the people gathered around Morrigan. "Not our jurisdiction anymore," he said in a confidential tone.

"What do you mean?"

"The feds are taking this one. Won't even let us into the condo. Something strange went down in there last night, but so far no one's talking about it."

"Is Gregorius still inside?"

The man looked back toward the group again, then said, "No, I think they brought him out."

I was surprised I hadn't seen him, then. As far as I knew, his clearance went to the highest level. I'm talking limitless, imaginary levels of clearance. He must be fuming.

"May we see him? He asked us to come."

The man, who'd been looking less rigid by the second, suddenly froze. "He did?" He frowned, then said, "I'm not sure, but let's find out. Come with me."

To my dismay, he led us to the group surrounding Morrigan. The tall, mustached man she was speaking with must be the investigator in charge.

"Director," the officer said, "excuse the interruption. We have two consultants here. Said Gregorius asked them to come."

I had an uneasy feeling. It had almost seemed like he was speaking to—

"Thank you for bringing them to me, Nielson," Morrigan said, eyeing Caden and me. "I'll take it from here." She turned to the man she'd been speaking to and nodded. "I want a preliminary autopsy by this afternoon. The irregularities—"

"What the hell is going on here?" I demanded, drawing the stares of the surrounding officers. I didn't care. This whole situation was spinning out of my control even faster than was usual when Morrigan was involved. "Where's Gregory?"

I saw several of the officers stiffen. Morrigan turned slowly to regard me, the very model of exaggerated patience. "That isn't very sensitive of you to say, Mr....?"

"You know who I am, Morrigan."

"Ah, yes. Emery Luple. Gregorius's right-hand man. Your reputation for irreverence precedes you, I'm afraid."

"Where is Gregory?" I bit out. But the horrible truth was starting to dawn on me. I could see it in the officers' averted gazes, their rigid postures.

"It's okay," Morrigan said to the gathered folk. "He's understandably upset. Let him see for himself."

She gestured to the sheet-wrapped form.

No.

I licked my lips, then strode over to the corpse. I resisted the urge to rip the sheet off the body, to expose their lies. Instead, I carefully pulled back the white cloth.

No, no, no, nooooo.

It was him. Gregory Gregorius. He was almost unrecognizable in death. His head was shrunken and wasted to the point that it looked more like a skull, cheekbones standing out starkly, lips shriveled and pale. With his skin emaciated and the pigmentation drained, his flesh looked like old, worn parchment over nonexistent muscle and too-thin bone. The silent confidence he exuded was gone. In its place was an emptiness, a profane *lack*.

Just another body, another crime scene.

Not my friend. Not the Watchman incarnate.

Peeling back the sheet further revealed faint, purplish lesions on his throat and up the side of his jaw. They'd paled to almost nothing as the rest of his life force had been drained, but I could just make them out. Like he'd been strangled by a collection of strands held tight against his throat.

Like hair.

The Mare. It *had* to be the Mare. She'd strangled him while he slept and drained him of his essence. Just like she'd done to Amara's horse, Spray.

Seeing the near-skeletal body of my friend, a towering wave of emotion built on the horizon. An entire storm front of rage, and behind that, a vast abyss of despair.

There wasn't enough room in my heart, or in my soul, or in my entire *being* to contain all that emotion. It would bring me to my knees. Maybe I'd recover, or maybe I'd just stay there, bowed beneath the weight of hopelessness for 1,001 days.

No. Gregory would be disappointed if you let this break you.

But he'd been disappointed in me before.

Caden came up to my shoulder, and I heard his sharp intake of breath. Thankfully, he didn't try to touch me.

Only because he believed in you, Emery.

It wasn't words. It was a feeling. Like Gregory was right there, conveying what he felt.

Morrigan was watching us, radiating professional concern. Her façade did not lower for an instant, but I knew she was gloating. Her mock compassion was an affront to everything Gregory stood for. "I'm sorry for your loss," she said with exaggerated sympathy.

My hands curled into fists.

No. Gregory wouldn't want vengeance; he'd want justice.

And he'd want to make sure those closest to him were okay. He'd devoted his life to it, in fact.

A pit opened up inside me, swallowing all emotion, all cares, all tears. I turned to Caden, but it was like I was watching someone else do it. "Can you heal him?" I asked, my voice ragged. Maybe I didn't ask it quietly enough. At the moment, I couldn't summon enough energy to care.

Caden shook his head, tears standing out in his eyes. "No, Em. I'm so, so sorry."

I felt a small hand slip into mine. Thinking it was Caden's, I squeezed, but my fist closed completely. It took me a moment to realize the hand had been too small.

Iris. The Ghost. She was here, too.

And then I felt a hand on my shoulder, heavy and warm. I shrugged it off angrily, but it didn't dislodge. It remained, as stubborn and steadfast as ever.

I turned to look, but there was nothing there.

It's going to be okay, that touch said. And *It's up to you, now. Protect them.*

I felt tears prick my eyes. "I will." The words were barely audible.

We'll meet again.

"I know." It would have to be enough, for now.

Then, one more thought reached me. The heavy hand on my shoulder withdrew, and Iris's ghostly fingers slipped out of my grasp.

I am proud *to be your friend.*

*T*en things.

The day passed in a haze of activity, but I remember only ten things.

It's strange how death affects us. Everyone seems to deal with it in their own way. For some, it leaches the world of color. For others, it spurs them to find new meaning in familiar, comfortable things. Sometimes it means listening to a song and truly hearing its lyrics for the first time. Or catching a whiff of an aroma you never before linked with the person you lost.

Some find comfort in prayer. Some seek it in the arms of their loved ones. Some seek it in solitude. Some continue their routine, hoping to distract themselves.

Death is sadness. And love. Sometimes it is holding on, sometimes it is letting go. Often, it's both.

There is no one right way to handle death.

For me, the day Gregory Gregorius, the Watchman incarnate, died was a day of ten things.

Gregory's condo, and what I found there.

A black cat.

The roar of an airplane.

My mom's face when I broke the news.

A fire in the hearth.

A text message.

A trio of puppies.

A message sent to the Incarnate Watch.

Caden's embrace.

And that ghostly hand on my shoulder.

~

The First Thing

*C*aden and I, with supervision, were permitted to enter Gregory's condo. Morrigan and her team—*her* team—had already combed through everything, so we weren't expecting to find anything damning.

The space was spartan, which was unsurprising. Everything was meticulously organized, from the microwavable dinners stacked in the freezer to the generic pictures positioned precisely on the walls.

Gregory had been a man of simple tastes. This wasn't his Sanctum, though. That would now be gone, but I could tell this hadn't been it. Knowing him, it had probably been his office.

The only thing that caught my attention was the dream catcher I found in the dresser drawer. Its presence snapped my mind back to last night, when Nyx had entered my dream. *After* I'd hung the dream catcher.

It hadn't worked. The talisman hadn't kept Nyx at bay. Nor, it seemed, had it kept the Mare from entering Gregory's apartment while he slept.

There was a mystery there. One I'd need to solve.

Not today.

~

The Second Thing

*N*umb, Caden and I left the crime scene.

Director Morrigan walked us to my car, accompanied by two officers. Now that I knew she'd co-opted the crime scene, I realized the officers weren't all in uniform. Probably federal agents, then. Who, bewilderingly, worked for Morrigan.

What had I missed?

I shouldn't have been surprised, damn it. But despite hundreds of years of experience, I continued to underestimate her. In this case, I'd underestimated her reach and authority. Those things, along with wealth, were direct paths to power. Why *wouldn't* she work for the FBI?

At the moment, I didn't care. I'd deal with that tomorrow. Today belonged to the Watchman.

But a small corner of my mind hoped that she didn't *really* work for them; that she'd used her powers to impersonate a director or just make mortals *think* she had that level of authority.

It didn't matter. Not today.

She spoke to us. We responded. The banter wasn't important. The only thing that mattered was that in the yard behind her, across the street from Gregory's condo, a black cat watched us. When it caught me looking at it, it dipped its head in shared sorrow.

The Ijiraat. In his own way, he'd come to pay his respects to the Watchman.

Morrigan said something underhanded. The kind of thing that would normally set my blood to boiling. I didn't engage. But I noticed the cat's ears prick forward, saw its eyes as it raised its head, listening intently.

Interesting. Had he caught a glimpse of Morrigan's carefully concealed wickedness?

I bid the officers and Morrigan goodbye. Promised we'd be in touch. Accepted her business card.

And when I looked back at the yard, the cat was gone, and a black bird was flying away on the horizon.

~

The Third Thing

*A*ll I remember of the drive home was an airplane passing overhead.

I'm not even sure whether I remember seeing the jet or only heard its distant roar. I just remember thinking about the hundred or so people flying overhead who had no idea of the monumental pain and loss I was suffering in that moment. They were simply traveling on an ordinary Saturday, no more or less significant than any other.

It seemed wrong to me. Like all the planes should've been grounded for the day out of respect for Gregory's life, or something absurd like that. How could the world keep spinning and not stop to give me this moment to grieve?

But there was a sense of comfort in that, though. Tomorrow was inevitable. Not even death could stop its inexorable approach. Billions of people were going about their lives right then, completely unaffected by Gregory's loss. But they carried their own weights and tragedies that I'd never know.

The normalcy of a plane passing overhead made today more special, not less. It was a reminder that this was not the end of the world. That the loss I was feeling was uniquely my own but could be understood by everyone.

I liked to think Gregory would have seen the airplane as a reminder that there were many people out there he needed to protect, whether or not he knew their identities or their stories.

That was my burden now. For 1,001 days, I would bear that cross for the both of us.

~

The Fourth Thing

I think I wanted to put it off but knew I wouldn't. I think I considered calling her but knew I shouldn't. And I think Caden drove me there without even asking, because he knew I *could* do what I had to.

I don't remember pulling up to the house or walking to the front steps. I just remember Mom's pleasantly surprised face when she answered the door. She must've invited us in, because we were in the kitchen when I told her what had happened.

Her face went through a series of emotions so distinct that I could write a poem about each.

First was disbelief. That stunned, blank look of surprise, the tiny furrow between her brows.

Then came pain. Her face crumpled, tears welling in her eyes. The quiver of her lip, followed by the firm set to her jaw.

Last was compassion. Her eyes widened, and she opened her arms. I sank into her, accepting the medicine that is a mother's hug. She and Gregory had started dating, but they'd only met a little over a week ago. He'd been my friend for much longer, and she knew that —even if she didn't know for *how* long.

We shared each other's pain. We shared love, too. Our love for each other, and our different brands of love for Gregory.

~

The Fifth Thing

e ate lunch, and it was a mechanical thing. Normally a home-cooked meal, even something as simple as a sandwich, was warm and comforting.

Today it was nothing more than a necessity.

At some point, Mom lit a fire in the living room hearth. I could barely remember the last time she'd done so, and I must've told her that, because she sobbed a little laugh and told me that it had been but a few nights ago, when Gregory had come over.

We sat and watched the flames devour the pieces of paper Mom fed them, watched them curl and blacken before flaring bright and burning out quickly.

The heat must've reminded my mom of a warm and comforting evening, but my mind was taken somewhere else entirely. To a memory I never thought I'd think upon fondly. To watching my office building go up in flames.

It had been where I'd met Gregory Gregorius for the first time this incarnation. He'd approached Rachelle and me and introduced himself, not knowing if I'd recognize him. I could just imagine his uncertainty at my new, young body. Too young for all the memories he probably hoped I'd have.

I'd shaken his proffered hand, and our times together had flickered through my mind like a movie reel. I'd instantly felt safer with him at my back.

In a few years, I'll find you, Gregorius. Just like you found me.

I don't remember leaving, but I remember thinking that I hoped Mom would be okay. I don't think Caden would have let us leave if that weren't the case.

~

The Sixth Thing

*C*aden was driving us home when my phone buzzed. I knew it was a text message, and I also knew I didn't want to look at it.

I didn't want to be pitied. Today wasn't about me. It was about him.

I looked at it anyway.

I AM NOT PROFICIENT IN HUMAN EMOTIONS, EMERY LUPLE, BUT I WISH FOR YOU TO STOP SUFFERING. I OVERHEARD GREGORY GREGORIUS SPEAKING WITH YOUR MOTHER LAST NIGHT. HE TOLD LYNN LUPLE HE'D NEVER KNOWN A BETTER PERSON THAN YOU. ALTHOUGH I DO NOT EXPE-RIENCE EMOTIONS MYSELF, I BELIEVE THIS MEANS THAT HE CARED FOR YOU, AND MY RESEARCH CONCLUDES THAT INFORMING YOU OF THIS SHOULD BRING YOU COMFORT.

Not for the first time and not for the last, I believed Artie under-stood emotions better than he gave himself credit for.

THANK YOU, I texted back. AND I'M SORRY.

IT CONSTANTLY AMAZES ME THAT HUMANS CAN SAY SO MUCH WITH SO LITTLE. YOU ARE EXTRAORDINARY, EMERY LUPLE.

∽

The Seventh Thing

*W*e made it home.

Beard, Mittens, and Mask greeted us with their customary enthusiasm.

I'm sure Caden let them out. Fed them. Refreshed their water. Did all the things that needed doing.

What I remember is sliding down the wall until I sat on the floor, where three puppies piled into my lap and licked my face.

I remember Caden joining us and our little family huddling on the floor by the garage door.

The puppies needed us, relied on us for everything.

Right then, I realized we needed them. Their effortless exuberance. Their joy and their unconditional love.

What was death to a puppy? Even these exceptional ones, so good at picking up on my moods, wagged their tails and pawed at our hearts. They didn't understand that their humans weren't in the right place to give them scratches. Their humans were there! Of course it was time for scratches!

For playing.

For kisses.

Maybe they *were* picking up on our mood. Maybe they knew, better than we, what we needed in that moment.

~

The Eighth Thing

Some time later, our phones alerted us that we each had a new email.

It was a video message to the members of the Incarnate Watch.

And it was from Morrigan.

I didn't want to play it, and Caden didn't want to watch it, but we both knew that of everything that happened that day, this might be the one thing we couldn't bury our heads in the sand and ignore.

He hit play.

Morrigan addressed the Watch. She spoke about Gregory and used words like *tragedy* and *sacrifice*. She used words she knew nothing about, like *good guy* and *hero*.

Most importantly, she identified his killer: the Mare incarnate. I think I felt shock that she'd surrender that information so easily.

The mortals would never know what had befallen Gregory Gregorius, but we, the members of the Watch, would know. Would stand vigilant against the Malevolent incarnates that prowled the edges of the Watch's light.

She even had the audacity to remind them that the Watchman had been our chief officer of security. And to promise that, if she won their support, she had an incarnate capable of stepping into the role.

Caden was dismayed. He'd dreamt of inviting Malevolents into the Watch, of creating unity.

I just felt numb.

Morrigan wasn't done. She requested the address of every incarnate in the Watch so she could send them talismans against the Mare —dream catchers. Saying that the Mare couldn't strike if they simply hung one of her dream catchers wherever they slept.

It was a simple ruse to get their addresses, I thought. Especially since the dream catchers didn't even work. Did Morrigan know that?

It wouldn't matter to her, I supposed. She appeared to be giving the incarnates what Caden had promised: security. It was a message inspiring trust in her leadership—communicating the events of the day, forging a path forward, and reminding the others that Morrigan, not Caden, would keep them safe.

Dream catchers, *again*. Why would Morrigan promise they'd work when they clearly didn't? Was her aim so short-term, simply to get to the next vote?

I dwelled on that for a while, staring at the wall.

Caden excused himself so he could work with Artie to follow up with a message of his own. I wanted to support him, and at that moment, I would best achieve that by staying away.

I couldn't help but think that with the Watchman dead, Morrigan had already won.

~

The Ninth Thing

I lay in bed on my side with my legs tucked up, my arms hugging them to me. I was staring at the picture of me, Caden, and Rachelle from New York—though I really wasn't seeing it.

Maybe I dozed.

At some point, I felt the weight of Caden's body sink onto the bed behind me. He settled against my back, wrapped his arms around mine, and pulled me close.

He enveloped most of my body.

He enveloped all of my soul.

I cried, then. With his breath on the back of my neck, safe in his arms, that pit inside me finally began to retch up some of my undigested emotions. They wrenched their way out of me, shaking my shoulders and making me shudder all the way down to my toes.

He didn't say anything. He didn't have to. I'd never felt so heard.

At some point, I fell asleep.

～

The Tenth Thing

I am proud *to be your friend.*
Me, too, Gregorius. Me, too.

29

"*I*'m so sorry, Em."

I found myself in a comfortable, familiar room. It was *oddly* familiar. The details were vague, but I could tell there was a hearth with a crackling fire. It emitted the idea of warmth rather than actual heat. Similarly, I sat in an armchair that gave the illusion of plush comfort, but if I focused, I came to realize I couldn't actually *feel* the soft cushion against my arm.

The Lucid. I was dreaming.

Sitting across from me was Nyx. Our chairs faced each other and had been pulled so close together that our knees were touching. I considered moving my leg to break the contact, but in my current state, it felt good to have the warmth and pressure of another person so near.

I nodded, not trusting my voice. The lump in my throat was all too real.

"I know he meant a lot to you. We'll make Morrigan pay."

"He didn't approve of you," I found myself saying. "He thought you brought chaos with you. Into my life."

Nyx smiled softly. "I do."

Here, in the Lucid, I could feel his glamour like a subtle film over the entire room. It softened his hard muscles, made him look less menacing. The room was lit only by the hearth, flickering orange and yellow light playing on Nyx's smooth cheeks.

"You do," I agreed. "And my life has enough chaos in it. More, now. Gregory was order. He brought structure into the messiness of my life."

Nyx's blink was slow, mesmerizing, and I found my eyes drawn to his lashes for some reason. Details in the Lucid were strange— they often made no sense when described after the fact, but all the sense in the world while sleeping.

"You gave him something, too, Em: spontaneity. When the best-laid plans go awry, there's no one I'd rather have at my back than you. I know the Watchman felt the same way."

His glamour tickled my nose. There were no smells in the Lucid, but my mind manufactured Nyx's scent. Of lightning, of midnight, of danger. It should've triggered alarm bells in my mind, but instead I found myself inhaling. His glamour enfolded me like an embrace, and after the day I'd had, I needed a hug.

I needed more than a hug. Would it be so bad to be held?

Something in the back of my mind tried to remind me that I'd fallen asleep that way, hadn't I?

I shook my head to clear it of glamour—and pesky thoughts. I froze, though, when I felt Nyx's hand on my knee.

"He'll be missed," he said in a melancholy tone. His hand slid a little farther, resting on my thigh. "I'm here. Whatever you need, you have my support, Em."

"Don't call me that," I said, but it was just a reflex. My words held no passion. I'd had too many strong emotions coursing through me that day to add another to the mix. Besides, this room was calming. It didn't remove or even really dim my pain, but it soothed it. Like someone kissing your wound to take away its sting. It wasn't a remedy, but somehow the pain felt more bearable.

"Of course," he said, squeezing my thigh ever so slightly. I wanted to lean into that pressure. "Anything you need."

I need to know how this happened, I thought. But the Lucid tugged at the knot of my conscious question until it unraveled.

"I need..." *To know how the Mare escaped.* Again, the thought evaporated, replaced by Nyx's intoxicating scent. The room had darkened, the fire in the hearth reduced to glowing embers. Our chairs nearly touched, and it seemed a cozy, intimate darkness. When had my legs become caught between his?

"What do you need, Emery?" he whispered. He was leaning in, and the hand that wasn't massaging my leg slid up to cup my cheek. His fingers were hot against my skin. I felt myself sink into the contact.

Nyx opened his mouth, and I watched his tongue dart out to wet his lips. "Tell me what you *need*."

I felt enfolded in his touch. The sensation of my pulse racing flushed through me. It shouldn't have been possible to be so aware of my physical body in the Lucid.

I reached up to where he was caressing my cheek and brushed my fingers against his. I felt his sudden intake of breath, saw his pupils expand as my fingertips ghosted over his flesh. I couldn't speak around the lump in my throat, but that lump was no longer wholly sorrow. "I..."

My fingers trailed down Nyx's arm, stopping at the elbow. Hadn't he been wearing a shirt a moment ago? I tried to blink away the nonsensical nature of the dream, to think logically, but I couldn't focus with Nyx so near me. He probably hadn't been wearing a shirt, anyway.

My eyes trailed over his soft, lean stomach and up his smooth chest. I could feel his hand sliding up my leg, but the moment I thought about it, the awareness flickered away like a leaf in a breeze.

I continued to draw a line up Nyx's body, taking in the soft curve of his jaw and the boyish smile he wore beneath sparkling eyes.

"Tell me, Emery," he said in a breathless voice.

I shuddered. "I..."

Boyish smile?

That wasn't right, was it?

"Yes?" His fingers trembled on my cheek with nerves and something else... excitement, I thought.

My anxiety melted back into the recesses of my mind. Nyx was trying to give me comfort in the only way he knew how. He could sense my despair, and he wanted to help me. I was sure of it.

Except...

No one would ever call Nyx "boyish."

Confused, I slid my eyes over his body again. Tender skin, slim physique. So beautiful and comfortable and familiar. But it was wrong, somehow. I marshaled my thoughts, fighting through the heavy cloud of my emotions that begged me to *stop* thinking, to just allow myself to be consoled...

Tender skin, slim physique? Nyx was all hard muscle and raw sensuality. Since when had anything about Nyx been *soft*?

He was modifying his appearance. Within the Lucid, within *his* Lair, Nyx possessed control over perception. The cozy room. My sensations. The smell.

And what he looked like. Right now, he was altering himself to look more like...

Caden.

The spell shattered. I knocked his hand away and bolted upright in my chair, breaking our contact. The flames in the hearth roared back to life, flooding the room with light.

Nyx was suddenly standing, too, his natural form revealed in the garish light from the fireplace. The silken look of yearning had been replaced with a lustful hunger. I took in his appearance, but this time with cool detachment. He stood tall, firelight and shadows playing over his slick, olive skin. He wore nothing but a loincloth, and the way the darkness pooled around him gave the impression of folded, batlike wings and a curled tail.

I wasn't just seeing Nyx. I was looking at the Incubus incarnate.

He *had* sensed my despair, but his instinct hadn't been to offer comfort or compassion. He'd mistaken my emotions for weakness and, like the predator he was, he'd chosen to pounce.

"That was your opportunity to do the right thing," I told him, my voice low. "You missed it."

"Mm, I can still help you." His voice was molten emotion: heat, fury, passion. His eyes gleamed with desire.

"You can," I agreed. I saw a wary eagerness creep into his expression. "You can tell me how the Mare escaped after attacking Matlas."

His eagerness evaporated. "She eluded me. I didn't think she could travel through the Lucid. She ran, and I pursued her." The fire reflected in his eyes. "I appear to be losing my edge."

"And she happened to escape through *Gregory's* dream?" I demanded. "Did you chase her in that direction, Nyx? I know there was no love lost between you."

He looked away. "No, Em. I—"

"Do *not* call me that."

"Why not?" he snapped back at me. "If I can't have you in the present, I damn well refuse to give up our past. You cannot erase me from your story, Protagonist. You loved me, once. *More* than once."

"So what?" I was yelling, I realized. I didn't care. So many emotions poured from that pit inside me. Some of them relevant, some not. "Even if I did, everyone is entitled to mistakes!"

"You'll make this *mistake* time and time again! You can't get enough of me! Your little angel may give you peace, make you think he's enough. *Fine.* I'll share. He can give you peace, soothe your mind. I'll take your body. Give you fire and satisfaction he can't hope to match."

"You think so little of my loyalty?" I spat.

"I don't give a shit about your loyalty. I don't even care about your body. It's just a means to an end."

"Then what the hell *do* you want, Nyx?"

"*You!* Your heart! Your love! I'll share it with that damn Guardian Angel if I have to. But I claim at least half of it."

I shook my head. "Claim? Listen to yourself. I'm not a thing to possess."

"I possessed your heart once before. You were happy to be mine."

"Because I *gave* it to you!" I shouted, and for some reason I felt like crying. "It was my choice, not yours!"

"Choice?" The word was bitter, flung from his lips with spittle. "*Choice?* You think it's my *choice* to share you with that pathetic excuse for an incarnate?"

"Careful," I growled.

His lip curled. "Screw you. I've been nothing but careful. You think *my* glamour is duplicitous? You spend so much time around Caden, you don't even see it anymore. How it curls around you, soothes your doubt, makes you see him as innocent, so damn sincere. He's *using* you. Seducing you. At least I admit it. At least you *know* when I'm making you mine."

I swung. In the Lucid, it took no time at all. I was suddenly on him, fist angling into his gut.

Nyx came in with a punch of his own. It caught me in the side and drove me to the ground. There was no real pain, but the illusion of it consumed me, leaving me unable to take a full breath.

"See?" Nyx said, towering over me while I wheezed. "I know you better than anyone. I know your every move. I know you better than he does. Rant and rail against it all you like, *Em*, but half of your heart belongs to me." I felt myself lifted to my feet, and his lips pressed against my ear. "Which is only fair," he whispered, "since you already own all of mine."

Tears slid down my cheeks, but I'm sure they were just from the imagined pain of his punch. "Nyx..."

"I'm not the cruel one here," he said softly, then shoved me away from him.

I stumbled backward several steps before regaining my balance. "I'm sorry, Nyx. I didn't understand the depth of the hurt I've caused you. I—"

I froze. Behind him, in the open doorframe that marked the entrance to the room—which hadn't been there before, I was fairly certain—was a hunched-over silhouette. A woman, with long, trailing hair.

The Mare.

She looked up at us with wide eyes, evidently surprised to find us conscious within the Lucid. In that infuriating dream logic, I couldn't make out her facial features, even though I could see her eyes dart back and forth between Nyx and me.

She spun and fled.

"The Mare!" I said, pointing.

Nyx turned and, I hoped, caught the fleeting glimpse of her retreating back. The hallway she ran down emitted too much light, a tunnel of it, so that she seemed to disappear into whiteness at its other end.

Nyx roared and flung out his hand. With a jolting sensation, the hallway suddenly flung itself *at* me and swallowed us, and I realized he was reorienting our positions in the dream to pursue the Mare.

She'd disappeared through a still-closing wooden door at the far end of the hallway, and it rushed toward us with alarming speed. It opened, and we suddenly found ourselves in a forest not unlike those found in the Pacific Northwest. Green and lush, with ferns and undergrowth choking the roots of proud evergreens.

"Where'd she go?" I asked, spinning around at every noise and crack from the forest floor. The Mare had chosen this terrain to escape us, I was sure of it.

Nyx snarled, and the skies opened. It was suddenly raining, a downpour, and even as I watched, the water hit the trees and *spattered* them like they were nothing more than a freshly painted canvas and some godly artist was pouring water across it. The greens and grays and browns of the forest began to bead and mix—first just the colors, but then the actual *trees* began to run together and wash away.

Nyx's control over the Lucid was immense. The Mare had come to the forest to hide from us, so he simply washed the woods away. I felt awed. He was so strong, so in command. An incarnate in his element.

The whole forest melted away, leaving only a field of empty grass. The snow-tipped mountains in the background remained untouched, however, and I could see the Mare's retreating shadow against the base of those mountains.

I indicated her fleeing form. "There!"

Nyx, still clad in his loincloth, coiled his muscles. Then he grabbed my hand, and we sprang forward. A single bound took us soaring through the sky, empty plains zipping by beneath us. There was no sense of wind resistance in the dream, no whooshing of air. Only motion, unsupported by the sensations it usually involved.

The Mare was loping on all four limbs like an ape, long banner of hair streaming behind her. I looked ahead to see what she was running toward and saw a tiny cabin tucked away at the base of the mountains. It looked vaguely familiar—a place I'd been? She looked over her shoulder at us and put on a burst of speed. The distance between her and the home shrank. At this rate, she'd hit the cabin in heartbeats.

We landed several paces behind her, and I dove at her ribbon of hair, trying to get a handful of it and drag her to a halt. She spurred herself forward, and I just missed. Behind me, Nyx flung out a hand, and the ground between him and the Mare simply *fell away.*

In response, the Mare leapt into the air and toward the cabin's firmly shut door.

At a gesture from Nyx, a crack in the earth encircled the entire cabin. He was going to sink the whole thing into the ground.

The Mare elongated and shrank in midair, becoming as thin as a pencil. Thinner. A razor. *Thinner.* She became a single strand of long, long hair that shimmered like a gossamer strand of a spider's web.

The cabin tilted, timbers groaning and cracking as the earth buckled around it. It was a race between the Incubus's will and the Mare's speed.

The Mare slipped through the keyhole in the cabin door just as the entire structure collapsed into the sinkhole Nyx had created. Wooden beams and immense stones crashed together, sending up a plume of dust and debris. In the Lucid, however, it dissipated unnaturally fast.

Nyx and I were suddenly standing at the lip of the pit. As we looked down into it, there was no trace of the cabin's wreckage or the Mare.

"She escaped?"

His fists clenched. "It appears so."

Silence stretched between us, then I put a hand on his arm. "Nyx—"

He shrugged it off. "Don't." He forced a smile that, even in the Lucid, looked pained. "We've said enough."

I nodded. "For now."

"For now," he repeated softly. Then he began to walk away. "Wake up. I concede this fight. We'll speak again soon. Be with your precious angel." He turned and smirked. "*For now.*"

I awoke with a start. I was in bed, my head cradled in Caden's lap. He looked down at me when my eyes opened. "You're okay?" he asked softly.

I shook my head and squeezed my eyes shut. "You knew?"

"Yeah." He rubbed his thumb across my cheek.

"And you didn't wake me?"

He leaned down and kissed my forehead. "You needed to hash things out, I think."

Tears pricked my eyes. "You still kept watch over me," I whispered, infusing my words with gratitude.

"Of course, beamish boy. Since our first night together. Now, hush. It's time to sleep."

I felt some of my tension and stress melt away. It had nothing to do with Caden's powers. At peace for reasons Nyx would never understand, I allowed dreamless sleep to take me.

I'm feeling a bit conflicted about incarnates. On the one hand, it's incredibly cool to know that supernatural beings walk among us. On the other hand, they're terrifying! I'm still sore from my time possessed by the Mare.

Worse, there's no one with whom to talk about it. Rachelle's amazing, but she doesn't seem to understand how frightening it is to have beings walking around that can snuff your life out with a snap of their fingers. I think I finally understand how an ant feels. I could just be minding my own business and then, wham, a shoe could come from nowhere and smash me flat. That's probably more literal than I intended, too, since I'm assuming the Giant incarnate is out there somewhere.

Sometimes I just want to take back my ignorance and bliss.

Don't get me wrong, it's still awesome being one of the very few mortals trusted with knowledge about incarnates—even though it really puts a damper on going to a nine-to-five job to eke out a living. Knowing what else is out there, the impact I could have on society if I had unlimited lifetimes... it's staggering.

It's also a Pandora's box—the Pandora's Box?—of possibilities: for example, does the Alien incarnate exist? If so, does that mean that life can be found on distant planets, or is the Alien just a product of speculation?

What an odd existence they lead. They must remain unrecognized, but at the same time they're the worst-kept secret in history; there are literally thousands of stories about them. And, if I understand reincarnation correctly, these stories need to remain in circulation to keep the incarnate alive. It's an entirely new level of existentialism.

~

The next morning, I harnessed my inner Gregory Gregorius. To get him justice, I needed to think like the Watchman. I had a laundry list of things to investigate, beginning with his murder. Which meant I needed to discover the identity of the Mare. And I'd be damned if I didn't reveal Morrigan's hand in his death.

Nyx hadn't been completely honest with me. After our fight in the Lucid, I was beginning to understand the depths of his feelings. Armed with that knowledge, I reconsidered the lengths he'd go to in order to win back my... affections. Today, I resolved to find out.

Caden and I sat in a conference room at E-Pluribus HQ, waiting for the others to arrive. It being a Sunday, the building was mostly empty, but Artie had secured us access. It didn't hurt that we had an in with "Micah Asker," the CEO. Sadly, the real Asker was dead, but Mikey, the Android incarnate, was impersonating him. He was currently on a break from work in order to better learn his new responsibilities but had given us unrestricted permission to use the building. I'd chosen this location today, however, because I wanted to have a conversation with Nyx, and keeping him away from our home seemed like a good idea.

We heard voices approaching, and Caden gave me a quick smile of encouragement. He'd called out of work for the next few days. To take care of me, I knew. I'd already decided to spend that time taking care of him, too.

Caden. Gregory. The Mare. Those were my top three priorities.

I was harnessing my inner Gregory Gregorius, but I was still doing this my way. I needed my friends. "I need your help, Artie," I said aloud. "Because after yesterday, I need all my friends."

"I am at your beck and call, Emery Luple," he responded from the speaker system. His tone was still a bit flat, but lukewarm was better than it had been. I suspected he was unaccustomed to feeling hurt, and thus my words had cut deeper than they ordinarily would. He was already well on his way to forgiving me, but he needed time to process his newfound feelings. So be it. With all the emotions I'd been contending with, I could hardly begrudge him his.

I'd chosen this location, in part, as an amends to him. E-Pluribus was, after all, his home.

Rachelle and Matlas entered the room. It had wood paneling on three sides, though the wall to my right included a large bank of windows overlooking the courtyard below. The final wall was made entirely of glass and faced into the building, giving us a rather boring view of empty cubicles and hallways. The glass was punctuated by whorls and frosted panels to impart a semblance of privacy to those within.

Mask, Beard, and Mittens greeted Rachelle and Matlas affectionately. Yes, we'd brought the puppies. They'd been incorrigible this morning, whining and yipping at us as we prepared to leave. Since we'd been so busy lately, neither of us wanted to leave them alone for the day again.

It was fascinating how in sync the three of them were. Oh, they separated on occasion, but it was rare. Most of the time, they didn't want to be far from one another, and whatever one of them was interested in usually attracted all three.

"Hey, pups," Rachelle said, scratching each behind their ears before settling at the conference table. "Oh, and hey, guys."

She and Matlas wore subdued expressions, somberness hanging around them like a cloud. After sitting, they turned those compassionate eyes on me. They were concerned with how losing Gregory was affecting me. I didn't want to see pity on anyone's face, but I accepted the love behind their gazes.

"I asked you here to help me find justice for Gregory," I said. My voice was too neutral, but it was the best I could manage. To lighten things up, I added, "And because I knew if I left you out of this,

Rachelle would kill me." She didn't smile. "Then wait 1,001 days and kill me again."

A tiny smile, that time. "Good," she said. "I've trained you well."

"Shall we get to it, then?" Matlas asked.

"Not yet," I said, shaking my head. I felt Caden slip his hand into mine. "We're not all here yet."

As if on cue, Nyx sauntered in.

He stood at the entrance, refusing to look awkward despite the uncomfortable energy that infused the room. Then Caden stood and gestured to a seat. "Hey, Nyx. We all just got here."

As the only people standing, the two of them drew everyone's eyes. I might have thought I'd be tempted to compare them, but evidently that time had passed. Nyx glided across the room and lowered himself into one of the seats Caden hadn't indicated, not far from me. He somehow made it look like he was casually lounging despite the rigid office chair.

Rachelle watched him with compressed lips. Matlas's eyes widened and tracked his movements the way a rabbit might watch a wolf. Caden settled himself comfortably next to me, unbothered by Nyx's presence. He didn't take my hand or wrap his arm around me, didn't make any protective—or possessive—gestures. He just turned to me and asked, "Is everyone here?"

I surreptitiously glanced at the windows on the right, behind where Rachelle and Matlas sat, to where a raven perched.

I'd texted Ray this morning and told him to listen outside the window. The Ijiraat had, for reasons unknown to me, aided me throughout the week. By inviting him here, I was extending an olive branch and hopefully returning the favor. This whole thing had begun with the death of his friend's horse, after all.

Admittedly, it was also my last-ditch attempt to get him to join the Watch.

"We're all here," I said.

Even the puppies had found spots around the room, lying comfortably, heads on paws. It may have been my imagination, but they seemed to mostly watch Nyx, too.

"I know I'm a treat to look at," he said, amused, "but are you all just going to stare, or are we here for another purpose?"

"We have a few mysteries on our hands," I said. "We're here to solve them."

"The Mare killed Gregorius," Nyx said. "There. I solved your mystery."

Rachelle rolled her eyes. "Please. That's like saying 'He was shot.' We don't know who the Mare is during the day. We need to figure that out, then take her down."

"There have been two different methods of killing," I said, trying to steer us in the direction I wanted to take the conversation. "There's a reason for that. Either the Mare is changing up the way she murders in order to throw us off her trail, or there are two murderers."

Matlas tore his eyes away from Nyx. "Two MOs. What are they?"

"Spray and Gregory were killed by having their life force drained. We know that the Mare wraps her victim in her hair and feeds until there's almost nothing left. I saw firsthand the markings on Gregory, where the Mare's locks had tightened around his throat. Jerry, however, was stabbed to death, presumably by his sleeping wife. Which is also the way the Mare tried to kill Rachelle, using Matlas."

"Were there any hair marks on the other bodies?" Matlas asked.

I tried to remember. "Not that I can recall. But I wasn't really looking for them at the time."

Nyx sat up straighter. "You think there are two incarnates involved?"

"I don't know." I met his eyes. "What do you think?"

"One murderer," he said without hesitation. Then he shrugged. "Maybe she's getting help from Morrigan, though."

He said it with such conviction, I almost believed him. Was it odd that he so quickly pointed the finger at Morrigan? Two days ago, he'd told me I needed to stop focusing on her.

Matlas was looking back and forth between us. After a moment, he ventured, "Two incarnates? I'm still learning, but could it be the same person?" He wilted a bit as everyone's eyes turned to him.

"Go on," I said.

He gave me a blink-and-you'd-miss-it smile. "Well, you said the Mare is another incarnate during the day, right? What if she's the same incarnate as the one 'helping' the Mare?"

"That would be brilliant," I admitted, "but I don't think it's possible. Not unless the Mare can shift back and forth at will during the night."

Caden tapped his fingers on the table. "It's something we shouldn't necessarily rule out, though."

"What if she doesn't shift at night, specifically?" Rachelle said. "What if she's the Mare while in the Lucid, but she's another incarnate here in the land of the awake?"

"That's a mouthful," Nyx commented. At her annoyed look, he cracked a grin. "I didn't say that was a *bad* thing."

"What if the Mare has been getting help from a dream incarnate?" I asked, watching him closely.

"Ah. So that's why you invited me. To make an accusation, or for my expertise?"

"Why don't you tell me?"

"Play nice," Caden said in a mildly reproving tone.

Nyx showed his teeth. "As long as we get to play."

"Either way, it's a lot of what-ifs. Let's focus on something you *can* answer," I said. "Nyx, why aren't the dream catchers working?"

He lifted an eyebrow. "Noticed that, did you? Calm yourselves; it has nothing to do with me. Morrigan did something to disrupt the Asibikaashi's power. Using her newfound friend, I'd imagine."

I frowned, but Caden nodded. "Hope, you mean."

"What a good and smart boy you are," Nyx said. "He *must* keep you around for your brain."

"At least he keeps him around," Rachelle snapped. "I hadn't even heard of you a few days ago."

"I don't mind being someone's best-kept secret."

"Enough, both of you," I said. Hope. It made sense. As the former leader of Vox Populi, she'd know our weaknesses and fatal flaws better than anyone. "Are you suggesting she *killed* the Asibikaashi incarnate?"

Nyx considered the question. "A possibility, but I don't think so. The Asibikaashi resides almost exclusively in the Lucid, only venturing into the physical realm on rare occasions. My guess is they did something to disrupt her flow of power."

"How would Morrigan, or Hope, manage something like that?" I asked.

"If I knew that," Nyx said dryly, "I would've done it ages ago. It effectively removed my most frustrating obstacle."

Caden shared a glance with me, then faced Nyx. "So you have an interest in the dream catchers not working."

He flashed a grin. "It worked out well for me. But I was not involved."

"Maybe it was the Sandman," Matlas volunteered. "Rachelle told me he was with Morrigan at your meeting. Morrigan might have used him to get her hands on—"

He cut off. All three dogs had lifted their heads in unison, then begun to growl. Just as when Nyx first appeared on my doorstep, their growls threaded together to create something more menacing than the sum of its parts.

"Did somebody say my name?" a thin, amused voice asked from one corner of the room.

We all spun. There wasn't even a door over there.

"That's a neat trick," I said, striving to slow my heart rate.

The Sandman's gaunt frame lent him a sense of exaggerated height. He inclined his head, sending his wispy hair swaying. "You would do well to take heed of whom you invite to your meetings, Emery Luple."

"I didn't exactly invite you," I said, keeping my tone level.

"No, indeed," he acknowledged in his threadbare voice. "Yet here I am. Two dream incarnates to answer your questions."

The dogs, picking up on my reaction and Caden's, ceased their growling. Had they done that in unison, too?

Nyx leaned forward. "You would confess your role in this? We're listening."

The Sandman's lips pulled back in a quivering smile. "Morrigan, the Protagonist, hired me to protect her against the likes of you, Incubus. Your powers over slumbering souls have no effect on those under my spell unless I permit it."

Nyx made a disgusted sound. "She needn't have bothered. I'd never stoop to seducing Morrigan. I have standards."

"You're seeking the Mare?" the Sandman asked me.

"I am. Do you know where she is?"

"Not at the moment. Last night, though, she was with the Witch."

I blinked. "In Maine?" I asked. "You're sure?"

He tented his long, spindly fingers. "I'm certain she was with the Witch, yes. Though not in Maine. In Seattle."

"What?" I couldn't believe what I was hearing.

"She's been sleeping here every night for at least a month. I cannot verify her whereabouts during the daylight." His lips twitched. "I only visit at select hours."

Sleeping in Seattle every night was pretty damning evidence that she'd been here the whole time. "Artie, how did we miss this?"

"I cannot say for certain," Artie replied with an irritated huff. "She was careful, I can see now. She went 'off the grid,' as you humans like to say. I'd rendered the probability that she'd left Maine unlikely. She didn't use credit cards to purchase airfare and has forgone the utilization of traceable electronic payments."

"Are you sure? Maybe she's using an alias."

"I considered the possibility and ran a probability algorithm to predict the likeliest pseudonyms a moment ago. Checking the top thousand results against electronic currency transactional databases." He paused. "No luck."

Well, shit.

Agatha had joined the Watch only a week ago and telecommunicated from somewhere. The fact that Artie couldn't trace the signal to a computer reinforced my theory that she was using a cauldron or some other mystical medium to communicate with us.

"I apologize. I would have informed you if I had thought the data to be relevant," Artie continued. "The statistical possibility that she would be in Seattle, no less, is exceptionally low."

Oh, Artie. He was wrong; it was exceptionally *high*. The story of the Protagonist and the Antagonist was coming to a head once again, unveiling day by day. Anyone *not* in Seattle wouldn't even be a player in the ensuing action.

"Any chance the Witch was killed and replaced?" Rachelle asked. As we all turned to her, she put her hands up defensively. "I know it's dark, but we should consider it. Her usual habits just changed overnight? Something's up."

The Sandman watched her for a moment, then said, "She is authentic."

"Okay," Rachelle accepted. Then her eyes narrowed. "Why are you suddenly Mr. Helpful, anyway? I thought you were Team Morrigan."

"I made no declarations of loyalty," he said. "I will continue to honor my deal with Morrigan, but I'm more concerned with your intentions regarding a fellow dream incarnate."

"You want to protect the Mare?" Caden asked. His inflection suggested he understood the Sandman's aims.

"If she's innocent."

She wasn't innocent. At the very least, she'd killed Gregory. But I was beginning to wonder about the others. There were too many question marks in my notebook. The Mare. Murders with two different methods. Nyx's angle. Morrigan's angle. Hope and the Sandman, both of whom had been surprisingly neutral so far. Hell, even the Ijiraat's role in all this was hopelessly unclear to me. I glanced at the raven sitting on the outside ledge of the window. He'd saved me from Morrigan and her goons in the graveyard, after he'd made it clear he didn't like me. Why had he intervened?

And now it turned out the Witch had been in town all along. Why didn't she want anyone to know? What was her game? Was she involved in all this or an unexpected ally in the eleventh hour?

"Oh my," Artie said, interrupting my thoughts. "I found more data that may be bad news."

"Lay it on us," I told him.

"In some legends, it appears the origins of the Mare—or the 'Mara' in the traditional Nordic pronunciation—are rooted in witchcraft. One mythology in particular attributes the creation of the Mare to a witch being separated from her animal familiar for too long or by too great a distance."

"Fantastic." So the Mare's and the Witch's history intertwined. The chance that she'd be a surprise last-minute ally was beginning to look less and less likely. I looked between Nyx and the Sandman. "Did you know that?"

Nyx shook his head, but the Sandman gave a thin-lipped smile.

"I need you to tell me what you know," I said. "My friend, Gregory Gregorius, was killed. I can't let anything else befall those I'm supposed to protect. Will you help me?"

The Sandman considered, his sunken eyes measuring each of us before finding their way back to me. "Judge her with a forgiving heart, Loophole," he said at last. "I will give you her loc—"

"Emery Luple," Artie interrupted, his voice quick and loud.

No, Artie. Not now. I was so close to getting somewhere with the Sandman. But I couldn't silence Artie, not after the events of the past few days. I had to trust him. "Yes, Artie?"

"Security footage from the lobby shows Morrigan has entered. And she's not alone."

I turned to the Sandman. "We were getting along so well. Why'd you have to go and invite her?"

He looked puzzled. No, I realized, he looked *alarmed*. He was either a very believable actor, or he hadn't been the one to summon her.

Caden stood, his mind a few steps ahead of mine. "Rachelle, Matlas, come here," he said. We all stood, and the two of them took a step or two closer to us. "Stay near me," he said.

"Where is the Mare?" I asked the Sandman urgently.

He looked at me, then shook his head in apology. "Better to see how this plays out, I'm afraid."

I clenched my hands into fists, and next to me, Rachelle looked ready to punch someone. *That's my girl.*

Then I saw Matlas's expression. He looked around at the gathered incarnates with fear, showing the whites of his eyes. Forcibly relaxing my posture, I turned to him. "Don't be afraid."

Rachelle looked sharply at me, then, realizing I was speaking to her boyfriend, nudged him with her elbow. "Hey, Atlas," she said.

"I'm not going fraidy-cat on you all of the sudden," he growled. He made an obvious effort to take a few deep breaths and cast the fear away. Or at least to hide it.

The puppies were on their feet, ranged in front of us, staring at the door.

Morrigan walked down the hallway on the other side of the glass wall, a good half-dozen people in her wake. They were a collection of feds in suits and police officers, all armed.

The door opened, and they flooded inside. "Oh my, what a scene," Morrigan said as she entered. Her eyes flicked about, registering each of the people at the meeting. Her eyebrow arched at the growling puppies before she met my gaze and smiled brightly. "Emery Luple. You are under arrest for the murder of Gregory Gregorius."

"It's okay," I told my friends, not fighting as I was handcuffed. The man was not gentle. "I'm innocent, we all know that. Call..." I trailed off. I'd been about to say "Gregorius." "Call the Watch," I said instead.

The man cuffing me snapped, "You have the right to remain silent." He jerked my hands roughly, leading me from the room.

"There's no way you have evidence against him, Morrigan," Rachelle said fiercely. "We both know Emery didn't do this. What's your angle?"

"Why, justice for Gregory, of course."

Hands patted me down and liberated me of my wallet, cell phone, and keys.

Seeing that the agents didn't care about her objections, Rachelle changed tactics. She took out her phone and began to record the arrest. "Emery Luple is being falsely arrested by Morrigan," she said loudly, following us as they led me toward the elevator. "No warrant, and they're not even reading him his full rights. This is a sham..." She followed us all the way down to the street level, commenting on the injustice of the situation.

"Someone deal with her," I heard Morrigan say to one of her agents.

"Morrigan," I said quickly, "I'll go peacefully, but only if you leave them out of this. They have nothing to do with me, you, or Gregory."

She considered my words, her lips quirked in the barest trace of a smile. "I do so appreciate your cooperation." I hoped that meant she was accepting my deal, but I wasn't able to find out before her agent crammed me into the back seat of a police cruiser.

From within, I watched as Morrigan spoke with my friends. The Sandman evidently hadn't followed us downstairs, but Nyx stood behind Caden and Rachelle, arms crossed, surprisingly furious. Angrier even than Rachelle. I half expected Morrigan to start smoking from his heated glares.

Even Caden's usual composure had cracked, his eyebrows drawn into angry glowers. He kept looking in my direction, as if afraid he'd lose me if I left his sight. Matlas was quiet, but I saw his eyes flitting from face to face, noting details the others undoubtedly overlooked. He even pulled out his phone and snapped a shot of the car I was in. Artie would be able to track me with the plate number, I realized. I was growing more and more impressed by Matlas's quick thinking—which he retained even while under pressure, it seemed.

The car's engine rumbled to life, and I watched my friends grow smaller in the rear windshield. We took a corner, and they were gone.

I leaned back and wondered why I felt so numb. Maybe I'd just run out of emotions after yesterday and this morning. As I sat there, a feeling of resignation settled over me. Just like that, Morrigan had won.

I had to hand it to her: she'd played her cards perfectly. First, thrusting Nyx back into my life. She'd thrown my world into chaos to distract me, to ensure I was too busy dealing with him, Caden, and my feelings to watch her with the vigilance she knew I otherwise would. Then she'd ambushed us in front of the incarnate community and stolen our support by solving problems she likely instigated in the first place. She'd undermined our authority and called our competence into question. If I'd had any hope of turning the tables on her, she'd destroyed it with Gregory's death. I'd thought her next move was going to be winning the presidency. But to also frame me for his murder?

Brilliant. Despicable, immoral as hell—but brilliant.

I didn't fear for my life. She'd arrested me with mortal agents, which reduced the likelihood I'd be driven someplace quiet and killed, my body dumped in a ditch. These were officers of the law, likely duped by Morrigan rather than knowingly working with the Antagonist. This whole thing stank of posturing, of maneuvering me into position. What I needed to figure out was whether she was removing me to keep me from interfering with her plans or placing me in the middle of a new scheme.

That...

That was *all* I needed to figure out.

For what felt like the first time in far too long, I found my mouth stretching into a smile.

Morrigan had made a mistake.

I'd been consumed by the larger picture, overwhelmed by trying to fit together the storm of puzzle pieces she'd thrown at me. I'd been incapacitated, I realized now, frozen into inaction because I'd had too many choices to explore, too many damn question marks in my notebook.

In arresting me, she'd narrowed my options to a manageable number.

I felt... peace. How ridiculous was that? I was being falsely arrested for the murder of my friend. But Morrigan's action, as aggressive and underhanded as it was, gave me something to *do*. Action was my playbook, what I excelled at. Knowing I would soon be facing Morrigan shoved away the despondency I'd been feeling since losing Gregory and sharpened my mind. I needed to be alert and ready. There was, suddenly, only so much I could control, but that narrowed my focus, making it possible to absorb any twists thrown at me, to take them in stride. For the first time since I'd pulled back that sheet and seen Gregory's face—no, earlier than that; since Nyx had shown up on my doorstep—I felt like me.

So Morrigan had arrested me. She'd accused me of a murder she likely orchestrated herself. She'd ambushed me, had me handcuffed, and was now having me driven to a destination unknown.

Bring it on.

I knew the smart thing would be to start constructing counter-measures in my head, but I found myself not wanting to overthink. Even though I should be plotting loopholes for what Morrigan had in store for me, I was *tired* of thinking, of trying to outsmart her. I wanted to *outplay* her. She undoubtedly had a contingency for every possible outcome, but that was kind of my point. I wasn't Morrigan— and that was a good thing.

The Mare's identity. Hope. The Asibikaashi and her dream catchers. The Sandman and his mysteries. Nyx and the million feelings he invoked. Winning Caden the presidency of the Incarnate Watch. The Witch and why she was in Seattle. Amara's horse, Spray. Why the Ijiraat saved me. Susan and Jerry.

Gregory.

I put them all in a file in my brain labeled "Tomorrow's Problems... If I'm Still Alive."

A short time later, we arrived at a two-story building that looked renovated rather than modern. The car's door was opened, and I was escorted into the facility. The glass door proclaimed the building to be the Pacific Detainment Center. It reminded me of a courthouse, with security monitors and locks on the heavy oak doors. The floor was tile, the windows were barred, and I had to walk through a metal detector before being brought before a clerk so engrossed in his work that he didn't immediately notice our arrival.

"Hey, Carl," the agent at my elbow said, "We're parking this one in the director's room."

Carl blinked, looking up at us. His thick glasses magnified his eyes, giving him an owlish look. "I need to book him first."

The other agent with us stepped forward, depositing my items— including my ID—in a tray on the counter. "Start the paperwork. The director was quite clear."

Before Carl could object, the two agents escorted me through another door and past rows of mostly empty cubicles. Rounding a corner, we came to a locked wooden door with no discernible difference from the others, except for the nameplate in red—the others had been a subdued brown.

MORRIGAN ANAND.

The door was unlocked with a code, and we entered, no fewer than four agents guiding me toward the back where another door—this one replete with a sliding viewport—had to be unlocked. Behind this was a private prison.

It was a converted area, having originally been two conjoined offices by the look of it. The wall between them had been torn down, elongating the space, and thin metal bars added to define and separate the cells. Each of the three had a toilet, a rudimentary sink, and a portable cot. There wasn't much space, but otherwise the cells weren't half bad.

I was placed in the middle one, the door was locked, and I was left alone. The voices receded once the door was closed, and as the minutes passed, I began to wonder if they'd even left anyone to watch me.

More minutes ticked by. I say that metaphorically, because there was no clock and my phone had been confiscated.

I stretched as best I could, then paced the small cell. I investigated to the best of my ability. The toilet reminded me of something you'd find on a plane, the cot was sturdy and well-made if a little stiff, and the sink was operated by a foot pedal, but the water pressure was actually decent. I spotted several security cameras in the ceiling and in the corners where the ceiling met the wall. They gave no indication that they were on.

My biggest complaint was... *boredom*. An hour or maybe longer slid by, and my wrists chafed against the metal.

Finally, I heard a code being entered on the other side of the door, and then Morrigan herself walked in.

She wore red, the color I usually associated with her. At least, this incarnation of her. Whether that was her favorite color because it was the color of blood, I wasn't certain.

She hadn't come alone.

Hope stood at her shoulder, white-blonde hair tied back into a ponytail, wearing combat fatigues and a black tank top. To blend in with Morrigan's other mercs, perhaps. Of which there were two in the room, dripping with weapons. Not her federal agents, these guys.

That wasn't all. Two others, obviously incarnates, had shuffled in behind Morrigan and Hope: the Pirate—immediately recognizable by his eye patch, beard, worn coat, and skull-and-crossbones *pirate hat*—and a woman I couldn't immediately place. She had dark hair tipped in bright blue, dyed to match her striking eyes. Her skin was rough and dry, textured not like flesh but like barren earth. She was also holding up a phone, recording the encounter.

"I do hope you're comfortable," Morrigan said. "This is hardly my favorite place to play the role of hostess, but I must admit that seeing you behind bars lifts my mood."

"We both know I didn't kill Gregorius, Morrigan. He was one of my closest friends. So, what's your angle?"

"Oh, very good. We're streaming to the Incarnate Watch, Emery. I promised to provide them with some entertainment."

Who did she think she was messing with? I had my own internet show. "Hello, friends," I said to the camera. "I don't know what 'evidence' she manufactured, but I assure you I'd never harm my friend." To Morrigan, I said, "Release me and I'll prove it."

"I'm afraid you won't find many friends on the other side of this stream," she said. "These are the members of the Watch you haven't had the opportunity to meet yet."

A chill went through me. Had she really recruited so many to her side already? Enough to swing the vote in her favor? More?

"Say hello to two of them. The Pirate and the Rusalka."

"I regret we couldn't meet under better circumstances," I said. I'd had several run-ins with the Pirate before, as it happened; my mind threatened to pull me into a memory or two, but I shoved the sensation aside. Now wasn't the time.

The Rusalka incarnate was a different story. I knew *of* her, but we'd never met. She was another sea incarnate, sort of a cross between the Mermaid, the Siren, and the Nymph.

If Morrigan had more incarnate allies, as she was implying, why bring just two, I wondered. Two of the people with her right now were mortal mercs; if she had recruited other incarnates to her cause, why not bring them instead? My eyes narrowed. Could it be a ruse? Everything with Morrigan was smoke and mirrors, right up to the smoking gun.

"You're bluffing," I said, injecting confidence into the words. "Congratulations on finding two new incarnates. What a feat. I'd clap my hands, but, well, they're a little tied up at the moment."

Morrigan's dangerous eyes glittered at me. *Careful, Emery. Don't get too cocky.* "There's the witty banter they all came for. Bravo." She leaned forward. "Unfortunately for you, I'm dead serious about my new friends. Including the little birdie who told me where you and your friends were meeting."

Little birdie? *The Ijiraat.* What the hell? Why had Ray saved me in the cemetery just to turn around and stab me in the back? What was his part in this?

I put the question into the folder in my brain. A problem for Tomorrow-Emery.

Morrigan turned to the woman at her side and addressed the phone's camera. "You've seen that I can deliver on my promises. I've detained the Loophole. I have weight and value with the authorities. As your president, you would have these resources at your disposal. Think on that, while I have a private chat with the Loophole."

She nodded to the woman. The Rusalka lowered the phone, blew me a kiss, and left the room, the Pirate going with her.

At a head tilt from Morrigan, one of the mercenaries stepped forward and said, "Step up to the bars and turn around. I'll remove your handcuffs."

I raised my eyebrows. I recognized him from our tussle in the cemetery. The skinny guy, the one I hadn't been able to tase. "Just like that? I'm free to go?"

"You're free to have your hands back, if you step up to the damn bars."

I didn't need to be told twice. Well, I didn't need to be told three times, I guess. I felt the metal click and twist on my wrists, and then they were finally free. I rubbed them, unhappy at the deep grooves the metal had left in my flesh.

"Leave us," Morrigan commanded.

"You're sure?" the man asked.

"Hope will stay with me, and we're on camera. I'm the Protagonist, and he's behind bars." She turned cold eyes on the man. "And if I ever have to explain a command to you again, it'll be to explain why your tongue is not a prerequisite for this job."

He saluted quickly, and the mercs disappeared through the back door.

"Say what you will about Vox Populi," Morrigan said to Hope, "but at least they follow orders without remark." While she spoke, she fished something out of her pocket. My phone. She held it out to me.

"Enter the password, then hand it back to me."

I didn't reach for the phone. "Why?"

She looked pointedly at Hope, who pulled her handgun from her holster and handed it to Morrigan. Morrigan took the gun with a gracious, "Thank you." Then she calmly raised it and pointed it at my forehead.

"My security cameras do not have audio capabilities," she informed me, "and are not transmitting live footage. Take your phone, or get a new one in 1,001 days. The choice is simple."

It wasn't an idle threat. Morrigan would shoot me just because I'd scorned her. And she'd doctor the evidence later to cover her ass.

I took it, unlocked it, and handed it back to her. I glimpsed that I'd received a text from Rachelle, but I didn't see more than HANG IN THERE before Morrigan snatched it away.

"You see?" she said with a smile. "That wasn't so difficult." She handed the phone to Hope. "Check it."

I stood there awkwardly, doing everything in my power to ignore the gun aimed at my head while Hope leisurely went through my phone, not speaking for two full minutes. Then she shrugged and said, "Nothing but a text from Rachelle. No coded message. His photos, apps, and the rest of the text chains are conspicuously missing."

"The Artifact's doing, no doubt. No matter." She considered me. "Let's not be rude. Text Rachelle back."

I felt a spike of alarm, but I swallowed it back down. Artie was undoubtedly overhearing our conversation. He'd make sure Rachelle knew that the text came from Morrigan, not me.

"What do you want it to say?"

"Unum, give Rachelle our current address and extend an invitation to come visit Emery. He's feeling lonely."

"It won't work," I said quickly. "Rachelle won't—"

"Oh, I think she will. Brave, that one. But too young and impetuous to appreciate the difference between courage and recklessness." She paused. "Unum?"

"Sent."

She nodded at Hope, who tossed the phone on the ground. I winced at the crack. Then Hope ground it beneath her heel.

She took her time. My phone was reduced to a crushed pile of glass, metal, and plastic in minutes.

"Now that no one can overhear us," Morrigan said as if nothing had happened, "I have a proposal for you."

"A proposal? To do what?"

"To solve our problem, of course. The Mare."

I didn't give her the satisfaction of showing my surprise. "She works for you," I said, as if it were the most apparent thing in the world.

"Obviously."

I couldn't quite contain the barest hint of a reaction at how readily she'd admitted that. Her slow smile told me that she'd seen my surprise, too. Shit. "Clean up your own messes."

Morrigan considered that response with a cocked head. Then she nodded. "Very well. I'm only here as a courtesy to Nyx. I'll inform him of your decision to remain incarcerated."

"Why would you owe Nyx anything?" I knew the answer. I knew it, damn it, and I asked the question anyway.

"For his role in distracting you, of course."

I refused to give her the satisfaction of asking if they were working together. "I'm not distracted now. Even bringing Rachelle here won't be enough to throw me off the scent. I know you have the Asibikaashi."

Her eyes twinkled with amusement. "So my pet's been talking? I'm hardly surprised—he'd tell you anything to ingratiate himself."

"I know where you stashed her."

"An empty boast. We both know I'd hardly trust him with that information."

"I didn't need him, Morrigan. I figured it out on my own. I must admit, creating a prison to which only the Protagonist and the Antagonist have the key is genius. Too bad you can't use it to lock *me* up."

"I see someone has been using his head for a change. Congratulations."

I glanced around my prison cell and spread my hands. "Thank you for providing me with the time and space to meditate. A mistake Nyx wouldn't have made. I can't believe he'd stoop to work with you."

"What can I say?" Her mouth widened into a smile that exposed her teeth. "I made him an offer he couldn't refuse."

"Then make me a similar one."

Her eyebrows shot up. "A willingness to negotiate? Pinch me."

I folded my arms. "Make me an offer, or get out. I don't have time for this."

Morrigan looked around the cell and then cracked a laugh. "Oh, kitten, you've gotten rather good at this. Reminds me of some of our greatest adventures together. Clever repartee, swashbuckling, gunfights, traps within traps, and at the end of it all: the *climax*. You and I, together—though, admittedly, not always for the epilogue."

"You want to solve the problem of the Mare in order to look like a hero in front of the Incarnate Watch."

Morrigan shrugged. "A perk, certainly, but nothing more. As I've already demonstrated, I have the vote in my pocket."

Assuming she wasn't lying. I refrained from narrowing my eyes, trying my best to think furiously but give no outward indication that I was doing so.

She'd set the Mare loose in Seattle before the Watch voted, setting proverbial fires that she could then extinguish. She wanted my help to capture the Mare and parade her victory in order to appear a hero to all. Why did she need my help, though? There was more to this. Winning the Watch was too simple. Too *small*. Even with Gregory's death—not an insignificant feat—to relinquish her weapon when we still didn't know the Mare's identity was foolish.

I was missing something.

"Why do you need my help?"

The gleam in Morrigan's eyes told me that I'd asked the right question. "I don't."

"But...?"

"But you're more use to me alive than dead."

I wasn't sure I believed her. She wanted me pliable, willing to help her in her quest to find the Storyteller, a man whom she mistakenly believed was our shared father. But she was infinitely patient, and if my current incarnation proved too much trouble for her, she'd certainly be willing to wait 1,001 days for a weaker, more amenable version.

I shot her a flat look. "All right, I'll bite. What's your plan?"

Morrigan reached through the bars and patted my cheek. "Good boy. I knew you'd see reason." It was so fast and so unexpected that I didn't even get a chance to knock her hand away. "You'll stay in this cell tonight and sleep while I watch over you. You and Nyx will lure the Mare to your dream and force her into the physical realm, where her powers are weakened."

"Why my dream? Are you too cowardly to face her in the Lucid yourself?"

"Despite our temporary alliance, I do not trust the Incubus to adequately protect me while I hunt her in the Lucid." She lifted one eyebrow. "But we both know he won't let any harm befall you."

"All right," I hedged. "But we can at least do this somewhere more comfortable than a cell."

Morrigan was shaking her head. "When you force her out of your dream, she will appear here, in the physical realm. A cell is the perfect place to ensure she cannot escape."

As usual, she'd thought of everything. "You can't honestly expect me to go to sleep while you're in the same room. I know the difference between brave and reckless."

"Color me skeptical. Regardless, it's nonnegotiable, I'm afraid. Someone needs to wake you when the Mare is in the cell, to prevent her from escaping back into the Lucid through your dream. And it must be me on the camera, so the Watch understands this was my plan."

I shook my head. "You're losing your edge if that's your best attempt at persuasion."

Hope laughed, a bitter sound. "I told you, Morrigan. We're going to have to—"

"I know." Morrigan sighed, massaging her temple. She inhaled sharply through her nose. "Very well. I'll permit your Guardian Angel to watch over you. Nyx in the Lucid, Caden in the physical realm."

I snorted. "Lock up both me and Caden? Forget it."

Morrigan stared at me. "I'm being more than reasonable. I have no ability to hold him here, and we both know it."

"You have no right to hold me here, either, yet here we are. Caden stays out of this."

"You underestimate your friends' distrust of me," she said with a flicker of annoyance. "If I don't invite him, I'll need to devote my entire team just to keeping him out. You cannot hope to understand the paperwork and cost associated with that. One way or another, I suspect Caden will end the night in this cell. I'd have that be on my terms, if possible."

"What makes you so sure the Mare will even fall for this trap?"

"Oh! Did I forget to mention? You're her next target, Emery. The arrow has already been released from its bow, so to speak." She glanced down at her ostentatiously expensive watch. "One way or another, you have three hours until the Mare is here."

"Ah."

"Like I said, I prefer things on *my* terms."

*A*t least two hours passed while I sat in that cell, my jaw aching from clenching it. I'd accepted Morrigan's deal, and, in exchange for my telling the Incarnate Watch that she'd found the way to defeat the Mare, she'd free me.

We both knew she probably didn't have much choice, since the evidence would exonerate me in the end. But I had no doubt she'd make my life hell in the meantime, and I wasn't *entirely* convinced she couldn't create enough evidence to seal my fate, if provoked.

The only thing I'd insisted on was that Caden not be involved. The idea of Morrigan and Caden alone in the room while I slept, unable to intervene if she turned on him, gave me the shudders. Caden's powers of protection were incredible, but he lacked the ability to guard himself. It wasn't his fatal flaw, precisely, but it was an exploitable weakness.

In order for Morrigan to accept that part of the deal, she'd made me record a message—on Hope's phone—for Caden, informing him of my decision and pleading with him not to storm Morrigan's complex tonight. Knowing it might hurt him, but hoping he'd understand, I'd told him that Nyx was with me and he'd keep me safe. I cringed at the idea of Caden thinking I'd chosen Nyx over him. In truth, I was simply more willing to throw Nyx into harm's way. Especially after discovering he'd been working with Morrigan all along.

In the end, I would have to accept the ramifications of my message.

Even if Caden was furious with me. Even if he hated me. Even if...

I took a deep breath, surprised at how morose I felt. I was being ridiculous. It was *Caden*. He'd understand.

I heard the sound of the code being entered at the doorway, but wrapped up in my own mind, I didn't immediately register it.

"You look deep in thought," a voice said from the doorway.

I looked up, surprised. It was Rachelle. "You don't have to sound so shocked," I said. I stood. "What the hell are you doing here?"

"Nice to see you, too." She stepped up to the bars. "You seriously volunteered for this? A plan of Morrigan's? Did you hit your head or something?"

"I'm confident Nyx and I can handle the Mare."

She swatted me on the arm. "I'm not worried about the Mare, you jerk. You're going to be *sleeping* in a room with no one else in it except Morrigan." *Don't remind me.* "If you die..."

"I know, I know," I said, striving for a light tone. "You'll wait 1,001 days and then kill me."

"Damn right." She gave me a hard look. "Don't do that to Caden."

"I don't plan on it."

"Do more than that. Don't let it happen." She reached through the bars to give me a hug, speaking quickly, voice hushed. "I have a plan to help. Nothing like a jailbreak. Just know you've got someone watching over you."

"Don't do anything rash."

She stepped back and said, "Me? Never."

I thanked her. "Rachelle, have Artie contact the authorities immediately if you're not allowed to leave these premises."

She rolled her eyes. "Like I'd come in here without a plan? Please. I'm not *you*."

I grinned, and we said our goodbyes.

Another hour must've passed, because someone was putting in the door code. It was showtime—

"Hey, Em."

My heart nearly jumped out of my chest. "What are you doing here?" I demanded.

"We need to talk," Caden said, entering and closing the door behind him.

"You know I didn't choose Nyx over you, right?" The words just spilled out. Must've been bugging me more than I'd thought.

He hovered beyond the bars, looking down. "Of course I know that."

"You're mad because I took this choice away from you?"

"I'm not mad." He still didn't come any nearer.

"Then what?" I asked, feeling unnerved. The way he was standing there, nervous, was making me far more worried than anything else that had happened today, and that was saying something.

"Em, I'm—" His voice shook and he looked away, obviously fighting tears.

I stood there, the thin bars feeling more like a gulf between us. My heart was in my throat. What was wrong?

"I'm *terrified*," he said, his voice breaking. He surged forward and held the bars, shaking.

I reached out and wrapped my arms around him as best I could. "Hey, now," I whispered. "It's going to be okay."

"Is it?" He swiped at his face. "Em, you're going to be completely at Morrigan's mercy. You think she's not going to kill you? There'll be nothing, no one, to keep you safe. *I'm* the one who would stop her. Me. Your Guardian Angel. Why won't you let me?"

I rubbed his back soothingly, worried at the tears that shimmered in his eyes. "This trap might not be just for the Mare," I said.

"Which is exactly why—"

"It could be a trap for *us*," I said gently. "Morrigan doesn't want me dead, she wants me broken. Compliant."

"She'd never be able to break you."

"There's one thing that would do it," I breathed.

His expression softened for a moment. Then he stiffened. "So you get to protect me, but I'm not allowed to protect you?"

He had a point. "What would you do if the roles were reversed?"

"What would *you* do if the roles were reversed, Em?" He reached up and cupped my cheek.

His glamour coaxed truth from those he questioned. Armed with that knowledge, I could fight it. But I'd learned over the last several months that I had no reason to. I loved him, and while I was entitled to my privacy, I'd found no reason to outright lie to him.

Now, for the first time since New York, I found myself questioning. Nyx's words about Caden manipulating me flitted through my consciousness unbidden, unwanted. *Was* Caden unaware of the way his glamour affected me? Or did he sometimes use it to... encourage things to go his way?

I tried to shove Nyx's traitorous words away. Trust was a round-trip flight. And as far as I knew, Caden had always been honest with me.

But you can't know for sure, can you? Nyx's voice whispered. *His glamour makes him look so innocent.*

Caden looked away. "It's okay. You can lie. I might, if it meant saving your life."

But the tears were back, unshed and bright.

I'd endured the psychological horrors of the Thirteen Steps to Hell. I'd resisted seduction by the Incubus. I'd banished the haunting eyes of a past lover, murdered in front of me. Cast off the trauma of three lifetimes.

I could not survive the anguish in Caden's eyes, knowing I caused it.

"If it was within my power to keep you safe, nothing would harm you while I stood watch." He met my eyes, the stirrings of hope behind the tears. "I don't always have that power, Caden. But I have it now. I can keep you safe." My own eyes felt hot. "Please let me."

"I can't just sit at home while you're in danger. Don't ask that of me."

"If you step into Morrigan's trap, we could both be killed."

"I can take care of myself, Em."

"*So could Gregory!*" I said it too loud, my voice cracking. "He could handle just about anything, but we lost him anyway. *I* lost him. I can't go through that again. Not with you."

He leaned his head forward, able to partially squeeze through the bars and rest against my chest, his hair brushing my chin and mouth. He stayed like that for a time, quiet. My heart decelerated back to a normal tempo as I stood there with him.

"This might be our first fight," he mumbled at last. "And I don't know how to resolve it." He pulled back to look up at me with a stubborn expression. "I'm not willing to just give in. The stakes are too high."

"I wholeheartedly agree with you." I released a short, frustrated laugh. "What a weird fight."

"Should we... compromise?"

"I've heard of that. Supposedly it's a mythical solution to maintain peace in relationships."

I was holding him close, trying to convey my love and fear in a single embrace. I felt his shoulders bob in response to my words. "Mythical, huh? The Compromise incarnate?"

"I'm listening."

"We do this as we've done everything else. Together."

"That's... not really a compromise. That's just a rephrasing so you get your way."

"There's a reason the Compromise is mythical, Em."

I sobbed a laugh. "I love you. But you need to leave."

He shook his head. "If we die," he said, very softly, "we do that together, too."

"She won't kill me. She wants me alive. And she wants the presidency; killing me would cost her the vote."

Caden grabbed my head and forced me to meet his eyes. "I would give up the presidency in a heartbeat if it meant you'd be safe. Don't you dare talk about becoming a martyr."

"If something happened to me, you could find me in 1,001 days, you know. You aren't mortal. You wouldn't forget all about me."

He shook his head. "What if you come back as a toddler? Or married and in love with someone else? We found each other in this lifetime because we're *meant* to have this lifetime together. I believe that."

"Good," I said, trying for a smirk and unsure of my success. "Then there's really no reason for you to worry about tonight, is there?"

Since his hands were still on the sides of my head, he pulled me down into a kiss. "I love you," he said against my lips. I tried to reply, but he was just too proficient at kissing. "And I really hope you'll forgive me."

"What?"

"Visiting hours are over," Morrigan said from the doorway. "It's too late, Emery. The Mare is here."

I ground my teeth together. "Then I'll refuse to go to sleep."

"You won't." The thin voice preceded the Sandman as he glided into the room. He flung his hand forward, and an explosion of powder hit my face, expanding outward in a cloud. "Sweet dreams."

Everything began to fade, my vision narrowing to Caden's anxious face. He'd caught me, I realized, and was lowering me to the cot. He must've slipped into the cell while I was reeling from the Sandman's attack. "I'll watch over you," he promised, brushing a lock of hair from my forehead. "Just like our first night together. Now hush. It's time for sleep."

*M*y eyes opened slowly.

I was in a meadow, cushioned by wild grass. I could hear water burbling gently nearby, and the smell of jasmine hung like silk in the air. I sat up, the movement requiring no effort, and looked around.

The clearing was gilded in moonbeams and starlight, petals and seed fluffs dancing gently in a breeze I couldn't truly feel. The deep, dark sky held an infinite swath of glittering stars that bathed me in their soft illumination. To my right, a small waterfall fed a stream that circled three-quarters of the meadow, the brook a sparkling ribbon beneath the glow of the moon.

I knew this place of eternal bloom. It was *our* place, a place that shouldn't exist, a place that could only exist within the Lucid. A Sanctum and a Lair, fused.

The expected silhouette drew my attention.

The Incubus rose from where he'd been lying on his back atop a bed of vibrant blue coriander flowers. He stretched like a cat, the moonlight sculpting his perfect muscles. I expected to feel his glamour teasing my flesh, tugging on the strings of my desire, but I felt nothing. Before me was simply a beautiful man, nude, tempting me only with the memories of our time spent here together. Fond, guilty, blush-inducing memories.

Not a man. The Incubus, his olive skin a deeper, almost rust-bronze hue. Flushed with heat, his eyes twin embers, his body inhumanly flawless. He'd come to me as himself. No glamour. No tricks.

Just Nyx. The person I'd loved, once.

I drank him in. Had he begun with this, days ago, perhaps it would've worked. Perhaps I would have convinced myself that sex in a dream wasn't *really* infidelity, not a betrayal of the guy I loved. I'd like to think I would have resisted, but I'll never know.

Right now, all I could think about was Caden. He was alone in that cell with *Morrigan*. All I cared about was catching the Mare and returning to him. I couldn't give Morrigan the time to act or to think. Caden was probably still holding me in the physical realm, watching over me while Morrigan watched *him*. Would she uphold her end of the deal? I knew she wanted the Incarnate Watch, that she would use the capture of the Mare to accelerate her plans. What I didn't know was whether that was the extent of her scheme.

Even if it were, would she be able to resist taking advantage of our vulnerable position? Even if she intended to honor her bargain, she might change her mind when she realized what I'd already come to understand: we were defenseless, completely at her mercy. She could kill us both, right now, with barely any effort.

Then she'd have 1,001 days to scheme without worrying about our interference. Could she let this moment pass? I—

An arm snaked around my waist and another over my shoulder, muscular limbs that glowed softly in the bright night. I hadn't even seen Nyx move, but this *was* the Lucid, and things sometimes happened in stilted moments rather than as a seamless sequence. He was now standing behind me, and he pulled me back against his body, his scent filling my nostrils and sending a wave of goose bumps down my arms despite my resolve.

"Remember this place, Em?" he whispered in my ear, his breath tickling my cheek. "We could make new memories here."

Ignoring his naked body took more concentration than I'd thought it would. I couldn't blame his glamour, this time. In this place, buried somewhere deep in my subconscious, I could admit that I was attracted to him. That he roused feelings in me I only felt around him.

That didn't make me the monster I thought it had, as long as I stayed true to Caden. I loved him, and I wouldn't betray his love. All else was immaterial.

"We will," I promised him, gently removing his hands from my body and stepping out of his embrace. Turning to face him, I said, "We'll make new memories right now. A friendship. And it begins with an alliance created for an unlikely goal: you and me, teaming up to save Caden."

I saw him flinch, though he tried to cover it up with a self-deprecating smile. "Does our place mean nothing to you now?"

"We've had this conversation, Nyx," I said, sighing. "I want us to stop hurting each other. Let's put the past where it belongs: a memory we both think of fondly." I placed a hand on his shoulder and saw the surprise and longing in his face when my hand touched his naked flesh. "Help me catch the Mare and keep Caden safe. We can remain in each other's lives. You can join the Watch and be a part of building a future for all incarnates. The Protagonist, the Guardian Angel, and the Incubus: a team-up for the ages. I could learn to love you again, as a friend."

"As a *friend*," he repeated, flatly. My hand suddenly gripped cloth, his nudity vanishing beneath his modern-day dark jeans and tight T-shirt. Like he'd donned armor. I could feel him trembling under my hand. "I would rather be your enemy and your dirty little secret than a *friend*."

I shook my head in frustration, pulling away from him. I didn't have time for this fight right now. "Why are you unable to accept any other form of love?"

"It literally sustains me, Em. I'm starving, and you're flicking me crumbs."

"If all I do is hurt you, then maybe you're right. Maybe all we'll ever be in this lifetime is enemies. But the choice is yours."

He looked up at the expanse of stars, his face raw with the pain of rejection. "Why do you have to make this so hard? The problem isn't you and me. I've been waiting for you to realize what I already know: it's *him*."

"Caden?"

"*Stop saying his name in our place!*" he snarled, the stars and moonlight flaring red. Emotions often changed perception within the Lucid, where natural law succumbed to passion. As I watched, his shadow grew and contorted, reflecting a winged creature with a wickedly barbed tail. Nyx himself, however, remained unaltered.

The space between us had grown, and I couldn't tell whether that was a product of the Lucid or I'd taken a few involuntary steps backward.

"You need to release your hatred of him," I said, striving for calm. "*I'm* the one who hurt you, Nyx. If you must hate, then hate me."

"I've tried," he said icily.

I didn't know how to respond to that. "I'm sorry."

"Those words mean nothing to me," he said, face darkening.

"They're all I have left to offer." I took a step forward, stalks of grass and soft flowers tickling my bare feet. "Change this place. We need a fortress, a place the Mare can't escape. A room with only one door, or a courtyard with a moat and portcullis. Something like that."

A flicker of guilt passed over his features before he buried it beneath his cool façade. "No."

I took another step closer. "I'm not messing around, damn you. If the Mare escapes, we might never be able to lure her back into a trap."

"I know."

I threw my hands up in frustration. "You're turning on Morrigan, is that it? She was unable to deliver the reward she promised you, so you're going to let the Mare go free?"

He lifted an eyebrow. My mounting desperation seemed to amuse him. "What makes you think she's unable to deliver?"

I stared at that arched brow feeling powerless and helpless—and furious at both. "Because I'm not going to change my mind!" I snapped. "My heart is not for sale." We glared at each other from only a pace away. Then I looked away in disgust. "Fine. When the Mare comes, I'll fight her alone. I'll find a way to keep her from escaping."

"You'd help Morrigan?"

I spun back around. "Yes. If it will stop the Mare from murdering more people, I'll help her." *If it will help me get back to Caden, I'll help her.*

He stared at me for a few long moments. "The Mare isn't coming."

I went cold. "What do you mean?"

"I mean she isn't coming to attack you. Nor is she coming to seek your aid, like the other night. She isn't coming *at all.*"

"Seek my—" I couldn't seem to form a complete thought.

The Mare had shown up in my dream and seemed shocked to see us in the Lucid. I'd assumed she was surprised because she'd been expecting to find me sleeping. But if what Nyx had said was true and she'd been seeking my help, there was only one reason she would flee: because she'd seen *him.*

No, that didn't make sense. Why would she come to me? How could she think I would help her—even *listen* to her—after she'd killed Gregory? Unless...

No.

Unless she *hadn't* killed Gregory.

I was suddenly grateful I was in the Lucid. In real life, I'd be having trouble breathing. Even so, the air around me seemed to thicken in response to my strong feelings.

The Watchman had been drained of his essence. If the Mare hadn't done it...

Oh, god. No, no.

I raised my eyes from the ground, slowly meeting Nyx's reddish-brown ones. The night sky had swallowed most of the stars, and heavy clouds rolled in front of the moon. The waning light deepened the winged shadow behind Nyx, the stark contrast thickening the shadow until it seemed more real than his physical body.

"You killed Gregory?" My question came out as a whisper, but it seemed to crack like thunder between us, electrifying the meadow.

"I'm sorry." Then his lips twisted into a bitter smile. "See? The words don't mean much, do they?"

I screamed. The pit inside me opened, and all my grief poured out in an avalanche of agony and loss. Of betrayal.

Of hate.

I rocketed forward, propelled by my emotions. Chunks of soil and clumps of grass tore up and into the air behind me. I closed the space between us and clutched at the collar of his shirt, balling it in my fist, jerking him viciously. Our noses nearly touched. *"Why?"* I roared. My voice reverberated with layer upon layer of emotion made manifest in the Lucid.

Nyx's nostrils flared, and though he didn't move, his shadow suddenly unfurled its wings. I felt an invisible weight against my chest like a physical blow, and I was hurled backward. I tumbled through the clearing, sending petals and blossoms scattering.

I stayed there, unable to get up, crushed beneath my emotions and whatever force Nyx was exerting.

"Why?" I asked again, voice ragged.

"I was hungry."

With a bitter cry, I pushed through the force and rose shakily to my feet. "You're a monster," I spat.

"Love scorned makes monsters of us all."

I was buffeted on all sides, caught in a storm of feelings. As weird as dreams could be, they often made an illogical kind of sense. In the Lucid, my repressed emotions had taken on a form of their own, tearing at me like shrieking winds. I knew I could stop it—they were *my* emotions—but a part of me wanted to surrender to them, to let them carry me away. I'd repressed them, and they'd grown stronger in their prison.

Nyx watched me with folded arms, half in shadow, half in light. He was cruelty and compassion. Anger and remorse.

He'd killed Gregory.

How could I forgive him? How could he think I'd *fall* for him after that? His deal with Morrigan made no sense.

The winds ceased abruptly as realization stole over me. I stood frozen, my emotions crystallized into ice by my train of thought.

It made no sense.

"Nyx." Dread welled in the pit of my stomach. "What did Morrigan promise you?"

He nodded as if he'd been expecting the question, guilt heavy in his eyes. "Caden."

34

"**W**ake me up!"

He shook his head unhappily. "No."

"You can still do the right thing, Nyx. Please!"

"I *am* doing the right thing," he growled. "Soon you'll be free of his manipulation, the twisted way you think of him. You'll thank me when your mind is clear of his bewitchment." He said the words with passion, but there was a tremor of uncertainty beneath them. Like I wasn't the only one he was trying to convince.

Maybe I could've exploited that if I'd had the luxury of time. I didn't. If Caden died, I might find him again after he reincarnated, but all the unique things I loved about him in this lifetime would be gone. Maybe I'd fall in love with the new Guardian Angel, but it would be like falling in love with someone else—a stranger.

Morrigan and Nyx had worked together to orchestrate this play, to maneuver Caden and me into vulnerable positions on a pretense.

"Nyx," I whispered. "Morrigan is likely to kill me, too."

"She won't," he said firmly. "She needs you alive."

"She needs me *broken*."

He softened. "I won't let her hurt you, Em."

"Killing Caden will do more than break me," I said, desperate. "It'll shatter me completely. Help me, Nyx! Don't let her do this. Don't be a part of it."

Emotion roiled in his eyes. "If something happens to you, I'll be here to pick up the pieces."

Even if he wasn't intentionally stalling, I felt like I was wounded and bleeding time. I'd tried to handle this the right way. Now, I'd handle it *my* way.

I poured my anxiety, love, and desperation into the Lucid. I knew some tricks to control the dreamscape, though I was nowhere near as proficient at it as Nyx. My emotions shimmered into a physical manifestation. A simple wooden door appeared in the meadow, like something you'd draw while playing Pictionary.

All I had to do was walk through it, and I'd wake up.

I took a step.

The door wrenched to the side, then shot into the sky like some giant's invisible hand had plucked it and was now holding it, suspended, thirty feet in the air.

"I'm sorry, Em," Nyx said from behind me. "I can't let you leave yet."

Fury flashed through me, but I pushed the emotion out of my chest and into the Lucid. The clearing began to rumble, the ground rippling. An enormous staircase tore out of the earth at my feet. I began to scramble up the steep incline before it was even fully formed, each step taking shape beneath my foot as I raced up toward the floating doorway.

I moved with a speed I wasn't sure I possessed in the physical realm. The doorway loomed closer as I ascended each step. I could make it!

The doorway stopped getting closer.

I continued to rush up the stairs, but the doorway stubbornly refused to get nearer. *What?* I stopped for a moment in surprise, and I fell farther away from my destination. Nyx had turned my stairwell into a down escalator, the steps tumbling away into the earth below. It felt like a nightmare where you knew you *should* be able to get away, but your feet just stopped carrying you forward.

With a roar, I leapt from the staircase, angling for Nyx. If I could distract him long enough, perhaps I could surprise him and escape. It would only take a moment.

I soared through the air, slamming into him with crushing force. He crumpled beneath me with a gasp. I should've followed up my attack, but I was a little stunned I'd managed to jump him in the first place. I'd seen him move faster than a blink in the Lucid. Either he was more distracted than I thought, or I was better at controlling the Lucid than either of us expected.

He squirmed beneath me, pinned. He tried to gain leverage by tugging ineffectually at my legs. I maintained the pressure, surprised at his lack of strength. Then it dawned on me that time spent grappling with him was time spent *not* racing for the doorway. He wanted to keep me in the Lucid, and I suppose he didn't care how.

With a curse, I leapt off him and sprinted across the meadow. Pumping my emotions into the Lucid again, I abandoned the doorframe hanging in the air and created a new door. As it shimmered into existence, it looked like the front of our townhouse.

Something snaked around my ankle and jerked me backward. Before it could drag me too far, I reached out and snatched the door handle. I was suddenly horizontal in the air, stretched out between whatever had my ankle and my grip on the door. I looked back over my shoulder and saw that I'd been lassoed with something like twine. It should have dug unbearably into my leg, but pain didn't work normally in the Lucid.

My muscles protested as I poured all my energy into pulling myself toward the door. I didn't budge an inch.

Furious, I summoned a blade into the hand not gripping the door handle and brought it down, severing the line. I fell to my knees in the soft grass. Springing to my feet, I turned the handle.

It didn't turn. It was... locked?

"Looking for these?"

I spun to see Nyx standing across the meadow, jingling my keys in his hand. It was absurd. This was *my* doorway, and the only thing standing between me and consciousness was a house key?

And the Incubus.

The blade in my hand shimmered into a set of keys, and I rammed one into the door triumphantly. But as I turned it in the lock, the key became glass and shattered.

I hadn't truly expected it to work, but I used my mounting frustration to create a loophole back to consciousness. Doors didn't have to *look* like doors. A manhole appeared beneath my bare feet. I created it without its cover, so I fell through it immediately.

Bye, Nyx.

I jolted to a stop, my feet splashing in cold water. Looking down, I saw he'd changed the manhole into a puddle.

Loosing a wordless cry, I darted back across the clearing, reaching Nyx in a blink. He still held out my keys tauntingly, and I was certain he expected me to make a grab for them.

Instead, I aimed a punch at his face.

He sidestepped the blow. Faster than thought, faster than lightning. Much, much faster than me. But he'd done this last night, when I'd swung at him and he'd dodged my punch. Then, he'd countered with one of his own.

I wasn't *that* slow of a learner. I caught his wrist as he drove his fist toward my gut.

Time seemed to stand still.

This exact sequence. It wasn't the second time I was experiencing it, it was the *third*. In Matlas's apartment, when I thought I'd been fighting the Mare inside Matlas's body.

It hadn't been the Mare at all. It had been Nyx the whole time.

Matlas's words popped into my mind like fireworks. He'd thought he'd been fighting her, but he'd really been fighting *me*.

Oh, shit.

I dropped Nyx's hand and backed away, eyes widening. When I'd tackled him earlier, when he hadn't resisted—had that been because I'd actually tackled Caden? Had I just thrown a punch at my angel?

An acidic thought scorched me: how fitting for Morrigan to watch me kill Caden myself.

Nyx cried out and rushed me, trying to reengage. I put up my hands to ward him off, but I didn't fight back. He slapped me across the face, but the sting was ephemeral, a thing belonging in a dream rather than the real world. I refused to retaliate, so he began throwing himself at my fists. I shoved him away, cringing as I considered the superhuman strength Matlas had displayed during our fight.

Had I just sent Caden flying through the cell?

Damn it! The Lucid twisted natural law, and apparently that was enough to augment attributes in the physical realm. I wasn't sure whether it was some sort of supernatural transference of energy or whether it was something simpler, like tapping into unused reserves of adrenaline. I didn't care. I needed to get away.

Nyx lunged at me, and I recoiled. He fell on me and pummeled me, trying to provoke me into fighting back.

I didn't know what to do. If I fought Nyx, I'd hurt Caden. If I didn't wake up, Morrigan would finish him off herself. Was she watching from outside the cell, mocking Caden even as I slept?

I needed something to distract Nyx long enough that I could create a doorway. But what?

"Give up, Em," Nyx said, his voice rough with emotion. He tried to smack himself with my fists, and I was forced to pull against him. We wrestled in the most bizarre anti-fight I'd ever been in.

I didn't respond, desperately trying to come up with a plan. In the Lucid, creating anything with sentience was extremely unpredictable. Just like in dreams, imagined people and creatures didn't often act in logical ways. If I created an ally, they could become my enemy just as easily. I was already struggling to *not* fight one foe—I didn't think I could manage it with two.

"You're in *my* element."

He was right. But...

"Sandman!" I cried.

"Submit, Em!"

Tears leaked out of the corners of my eyes. "I can't."

"Did somebody say my name?"

I nearly sobbed at hearing that reed-thin voice.

"Leave us," Nyx snarled. "This doesn't concern you."

"You were hired to protect the Protagonist from the Incubus," I said, trying and failing to roll out from under Nyx without shoving him off me. "*I'm* the Protagonist! Morrigan lied to you. Help me, please!"

The Sandman didn't immediately respond, and I couldn't see him to gauge his reaction. I funneled my mounting frustration and terror into the Lucid, and my emotions manifested as webs of roots and vines. They slithered over Nyx and pulled him off me, holding him back. I scrambled to my feet.

Nyx made a gesture, and the vegetation entangling him puffed away into smoke. He lunged at me again.

The Sandman was suddenly there. He didn't move like a man; he moved like a thundercloud, robes and black cape billowing around his bony form. "Go!" He met Nyx midleap, the Incubus roaring his rage as the two dream incarnates collided like forces of nature, a thunderclap flattening the grass and sending blossoms tumbling through the air. I braced myself, arm in front of my face, as the concussion washed over and through me, threatening to knock me off my feet.

Actually...

I let go, and my feet left the ground. I rode the invisible shock wave back toward my door, the one that looked like my house. Fueled by my feelings, it expanded and grew into the townhome's garage entrance, but I directed my will into it and omitted the garage door itself so Nyx couldn't keep me from dashing through.

The meadow shrank as the mouth of the garage rushed to meet me. This time, I *would* make it. *I'm coming, Caden!*

I wouldn't be too late. Morrigan expected me to sleep for hours.

I'd wake up, I'd protect Caden, and he'd protect me. We'd walk out of this alive, the same way we always did: together.

From behind me, I heard a shout, but even if Nyx had won his fight with the Sandman, I'd made it.

As I took my first step across the threshold, I slammed into something hard and unyielding—a physical barrier that hadn't been there a moment ago.

Nyx. He'd just *appeared* between one blink and the next, as though he could be wherever he wanted to be.

A howl tore from my throat. My momentum carried me into his chest, and I caught at him out of reflex, then rebounded off him.

I stared at his chest in horror.

Somehow, as he'd materialized in front of me, he'd also placed a knife in my hands. A saw-toothed blade the length of my forearm.

And it dripped crimson blood.

I'd slammed into him, unknowingly plunging the blade deep into his chest. Into his heart. Then I'd rebounded, still holding the knife's handle—so that its serrated edge had ripped out of his chest, leaving a horrifying, ragged wound.

In the physical realm, that wound would be pumping blood all over the cell.

Here, in the Lucid, there wasn't even a stain spreading across his thin, partially shredded shirt.

Nyx stared at me as the Lucid began to collapse at the edges of my vision, as consciousness pulled me, finally, awake.

"I'm sorry, Em," he said.

Now, after all my efforts to return to the physical realm, I shied away from it, wanting to stay here in the Lucid. Wanting to never awaken. I knew what I would find when I did: Caden, bleeding out on the floor.

As I woke, I heard a woman's quiet sobbing growing clearer. I heard ragged gasping. I felt the slick handle of a knife in my fingers. I hadn't had a weapon in the prison cell, but Morrigan would've put one in my hands.

I was looking down at my feet, the Lucid and the physical realm overlapping for the briefest of moments. Then the meadow was replaced with the tile from the cell, a crimson puddle spreading at my feet, staining my shoes and the floor.

Through my tears, I looked up to meet the dying eyes of the boy I loved.

orrigan.

Morrigan.

I looked up and met her wide, surprised eyes.

She crouched within arm's reach, of course, bent over the ground, paying no attention to the lifeblood flowing out of her and pattering on the tile. She just stared into my eyes, drawing short, ragged, shuddering breaths.

I experienced a moment of surreality. Surely I was still dreaming. The Lucid must've manufactured this vision, placed Morrigan in front of me. That's why she was gushing red all over the floor—it was the color I'd always associated with her. Those kinds of details only happened in dreams, didn't they?

I was frozen. I was still frozen when she leaned forward with a willpower I'd never witnessed before. When she whispered, gasping, the last words I'd ever expect: "You've got mail."

Then her lips twisted into a hideous smile. Her face was leached of its color, making her scarlet lips stand out vibrantly, indecently vivid. "Bravo."

She collapsed.

Not Caden. Morrigan.

I'd killed Morrigan.

I felt a wave of relief, followed by a surge of anger. As the blood pooled on the tiles, I couldn't stop thinking that it had almost been Caden.

A wave of guilt at my relief caused me to stumble. What would Caden think? I was the Protagonist, his hero, damn it. Even if she deserved this death, I needed to be a better person. I needed to help her.

That thought finally thawed me. *Caden.* He could heal her. She'd lost so much blood, but his powers were magical. I leapt to my feet and spun, looking for him. My movements were jerky and frantic, emotions coursing through me. *It had almost been Caden.* That had been Nyx's plan all along.

My eyes alighted on Caden, still in the cell. But what I found, my mind didn't immediately make sense of.

He'd taken my position on the cot. He was unconscious, on his back, arm draped over the edge and dangling to the floor. Sitting on his chest was a withered creature, more hair than woman. Her long, colorless locks spilled over Caden, wrapping him like bandages across his chest, waist, wrists, and throat. Her shoulders convulsed with sobs, low keening sounds escaping her as she wept.

Panic drove me forward to inspect Caden, terrified I'd find his body emaciated beneath her.

He appeared healthy, though his eyes roved beneath his closed eyelids as if he were in distress. A nightmare.

I understood, then. The Mare was keeping him sedated. Morrigan hadn't left anything to chance: I would've murdered him in my sleep, and Caden, trapped by the Mare, couldn't have fought back or protected himself.

My blood went cold. That's what had happened to Jerry and Susan. They had been a test run.

The knife was still in my hand, and I leveled it at the Mare. "Release him." My voice was iced fury.

She responded immediately, the tendrils of her hair writhing as they retracted from Caden. She withdrew to the corner of the cell, trying to stay away from Morrigan's body.

I tossed the blade on the tile, ignoring the loud clatter and the Mare's flinch. I leaned over Caden and shook his shoulders. "Wake up, Caden. I need you."

He didn't stir.

"Caden!" I said, shaking him a little harder. "Wake up!"

Nothing.

I spun on the Mare. "What's wrong with him? What did you do?"

The pitiful creature shook her head. "Nothing," she said in a dry, raspy voice. Now that I had a clear look at her, she didn't resemble any of the female incarnates I knew. Her features were sunken and skeletal. She looked more like the Sandman than anyone else.

"Why won't he wake up?"

"I sat on his chest," she said, ducking her head. "Keeps them under. But he'll wake in time. Before morning."

"That's not soon enough!" I looked back at where Morrigan lay. "She'll never make it."

The Mare tried to hunker into herself. "She's already dead."

I stared down at Morrigan's blood coating my right hand. I didn't want to be a murderer. Not *this* Emery. I liked myself for the first time in lifetimes, and I didn't want to be stained with blood. Not even hers. "No."

That wasn't it, though, not really. The red wave seeping across the floor had almost been Caden's. The blood on my hands—it could've been *his*.

His sleeping face was almost too still. In that horrible cell of death, it was too much.

The emotions inside me towered, threatening to topple. Horror at the bloody mess. Terror at almost stabbing the man I loved through the heart. Overwhelming relief that I'd killed someone else—*anyone* else. Disgust that I could feel *relief* at murdering someone, even her. Hatred for what they'd done to me, who they'd made me become— Morrigan's killer—and far worse, who they'd *almost* made me become.

Caden's killer.

A sob. Mine?

This was Nyx's fault. Right? I hadn't intended to kill anyone. Didn't that matter? Didn't that mean something?

Nyx.

His fault.

I stared at the body—the corpse—on the floor. It wasn't Morrigan. *Morrigan* was something alive, something vivid. A hateful force, but always, always animated.

I'd killed the spark in her eyes. I'd taken that, the force that made her who she was. And I'd almost taken it from Caden.

I retreated into myself. Felt other Emerys' minds wake.

Nyx. It was *his fault.*

Emerys flooded from the recesses of my subconscious, pouring forth in a torrent of past minds. They fought and scrabbled and rolled over and into one another, blending into a fusion with a singular goal: find Nyx.

His fault.

This was channeling on a whole new level, pain and emotions blessedly washed away on a tide of other Emerys.

We had bloodstained keys in our hand. Blood was so warm. It pulsed with something almost alive, the closest thing to Life incarnate. Ironic that it so often accompanied death.

A knife was in our hands.

I hadn't intended to kill Morrigan. An errant thought. We'll carry your pain. Put the blame on him. And then, on *us*.

A gun. Morrigan's. Loaded.

The cell was unlocked.

Having gotten through the building, we found ourselves scanning the mostly empty parking lot, gun tucked into the back of our waistband. Our knife no longer dripped blood, but it was still bright red in the light from a nearby streetlamp.

We would be strong enough for present-Emery. We'd killed before; we could do it again. It was best done with respect, true, but sometimes your enemies didn't give you that opportunity. We'd had to kill Morgan and Morrigan before, and they'd ended our life, too. Present-Emery killed Morrigan, but present-Emery was more concerned with justice than pragmatism. That was good. We envied those who could afford ideals like justice. We'd fought, we'd *killed* in days past so that one day we could hold such ideals.

Who are you? I thought.

The voice was meek, afraid. We understood. We were always here, always watching. Always accessible for moments like these, able to lend our knowledge or our skills. Today, we would lend our strength.

There, across the street, was a car. Someone was in the front seat.

Nyx.

We are justice in motion. We could be that for him.

We stalked across the parking lot, unsurprised when the car's headlights flared to life.

Options skittered across our minds, a storm of analyses. Steal the car in the parking lot and give chase. *No keys.* No problem. No, lure him back later. He'll come back to us, and we'll be waiting. That'll take too long. You cannot stop the momentum of justice. Call the police, set up a barricade. License plate number? Vehicle make and model? Yes, we've memorized them; call law enforcement. Then what? No, we must get vengeance. *Justice,* you mean.

Too many voices clamored in our head.

The engine roared to life as we considered. A moment later, it sputtered and died.

Engine problems? We smiled. How convenient.

Our face contorted. Some of us wanted to keep smiling. Some of us wanted to shake our heads in amusement. Some of us just wanted this over with. Some of us wanted to warn Nyx to run—but they were quieted by the majority.

Only helpful Emerys, please.

Nyx—it had to be Nyx—tried the engine again, but it refused to turn over. He abandoned the car, opening the driver side door and bolting.

We watched him flee through compound eyes with overlapping minds.

Shouldn't we let him go? We loved him, once.

He's a Malevolent.

So?

He took away our choice. Killed our enemy. *Killed*, period. He's a monster.

We hunt monsters.

We tore after him, impressed with the fitness of this body. We reached his Mustang and leapt onto the vehicle's hood, the Incubus's fleeing silhouette but one more quarry in dozens of hunts.

We could ride him down like we had the Ceryneian Hind, but we'd need a horse. This Mustang would not suffice. Should we give chase and wrestle him to the ground as we had the Rakshasa when he'd bolted from his Territory?

No, think of the Ghoul in Ipswich. Ah, yes. We hurled the knife at his retreating form with a precision born of several minds.

The knife sank into Nyx's right calf, and he crashed to the ground in a spray of bark and earthen chunks.

We hopped off the car and began stalking him. He cursed and struggled back to his feet, limping away. He was as resilient as the Revenant had been, we thought with respect. Several of us, unhappy with our willingness to employ such violence, had retreated back into the recesses of Emery's mind. Good. We couldn't afford dissenters.

The Incubus was hop-skipping away from us. We snapped the handgun up and fired. Thunder cracked through the night, and the bullet tore through his left leg. Nyx, predictably, collapsed.

Even our most aggressive incarnations didn't relish violence. We would not draw this out, wouldn't torment him. We would dispatch him and get justice for Morrigan. *And Gregory.* Yes, yes, Gregory. *Susan and Jerry, too.* Who? It didn't matter. We were claiming justice for all of them, and most importantly, for ourselves.

For me?

Of course.

We made it to where Nyx sat on the ground, grimacing in pain.

"Em, I'm sorry," he said. There was no real pleading in his voice, just misery. "When the hell did you get so good at—"

He cut off as we raised the gun to his head. We were three feet away. We couldn't miss.

"Channeling?" he asked, softly.

He thought he knew us so well!

Doesn't he?

Nyx nodded slowly. Eyes never leaving ours. "I can see it. Only you, yet I feel like I'm being stared down by a crowd."

Our finger was on the trigger, but we watched him. Would he say something to try to save himself? To explain his actions?

Do we care?

I do.

He looked meek, huddled there on the ground. We had loved him, many of us. Some of us despised him, but that was a form of passion, too. He was impressive, we all had to admit. He'd taken a knife and a bullet and barely so much as winced.

Our finger hesitated on the trigger, the gun still pointed at his head.

Could we really kill him? To end his life would be a tragedy, to take such beauty from the world. To extinguish a spark so bright, so lovely, warm and—

His glamour. He was clouding our senses. He sought to manipulate us.

We squeezed the trigger.

hunder detonated, resounding through the night.

We stared at Nyx.

A bullet hung in the space between us, caught in a curtain of light.

"Please don't hurt him," a voice said. Taking our eyes from Nyx's astonished face, we saw a young, blond man standing with hand outstretched.

Caden. Our angel.

Protecting *him.*

"Emery, you aren't yourself. Come back to me." His words settled around our shoulders like a physical weight, a command as much as a plea.

He was using his glamour on us, too.

I don't care, a group of us railed. *He doesn't do it to harm me.*

Naivete. Doing the right thing was hard. It required a depth of conviction. We would be Emery's strength.

"Emery," Caden tried again, his voice softer. "Don't do this. Don't become a monster on his account."

Nyx muttered something, but it was lost as we considered.

"I am not a monster," we said, struggling to get the words out of a mouth that, despite being empty, felt stuffed with marbles. No, not marbles. Voices. That was it: there were too many voices. "I *hunt* monsters," we managed.

"Sometimes. But it doesn't define you." He took a step toward us. He was weak, we saw. Barely able to stand.

We could use this.

Our eyes were intent on his, but our arm hadn't wavered from where it held the gun, aimed directly at Nyx's head.

Backlit by his own luminescence, Caden's seafoam eyes seemed almost to glow. "You're the Protagonist. You're my hero, remember?"

Yes!

"Why do you seek to stop me?" we grated. "He kills without remorse." We felt guilt. But we were strong enough to stomach it.

"Killing him will destroy you, Em. Killing isn't an acceptable answer. Life is too precious to snuff it out simply because his actions offend you. You know that." His voice dropped to a whisper. "Please. You aren't a murderer."

"Morrigan."

"You didn't kill her," he said firmly, stepping nearer. He was only a few steps away, now. "Nyx killed Morrigan. He'll answer for his crimes. But not like this."

"This is *right*."

We expected tears, but while his eyes were bright, his face was calm, his voice resolute. "It isn't. Em, you told me a few days ago that the right choice isn't always the easy one. Don't take the easy path. Resist it."

Easy? Killing the Incubus was not easy. His death would weigh heavily on us. We understood what was lost upon each death. We understood it better than anyone. We were dead already, the lost returned for but a brief moment. We'd given up our lives so that present-Emery could exist. So many personalities, so many minds ground to pulp to fertilize the ground for the current incarnate.

We knew the sacrifice.

That was why we knew Nyx must die. He'd lived in this incarnation for hundreds of years. This incarnation did not hesitate to kill to achieve his ends.

Maybe the next one would.

We fired three more times. The barrier rippled with shimmering light, stopping the bullets inches from Nyx's wide-eyed face. The barrier dimmed each time.

"*Emery*," Caden pleaded, "stop. The Incubus is under my protection. But I came here to protect *you*." His voice broke on the final word, and the jagged piece of it pierced our soul, like it was meant for us alone.

"Me?" we asked.

Me.

We were conflicted. Caden was our angel. We trusted him more deeply than anyone we'd ever known before.

"I can't maintain this barrier much longer," Caden said to Nyx, back in control of himself, eyes not leaving ours. "You need to flee."

Nyx gave a caustic laugh. "Not an option."

"This isn't Emery. Nyx, you know that."

"Why do you care?"

The Guardian Angel didn't answer immediately. "Because Emery cares for you. He sees something good in you."

"He's mistaken."

We tended to agree.

"No," Caden whispered with the barest shake of his head. "He's not wrong. I wish you could see the light in yourself that he does."

We wanted to believe Caden's words. But it felt like every time we opened our heart, it bled.

Nyx made a rude sound. "Just let him kill me."

Caden's face hardened. "Not an option," he echoed.

Better not to feel at all, we decided. Better to channel, to let others shoulder our burden for a time.

I don't believe that, do I?

Yes, we did. We were strongest together.

Caden took our free hand in his. "I love you."

"I love you, too." That hadn't been hard for us to say. With Caden so close, this was our opportunity to remove the barrier of light that protected our quarry. Dozens of different ways to attack sprang to our minds. We could end this! We could even do it in a way that left our angel unharmed. Why did we hesitate?

"Come back to me. Be my hero. Be *you*."

We expected tears. All we saw was determination and love. But we knew him too well; we saw the unshed glimmer in his eyes, saw the pain he tried to bury beneath the calm exterior he projected. We saw through the glamour, saw through the Guardian Angel. To Caden.

We had endured the siege of Troy. We had resisted the Siren's alluring song. We had led armies into unwinnable wars and emerged the lone survivor. We had undergone trials at the hands of the gods, survived dozens of assassination attempts, and battled endlessly with the Antagonist.

Through it all, we had survived.

We could not survive the anguish in Caden's eyes, knowing we caused it.

Like a dream receding from a waking mind, the horde of Emerys retreated, leaving only one, emotionally drained Emery at the forefront.

Me.

I lowered the gun, surprised at how much my arm ached. Did I feel no pain when I was channeling?

Caden smiled at me, face softening. "Hey, beamish boy." Then his eyes rolled up, and he collapsed.

I caught him as he stumbled and fell. He'd been tapping the dregs of his reserves, apparently. He groaned as I lowered him to the ground, his eyes flickering half-open. "Nyx," he mumbled. "Need to heal..."

"Oh, for the love of sin," Nyx grumbled. "Is he always this obnoxiously helpful?"

"He just saved your life," I said quietly. I couldn't keep the edge out of my tone, though. I was still furious with him. No, "furious" was too gentle a word. He'd murdered Gregory and nearly killed Caden. Right then, I still thought he deserved the execution I'd almost delivered. Not for Morrigan's sake, but for Gregory's.

"I didn't ask him to."

I was silent, cradling Caden against me. The only sign that Nyx was injured was his slightly heavy breathing. He ripped strips of cloth from his clothes—which didn't really alter the shredded appearance of his outfit—and created tourniquet-style bandages for his legs. Then he sat back.

"I know it's not worth anything, but I *am* sorry."

I didn't answer. I'd seen his remorse in the Lucid. I knew he felt guilt.

It just wasn't nearly enough.

I sighed. "You saved Caden, didn't you?"

He looked at me. "What makes you say that?"

"He was helpless. The Mare had him pinned down." That wasn't really the reason, though. It was the surprise in Morrigan's eyes before she'd died. The shocked look of someone who'd lost a game they'd been certain they'd already won.

And Caden's words. That there was good inside Nyx. He was wrong about me being able to see it, though. That was the Guardian Angel's superpower, not mine.

Nyx shrugged. "It would've destroyed you, Em."

I nodded. "I'd get someone to look at those legs."

I stood, gathering Caden in my arms. He was heavy, but I'd have managed it if he'd been made of lead. He sleepily wrapped his arm over my shoulder, and that helped. I cradled him to my chest, his head resting against my heart.

Then I headed back toward the parking lot.

"Emery?" Nyx called after me. "You didn't ask why I killed Morrigan."

I know. I didn't want another reason to hate him right then. And I especially didn't want another reason to start forgiving him. Worst of all, I didn't know whether I'd be able to handle it if he said he'd done it for me.

So I did what I should have done the first time he'd shown up and every time thereafter.

I walked away.

Caden woke up as I parked the car. Luckily, he'd had his keys on him, so I hadn't had to go back into the building and see the corpse of my nemesis. I'd let the mortals find her body and trust my Protagonist powers to keep things in check. Even if it made a horrible scene, they'd forget about her shortly after. The mysteries of the Protagonist and the Antagonist did not remain in the minds of mortals after our deaths.

I suspected the Mare would've already been gone, but I wasn't in any hurry to see her again, either.

"Where are we?" he asked quietly, looking out the window. "The cemetery?"

"I have some unfinished business."

He sat up. "Not alone, you don't."

"I appreciate it, but it isn't necessary for you to come with me. Stay here and rest. I'll be back in a few minutes."

I could see the argument behind his eyes, but he must've seen something in my face, because he nodded and rested his head back on the seat. A few moments later, he was snoring softly. Maybe he hadn't seen anything after all. Perhaps he just needed rest.

I got out of his car, taking his phone with me. He'd left it in one of the cup holders, and I could only assume Artie had alerted him that my phone had mysteriously gone off the grid, prompting Caden to leave his behind when he entered the facility.

"Artie," I said as I walked into the graveyard.

"Emery Luple!" The voice that greeted me was far cheerier than my somber mood and surroundings. It felt like balm on a wound, though. "I must confess, I feared the worst. Are you... well?"

I snorted, unsure how to answer that. "I don't know, Artie. But I will be." I reached the first flight of steps and descended to the second level of the graveyard.

"I am pleased to hear you say as much."

"Artie, will you please inform Rachelle and Matlas that I'm fine? We'll pick up the puppies in an hour or so." I hesitated, then said, "Tell them Morrigan is dead."

"They undoubtedly already know about Morrigan," Artie said. "I'm more than happy to pass along the entirety of your message, however."

I came to a stop on the grass. "How would they already know about Morrigan?"

"The live feed, of course."

I felt my heart skip a beat. "What live feed?"

"The one from the security cameras. Rachelle told me she informed you of her plan to stream the security footage to the Incarnate Watch in order to ensure Morrigan upheld her end of the bargain. I was able to establish the connection before you fell asleep."

"And you streamed it, live, to the Watch?" I asked incredulously.

"Indeed. Just as Rachelle Grey instructed. Did I misunderstand the mission?"

I felt my heart sink. "No," I said. "Morrigan said the cameras weren't live."

"Indeed they were not, initially, but they still backed up data to a server. I was able to connect to that and change the core functionality of the security tapes. I must admit, however, that I do not understand everything I witnessed. Why did Caden Malek fall asleep and remain so despite your attempts to wake him?"

"Because the Mare was..." I trailed off. I began walking again, if for no other reason than to vent my frustration through motion. "Artie, did you see the Mare?"

"I have not been successful in locating her, no."

"I meant in the room, on the security camera. Did you see her?"

"I'm sorry, Emery, I don't know to what you're referring."

I'd suspected as much. Nonhuman incarnates rarely showed up on camera or any other form of technology. To the members of the Watch viewing the footage, it would have appeared that Caden fell asleep of his own accord... and I'd stabbed Morrigan without any provocation.

Damn it! Somehow, Morrigan had spun the trap Rachelle had set for her. Her Antagonist powers at play, no doubt, turning the tables even after she'd lost. Now the whole Watch would think I'd murdered her.

You did.

No, I told myself. *Nyx* did. I needed to forgive myself. I—

I wasn't ready to.

That was okay. Time was something I had in abundance, now.

I walked the rest of the way in silence, arriving at the Thirteen Steps a few minutes later.

After my fight in the Lucid, the clearing seemed ordinary. Even when the fog came rolling in, unnaturally thick. I shrugged off the sense of dread that told me I'd entered a Malevolent's Lair and pushed through. Unlike the last time, when I'd followed Morrigan and Hope here, the Steps were open.

"I was wondering which one of you would come," a voice said.

I flinched. I hadn't seen the figure sitting on a rock on the edge of the clearing.

"What now?" I asked, my voice hard.

"Peace," Hope said, raising her hands to show she wasn't armed. "I don't want any trouble."

"Why are you here?"

"I'm waiting, obviously."

"I can see that. But what are you waiting *for*?"

"You, apparently." She sighed and shook her head, white-blonde hair brushing her shoulders. She seemed more natural now, more like the commander and leader than the simpering woman who'd served Morrigan. "You're the Protagonist, aren't you?"

I watched her for a few long moments. Then I shrugged. "I am."

"Well, shit."

For some reason, I found that funny. I laughed, a cracked, mirthless sound. "Sorry to disappoint."

"In some ways, I'm relieved."

"How so?"

"Morrigan stood for everything I despised as the leader of Vox Populi. Manipulative and arrogant, with no regard for human life. If she was the *best* of your kind..."

"The Protagonist is not the best of our kind," I said, a bit too defensively.

Hope grunted. "I didn't expect you to be humble. Our experience together taught me otherwise."

"I'm not humble, Hope. I'm flawed. I'm just wise enough to know it."

She weighed me with her eyes. "That makes you wiser than many."

"Are you here to keep watch on your prisoner?" I asked.

Hope's eyebrows arched. "Not quite. The prison itself was, as you can imagine, sufficient." She sighed. "You probably won't believe me, but I came here as penance. A form of self-flagellation, as it were."

"This place terrifies you." It wasn't a question.

"Yes. But not because of the nightmares. Not because of the torture. This clearing scares me because it is a place of transformation for me. Change terrifies me more than anything else in this world. Especially when it challenges all I've ever held sacred." I was surprised to hear raw emotion in her voice.

"You expect me to believe you've turned over a new leaf? A 180-degree about-face, just like that? After countless lifetimes hunting me and my kind? *Our* kind?"

"No." She was staring beyond me, seeing something I couldn't have, even if I'd turned around. She was looking into the past—and, maybe, just a little bit into the future, too. "I don't even believe it myself, so how can I expect anyone else to believe it for me?"

I considered that for a moment, then inclined my head. "If you want to start believing it, if you want to make amends to those you've wronged, then join the Watch." I knew it was what Caden would say. I'd think he was naive for trusting her, but trust had to start somewhere, didn't it? Oh, I'd keep an eye on her, keep my guard up. She'd fooled me utterly last time, and I wouldn't soon forget that.

It wasn't forgiveness. Not really. But it was the seed of reconciliation, and right then, I needed to believe that someone out there deserved it.

Heh. I hadn't started with the low-hanging fruit, had I?

"I won't be offended if you don't accept the offer," I added. "As long as you don't go back to your old ways."

"There's no going back," she said. "Besides, I don't think I'm able to be so far from my Sanctum." She indicated the clearing.

Sanctum was absolutely a stretch, but I didn't point it out. "I'm going to release her now."

She nodded and stayed where she was, contemplative.

I stepped up to the Thirteen Steps to accomplish what I'd come here to do: free the Asibikaashi incarnate. I'd realized after our conversation at E-Pluribus that Hope and Morrigan had done something to disrupt the flow of power between the Asibikaashi and the dream catchers. If they hadn't killed her, I reasoned, they must have captured her. Since she resided primarily in the Lucid, they'd have to have found a way to prevent her from returning, to keep her locked in the physical realm.

Wherever Morrigan and Hope had originally stashed the Asibikaashi hadn't been working, which explained my dream the night before Morrigan arrived at the Watch. I'd seen a black spider swallowed by a crow. That had been the Asibikaashi trying to tell me that she'd been taken by Morrigan. The next day, Morrigan had scoped out the Thirteen Steps, and it had taken me a while to piece together why. It wasn't until I'd been stuck in the cell for hours, given nothing but the opportunity to think, that I'd realized I hadn't had another dream. The Asibikaashi hadn't been able to send me another one the following night, the same night Morrigan had visited the cemetery.

Morrigan had realized if she locked an incarnate in the Thirteen Steps to Hell, they'd be trapped, because only two people held the "key": the Protagonist and the Antagonist, the only incarnates known to be capable of opening the Steps. I thought the Asibikaashi had even tried to warn me about the Steps, having placed me on a tower in the dream, where I fought to get to the stone hatch and the steps beyond but was unable to before the crows—Morrigan—swallowed me.

Maybe I was looking a little too deeply into the metaphor. After all, that would mean the Asibikaashi had at least some power to glimpse the future.

I stepped up to the lip of the stairwell.

As I looked down into the staircase, thirteen steps descended, ending in a blank wall. On the top step, like she was waiting for me, sat a fat black spider.

"You're free," I said.

I received an imprint of emotion as a response. It was powerful, and alien in the way it surged through me. It forced all other feelings from my head, then put new ones directly into my brain.

Gratitude. In my mind, I saw the unfurling appreciation of a plant receiving water and sunshine. *Peace.* An ocean of tranquility. I saw a mountain's contentment at being stone, standing tall, its peaks majestic. I gasped—it felt like *ages* since I'd experienced peace.

"The Thirteen Steps didn't even faze you, did they?" I said.

Mirth. I saw the burbling of a playful stream. I found my mouth stretched wide in a smile, and the sensation lingered even after I realized that the spider had disappeared.

Back to the Lucid, I guessed. The Asibikaashi incarnate was more than a spider, of course, and more than most incarnates. She was the reflection of a sacred being, which made her nearly a deity, offering peace and protection at night.

I stepped back and away. Then, feeling better than I had in a while, I began to pick my way out of the clearing.

"Is Morrigan dead?" Hope called after me.

I hesitated. "Yeah."

"Nyx killed her?"

I turned, pleased that the sensations of peace hadn't fled entirely. "Something like that."

Howdy, y'all.

The week's been stressful on all of us, I reckon. After watching that video, we weren't sure what to think. Rachelle told us to hold our horses, that everything wasn't what it seemed, but I've got to be honest: there wasn't a whole lot of room for interpretation.

We saw the Sandman put Emery to sleep, while Caden watched over him. It was a long, boring twenty minutes or so, then Caden just sort of fell over. And he was out like a light, too, 'cause Emery suddenly got up and grabbed him by the front of his shirt and started shaking him, but the poor lad wouldn't wake up.

It gets a little muddied from there. Emery tackled Morrigan, somehow finding a knife on her, and I'll say this: Morrigan sure didn't seem overly bothered that Emery had armed himself. Emery's attention turned to Caden sleeping peacefully, and I swear he was fixing to do something terrible.

Something was off about him, too. Like the porch light was on, but no one was home. Morrigan got real close, and we all wanted to know what she was saying. Emery sank to his knees, then spun and stabbed her.

Only thing I can tell y'all is, I can't wait to hear what he has to say in his defense. Not sure it'll make a lick of difference, though. Might cost Caden the presidency of the Watch, too, which would be a shame.

Well, here goes. I must say, these Watch meetings are far more interesting than I thought they'd be.

~

"You expect us to believe you were being mind-controlled?" the woman asked, her unamused tone clearly expressing what she thought of that idea. Her lovely Japanese features were partially hidden behind an ornamental mask that covered the lower half of her face. It did not, sadly, cause her any difficulty in speaking.

She'd added her voice to those in opposition to my claims—aka Team Morrigan. Its other esteemed members appeared to include the Rusalka—the social media maven with the blue-tipped hair and matching eyes who reminded me of Melusina's evil twin—the Pirate, the Sandman, and the Ijiraat.

Ray's presence upset me the most. I'd tried to catch him in the hallway before the meeting began, but he'd brushed me off and then continued to keep others between us. I wanted him to explain why he'd bothered to help me in the cemetery if he was just going to report me to Morrigan in the end.

It was more than that, though. He'd been there—prowling about in one of his various animal forms—each time I'd faced something dangerous. I'd thought I'd been winning him over, that we'd shared something each time. Especially at Gregory's place, when I'd lifted the sheet and seen the body of my friend. I'd drawn comfort in the Ijiraat's presence, had been convinced he was watching my back.

I'd been wrong. Or it had been a ruse. Either way, I wanted to know why.

"Not mind-controlled," I said, striving for patience. "I was dreaming, and the Incubus incarnate took advantage of my slumber, using my body to attack Morrigan. In my dream I was struggling against him, but in the real world, I was struggling with someone else. I didn't know that person was Morrigan."

We were back at E-Pluribus for this meeting, taking advantage of the greater space and the more professional atmosphere.

The room was divided into two distinct sides. On the left were the aforementioned Morrigan supporters. In my corner sat Melusina, Maggie, Dagan, and Nimue. The Amazon sat with Hope at the end of the table, as if they hadn't yet decided where to put their allegiance. The other incarnates gave Hope a wide berth, but the Amazon didn't seem to mind her presence.

They were joined by two more familiar faces: Walt and Halona. the Kushtaka and the Thunderbird. Like Ray, Walt wore biker clothes, but that's where their similarities ended. The Kushtaka was older, his hair more gray than black, his lined face grave and his eyes piercing. He was shorter than I remembered but had a solidness to him that I would've appreciated a lot more if he'd been firmly on my side.

At least he and Halona sat in the undecided camp. Beggars can't be choosers.

Halona was exactly as I remembered, a dark hawkish bird with feathers the color of the sky during a thunderstorm, lightning peeking out from beneath them. She perched on the back of a chair, her fantastical appearance pulling at my attention even though she hadn't said a word since the meeting began.

Rachelle and Matlas sat at the side of the room, in chairs placed against the windows. I would've argued against the literal sidelining if I weren't already defending my own hide. Speaking out on their behalf wouldn't do them any favors until I'd cleared my name with the other incarnates.

Neither Kolby nor Iris had made it. I tried not to take that personally. But they, as well as Gregory, were sorely missed.

Agatha was absent, too, though the laptop she usually called in on was on the table, firmly closed.

"Did you know the Incubus could do this?" Dagan asked, frowning.

"No," I answered, grateful to have a voice on my side. Well, maybe *my* side was a little presumptuous, but at least he wasn't sitting with the Pirate. "At the time, I thought it was the Mare."

"I can confirm Emery was sleeping," the Sandman said in his reed-thin voice. We hadn't spoken since he'd tried to help me in the Lucid, and I realized I owed him a thank-you. And an apology. And probably a much more thorough explanation. I cringed. No wonder he'd entered among the incarnates supporting Morrigan. Still, his comment almost sounded like support.

At least he wasn't wounded. I would've felt awful if he'd shown up to the meeting with something broken.

"We all saw him hit the hay," Maggie said. "The question is, was he still asleep when he put the knife in Morrigan."

"The footage is inconclusive," Dagan said. "Sleepwalking can mimic consciousness. What we need is a witness."

Caden swallowed as attention in the room settled on him. "I was there," he said, "but the Mare showed up and put me under. I didn't wake up until after Morrigan had passed."

Had passed. What a peaceful way to put it.

"Your story is not in question," Dagan said with a smile he probably meant as comforting. "You were clearly asleep. While the Mare was not visible in the footage, we all agree events must have transpired as you recounted them. We all saw Emery try to rouse you to no avail. Whether it was visible or not, we believe you when you say an incarnate was present."

"But you will not extend the same faith to Emery?" Caden asked.

Dagan stiffened. "I am doing what I can to clear his name, provided he truly is innocent."

I'd been dreading this. I didn't know what to expect. Pity at having been tricked into killing Morrigan? Condemnation for ending her life? She *was* Caden's rival for the presidency, after all. Would they be disgusted I'd ended a life after touting the need for protection and safety? Disappointed that I hadn't found another way?

"Is he not the Loophole?" the masked woman said. "Are we really going to allow him to use one to avoid taking responsibility for a murder he committed?"

It all made me sick to my stomach. Morrigan hadn't even known she was being broadcast, yet somehow the footage perfectly incriminated me. Thank goodness Rachelle had only streamed the footage to our friends in the Watch, or I'd likely be in trouble with mortal officials, too. Without Gregory to bail me out, what were the chances I'd be exonerated of two murders in the same week?

At least Artie hadn't forsaken me. Maybe he understood better than most what it was like being used as a tool for murder. Maybe he was just a good friend. Either way, he'd fabricated reports as "Morrigan Anand" to secure my release and clear my name—at least with the mortals—regarding Gregory's death.

So here I was, waiting for the Watch to decide my fate, right before they decided Caden's. The timing was terrible. If things didn't go my way, Caden would lose everything he'd worked so hard for. The Watch would not abide a leader who, in their eyes, condoned murder.

"He didn't murder anyone," Rachelle snapped. "Aren't you listening? It was Nyx."

"Aye, we're listening, lassie," the Pirate said, "but we aren't liking what we're hearing. And meaning no offense to yeh, but his loudest defense coming from mortals isn't doing a lot of good for his case, savvy?"

"Being mortal's got nothing to do with it," Maggie said, bristling. "Rachelle's been a member of the Watch since before either of us joined, Bart."

The Pirate stroked his matted salt-and-pepper beard. "It's Longbeard, Selkie. Don't be making me remind yeh again."

Her cheek dimpled. "Then maybe try growing it out."

"Enough," Dagan said. He turned to me. "Emery, you admit to stabbing Morrigan through the heart?"

My breath caught. "Yes. When I woke up, the knife was in my hands and Morrigan was crouched in front of me, wounded. Her blood was everywhere. But I swear, I didn't intend to kill her."

"Yet you ran?" the masked woman asked. "The guilty do not often run."

"I didn't *run*. I went to find the Incubus, to bring him to justice for the crime he'd committed."

The woman's immaculate brows lifted. "Why didn't you say so? Bring him forth, then."

I ground my teeth. "I was unsuccessful."

Ray watched me with narrowed eyes, but so far he hadn't said a word. He'd sat on the Morrigan side of the table, but only the Rusalka, the Pirate, and the Japanese woman—I really needed to get her name—had specifically spoken *against* me.

"Then how do we know you're telling the truth?" the Rusalka asked.

"I was there for that part," Caden said. He stood beside me, presenting a unified front to the others. Showing his support even if it cost him everything. I had asked him not to do it, but he'd steadfastly refused. "Though I was sleeping when Morrigan died, I later found Emery in pursuit of Nyx."

That was putting it mildly.

"Yet he eluded you both," the masked woman said to me. "How did you even know where to find Nyx?"

"I have a history with him," I said, trying to pull my voice out of the growl it threatened to fall into. "When he enters the Lucid, his physical body is nearby."

Several heads turned to the Sandman, who inclined his slowly. "He speaks truly. In addition, some incarnates, the Incubus among them, possess the power to physically enter dreams. But whether projection or corporeal, both require proximity to the dreamer."

The Rusalka yawned. "I'm bored. Let's just agree that he killed her and move on."

"I will not stand for your insolence, Ru," Dagan said in a reproving tone. "If the Watch is to stand for something, it must hold its members accountable. Determining Emery's guilt or innocence is integral to upholding our new tenets."

I looked back and forth between Dagan and the Rusalka. *Ru?* He'd spoken to her like a father might speak to a wayward daughter. Was there a past there I'd been unaware of?

"Many people drown in the ocean's tide," Nimue said into the silence. "Yet we do not hold the sea accountable. Few among us have escaped committing violence. In our longevity, it finds us eventually. Ever before, we've washed our hands of the guilt. Before us stands a man who sees the value of life, who knows right and wrong. I would not hold him accountable."

"Aye, but would the lad hold yeh accountable, were the tables turned?" The Pirate glared at me. "Yeh can't have your rum and drink it, too."

"You're forgetting," mask-woman said, "that he did not kill just *anyone*. He killed the Protagonist. This warrants greater recrimination than another victim might."

I stole a glance at Hope. Her eyes met mine, then cut away. She wasn't speaking against me, but evidently she wasn't yet ready to be my ally. At least I hadn't been counting on her.

I noticed that Halona had caught the exchange between Hope and me. Nothing escaped those eagle eyes, it would appear.

Great. All I needed was her thinking I was allied with the former leader of Vox Populi.

"I don't know what else to tell you," I said, wishing I had some proof that Morrigan wasn't their beloved Protagonist. But if I tried to reveal my true identity now, it would go horribly wrong. Not only did I have zero proof to offer them, but it would look like I was claiming the title to escape justice and cast shade on Morrigan. Not to mention I'd been lying to my friends this whole time. If Gregory were still alive, maybe his relationships with the other incarnates would've provided enough support, backed up my claims. But Caden, Rachelle, and Matlas were too closely aligned with me to appear unbiased, so the others wouldn't accept their endorsement as evidence I was telling the truth. "I've admitted my wrongdoing and told you the circumstances behind Morrigan's death." I refused to call her the Protagonist. "I told you it was a tragedy, that I'm sorry events turned out the way they did. I can offer you nothing more than my apologies." That reminded me of what I'd said to Nyx. Which worried me; *that* hadn't ended well. "I'm the chief officer of relations. You'll need to trust me if we're to move forward. If you can't, it would be best to strip me of my title now. I cannot help the Watch achieve our goals if my integrity is in question."

"Pretty words will not earn back your reputation," mask-woman said.

Ray spoke for the first time. "I agree. In my experience, actions speak louder."

Caden shot to his feet, red spots dusting his cheeks. "Actions? I met Emery when he flew to New York to stop the Ahedrian murders." He pointed at Rachelle. "The day he met Rachelle, he saved her from the wrath of the Genie, and his home was burned to the ground as his thanks." At Matlas. "Earlier this week, he saved Matlas from several mercenaries with orders to kill him just for being in the wrong place at the wrong time. Then, later that night, he saved *both* of them from the Incubus, who possessed Matlas while he slept in an attempt to murder Rachelle." Point. "He met the Mermaid while rescuing her from being kidnapped. He saved me from capture by Vox Populi, storming their yacht to rescue me. He saved the lives of countless mortals at Rikers prison, then saved incarnates from Vox Populi.

"You want *actions?* Emery Luple is the *soul* of this Watch. He's the reason I dare to dream of a world where incarnates can find peace and safety. Because while we *dream* about it, Emery's making it happen each and every day. His *actions* are the ideals we're just starting to build here."

He trembled with emotion. I put my hand on his arm in gratitude, hoping he felt the love and appreciation I tried to convey in that touch.

Melusina had a little smile on her face, her eyes distant. Maggie had been nodding along at Caden's words. Rachelle and Matlas held hands, gauging the others' reactions. Dagan appeared moved, his eyebrows raised and his lips pursed in a considering frown. The Sandman weighed me with sunken eyes. Ru and the masked woman looked unconvinced, while the Pirate scratched a scar on his cheek. The Undine and the Amazon exchanged glances, and Hope stared at the floor, her face hidden. Walt and Halona were watching Ray.

The Ijiraat harrumphed. "More pretty words," he said. "Prettier than the last, I admit. But you forgot a few actions, Caden. He may have saved all the people you mentioned, but he killed the Protagonist. He promised to help my friend find justice for her slain horse but then—together with you—defended the incarnate responsible. Turned your weapons upon me." He shook his head in distaste. "Emery stood accused of killing Gregory Gregorius. He sought to collude with the Incubus against Morrigan and her allies, to win the Watch through deceit. He contacted me to be complicit in it. When all of that failed, he murdered her."

"No!" I snapped. "How can you say that, Ray? You were there when I was investigating Susan and Jerry. You were there when I found Gregory—" I cut off, swallowing hard. "You witnessed the truth again and again, so why do you spew these lies?"

He stared at me. "I don't know what you're talking about. I've been nowhere near you until you called me to eavesdrop on your meeting."

"But you're proving his point," the Rusalka said. "You'll say anything to get out of this."

"What? Ray—"

"No. We've heard enough. Let's proceed with a vote. The Loophole asks us to judge whether he should keep his title and position in the Watch. I think we should oblige."

The masked woman shook her head. "If the Watch is to prosper, it must trust its members, not only its leaders. Stripping him of his position is not enough. I believe his future in the Watch is what should be on the table."

"You have a lot of opinions for your very first meeting," Rachelle noted.

"Had it not been for the Loophole, these opinions would be voiced by the Protagonist. Alas, she cannot be here. Someone must speak on her behalf."

Dagan frowned. "I will not agree to removing the Loophole from the Watch. He has played an essential role in establishing it. But"—he met my eyes—"I do agree that your actions have called your character into question. Until everyone can again place their confidence in you, your effectiveness as chief officer of relations will suffer. I believe it is for the best that you voluntarily step down. If you do, then I concur with the Undine and say we set aside this unpleasantness and proceed with the meeting."

I hesitated. "If I step aside, won't that be seen as an admission of guilt?"

"I suspect that most of us will see it as a responsible decision made for the good of the Watch." Dagan's face hardened. "What do you say?"

This wasn't what I'd expected. I'd been hoping to win over the majority of the room by explaining what had happened. That Nimue, Dagan, and the Amazon would understand the mitigating circumstances and be swayed to absolve me of fault. In spite of their unreadable expressions, I thought I'd been succeeding, but Dagan's challenge threw a wrench into things. Now if I didn't step down voluntarily, if I forced a vote, I'd be seen as less reasonable, less *honorable*. Which might cost me the vote.

Which, in turn, might cost *Caden* the vote.

Worse, I couldn't fault Dagan's logic. If I were in his position, I'd be moved by the accused stepping down of his own accord. It made sense.

I glanced at Caden. I remembered our conversation about how he thought he was being selfish because he wanted to be the one to spearhead the Watch, to drive it forward and shape it into his vision for a better world. I'd told him that he wasn't selfish.

How do you know I don't want the credit? he'd asked.

Because I'd want it, and you aren't me. And I love you for that.

This was my chance to be selfless. To put Caden first. If I stepped down, it would swing Dagan. Maybe the Amazon, or even Walt and Halona. It would be worth it if they voted for Caden to be president.

Now that it was about to be taken from me, I realized that while I wanted to be a part of this, I *could* let it go if it meant Caden could live his dream. For the first time in this hell of a week, I'd put him first.

I opened my mouth.

The door to the room slammed open with a *crack*. "Not so fast!"

*E*veryone turned to face the newcomer.

She was... a stranger. Short and plump, at the twilight of middle age, she looked like an overstuffed scarecrow with her straw-like hair poking out from beneath a Kentucky Derby–style black hat. Her hooked nose rivaled the hat for supremacy of her face. She wore a dark top and a red-checkered skirt above sturdy boots. And the jewelry! She had more necklaces, bracelets, and rings than a department store rack, and little charms made of wood, metal, and bone dangled on chains clipped to her clothes and belt. When she moved, she jangled louder than Santa's sleigh. She looked like she'd be more at home at a Renaissance faire than in the office building of a transnational corporation, but her dramatic entrance held our attention regardless. Tucked beneath her arm was a comically large book with a thick leather cover and metallic bindings. In her other hand she held a fabric bag, not unlike the kind Mary Poppins toted about.

Even though I'd never gotten a clear image of her, I knew her at once: Agatha, the Witch incarnate.

"Sorry I'm late," she said, shuffling into the room. Her voice didn't really match her appearance. It was too big for such a short woman, robust and loud, as if every sentence ended in an exclamation point. She probably had a wicked cackle, though.

The Japanese woman turned her glare on Agatha. "You are interrupting important proceedings."

"Oh, good! Timed it perfectly, then." She stepped up to the table —between Ray and Longbeard—and heaved her enormous tome onto the wooden surface, the sound of the book hitting the table causing me and several others to wince. "I'm Agatha. The Witch."

I wasn't certain whether or not to speak up. She'd interrupted at a very timely moment, which made me think I should keep my trap shut. Especially given my powers of convenience. That said, she'd been misleading us about being in Seattle this whole time, and she was a wild card for which I couldn't yet account.

"I didn't know you were in town," Maggie said. "Welcome to the meeting. We're just wrapping up—"

"Oh, yes. I know precisely what you're wrapping up. And, I'm sorry to say, I'm about to *unwrap* just about all of it, I imagine." Agatha gave the room a toothless smile. Nudging Ray, she said, "Move aside, young man. Can't you see I need some elbow room here?"

Ray blinked, moving to make space for her out of instinct. He glowered a moment later, but the Witch paid him no mind. She was opening the book.

"Is this really the time to consult your spell book?" Dagan asked, his polite tone not quite masking his impatience.

"And is it safe?" Melusina added.

"Eh?" Agatha looked up, then chuckled. "Oh! This isn't my grimoire. These are my notes."

"Notes?" Rachelle asked. "Notes about what?"

"Why, about all of you, of course. Between all the secrets and politicking, I don't know how you expect to run an above-board community. No, one never can be too careful."

Ray cleared his throat. "I think—"

"You've been doing a poor job of it," Agatha interrupted, "and I'm here to set a few things straight. Starting with your misplaced anger toward Emery..."

I liked where this was going.

"... and why you *really* ought to be upset with him."

Hrm.

"I say we let the Witch speak," the Japanese woman said, her eyes glittering above her ornate mask.

"Thank you, Kuchisake-onna," Agatha said absently, her head buried in her book, finger running down her notes.

Kuchisake-onna? The name shot a spike of alarm through me. The Slit-Mouthed Woman incarnate was a Malevolent spirit from Japan. Very, very Malevolent. As in, cut-your-face-if-you-don't-say-she's-beautiful kind of Malevolent. What the hell was she doing here in Seattle? Looking at her with fresh eyes, I realized her identity should've been obvious. I guess I just thought I'd be able to pick out a Malevolent on sight, so she'd slipped under my radar.

It suddenly felt as if a loaded gun had been brought into the room. I couldn't stop stealing looks at her. I wasn't the only one, I noticed. Hope was watching her with suddenly wary eyes, and we exchanged anxious glances. The guarded look Dagan directed at the Slit-Mouthed Woman may have been an indication that he'd heard of her, too.

"Ah!" Agatha said. "Here we are. First things first, we need to clear the air. Four murders occurred this week: Spray, Jerry, Gregory, and Morrigan. On this we can all agree, yes?"

Maggie barked a laugh. "You'll be trying to get this lot to agree till the cows come home."

"Who are Spray and Jerry?" the Amazon asked.

The Witch held up a finger. "Excellent question, Lita. Spray's death was the Mare's motivation to take part in the subsequent murders, as well as the reason Ray doesn't trust Emery and Caden. Oh, and she was a horse. Jerry Myers was nothing more than a poor mortal pawn and a casualty of these foolish political games."

That didn't really answer the question the Amazon—Lita, apparently—had asked, but I was curious where the Witch was going with this. At the silence that met Agatha's statement, I took it I wasn't alone.

"Four days, four murders. Thursday, Spray; Friday, Jerry; Saturday, Gregory; Sunday, Morrigan." She held up a finger. "But how many murderers, hmm? That's the real question."

"One," I said.

"Ah." She gave me a sidelong glance from beneath the brim of her hat. "This question is not as simple as it first appears."

"Two murderers?" Matlas ventured.

"One could argue."

The Pirate chimed in. "How many monkeys are in this barrel, eh? Spit it out already."

"Things are finally getting interesting, Longbeard," Ru said, sitting forward. "I'll guess four different murderers."

"Oh, at least," the Witch replied.

"Was at least one of them the Loophole?" Kuchisake-onna asked.

"Nope." I caught my breath. Had she just exonerated me? "No, no, no. The *Loophole* did not kill anyone. But we'll get to that in a moment. The correct answer is that there were *five* murderers."

A ripple of shock passed through the assembled incarnates, whispers and confusion blooming in its wake. Agatha took advantage of the moment to place three glass globes on the table in front of her. Each sat on a metal base that kept the ball from rolling out of place. Milky, pearlescent fog began to shift inside them.

"Allow me to explain. We'll start at the beginning. Spray was killed by"—she paused, looking around the room for effect—"the Mare. Behold the damning pieces of evidence. Fact one: the victim's emaciated appearance, a result of having its life drained from it." In the first crystal ball, a watery image of Spray's corpse could be seen against the backdrop of the murky mist, like some sort of projector was beaming the image onto the mist. "That can really only be the work of two incarnates: the Mare or the Incubus. To determine which one, we must proceed to fact two: the twisted branches above the site of the attack, a telltale sign that the Mare has been feeding in the area." A faint picture of the interwoven tree branches that I'd seen at the ranch obligingly appeared in the second crystal ball. "And finally, fact three: the victim was a horse. This precludes the Incubus from having committed the crime, as he can only feed on humans." The third crystal ball remained a pattern of swirling mist.

"Where is the Mare, then?" Ray asked, his voice low.

"Oh, yes, another excellent question. I will reveal her identity in due time. But first, to prove another murderer was present, we must go to the talismans." The third crystal ball revealed mirrors affixed to the perimeter of the horse's pen. Then a dark silhouette hit one of the mirrors with a branch, and it shattered.

"The Sasquatch?" Ray asked.

Agatha leveled a look at him. "Do I need to replay the crystal ball? Did that silhouette look like *Bigfoot* to you? No, the only reason Bigfoot was around in the first place was the free meal." The corner of her mouth crooked up. "And because of *you*."

I flinched. She was pointing a bony finger at me.

"What did I do?" I asked.

She *tsk*ed and shook her head. "Not a good question, Emery Luple. You've achieved too much in too short a time for that kind of broad inquiry. In this case, however: you've empowered the wee folk among the incarnates. Those we often inappropriately call Prey. Your powers and your will to protect the meek have resulted in rapidly growing Safe Havens, which has encouraged migration. The Sasquatch, usually found far from human society, has ventured nearer and nearer mortal habitation as its Safe Haven has expanded."

Matlas was frowning. "Isn't that an oxymoron?" he blurted. "The Sasquatch encountered more danger because its Safe Haven is growing?" As the room's attention shifted to him, he shrank back.

"Shrewd, Mathew Atlas. Indeed, much that Emery does is a proverbial double-edged sword. Intention must be measured against results, I think, to properly determine his culpability."

"I disagree," the Undine said, her blue skin pulling tight around her apologetic smile. "We *Prey* alone should judge the worth of an expanding Safe Haven. It is not up to the Watch to determine its value, but to those of us who must live each day with its consequences."

Dagan shook his head. "Consequences that could reverberate

throughout the incarnate world deserve to be addressed by the entire community."

"Then who better than Emery to be the chief officer of relations?" Rachelle pointed out. "If he's responsible for the repercussions, wouldn't he be the best person to mitigate them?"

"We've yet to carry out the vote," Kuchisake-onna said in a hard voice. "Whether Emery retains his station is yet undetermined."

Ray sat forward. "Another murderer was present at Spray's death. Who was it?"

"The only murderer who was present at all four crime scenes," Agatha said. "Best you hear it firsthand, though." She clicked one long fingernail on the table. "For those of you who do not know, the Mare is only nightmarish between sunset and daybreak. The rest of the time, she's someone else entirely." She trailed off, her lips spreading into a knowing smile.

On cue, the door swung open.

The woman who entered this time was not a stranger.

Ray leapt to his feet. "Amara! What're you doing here?"

The woman looked at us with anxious eyes above deep, purple circles. She clearly hadn't been sleeping well. She looked much as I remembered her, with plain clothes and a rancher's hat. "Hi, Ray." She turned and dipped her hat in greeting to me, too.

"Oh!" It was Artie, his voice coming over the speakers. "Amara. A Mara. How clever."

I groaned. We'd been looking for an incarnate the whole time. I hadn't stopped to consider she might be masquerading as a mortal during the daylight hours.

"As I was saying, the Mare is an ordinary mortal during the day," Agatha said. "But at night she transforms into a Malevolent incarnate."

"I don't usually have any recollection of my nighttime activities," Amara said, looking at her feet. "So I didn't know I was the Mare until Agatha restored part of my memories. I'm so sorry for the harm I caused." She struggled to look up and meet Caden's eyes as she said it.

"Tell them what you told me about what really happened that

first night. The night Spray died." The Witch's voice was surprisingly tender.

"Is this really necessary?" Ray asked. "Hasn't she been through enough?"

"No, I'm okay, Ray. Thank you." She took a shaky breath. "The Incubus appeared in my dreams and forcibly changed me into the Mare. He and Morrigan wanted me to attack an innocent person, to drain their life force completely. I was *so* hungry. I hadn't transformed in *years*. I still, barely, managed to refuse. I didn't want to kill. So the Incubus said I could feed on him. I accepted his offer, drinking my fill. I kept asking if I should stop, but he demanded I sate myself, insisting that he was fine. So I did. I drank until there wasn't a drop left, yet still he stood before me, calm and healthy and strong."

She let out a sob. "I woke up over the wasted body of my girl, Spray. The Incubus had tricked me—I wasn't draining *him* at all. I'd feasted on her until she died. The talisman I'd hung to protect her was smashed to smithereens. I'd murdered my beautiful girl."

"I'm so sorry," Ray said softly.

The Witch gestured. "Tell them the rest."

"The Incubus told me I'd be working with Morrigan, that she would direct me where to feast. If I refused, he'd feed my other girls to my unquenchable thirst."

"How dare you speak against the Protagonist?" Kuchisake-onna said. "You tread on thin ice."

"Oh, she said nothing against *the Protagonist*." Agatha looked at me with a gleam in her eyes, and my stomach fell. She knew. How? "Well, there you have it. Who really killed Spray, then? The Mare or the Incubus?"

"Or Morrigan and me?" Hope interjected unexpectedly, her firm voice belying the guilty expression on her face.

Everyone turned to her. "I beg your pardon?" Agatha said. "Are you referring to your role in capturing the Asibikaashi?"

Hope nodded. "Morrigan and I took the Asibikaashi from the Lucid to remove the protection dream catchers provide. That way, the

Incubus and the Mare could go anywhere unhindered. Without the Asibikaashi's protection, we made everyone susceptible to attack."

"You admit your guilt freely?" the Sandman asked, his head tilted as if he hadn't been expecting that.

"Why shouldn't she? The only thing Hope's guilty of," Agatha said, "is her poor choice in bedfellows. First Vox Populi, then Morrigan."

"Morrigan told me we needed the Asibikaashi's help to manufacture dream catchers to protect members of the Watch," Hope said. "But I later learned that she'd lied to me. I overheard Nyx and Morrigan talking about how transforming Amara into the Mare took too much out of him. I realized our capturing the Asibikaashi resulted in the Mare turning each night without the Incubus's intervention."

"They sent me with the Incubus the next night," Amara said. "I was told to target Jerry Myers. I didn't kill him, though. I refused to feed on him. I just sat on his chest and wrapped him in my hair."

Agatha nodded. "There's proof enough of that," she said.

"The flowers on the bedside table," I said, seeing it clearly now. "They weren't all twisted up, like the tree branches had been. Proof you hadn't fed." If I'd noticed that sooner, would it have led me to recognize Nyx's hand in all of this? I doubted it. When it came to Nyx, I had an unfortunate tendency to ignore the facts.

"Exactly. The Mare didn't kill Jerry. Susan did."

"But she was being controlled by Nyx," I said, "wasn't she?"

"Oh, yes," the Witch said. "Nyx fed on her to replenish his lost energy, then used her to kill Jerry, who was unable to wake beneath the Mare's sleep paralysis."

Amara looked at the floor. "I had to," she mumbled. "They were going to hurt my girls."

"But *why?*" Ray asked. "What did Morrigan and Nyx seek to gain by a random man's death?"

"The Watch," Hope answered. "They were setting up murders they could then solve."

Agatha nodded. "Precisely. The first murders occurred to sow doubt among the Watch as to whether Emery and Caden could accomplish their goals. The subsequent murders furthered that agenda, while also showcasing Morrigan's competence in handling each case. The Mare was but a pawn in the greater game. Afraid for her horses' safety, she had no choice." Agatha's face turned down. "And neither did Susan. But you learned that during your visit, didn't you, Emery?"

"How do you know all this?" I asked.

"Why, I was keeping tabs on Nyx and Morrigan—but *you* kept cropping up in their wake." She stooped down and opened the top of the bag she had brought in. A moment later, a black cat jumped out and hopped up onto the table next to the tome. It sat down and, unintimidated by the number of people in the room, met my eyes. Then it dipped its head in greeting.

No way.

The cat leapt into the air and transformed into a raven between blinks, flapping its wings and landing on the Witch's shoulder.

"Meet my animal familiar," Agatha said. "Or, more accurately, Barnaby, the Familiar incarnate."

It all made sense. *Ray* hadn't been at Susan and Jerry's, hadn't saved me from Morrigan in the cemetery, hadn't shared that moment after Gregory's death. It had been Agatha and Barnaby all along. I'd never stopped to consider that *another* shape-shifting incarnate would be in town.

Moreover, the Familiar hadn't been following me around. He'd been following Morrigan at the cemetery and at Gregory's. Nyx at Susan and Jerry's.

"Hello, Barnaby," I said, feeling that the words were woefully insufficient after the things we'd shared. After Gregory. "Thank you... for everything."

Barnaby cawed and dipped his beak, then flapped over to the windowsill not too far from Rachelle before transforming back into the cat. Were those his only two forms?

"Amara, were you at Gregory's death, too? In your Mare form?" Dagan asked.

She shook her head. "Agatha wrote to me and told me to come to her. I visited her that night and learned the truth. Then, the next night, I went to visit Emery, to tell him what was happening and gain his help. But..."

"I was with Nyx," I said, nodding. I'd already figured this out. "You fled, terrified of the Incubus."

She sagged, looking at the floor.

"So, who killed Gregory?" the Triton pressed.

"The Incubus," I answered. "He admitted as much before Morrigan died."

"A half truth, actually," the Witch said. "Gregory was too much for the Incubus to handle alone, but Morrigan helped murder the Watchman. Barnaby witnessed it, and he was still present at the crime scene when you showed up. He saw Morrigan strangle the Watchman while Nyx drained him."

To simulate the marks of the Mare's hair around his throat. Fury like a flash in the pan left me feeling suddenly forlorn. But a small, fierce part of me was proud; Gregory had put up such a fight that it had taken both Nyx and Morrigan to best him.

"Nyx, Morrigan, and the Mare," Melusina said, ticking them off on her fingers. "That leaves—what?—two more murderers at Morrigan's death?"

"You forgot Susan," Matlas said.

"Oh. So *one* more murderer at Morrigan's death, then."

"Me," I said, realizing where this was headed. "I stabbed her, even though it was Nyx's fault. The same as Susan."

"But you said the Loophole was not one of the murderers," the Kuchisake-onna hissed, frustration beginning to peek through her otherwise calm disposition.

"So I did," Agatha mused. "Someone's been paying attention. The *Loophole* was not involved in any of this. In point of fact, the *Loophole* is not even in this room!"

I think she expected gasps, but instead she received a roomful of perplexed frowns and grumbles.

"Emery Luple is not the Loophole incarnate," Agatha continued.

"I'm not even sure such an urban legend exists, to be honest." She raised a finger and pointed it at me. "And here we've arrived at the moment you've all been waiting for. The truth."

Every eye turned to me. A weight seemed to hang in the air, collective breaths held. I wondered if they could hear my heartbeat in that sudden silence.

"Emery Luple is none other than the Protagonist incarnate."

The reactions in the room were diverse.

Melusina's eyes widened, then turned introspective as realization flooded over her. The Undine nodded to herself, as if this turn of events made sense. The Amazon blinked in surprise, then leaned forward to scrutinize me as though she were seeing me for the first time. Maggie looked chagrined, like someone had told her the answer to something she should've known all along and she was disappointed in herself for not having figured it out on her own.

Dagan glowered, clearly believing Agatha and not appreciating having been misled. I could understand that. I smiled apologetically, but his expression didn't change.

Ray's face had drained of color, and he looked bewildered. Like everything he'd believed was being turned on its head. He looked to Walt and Halona who, for some reason, didn't look too surprised. The Rusalka and the Pirate exchanged glances, but each came out of the exchange with a different reaction: Ru shrugged as if it didn't matter, while Longbeard's face scrunched up in what I think was skepticism. The Kuchisake-onna wore a sour face above her mask, but I suspected it was more because this news undermined her case than that she felt insulted.

And the Sandman looked visibly relieved. I got a genuine smile there.

"Hello," I said into the silence. "I'm sorry for deceiving you all. I'd planned on telling you, but Morrigan beat me to the punch, and then I figured you'd think I was lying."

"Who says you aren't?" Ru asked.

"Me," the Witch said. "And let me tell you, it wasn't easy to piece together. The coincidental timing of things between him and Morrigan had Barnaby and me going in circles."

"We, too, know Emery to be the Protagonist," Halona said in a high, feminine voice. "The Asibikaashi sent dreams to Walt and me last night, and I believe she meant for us to speak up on his behalf, even if it ruffled a few feathers." She spread her wings as she repositioned herself on the chair's back. "So to speak."

"Coincidences and dreams?" the Kuchisake-onna said, skepticism heavy in her tone. "If that is all you have to offer..."

"I think I can prove it," I said. Everyone fell silent. I turned to Lita. "I don't know which of the nine Amazonian girls you were, but I'm so sorry. My hubris got six girls killed that day. I should've hunted the Hydra on my own. You were right; tragedy follows me around like a puppy."

The Amazon looked taken aback. "You remember that day?"

I nodded, solemn. "I remember. I owe you more than an apology, but I do not know—"

"Stop. Six perished tragically, yes. But the Hydra had already claimed at least that many. Who knows how many more you saved? And the three girls who survived grew into a line of women who taught others how to best the Hydra. It never plagued Anatolia again."

"I could've brought one with me. One, I could've protected."

"The error was not solely yours."

"Did you die that day?" I asked, afraid of the answer but needing to know.

The Amazon smiled. "I was the fool who sent you on the quest in the first place. An old woman then, I was unable to challenge the beast on my own. I threw a feast in your honor, lamenting that I could not accomplish what I knew you could. I told that story not to shame you, but to verify your—well, Morrigan's—identity. You are who you say you are." She stood, slamming her hands onto the table to emphasize her point—as if she didn't already have command of the entire room. "Emery Luple is the Protagonist."

"Then who was Morrigan?" Ray demanded.

The focus of the room seemed to split, undecided who could best answer the question. Me? Agatha?

"My nemesis," I said quietly. "Morrigan is the Antagonist. Her powers work similarly to mine."

"How dare you!" the Kuchisake-onna cried, leaping to her feet. "How dare you sully her name with your foul words!"

"Peace," Caden said at my side, holding up a hand. "Our incarnations shape who we are, but we're not defined entirely by them. We can choose to change, choose good over evil. We all have that choice."

"Well said, Guardian Angel." I was startled to find it was Walt who'd spoken.

"And yet, how do we hold Emery accountable for the actions of four others?" Ray asked. I glanced at him. That almost sounded as if he'd reconsidered his original stance.

Agatha cocked her head. "Five murderers, yet only one was present at all four events, pulling the strings."

"Nyx," I said in a near whisper.

"Indeed. The Incubus incarnate," Agatha said. "I contend that we should hold him responsible for the deaths of all four and absolve the others of wrongdoing. The Mare was deceived and coerced. Susan killed her husband while being manipulated by Nyx. The Protagonist killed Morrigan through Nyx's machinations. And Morrigan paid for her crimes against Gregory with her life. At this time, it makes sense to lay the rest to bed."

"I see why Emery took upon himself the disguise of the Loophole," the Kuchisake-onna spat, "as he is slippery enough to get away with murder."

"I'm sure the Watch wouldn't mind putting it to a vote," the Witch said with a sharp smile. "Though we'd be remiss not to closely examine the deaths of those two young women in Osaka. They died the day prior to your arrival in the States, did they not?"

The Kuchisake-onna glared at Agatha but remained silent.

Nimue waved her hand, indicating the room. "We must admit we're all in the same boat. As I said earlier, every incarnate has committed violence at one time or another. Best to wash the slate clean, for all of us. And who better to begin the process than the Protagonist himself?"

"I couldn't agree more," Caden said. Then his usually soft features hardened. "But from this point on, the Watch *will* hold incarnates accountable for their actions. Murder and violence will not be our way. Against each other or against mortals."

"We should move on," Dagan said, his voice brooking no argument. "But before we proceed to the vote for the president of the Watch, I would ask Caden directly: did you know that Emery is the Protagonist incarnate? Were you complicit in his ruse?"

I swallowed, but Caden didn't hesitate. "I knew."

"But I asked him to," I said quickly. "He didn't do anything wrong."

"He put your interests before those of the Watch," Dagan said reprovingly. "Regardless of his noble intentions." He shook his head. "I'm sorry, but I will not give my vote to you."

Caden nodded, accepting the rebuke. "It's okay. We each have our own convictions. While I hope to earn back your trust, I respect your decision."

"Let's do this," Rachelle said from her seat. "A simple majority, right? All in favor of Caden as president of the Watch, raise your hands." She led by example.

Hands went up. Artie voiced his support over the intercom. Halona fluttered off her perch to noisily flap her approval.

"Wait," Caden said. Everyone froze, staring at him. "I appreciate your support more than you know," he said softly. "But so much has come to light today, and I realize that I'm better suited to another role."

"Are you sure?" I asked. Even though I said it softly, it carried in the quiet.

"I'm certain. Can you do me a favor?"

"Anything."

"Nominate me."

I understood. Caden had told me he didn't need the credit. All he wanted was to steer this thing forward, to make sure the Incarnate Watch stayed true to its dream.

To protect incarnates. To keep them safe. To be a light in the darkness.

"I would like to make a nomination," I proclaimed to the attendees, who waited expectantly. "I nominate Caden Malek, the *only* person I'd trust to fill the Watchman's shoes. Caden, will you be our chief officer of security?"

Dagan broke into a grin, which looked out of place on his usually stern face. "I second that. All in favor?"

Almost every hand shot into the air.

A cheer went up, and I pulled Caden into a hug as he exhaled heavily against my neck. Then he stepped forward and lifted his hands. "Thank you so much, everyone."

Rachelle hopped up from her chair and said, "Okay, but who's going to be president? Or is this going to be one of those council-led things?"

Caden shook his head. "We promised ourselves a president, and I think we should continue with that plan. I nominate Agatha, the Witch, as president of the Watch. She's more than proven herself competent."

The wave of hands in the air agreed with him.

*A*mong incarnates, death is a cyclical thing rather than an end, so funerals are not always expected. Moreover, with how averse to gatherings incarnates had proven in the past, funerals were not especially well attended.

Maybe because the protagonists of stories are so wildly diverse, or maybe because I'm quirky and unpredictable, I'd always felt differently. To me, the death of an incarnate *was* an end. At the very least, it was the end of an era. A farewell, with a promise to meet again at some unknowable future point.

Lifetimes and changes occurred in the meantime, though, so the meeting might be of two strangers with fond memories of one another but no real current connection.

Mortals understood. They treated life with the respect and reverence it deserved. Well, more often than incarnates did, at any rate.

Caden and I were challenging past practices. The Incarnate Watch was just the beginning. Hope's words about the terrifying nature of change came across as more authentically *incarnate* than she'd probably like to admit. Then again, I could sympathize—with how much drama my lives attracted, sometimes all I wanted was for things to stay the same for a time. In any case, I could understand why the Watch was, at its core, a scary progression for incarnates. It was change.

And it was working.

The proof was in Gregory's funeral.

It occurred on Wednesday, five days after the election meeting. Agatha assembled the entire Watch to pay their respects to Gregory Gregorius, the Watchman incarnate. I'd never seen such a gathering of incarnates and mortals. The incarnates were, of course, trying to blend in, with varying degrees of success.

I attended with my mom, her puffy, swollen eyes the only indication of how difficult his death had been on her. In part, this was the reason I hadn't wanted her and Gregory to date in the first place. His life had carried risks and dangers she'd never understand.

It weighed on me, making me wonder how she'd take it when I was the one who died. I hated to focus on it, but I tended to live shorter lifespans than ordinary mortals—a consequence of my exciting life—and it seemed unlikely that I'd outlive Lynn Luple. At least, as callous as it might be to say, the outlook for the next thousand days or so looked brighter with Morrigan out of the picture.

Morrigan.

I refused to acknowledge my complicated feelings about her today.

Today was for Gregory.

Or, perhaps more accurately, it was a day for those he'd left behind. A day for Mom. For Grant and Quinn, officers who had worked with him for years and who looked to him as a mentor. For Yamamoto, the medical examiner, and Dawson of Major Crimes.

Maggie and Melusina blended in quite well. They were dressed in dark, solemn blacks and grays, Melusina's bright blue hair tucked under a fancy funeral hat, though she'd forgone the widow's veil. Maggie wore her customary fur coat, but the black dress beneath it was conservative and formal. I came across them in the parking lot, before the service, and thanked them again for believing in me and Caden. They gushed about how we'd earned their goodwill and we had nothing to thank them for, but they also made sure to ask if I was doing all right.

Even distracted, Mom picked up on the odd intonations and pulled me aside after that. "*Are* you all right, sweet pea?"

"I'm good, Mom. Today's exactly what I need."

She gave me a sad smile and said, "I know what you mean."

I hugged her tight.

Which was when the Pirate walked by, dressed... well, in a swash-buckler's Sunday best. Which is to say, the same damn thing he wore everywhere else. Mom's mouth hung open as he tipped his pirate hat to her and continued on toward the main hall.

While a somber service, it managed to be celebratory, too. The sheer number of officers, agents, and medical staff in attendance had the funeral conductor scrambling to find more seating. It gave me a swell of pride, and a pang of loss, to witness the volume of love and loyalty Gregory had inspired. Gregory himself would've likely considered the event overblown.

Rachelle and Matlas paid their respects with us but also gave me and my mom the space to grieve in peace. Caden stayed near me, squeezing my hand and giving me small, supportive smiles that were meant just for me.

Watching the procession of honors bestowed on Gregory and listening to the accounts of those whose lives he'd touched brought me closer to understanding the facets of his personality I hadn't known. Mom had lauded his sense of humor, and I thought she'd been poking fun. But Grant, whose own anecdote about Gregory was short yet emotional, also talked about how she bonded with him in Tacoma *in spite* of his sense of humor. The assemblage had laughed at that, leaving me somewhat bewildered.

I'd been expecting the funeral to drag my mood through the mud, but it felt freeing. I guess it really was a farewell with a promise to meet again, and its formality brought with it a sense of closure.

The next day, the day of Morrigan's funeral, I stayed home. Caden went back to work, and I made coffee, trying to decide what kind of person would attend her memorial service. Her employees? Her agents? *Anyone?*

A mean-spirited part of me hoped no one showed up. She'd never valued life; why should anyone value hers?

Tough talk from the guy who almost killed her murderer in retribution.

I sat down at my laptop and opened my email.

There were twenty-six unread messages. Two of them caught my eye: one from Nyx, and one from Morrigan.

Nyx was gone. With the Asibikaashi free, the dream catchers were working again and he was unable to haunt our dreams. Happily, the Asibikaashi's presence was also enough to keep Amara from transforming into the Mare.

I opened the email from him first.

It was an electronic payment in the amount of two thousand dollars. The body of the email was short.

IF YOU WANT THE REMAINING THOUSAND DOLLARS, COME AND GET IT. I EAGERLY AWAIT THE DAY. UNTIL THEN, THANK YOU. AND SORRY.

YOURS, NYX

I couldn't help but smile. In part because of the message, in part because he was gone. I squashed the unwanted, unexpected pang of loss. My feelings for Nyx were something I could put aside. I hated the hurt I'd caused him. I hated the attraction I felt for him. But most of all, I hated that he could make me hate at all.

I'd rather love.

That's why I'd chosen Caden.

My eyes went next to the email from Morrigan. Impossibly, it had been sent an hour after her death. The subject line read, "Ta-ta."

My emotions regarding Morrigan were, as always, cloudier than the Seattle sky. The peace granted by the Asibikaashi and renewed at Gregory's service hadn't dissipated completely, but I couldn't shake a feeling that I was still waiting for the other shoe to drop.

Her last words festered in my mind. *You've got mail.* I'd been putting this off. At first I'd been distracted with clearing my name and having no phone, so avoiding my email had been simple. When my new phone arrived, I didn't sync it up to my account.

Today was Morrigan's funeral. It was time.

I stared at the unread email, my mug of coffee cooling on a coaster. The six sugar cubes and mountain of whipped cream were insufficient to mask the bitter taste in my mouth. The email had been sent one hour after her death. Taking a deep breath, I opened it.

EMERY, DARLING,

I CONGRATULATE YOU ON YOUR TRIUMPH. I AM DEAD, NO DOUBT DUE IN PART TO MY UNDERESTIMATION OF THOSE IN MY EMPLOY. HERE'S SOME FREE ADVICE: GIVEN THE OPPORTUNITY, NEVER FORM A BUSINESS PARTNERSHIP BY THREATENING SAID PARTNER'S CHILD. NYX WAS MUCH MORE ACCOMMODATING BEFORE HE FORCED ME TO PUT A BLADE TO AVERY'S THROAT. OH, LOOK WHO I'M TALKING TO—YOU'D KNOW A THING OR TWO ABOUT THAT, WOULDN'T YOU? SHE'S A TOUGH ONE TO KEEP TABS ON, I ADMIT, BUT AN INVESTMENT THAT PAYS DIVIDENDS COMMENSURATE WITH THE DIFFICULTY OF THE WORK. AT LEAST THE POOR THING HAS *SOMEONE* LOOKING FOR HER OUT THERE.

IF IT WAS HOPE WHO BETRAYED ME, THOUGH, DO ME THE COURTESY OF NEVER INFORMING ME OF SUCH, FOR I'LL BE MOST DISAPPOINTED IN MYSELF AND MY INABILITY TO ACCOUNT FOR HER *OBVIOUS* SIMPERING AND DUPLICITOUS TACTICS.

ALAS, EVEN IN DEATH, I'VE BESTED YOU.

HOW SO, YOU ASK? OH, KITTEN, I CONTINUE TO OVERESTIMATE THAT INTELLIGENCE OF YOURS. VERY WELL, I'LL SPELL IT OUT FOR YOU: I HAVE SOWN SEEDS IN THE INCARNATE WATCH, THE REAPING OF WHICH SHALL ONE DAY CHANGE THE COURSE WE'VE PLOTTED. THE WATCH ITSELF IS A MARVELOUS CONSTRUCT, I MUST ADMIT. TO GALVANIZE THE COMPLACENT INCARNATES OF TODAY INTO EVEN THE SEMBLANCE OF COMMUNITY IS NO SMALL FEAT. AS EVER, WE WORK BEST WHEN WE WORK TOGETHER, MY DEAR.

I REGRET THE CHALLENGES THAT PITIFUL BAND OF INCARNATES WILL FACE IN THE ABSENCE OF MY LEADERSHIP, BUT THOSE HURDLES WILL BE IRRELEVANT IN THE END. THE WATCH NOW IRREVOCABLY TREADS ALONG MY TRAJECTORY, TOWARD ITS ULTIMATE CONCLUSION. I KEEP HOPING YOU'LL DREAM BIGGER, BUT I'M EVER RESIGNED TO MUSTER THE EFFORT FOR YOU. THE WATCH IS NOT DESTINED TO BECOME SOME PALTRY

COMMUNITY, NOR A SO-CALLED SANCTUM CITY (AN ABYSMALLY TRITE NAME, BY THE WAY—I'M EMBARRASSED FOR YOU). NO, FATE HAS SOMETHING FAR GRANDER IN STORE FOR THE WATCH.

WHO KNOWS? IN TIME, IT MIGHT EVEN BECOME ITS OWN MYTH.

THE RACE IS ON IF YOU WANT TO TRY TO THWART MY SCHEMES, AND I'M EVEN WILLING TO GIVE YOU A THOUSAND-AND-ONE DAY HEAD START. PERHAPS YOU'LL SURPRISE ME AND ACCOMPLISH SOMETHING MEANINGFUL WITH THIS GIFT OF TIME. WILL YOU SHATTER YOUR GUARDIAN ANGEL'S DREAM JUST TO SPITE ME? I'M WAITING WITH BATED BREATH.

AS A FINAL PARTING GIFT, I HAVE SUBMITTED THE FORMS REQUIRED TO NAME YOU GREGORY'S NEXT OF KIN. HIS DEATH CERTIFICATE SHOULD ARRIVE IN THE MAIL SHORTLY, ALONG WITH A FRAME I PICKED OUT. WHAT CAN I SAY? IT JUST *SCREAMED* GREGORY.

TA-TA.

My name is Emery Luple, and I am the Protagonist incarnate. We're building the first Sanctum City, with support from those who dare to dream with us. A place where all are welcome to build a future for themselves unfettered by their past. But every once in a while, the demon of my past returns to test us. Nonetheless, we prevailed. Because together, we always do.

This is not the end of our story.

ACKNOWLEDGMENTS

Thank you, Class, for reading my book and keeping my childhood dreams of being an author alive. Your contributions and love have allowed me to embark on the happiest career adventure of my life—and I can't describe how much I appreciate you! Please know, whoever and wherever you are, that you are loved.

The first acknowledgment always belongs to my own beamish boy, my husband, James: Thank you for your unending love and support. For brainstorming plot elements before I've even begun writing. For listening to every chapter and asking, "What if you did *this* instead?" For working long hours so I can stay at home and tell stories to the world. For being there for me, always. I love you.

Next up is you, Mom. Thank you for reading every version and draft of my book. You delight me with your reactions, and our conversations about my growth as an author inspire me. And thank you, Dad, for reading even when there's work to be done just to show me your support. Mom's there to encourage me during the creation process, and Dad supports me through the production process. I couldn't ask for a better tag team of supporters.

And speaking of fantastic duos, I'd like to recognize my brother, Tyler, and Nick Rood. Thank you both for everything you've done throughout the series. Your combined insights push my writing, characters, and dialogue to greater heights—and while everyone benefits from your efforts, I especially appreciate how far I've come because of you.

This next thank-you is for my earliest readers and two of my best friends: Todd Arntson and Michelle Sasso. You haven't just helped me along in my journey, you've placed yourselves on this road beside me. No one else has been as willing to drop everything to help me succeed and flourish as the two of you.

Katie McDaniel, you also deserve so much credit for putting in late nights (plural!) reading my book and telling me how it reads and feels. Thank you for being proud of my accomplishments—your words of encouragement mean the world to me.

I'd also like to thank Vincent, our cat, for cuddling away my worries and anxieties—and especially for giving up the good old days of lounging around with James to instead spend time with me and my keyboard.

Thank you to my "proofers" and friends Linnea Mulvaney, Sunshine Dunning, Kevin Nolan, Peter Brown, Heather Conti, Lanae Oliver, and Sherry Arntson. Each of you provided something special and meaningful during this process—from your all-around support to your specific feedback. This book was written by all of us.

Speaking of all the people involved in writing a book, I'd like to give my warmest appreciation to my editor. If Emery needed to look up "the best editors" online, I'd expect Artie to insist there's really only one, and her name is Alicia Z. Ramos. I must've had the luck of the Protagonist to have found you on my first series, because you elevate my manuscript to levels that blow my mind. You are a technical wizard with an incredible eye for character voice, and you care more about the story, the characters, and even the author than I could ever hope for from a professional with whom I worked. Thank you for making the editing one of my favorite parts of this entire process.

Thank you to Jeff Brown (at Jeff Brown Graphics) for inspiring so many readers to pick up my book. Your cover designs are gorgeous and attention-grabbing, and I am so happy to have found you to represent my series. You also make the process easy and fun, and I'm always excited to see your final version.

A very special thank-you to my sensitivity readers. First up is Sofia Jarrin for insights into Native culture. You improved the authenticity of my writing about Native myths, urban legends, characters, and beliefs. Thank you for sharing your expertise and ensuring my writing was respectful—you've truly enriched my novel. And Lanae Oliver, thank you for paying special attention to my representation of Southern Black women—Maggie is one of my favorite new characters, and she deserved to be the best version of herself. Thank you both for deepening the representation and diversity in this series! I hope I made you proud.

As always, thank you to my incredible family: thank you Nancy, Pop, Ang, Steve, Maddie, Colleen, Cody, Lucy, Susie, Grandma, Teresa, and Terry for believing in me each and every day.

I can't believe we're wrapping up the acknowledgments of my third novel! Thank you to every person listed here and to all of you who took a chance on a new author. I can't wait to set out on the next adventure with you.

ABOUT THE AUTHOR

Justin Schuelke

I'm a Washingtonian living in the greater Seattle area with my husband, James, and our cat, Vincent. I graduated from the University of Washington with a degree in—wait for it—English. When I am not writing, I enjoy games of all kinds: board games, roleplaying games, video games, computer games, phone games... you name it, I'll play it!

Learn more about me at my website: https://justinschuelke.com.

Please subscribe to my mailing list for exclusive content, limited promotions, and more!